D0093834

THE LUCIFER CHORD

A Selection of Recent Titles by F.G. Cottam

Novels

THE MEMORY OF TREES *
THE LAZARUS PROPHECY
THE HOUSE OF LOST SOULS
THE LUCIFER CHORD *

The Colony Series

THE COLONY
DARK RESURRECTION
HARVEST OF SCORN

* *available from Severn House*

THE LUCIFER CHORD

F.G. Cottam

This first world edition published 2018
in Great Britain and the USA by
SEVERN HOUSE PUBLISHERS LTD of
Eardley House, 4 Uxbridge Street, London W8 7SY
Trade paperback edition first published
in Great Britain and the USA 2018 by
SEVERN HOUSE PUBLISHERS LTD

British Library Cataloguing in Publication Data
A CIP catalogue record for this title is available from the British Library.

ISBN-13: 978-0-7278-8803-7 (cased)
ISBN-13: 978-1-84751-922-1 (trade paper)
ISBN-13: 978-1-78010-978-7 (e-book)

All Severn House titles are printed on acid-free paper.

Severn House Publishers support the Forest Stewardship Council™ [FSC™],
the leading international forest certification organisation.
All our titles that are printed on FSC certified paper carry the FSC logo.

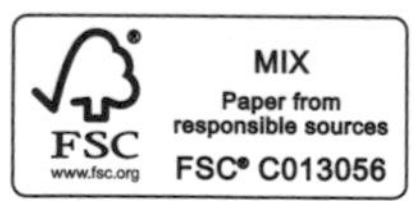

Typeset by Palimpsest Book Production Ltd.,
Falkirk, Stirlingshire, Scotland.
Printed and bound in Great Britain by
TJ International, Padstow, Cornwall.

ONE

Ruthie Gillespie had arranged to meet Michael Aldridge at the Riverside Café on Queen's Promenade. She got there slightly before their agreed time of three in the afternoon and she ordered an espresso and found a vacant table and sat and lit a cigarette and watched the river sparkle and toil in patches with current under vapid October sunshine. It was a Saturday and the cafe was quiet and there weren't many passers-by so when she sensed someone approach, Ruthie looked up and saw that it was him, quite tall and athletic-looking in jeans and a black leather jacket.

Ruthie smiled, thinking that much about his life had changed in the two and a bit years since their last encounter, but that his appearance wasn't among the things that had altered. He looked exactly the same as she remembered him. She stood to greet him, lost in that momentary limbo between air-kissing and a handshake, but he committed to neither. He just returned her smile and pulled out the chair opposite hers and sat down.

'This is a lovely stretch of the river,' she said.

'But you're not here sightseeing.'

'I wasn't sure you'd come.'

'Neither was I. Not until I did, and now I have.'

'Scared of seeing me?'

'Scared of how seeing you would make me feel,' he said.

'I think that works both ways.'

'Probably it does, Ruthie. Anyway, you look well.'

'Likewise, Mr A.'

'Why am I here?'

'I need a job reference.'

Aldridge frowned. He said, 'You write books. You write fiction for children and young adults and I read somewhere you've a book coming out aimed at grown-up readers. It's out at the end of the year.'

'How did you know that?'

'My daughter reads you.'

'How is Mollie?'

'She's thriving and you'll always have my gratitude for that, but why the reference? And why me?'

Ruthie put out her cigarette in the ashtray on their table and lit another with a pink Bic lighter.

'Old habits,' Aldridge said.

'Bad habits,' she said, exhaling with a sigh. She looked at him. She said, 'The past few months have been difficult for me. I don't particularly want to go into why. I need a change. There's a London-based research job. Once upon a time I did a research job for you.'

'I never paid you.'

'Not really the point, Mr A. The point is whether or not I was any good at it.'

'I couldn't put a price on what you found out for me, Ruthie. You know I couldn't.'

She looked at the tip of her cigarette, smouldering. She said, 'And the collateral damage?'

'I don't hold anything against you.'

'Well, that's a relief.'

'What's the job?'

'You've heard of Martin Mear?'

'Everyone over the age of thirty's heard of Martin Mear.'

'Not so sure that's true, Mr A. He died forty-odd years ago.'

'I doubt an hour goes by without a music station somewhere in the world playing a Ghost Legion track. It's like Hendrix or Elvis or that singer from the Doors.'

'Jim Morrison,' Ruthie said.

'Dying, for Martin Mear, was a great career move.'

'The Legion were managed by an American impresario named Carter Melville. Did you know that?'

'No.'

'Melville was a Rhodes Scholar. He first met Martin at university. He was there at the start of everything. Now he wants to create the definitive Ghost Legion box set. It's going to have a glossy brochure with a ten-thousand-word essay on the Legion. It's going to be the last word on Martin Mear and the band he created and led.'

Aldridge didn't say anything. Then he said, 'Why does Melville need a researcher, if he was there for it all?'

Ruthie grinned. She said, 'Melville was more participant than witness, Mr A. You know what they used to say about the Swinging Sixties.'

'Anyone who remembers it wasn't really there.'

'And the 1970s were even more excessive. Carter Melville's recollections from his Ghost Legion days are probably a bit vague. Plus he's not a writer. And rich people tend to delegate.'

'Is he still on ten per cent?'

'I should think substantially more. And the Legion still shifts five million units a year.'

'So the research job's a well-paid bit of digging?'

Ruthie looked out over the river and smoked. 'Not really why I want to do it,' she said.

Aldridge shifted in his metal chair. He said, 'Martin Mear was heavily into the occult, if the rumours are to be believed. He dabbled in black magic.'

'I think he did a bit more than dabble, Michael. That's not why I'm doing it either.'

'Except that you've experience with matters other-worldly, haven't you? We both have, since it was an experience we shared.'

'I'm not really expecting things to go bump in my night,' Ruthie said, 'not researching a bunch of dead rock musicians.'

'Are all four of them dead?'

She raised her eyes. 'All reunited and rocking out at the big stadium in the sky, presumably.'

'How did you hear about the job?'

'Someone I was at school with works in their Soho office at Melville Enterprises. I'm from a small town on a small island and people talk and she'd heard a whisper that I was in a bit of a trough. When she heard about this gig she thought it might be a good fit. It would get me out of Ventnor.'

'And out of the Spyglass Inn?'

Ruthie shrugged. 'You said I look well, but appearances can be deceptive.'

'Why don't you tell me about it?'

She didn't answer him. Instead she said, 'How does it feel, sitting there? Were you right to feel a bit of trepidation about coming?'

'It feels exactly as I thought it would, so I was totally right,'

Aldridge said. 'And sometimes being right offers no satisfaction at all. I'm afraid this is one of those occasions.'

'I'm sorry.'

'No need to be. And of course I'll write your reference. You're a brilliant researcher, Ruthie. I just hope for your sake that there's nothing really dark for you to uncover and expose.'

'I haven't got the job yet, Mr A.'

'But you will get it.'

'I wish I shared your confidence.'

'I'm a believer in fate, Ruthie. Our shared experience made me one. You'll get the job, all right.'

'In the meantime,' Ruthie said, 'can I get you a coffee?'

'I'm in the mood for something stronger.'

'That,' she said, 'might be a really bad idea.'

Ruthie was staying with her friend Veronica Slade at Veronica's flat in North Lambeth. When she got back there at just after five in the afternoon, there was no one at home. Resisting the temptation to cross the Portsmouth Road to the nearest pub with Michael Aldridge had been harder than she'd thought it would be, speculating on how their encounter might play out, earlier in the day. From the pub, after a few disinhibiting drinks, it would have been only a short walk to the flat he occupied in Surbiton. A short and reckless walk, she thought. He was an attractive man, but the entanglement wasn't what she had left the island for. She needed fewer complications in her life, not more of them.

At Veronica's place, she made and drank a cup of Earl Grey tea. She charged up her laptop intent on trying to start a fresh chapter of the novel she was working on. When the words wouldn't come, she didn't try to force them. Instead she checked her emails and saw that Michael had already sent the reference she'd requested he write. He'd sent it as a scan, printed on Aldridge Associates headed notepaper. Ruthie recognized the font, because it was Palatino Linotype, in which she habitually wrote on those days when the words would come. It was a slightly neat coincidence, she thought, thinking there was a sort of symmetry about it.

Except that Michael had confined himself to fact, if not strictly, she thought, to truth.

His reference explained that Ruthie had researched for him in the period of the Ashdown Hall restoration project near Brightstone Forest on the Isle of Wight. He said that her work had been thorough, meticulous and discreet. She was quick to grasp the specifics of a brief. She was courteous and persistent, a tricky combination to pull off. She was highly intelligent and totally professional.

Ruthie knew she had been less than totally professional with Michael Aldridge, but that her solitary failing on that score need not concern Carter Melville. It was a character flaw unlikely to recur researching a dead rock icon and his fellow band members. She was too honest with herself to blame drink for the episode. Drink had played its lubricious part, but she wasn't drinking now and didn't plan to any time soon. This had dismayed Veronica, who worked extremely hard and felt entitled to her evening fun. Veronica liked to let down her abundant hair. But for the moment, for Ruthie, abstemious was how things needed to be.

After printing off the reference, she reread it and then pondered on a response. Michael had written promptly and very generously and she knew that the correct etiquette would be to write a note back thanking him for taking the time and trouble. The problem was that he might interpret her doing so as opening a dialogue between them.

Was that so terrible? He was an unattached man, not some sort of contagious disease to be avoided at all costs. She didn't want to lead him on or encourage false expectations, but if she really wanted to avoid hurting him, then she shouldn't have cold-called him, asking a favour of him in the first place.

She blew out a breath, craving the cigarette she'd resolved she wasn't going to go into Veronica's small walled garden to smoke. The fact was, she'd had to ask Michael Aldridge for the reference. She hadn't practically speaking had a choice. Her work for him had been research and she'd done a bloody good job of it even though the outcome had been unexpected and disturbing. Short of forging a reference, she couldn't have got one relevant to the Ghost Legion project anywhere else.

She'd write him a thank you, Ruthie decided. She'd keep it brief and businesslike. Then she'd write a covering letter and bring up her CV and send everything to her contact at Melville Enterprises so that it would be there when her old school friend got to her desk on Monday morning.

When she'd done all that, and there was still no sign of Veronica, she did go into the garden for a smoke. It was dark by then. She could hear traffic noise and feel the autumnal chill and endured that slight feeling of confinement being landlocked always brought with it. She was very close there to the River Thames and so to water and space, but she'd lived all her life in a coastal town with the briny odour of the sea and the sea's alluring vastness inviting her eyes and she thought big cities choked, claustrophobic places.

When she went back inside, she tried to write again and found that now the words came fluently enough. She sat at the keyboard at the desk in the spare room with a view of the Hercules Road railway arches and the somnolent sound of steel wheel rims on steel rails failing to impede her thoughts or distract from the bright pictures painted on to her mind and channelled through her fingertips. On evenings like this one, and there'd been too many of them over recent weeks, Ruthie was grateful for her distracting gift.

She wrote until just after 9pm, when Veronica came in, carrying a bag of cream paper packages that sent the hot smart of malt vinegar trailing through confined space.

'I knew you wouldn't sort yourself out, so I got us fish and chips,' her friend called out. 'Get off your backside, Ruthie, before you take root. Get out here pronto and grab us a couple of plates.'

Ruthie saved her file and got up and sniffed.

Veronica had put their supper down on the kitchen counter and was unbuttoning her coat. 'You've been crying,' she said.

'You don't sound surprised.'

'Thin walls, love, and you talk in your sleep.'

TWO

Ruthie spent the next couple of days preparing for the interview she wasn't at all confident she'd get. Doing that was the best way of readying herself for it if she did. She didn't want to embarrass Jackie Tibbs, the school friend who'd tipped her off about the research job, with a show of ineptitude in front of Jackie's boss. If she got an audience with Carter Melville she'd arrive well informed. This preparation also distracted her from dwelling on recent events in her private life. She'd a tendency to that she kept rediscovering was as painful as it was futile.

Martin Mear had been intent on rock stardom, or at least intent on being a full-time musician and band member. His first group was Peacock Blue, a psychedelic outfit formed when he was in his mid-teens. They'd performed his first attempts at songwriting at pubs and the occasional disco in his home town of Shaftesbury.

At university, he'd formed Tallow Pale with two other students. The Pale, as they'd come to be known, were basically a folk-rock trio. Sometimes they performed with sit-in musicians and for some of their numbers, they invited women singers as guest vocalists. The Pale were Martin's baby, so this could have been a straight musical decision or it could have been a proto-feminist thing. Or it could have been simply that Martin was enthusiastic about women. Certainly, his later career suggested that this was the case.

The Pale built quite a festival following. They were considered a good live act, but they never got near a recording contract and broke up amicably enough as the core members began studying seriously for their finals.

That was in the spring of 1969. It wasn't until after graduation, in the autumn of that year, that Martin Mear began the four-piece project that would come to rule the rock world as Ghost Legion.

The Legion were offered a record deal after only a few performances. The four-piece line up seemed to have been the perfect vehicle for the songs Martin was writing by then. Ruthie thought they must have gelled immediately, must have possessed that alchemy that makes the truly great rock acts stand out from what was by then a sizeable and noisy and stridently ambitious crowd.

Their debut album came out in '70 and Ghost Legion would cut six in total. That first LP, *King Lud*, was followed by *Black Solstice* and *Exiled Souls*, all released at intervals of a year. But it was the latter sets of recordings that set them apart from their peers and endowed the Legion with their mystical status and reputation as a band creating songs that needed not only to be listened to, but somehow decoded, before they could be properly understood and appreciated. These three albums were never given titles. They were referred to simply as 1, 2 and 3, as though nothing in the band's history had preceded them. Nothing would follow them either, because shortly after 3 appeared towards the end of 1975, Martin Mear died.

Albums without titles weren't unprecedented when Ghost Legion failed to provide names for theirs. The Beatles brought out the White Album in 1968. The album that came to be known by the band's fans simply as Led Zeppelin 2 was released the following year. But the Beatles were jaunty and Led Zep bluesy and much less dark and more straightforward than Martin Mear's outfit. Where their songs tended to be collaborations, Martin's by contrast were all his own solo compositions. He wrote the lyrics and the tunes and he was the lead vocalist. By the time of 1, 2 and 3, he was an established star and the inclusiveness that had characterized Tallow Pale was a definite thing of the past.

Ruthie was studying a rare Pale-period photo of Martin Mear on her laptop screen at Veronica's flat just after 11am on Tuesday when her phone rang and she recognized the number on her display for Melville Enterprises and it was her old Wight school friend Jackie Tibbs, telling her she'd got her interview, asking was four o'clock on Thursday afternoon a convenient time. She replied that it was. She swapped pleasantries, knowing that Jackie's office was more than likely open-plan and that she'd have colleagues casually eavesdropping on the call. She said goodbye and cut the connection aware only that she was unaware of where any of this was really going.

She focused on the image on her screen, on the muscular, long-haired figure caught in the snapshot and frozen in time, attired in purple loons and a paisley shirt, not androgynous as had been the prevailing fashion among front-men then but instead, emphatically masculine. There was a six-string acoustic slung around his neck and his long fringe partially concealed his eyes, giving him a shy look.

Martin Mear had been anything but shy. She knew that about him, if she didn't yet know much else. She'd been listening to Ghost Legion as she worked, had played the albums sequentially and then gone back to *King Lud* and as close as she was going to get to the musical birth of the band. Most of the mad fan speculation about Martin and black magic centred on the later, nameless records. But it was Ruthie's abiding belief that the beginning of anything was always the best place to start if you could.

She scrolled through more pictures and came across one that made her heart lurch. It was Martin Mear pictured on Wight, the Needles and their red and white hoop-painted lighthouse behind where he stood on the clifftop against an azure summer sea. Of course, the Legion had played there, they'd headlined at the festival, hadn't they? For a moment Ruthie endured a pang of homesickness so strong and piercing it felt like a knife-thrust. She waited for it to pass, which eventually it did.

She wondered when this self-imposed exile of hers would end. Veronica had told her she could stay for as long as she wanted to. She supposed that it depended on the outcome of Thursday's interview, on whether she got what Carter Melville would inevitably term the gig. Securing the job wasn't life and death but would be of practical help in enabling her to stay away from home for a while. And she thought the more she learned about the enigmatic Mr Mear, the more interesting a figure he became. It was as though the more she discovered the less she was sure of, and Ruthie found that an intriguing contradiction. It was to her a challenge.

She looked at her wristwatch. Her appointment with the man who had steered Ghost Legion to their colossal commercial success was just over fifty hours away. She thought that the time between now and then might drag. But she busied herself with her own writing through Wednesday and boned up some more on the Legion on Thursday morning and the time of her appointment arrived fairly quickly.

Fate, Michael Aldridge had called it. Ruthie had time to ponder only briefly on that claim before the appointed hour was upon her. She did so on Wednesday evening, just before descending into sleep, aware of the thin wall to her right and Veronica Slade beyond it and the knowledge now that her troubled dreams had been heard. She knew too that Veronica cared about her, but that thought didn't really offer Ruthie much consolation.

'I wasn't expecting a Goth.'

'I'm not a Goth.'

'The ink tells me different. So do the threads.'

'I wear black because it's slimming.'

'Then there's the haircut. Jesus.'

'I'm interviewing for a job, Mr Melville, not auditioning for a part. It's not very PC for you to comment on my appearance.'

'I'm not a very PC guy. But you stand up for yourself and we're only forty seconds in.' Carter Melville pointed for emphasis. 'That,' he said, 'I like.'

Ruthie shrugged. She was there to secure a paid commission, not to have an argument.

'Tell me what you know about Martin Mear.'

'Rather less than I will if I get the gig.'

'Which isn't really answering the question.'

'He was arguably one of the biggest rock stars of the early 1970s. He fronted a band he formed called Ghost Legion. He was exceptionally charismatic. He did all the usual stuff they could get away with much easier back then and he also had what was alleged to be a fairly serious interest in black magic. He died like Janis Joplin and Jim Morrison and Hendrix did, when he was twenty-seven. There's some dispute about the circumstances of his death, but I don't know the specifics.'

'You don't know the specifics yet.'

'I'll acquaint myself with the specifics, should I get the gig.'

Melville appeared to ponder, swivelling in his leather chair behind the steeple of his fingers on the other side of a desk she thought the biggest she had ever seen. His office was like a trophy room. There were gold records on the walls, awards in gold and silver gilt cluttering wall-length shelves. Some kind of animal pelt still in possession of its claws was splayed across the marble floor. Ruthie assumed he'd shot its original owner himself.

'You got one thing wrong,' he said.

'Only one thing?'

'Martin wasn't arguably anything. He was the biggest, bar none. He was the outright winner of the swinging-dick competition without ever having to whip it out of his pants. There was absolutely no contest.'

'Mick Jagger might disagree with you. Robert Plant, too.'

'I was there, baby,' Melville said, after a pause. He dropped his hands and swivelled to face her directly. 'Nothing could touch him alive and nothing can touch him dead. Ghost Legion still shift close to six million units a year and Martin Mear *was* the fucking Legion.'

'You don't sound like you need a researcher at all. The salient facts all seem to be at your disposal.'

He chuckled at that. He looked at the chunky watch on its bracelet of yellow ingots adorning his wrist. 'Three minutes in and already I get sarcasm,' he said. 'Good for you.'

She didn't reply.

'I have zero objectivity where Martin is concerned. We met when we were eighteen and our lives were inextricably linked for the next nine years. Plus, I was a doer in what got done back then. I've got gaps. I've got a mess of blurs and intervals. One of your tasks will be to fill those gaps, accurately, dispassionately.'

She'd looked him up. Of course she had. He'd been born in Maine in New England. He'd gained a scholarship to study at Oxford, where he'd first met Martin Mear. He'd become a recording-industry mogul and somehow over the decades his accent had drifted softly into the mid-Atlantic. She got the feeling he swore more often, usually. He was self censoring on her account, she thought. He'd stop doing that should she get the job. Courtesy was an effort for him. Courtesy to this man was a drag.

Carter Melville gave Ruthie his spiel. He told her he planned the definitive collection documenting Martin Mear's musical career. This stretched from his experimentation with the early bands right through to the last studio recording completed by the Legion. It was to include alternative takes, stuff from the BBC radio archive, the celebrated bootlegs and much other material never before released. Everything was to be re-mastered and a version on audio-grade vinyl complete with original artwork and lyric sheets was going to be cut for the purists as a limited edition at a premium price.

A twenty-thousand-word essay would accompany the discs, perfectly bound as a glossy booklet and replete with photos, some of which were being published for the first time. It would be Ruthie's task to research and write those twenty thousand words. She would separate the reality from the hype, rumour and the apocryphal. At least, it would be her job to do all that if she agreed to the gig.

'The fee is twenty large. Do it right, sister, and I won't quibble.'

'Jackie Tibbs told me ten thousand for something half that length.'

'Yeah, but I changed my mind. Downloaded a couple of your books and did some browsing last night. You've a nice turn of phrase and you're very atmospheric.'

'That's when I'm writing fiction.'

'Which some of this shit is far stranger than.'

'A pound a word's a hell of a rate.'

He pointed at her. 'Lady, you'll earn it,' he said. 'It's also source material for the biography I plan to write about Martin myself next year. No one was closer to him and the public interest is just as intense now as it was on the day he died. It's an investment, baby. Where Carter Melville is concerned, method always accompanies the madness.'

She nodded. She wasn't sure if any of this added up terribly well. And wasn't talking about yourself in the third-person what megalomaniacs did? But she was already spending the twenty thousand pounds the project would earn her in her head. She said, 'What's the deadline?'

He smiled, properly this time, a brief smile that begged for its own encore from a man she saw with a jolt possessed surprisingly potent charm. 'Two months,' he said. 'Tell me you're on board, Ruthie. Please tell me we're pulling together on this. Don't disappoint an old man nurturing visionary dreams.'

'I'm in,' she said.

He told her then about the three people from Martin's old life prepared to discuss their part in that life and their impressions of the man they knew, publicly, for the first time. She took out her Moleskine and made notes. He gave her an envelope he said contained contact details for the three, adding that he would not feel comfortable committing anything so confidential to email.

'Email can be hacked and leaked.'

'This isn't espionage.'

'There's a lot of prurient interest still in Martin's life. If any of these people get cold-called by the press, we can kiss their cooperation goodbye. And I've worked hard to get it.'

'They'll expect my call?'

'They will once I've told them to, which I'll do as soon as this meeting is over.'

There was a silence between them.

'I'll see you're forwarded some expenses cash today.'

'Thank you.'

Then he surprised her. 'What do you know about Frederica Daunt?'

'I don't watch much television.'

'But you've heard of her?'

Ruthie said, 'In so far as any spirit medium could ever be said to be credible, she ticks all the necessary boxes. She appears regularly on sober programmes on the themes of mortality and bereavement broadcast on terrestrial channels. Her books sell briskly. She can fill provincial concert halls with respectful audiences when she tours. She has a huge and I think mostly sympathetic following on social media. She's articulate, good-looking and comes across as too convincingly posh to be a vulgar trickster.'

'Jackie scored big, recommending you.'

Ruthie didn't reply to that.

'Where do you stand on mediums?'

'Grief shouldn't be an industry. I don't believe in profiting from pain.'

He chuckled at that. He said, 'Carter Melville's shrink has been profiting from his pain for forty years. His lawyer, too.'

Ruthie wondered, did he talk about himself in the third person to his shrink?

'Frederica Daunt claims to communicate regularly with Martin from beyond. She sounds quite plausible. It seems a good place to start.'

'It sounds a highly dubious place to start.'

Melville chuckled again. 'Then it will probably set the tone,' he said. 'You should attend one of her meetings, check out what the old chick's up to, whether she's got the goods or whether it's just a crock,' he said.

'My hunch is she's a plausible fraud.'

He smiled. It was an ambiguous smile, one without much humour. 'Take this gig on and you might find your scepticism challenged, honey. You might find that happening on a regular basis.'

Ruthie was taking it on. She didn't like the chicks and honeys that were, with the babes and old ladies, the tedious way rock-industry dinosaurs like Carter Melville habitually referred to women. But the work sounded genuinely intriguing and the money was far too incredulously good to turn down. She couldn't yet face going back to her home on the island. This job gave her every excuse to avoid doing that.

THREE

Frederica Daunt's address was in the affluent riverside district of Chiswick. The house when Ruthie arrived there isolated in the gloom, sizeable enough almost to merit the term stately, suggestive that spiritualism was a more profitable practice than she thought something usually so bogus had any real right to be.

It was Friday evening. She'd called the medium on a contact number given her by Carter Melville as soon as she'd got back to Veronica's flat on Thursday afternoon. Though it wasn't explicitly said, she assumed her call had been anticipated. She thought that the only plausible explanation for Ms Daunt's diary being so improbably clear of engagements. She'd apparently kept it clear, waiting for the call.

Now, Ruthie sat in Veronica's borrowed car parked at the kerb, smoking with the driver's window open and the rain percussive on the roof and sodium lit in the rectangle of pale droplets falling to her right. There was a bottle of Febreze on the passenger seat to eradicate the tobacco smell later and Ghost Legion playing on the stereo, their songs becoming more familiar and more alien at the same time to her with every listen. She felt already that there was much more to this job than research and writing. She remembered once again what Michael Aldridge had said about fate. She finished her cigarette, closed the window, climbed out of the car and locked it behind her.

The bell chimed. The door was answered by Frederica Daunt herself, slender and petite in a green evening gown and a purple shawl, her hair tightly braided, skin porcelain-smooth over the cheekbones that made her look a good decade younger than her fifty years.

Her eyes were the same bright emerald as the gown, Ruthie

saw, in the light of the spacious hallway. Attractive eyes, a compelling gaze. Her hands fluttered in front of her. They fingered and tugged at the fringed and tasselled edges of the shawl.

She said, 'I'm not quite ready for you.' She crossed the hall and opened a door; 'If you wouldn't mind waiting in here, Ms Gillespie? I do apologize. I can assure you it won't be a long wait.' Her voice, familiar from TV and radio, still sounded surprisingly husky and deep emerging from someone with so slight a frame.

The room was panelled in oak. It was lit from its high ceiling, four lamps with conical shades screwed into short brass tube fittings casting a glare that prevented any shadows. The wallpaper was florid, something expensive, Ruthie thought, from somewhere like Liberty, in the style of William Morris. Its pattern overpowered the framed prints hung from the walls at precise intervals, making them pallid, bloodless. Rain worried the windows of the exterior wall in capering gusts. Ruthie already craved another cigarette.

She wondered if Frederica Daunt had gone to arrange her phony ectoplasm or rehearse the sounds that would emerge from cleverly concealed speakers. Once they sat down, the table between them might thump and vibrate. Maybe there would be a hologram of the deceased rock star. Modern technology would enable convincing effects, but awareness of its capabilities would just as much lessen their impact on someone already predisposed to distrust them.

The medium reappeared, framing herself in the doorway and coughing into her right fist. The hand was small and the fist so tightly clenched that the knuckles appeared bloodless under stretched skin. The cough had been a nervous reflex, Ruthie thought. She's tense, though she must have done what she's about to dozens of times before.

'I'm ready for you,' she said.

Ruthie rose from and followed. After a hesitation, she left her coat where she'd draped it across the arm of the chair. She'd anticipated a bit of ice-breaking, an offer of tea or coffee possibly even with a biscuit on the side, a prelude of domestic normality to relax her prior to the ritual proper. Evidently there was to be nothing of that sort forthcoming.

She followed the medium up three flights of stairs. The room she was shown into was small, its single large window heavily curtained.

There was a circular wooden table at which had been placed two opposing chairs. Séances were performances, weren't they? She was being treated to a solo performance and she'd witness it from the best possible seat.

There was nothing on the table. No crystal ball, no tarot pack, none of the paranormal paraphernalia associated with ghostly fraud. There was the smell of beeswax from wood polish, the scent her hostess wore, which she thought she recognized as the Guerlain fragrance Chamade. And there was the churchy odour of the three burning candles in wall sconces providing the room's only illumination. The table wasn't even antique. It looked like the stolid sort of item you might pick up from the furniture floor at a branch of John Lewis.

'Sit down,' Frederica Daunt said.

Ruthie sat. She rested her hands on the table top, where they immediately began to feel sweaty. She put them in her lap and watched the smears of moisture they had left on the wood evaporate and disappear. 'What happens now?'

'We wait.' In candlelight, with her tight smile, the skin on the medium's face looked momentarily shrink-wrapped. Then the smile was withdrawn and she closed her eyes and her breathing became sonorous and the room seemed to grow colder.

The window behind Frederica Daunt faced the road outside and beyond that, the night river. Ruthie could hear the drift of occasional cars from outside and below. The sound was faint and distant. The rattle on the panes of rain in fitful gusts was closer. But these exterior sounds did not provide the comfort of the mundane. They made her feel trapped and isolated from normality. The flame topping one of the candles tore like renting cloth and she felt an emotion she thought was quite troublingly close to fear.

Nothing happened. For what length of time nothing happened, Ruthie couldn't afterwards have said. Probably it felt longer than it was. It was an interval in which she grew no more comfortable than she'd been at its outset. If anything, the opposite was true. She could feel the steady acceleration of her thumping heart. She became more restive and anxious and the chilly air grew heavy as though something dangerous impended not far beyond the four walls confining them. Behind brick and plaster she had the sense this hazard squirmed and pressed, uninvited.

One of the candles snuffed out. After a moment, the others followed. Ruthie frowned, because this didn't feel like trickery.

Frederica Daunt slumped in her chair like someone suddenly become boneless inside their body. Her head rolled back and then canted to one side where it rested, the right cheek almost touching her shoulder, the tendons in her exposed neck like whorls of knotted rope. It was not a flattering look and must be extremely uncomfortable, Ruthie thought, assuming the medium was conscious and faking, which her breathing, like this new posture, suggested she wasn't doing at all.

She became aware of a sound. It was a low, faint, insistent buzzing. Almost imperceptibly, it got louder. She tried to determine where it was coming from, but even when it became quite insistently real, it had no obvious source. Instead it was all around her, like an aural fog.

The room grew dimmer as the volume of the sound increased. She knew that physics would suggest the opposite should be happening, even with the candles extinguished, as her eyes grew accustomed to the ambient light that must have been leaking at the edges of the heavy curtain through the window from the lit street outside. But the darkness became denser. This happened deliberately, as though invisible hands were wielding brushes, daubing the walls with a layer of gloomy paint.

The sound was a drone. It was the sort of singular, endless note characteristic of tribal music. It sounded as harsh and insistent as the note a set of bagpipes might produce, were the player capable of so endlessly sustaining it. It was growing in loudness all the time. It had become a shriek Ruthie did not think she could bear for much longer in the deafening charcoal smudge the space around her had now diminished into.

It stopped. It just ceased and the medium's head jerked and she woke with a startled look as a crash like gigantic cymbals shivered through the blackness.

Frederica Daunt screamed.

Ruthie had recognized the sound. It had been far slower and more drawn out and vastly louder and more vibrantly abrupt in that cymbal clash, but she'd heard it before and heard it only recently. It was the start of the first song on the second side of *King Lud*, the Ghost Legion debut, the album the medium could not have known she'd been listening to driving through the rain on the way to the séance. Its title, aptly, was, 'The Ruler Returns'. In the song, he did so by boat. As if to prove the point, from the river beyond the window, a horn emitted a single grave blast that groped over the water and through the night air to reach them.

Frederica Daunt's nose had begun to bleed. Fat droplets dripped from her nostrils and inked the front of her dress blackly. It was still gloomy in the room, but Ruthie thought the light had improved since the music had stopped. She thought that if this was a put on, it had been put on very professionally. What she really thought was that it hadn't been conjured at all. Not by them, it hadn't. Not by the two living people sitting and enduring it.

The medium looked like someone recently mugged. There was the blood, the paleness, the reel of assaulted shock in her emerald eyes. Ruthie didn't think anyone was this good an actress.

She got up and exited the room and found a bathroom along the landing where she wet a hand towel with cold water to provide the bleeding woman with a compress for her nose. She was shaken by what she'd just experienced and was struggling to find a rational explanation for. She was still sufficiently frightened for the job of first wetting and then wringing out the towel to be accomplished only clumsily, by fingers that didn't quite yet feel completely under her control.

Movement obliged her to glance up from the sink into the mirror on the wall behind it where she saw a ghastly, blood-soaked apparition, pale and fraught, wide-eyed and with a rictus grin of trauma distorting the lower half of her face.

Frederica looked a fright, but Ruthie's first thought was, At least she has a reflection, it means she's human and alive, doesn't it?

She hadn't spoken more than a handful of words to the medium since her arrival and got nothing further out of her before her departure half an hour later. She helped staunch the blood from her nose and steadied her jittery progress down the stairs. She seated her in what she assumed to be the drawing room and went back upstairs to make sure that the candles in the room used for the séance really were all extinguished. Going back in there was an ordeal. But she wasn't treated to any more strangeness. The room was still and quiet, smelling slightly of wax and singed wick and maybe, just slightly, the sour secretion of fear.

She found the kitchen and made tea. Had she not had the drive to face, she would have sought out something more potent. Houses like this one always had generously stocked drinks cabinets and a brandy or whisky would have been welcome. Tea would do, she thought, grateful that at least she was getting away from the place, able to put several miles between here and her night's sleep in North Lambeth. If, that was, she did sleep.

She made a strong breakfast brew and put sugar and milk into the mug she made for Frederica Daunt without asking about her usual preference. This was not a routine situation. The mug was grasped with a small smile between grateful hands. She waited for a while, until most of the drink had been sipped and swallowed. Then she spoke.

'Has it ever been like that before?'

The medium blinked before replying. Something seemed to recoil in her expression, as if her mind had moved on from the moment as a defensive reflex and considered dragging her back to it ungracious or in bad taste.

'I can't discuss what happened. I can't talk about it now. Not now, I can't.'

'Can I call you tomorrow?'

'You can if you wish. I might not be much help.'

Ruthie nodded. She stole a glance at her watch. It was 9.45. She waited another ten minutes, feeling slightly guilty but unable really to do anything more, reluctant to speculate on what had occurred until she was safely in Veronica's home behind a locked door. Then she rose and went for her coat and said goodbye to Frederica Daunt, who neither rose from her drawing-room chair to see her out, nor even met her eyes in nodding a curt goodbye.

The rain had only strengthened in the time she'd been in Chiswick. On reaching and unlocking the car she glanced back at the house she'd just left and thought it had the sombre grandeur and stillness not of an abode, but instead of some great mausoleum. She breathed in river air, gusty and dank, rank with tidal ebb and very welcome. She thought of the churchy smells in the séance room and a shudder ran through her she didn't owe to the cold. It was October, but the night, though wet, was mild.

She'd left a place of death. She was no longer convinced that

Frederica Daunt was any kind of fraud. The woman suffered for her art, if art it was.

Ruthie got into the car. She composed herself before switching on the ignition and lights and slipping the transmission into gear. She'd switched off the CD player on arrival. Ghost Legion's debut reposed within its slot loader. She'd reached the second side of the album. She could switch it on and hear a less loud and spectral version of the drone and cymbal intro to 'The Ruler Returns' than the one to which she'd been treated an hour ago. Or she could leave it un-played, which would probably be wisest.

Martin Mear could bellow and roar with the best of them, but he had whispered and crooned that particular vocal, when it finally insinuated its way over the strengthening melody. She did not want to listen to it there, alone in the car, with the gusting wind rocking the body slightly on its suspension and the rain drumming on her roof in an unfamiliar location, alone.

She took her iPhone out of her pocket. She had switched it off before ringing the bell at the house. She switched it on and saw that there were no new calls or texts or emails to have to reply to. She was tempted to make a call herself, to Carter Melville, to ask him just what the fuck kind of introduction the supernatural cabaret she'd just endured was to the subject she was supposed to be researching. She was damned sure the experience would not feature in the finished essay.

But she decided against doing that. She needed to sleep on the experience and Melville was not a counsellor or a nursemaid or a psychologist. Neither was he a psychic investigator. That was her role, should there prove to be any substance to the stories of the magic her subject's antics in life still apparently provoked after his death. Those stories were plentiful and persistent, weren't they? Frederica Daunt and the blood and wax of her séances weren't the half of it.

She'd call Carter Melville in the morning. She remembered that he came from New England. She wondered if he was related to the famous New England Melville who had written the great American novel of the nineteenth century, in *Moby Dick*. She knew that Moby the musician was related distantly to that Melville, thus the nickname.

She looked at her car stereo again. She wasn't restricted to that or to *King Lud*. Her new employer had given her all six of the Ghost Legion albums in all formats. She could have driven the route to the sound of any of them. But she decided she'd drive in silence. She was in the mood only for a stiff nightcap when she reached the bland homely refuge of Veronica's flat. She'd spend the journey trying to dissuade herself from drinking that.

FOUR

Ruthie had not wasted the first full day of her Martin Mear assignment. On the first morning, she'd put in calls to the three people identified on the single sheet of paper in Melville's envelope as being the closest to her subject in life. They were his daughter, April Mear, his girlfriend, the then notorious groupie Paula Tort, and Ghost Legion's chief roadie and all-round fixer and factotum, Terry Maloney.

Martin was only sixteen when his daughter was born. He was still at school, still regularly doing homework and a paper round in his home town of Shaftesbury. The mother was older, nineteen and a hippie drop-out living in a ramshackle rural commune. Martin had taken to pedalling over there on his bike to join in their scrumpy-fuelled jam sessions on his first semi-acoustic guitar. April was the product of a drunken fumble that went further than it should have.

Her mother died when April was six months old of a brain aneurysm and the girl spent the first five years of her life in an orphanage. Martin got her out of there on the day he signed his first recording contract and for the next seven years, despite his demonic reputation, had apparently been a loving and attentive father. April was only twelve when he died, but she remembered him vividly, it was said. And she cherished the memories.

Paula Tort was twenty-two when Martin died, Seattle-born and a rock-scene fixture since leaving home to follow a Stones tour at the age of sixteen. It was fair to say she'd been around the block and then some by the time the two hooked up five years later. But she looked like no one's idea of a tramp. The pictures taken back then showed a beautiful natural blonde with a full-lipped smile and cheekbones so sharp they looked capable of engraving glass.

There was never anything shop-soiled about Paula's appearance. Her sartorial style in the '70s was the gypsy look favoured by the likes of Carly Simon and Stevie Nicks. She and Martin shared two intensely romantic years that proved to be the last he would live. Now she headed up a fashion empire embracing everything from couture clothing ranges to luxury perfume. She was sixty-four, a handsome woman, single, rich and someone who had never before spoken on the record about her relationship with the dead rock god.

Terry Maloney had also prospered. Back then he'd done more than just cart gear for the band. He'd started out like that, loading the guitars and amps into the Bedford van in which he drove them to early gigs up and down the M1. But their rise was incredibly rapid and by the time of their pomp, they toured in a private 727 with the Ghost Legion logo etched in black and gold on the silver aluminium of its fuselage.

By then Maloney was booking itineraries, shepherding the band's women, haggling over the damage inflicted on hotel suites and negotiating discounts done on volume with local drug dealers wherever the band played. He arranged their biker security whenever they played stadium gigs and he kept their names and antics out of the papers when their misbehaviour threatened to exceed what was permissible even in exceptionally liberal times.

That was the principal contrast, Ruthie thought, between then and now. Then, the records and the live performances sold the band. Their music and stage presence made them famous and successful and rich. They couldn't rely on MTV videos to shape their identity and peddle their wares because all that was still over a decade away. They couldn't harness YouTube and Facebook and Twitter, because none of those routes had even been thought of.

Ghost Legion had never given an interview collectively and Martin had only ever given two as an individual. The band had never bothered to release a single. They had never done a Christmas special or a *Top of the Pops* appearance or even a charity gig. They had done everything on their own terms and had conquered the world that way and Terry Maloney had the inside track on how it had all been accomplished.

He was Sir Terence, now. He was the chairman of a merchant bank, a pillar of London's fiscal establishment. His home territory was the Square Mile. He was a member of exclusive clubs and a patron of two children's charities and the Tate Britain art gallery. He had a titled wife and two grown-up sons and a stately pile in Bedfordshire and he was about to speak, on the record, for the first time ever about his involvement with Martin Mear.

She was reluctant to pre-judge, but Ruthie couldn't see what Sir Terence had to gain from dragging up this lurid period of his own past. To his City peers it would seem scandalous, squalid and possibly even criminal.

April was a woman of fifty-four now, tall and slightly haughty in appearance, long-limbed, strong-featured and with Martin's luxuriant head of wavy auburn hair. She grew richer daily on the royalties rolling in as the only beneficiary of his will. She would naturally wish to set the record straight about the father she had loved unconditionally. With April, it would be a heartfelt tribute.

There was an iconoclasm about fashion-world values which meant that exposure of Paula's decadent past would only increase her industry kudos and bring added status to her personal reputation. No revelation, however salacious, could do anything other than further her credibility in a deliberately edgy milieu. But Ruthie failed to see any upside in going public for the man who had begun life as plain Terry Maloney.

She looked forward to meeting him, though. Of the three, he was the one who most intrigued her. It was early days, but she was having difficulty pulling the character of Martin Mear into sharp focus. She thought that of the three sets of recollections, those of Terry Maloney would possess the clearest detail and the most objectivity.

None of the three had yet got back to her. She had to be patient. Two of them were very busy people and all of them had waited a long time to break their silence on a subject over whom the speculation vastly outweighed any readily verifiable truth.

She drained her glass. She'd got back as houseguest in an empty flat on a Friday evening after a frightening experience and she'd succumbed to the temptation of Veronica's fridge and a glass of chilled Chablis. She drank it in the sitting room. She switched on the television. The programme being broadcast was the regional news. She kept waiting to see the house she'd left in Chiswick, lit by flashbulbs and news crew floodlights, delineated by yellow crime-scene tape, as a grim voice-over described the grisly suicide of the famous spirit medium who'd been its occupant.

They'd found her hanging from her attic rafters. They'd found her drowned, wrapped in her sodden purple shawl washed up at the edge of the river. She'd been discovered in a crimson-filled bathtub with her arteries opened by a razorblade or carving knife. She'd been stretched out stilly in bed, her counterpane a litter of empty pill bottles.

There was no such item, of course. The bulletin finished with a whimsical end-piece about a duckling being nursed into maturity by a Labrador after a Staffordshire bull terrier mangled its mother to death.

'Cut out the middleman,' Ruthie said at the screen. 'Mangle the Staffies.' She'd been cautious around dogs since being bitten by a Doberman six months earlier, walking off a hangover on Wight's Tennyson Trail.

She switched off the TV and rose to fix another drink. She would switch on her desktop and study the claims made by Frederica Daunt concerning her contact with Martin Mear. She hadn't done that before the séance because she hadn't wanted to attend the event in any way prejudiced, or with the sort of preconceptions that could blind you to what you were actually witnessing.

She doubted very much that what she had earlier experienced had ever happened to the medium before. She was tougher than she looked, if such events were regular occurrences. But what grief-stricken client, looking for contact with a departed loved one, would fork out hard cash for so sinister an ordeal as that? None, was the answer. Ruthie was more and more certain the event had surprised and troubled Frederica every bit as much as it had her.

Her computer powered up. Her homepage clarified. But before she could look for anything, her phone began to ring.

It was Carter Melville. He said, 'Couldn't turn in without asking you how it played out tonight, honey.'

'It's only just after eleven. I didn't think people in your world turned in anywhere near so early.'

'Give me a break, baby,' he said. 'I'm close to seventy years of age.'

She nodded, thinking about this. Melville had once been the same age as his best friend Martin Mear, who still looked slender and beautiful on the posters and on celluloid and who had never and never would reach the age of twenty-eight. She said, 'I've been thinking about April and Paula and Terry.'

'That would be Sir Terence, to you.'

'I can kind of understand why they're prepared to break their silence.'

'It's because the project has integrity. It's the last, definitive word.'

'What I can't understand is why they're prepared to speak to me. I'm nobody. Don't they want some famous rock journalist with a heavyweight by-line?'

'Celebrity writers bring agendas, Ruthie. They have opinions of their own and the egos to want to channel those opinions stridently through their subjects. They're victims of their own myth, too often mired in their own bullshit.'

'So basically I'll just be transcribing statements.'

'You're misunderstanding me. You can ask any of them any questions you want. I'm just trusting you to ask the right questions for the right reasons and they will be too because I've told them that and because they've seen your resume.'

'Martin doesn't strike me as all that black and white.'

Melville paused before replying. He said, 'And you haven't answered my question. How did it play out tonight?'

'It was odd, Mr Melville.'

'Carter, baby, please.'

'It was odd, Carter. It was scary too.' She told him what had happened, its apparent effect on the medium, her suspicion that the event had been both genuine and unprecedented.

Again, he hesitated before saying anything. Then he said, 'Cold feet?'

'Not at all,' she said.

'Cool. That's my girl. Sweet dreams, Ruthie.'

She reached for the curtain behind her monitor, stretching over the width of the table to open it a chink and look at the night. Rain, made silent by double-glazing, spattered on the outer pane. It dribbled and blurred the view.

She looked to where Veronica's car was parked, on the street below, and frowned because she thought she saw the green light glowing under her dashboard that would signal the CD player was switched on and playing the contents of its slot loader to an audience of no one. It was a trick of the light, night refraction, some random collusion of neon and wet glass. What would be the point, otherwise? She didn't know all that much about magic, but she assumed that its practice required some sort of purpose.

FIVE

King Lud had been written and recorded over the late summer of 1969. Martin had got the money from somewhere – Ruthie would eventually have to try to determine exactly from where – to hire mobile studio equipment and set it up in a derelict house on the edge of Brightstone Forest on Wight. Ruthie learned this thinking Mear's Wight connections were strengthening in her mind and then remembering Michael Aldridge's words about fate.

Playing all the instruments himself, he laid down the album's seven songs on a four-track tape machine and got an engineer he knew at Abbey Road to mix the finished record before having a thousand copies pressed.

Someone from the Shaftesbury hippy commune where his daughter had been conceived contributed the cover artwork. He persuaded a handful of influential record shops to take and display a few copies. Within a week the entire production run had sold out and they were re-pressing as fast as four plants given over to the job could stamp and package the discs.

The *King Lud* of the title was a legendary ancient King of London, and London, at various times in its rich history, provided the thematic basis of the album. 'The Ruler's Return', the track to which Ruthie thought she heard the intro at the séance, wasn't about this titular king. It was a song about a druidic high priest returning by barge up the Thames to the capital at the time of the Roman occupation.

His mission was to enchant the occupiers, who had driven out the old religion, filling their minds with poisonous dreams so they died as they slept in the night. The drone was meant to symbolize a druidic death march. Instruments producing such sounds had been used at their ceremonies of human sacrifice. The Ruler of the old faith in England was about to sacrifice his enemies and the drone delivered him and their impending deaths. The cymbal clash marked the rude moment of departure from mortal life.

It was grim stuff. It was no more sinister than the folkloric material Fairport Convention had interpreted on their landmark album *Liege and Lief*. That release too would deal with witchcraft and curses and the restlessness of those who still stirred beyond their mortal death. But the house in Brightstone Forest had been huge and derelict with a bad reputation. Martin had been there alone, without the provision of heating or lighting, when he wrote and recorded *King Lud*. Little wonder the music evoked the mood it did.

These thoughts ran through Ruthie's ruminating mind early on Saturday morning. She hadn't hit Veronica's Chablis bottle hard the previous night. She'd slept surprisingly well. Veronica wasn't there, had slipped off for a long weekend in Normandy with her French boyfriend leaving for St Pancras and the Eurostar straight from work. She was alone there and would be until Monday evening.

She turned her attention back to her computer. She sourced and read a few feature articles about Frederica Daunt. Their character was essentially soft and sympathetic. She was not made to look in any of them like a crank or a fraud, profiteering from the gullibility intense grief tended to inflict on those mourning lost loved ones.

Instead she was portrayed as a sensitive and compassionate woman putting a selfless gift at the disposal of those who needed it most.

She had a connection in life with Martin Mear. Or at least, she claimed she did. Her father, Sebastian Daunt, had been a member of an artists' colony in Dorset, not far from the Dorset town of Shaftesbury in the 1960s. He had done the cover artwork for the Ghost Legion debut, *King Lud*. At least, he claimed he had. There was no design credit on the sleeve.

'Small world,' Ruthie said to her screen, aloud.

The Martin Mear who came to the medium to communicate from the other side did not deliver portents of droning death, either. He sounded sweet and harmless and as devoted to Frederica as might be a surrogate son.

Did the dead not age? Ruthie supposed they didn't. Alive, Martin would be two decades older than the medium who'd described his puppyish visitations. But he wasn't alive, was he? He was and would always be twenty-seven, like Hendrix and Jim Morrison, both of whom he had known in life and it was said had rubbed along with pretty well.

Whatever, the ghostly Martin experiences described by Frederica in these interviews bore no relation to the sinister event Ruthie had experienced in Chiswick the previous evening. Her instinct was that this stuff was all wishful thinking intended to generate trade and that what she had undergone, by contrast, was a real and powerful psychic experience.

The obvious, further and uncomfortable conclusion was that it had been staged specifically for her. Martin Mear had never bothered to conjure a posthumous performance such she'd endured for the sole benefit of the medium. She wanted to call Frederica Daunt and have that suspicion denied or more likely confirmed, but she'd left the woman in no condition to chat casually on the phone and anyway, it was too early in the morning to try to interrogate her yet.

She thought Sebastian Daunt's artists' colony probably the same ramshackle commune of hippie caravans at which April's mother had lived back in the days before her premature death. Martin had been familiar with that place. It might have even been a sort of second home for someone intent on living the life of a performing artist intent on pushing the boundaries of convention to their limits. It was where he had learned to play his guitar before a public of sorts. It was where he had extemporized musically and first encountered sex and probably drugs and their impact on his own burgeoning creativity.

King Lud had not come out of a vacuum. It had come out of an isolated and abandoned mansion on Wight, a place allegedly haunted on the edge of a gloomy wood, remote from the nearest habitation. Ruthie decided that she would fetch the disc from the car and give it another listen. The CD sounded much fuller than the music file of it on her phone. There was more detail, more of what audiophiles termed bandwidth. And Veronica's flat housed a high-end hi fi system, all Naim components lovingly assembled in Salisbury and bought a few years earlier with one of Veronica's auction-house bonuses.

She was humming the melodies from the album an hour later as she brewed her mid-morning coffee quite able to see how it had become so successful. As the 1960s reached their end, as pop aged and evolved into rock, it had answered the unspoken need for something deeper and more beguiling than what the Beatles and Beach Boys clones were churning out at the moment of its release. It had seized and defined a mood no one had known until then was upon the record-buying public.

The success of *King Lud* enabled Martin Mear to recruit the musicians of his choosing as band members. They were a conventional enough foursome; with a rhythm section of bassist and drummer and a keyboard player on piano, organ and later Mellotron. Martin sang lead vocal and played lead guitar. In either role, he suffered by comparison with no one.

Ruthie had only just finished her coffee when Frederica called her, agreeing to see her at three o'clock the same afternoon, on neutral ground at a riverside pub at Barnes. It was the weekend and therefore Ruthie assumed a day off for her. This was a presumption though that felt immediately foolish, because the notion that the dead paid strict attention to the calendar seemed absurd. The medium sounded improbably bright on the phone and Ruthie was slightly surprised to discover they were now on first-name terms.

'Standing on ceremony seems a bit pointless after last night's occurrences.'

'I suppose it does.'

'You saw me at my worst. I've never been reduced to such a state. Sorry about the blood.'

'I've never been particularly bothered by the sight of blood. Also, I wasn't the one doing the bleeding,' Ruthie said.

'You were exceptionally kind.'

Ruthie didn't know what to say. She said, 'Maybe I'm a kind person.'

'I don't doubt that you are. It's one of the reasons I've agreed to meet you today.'

The sun shone palely on the Barnes afternoon. Sixes and eights toiled over their oars, barked at through megaphones out on the still water. It was warm enough for them to sit outside in the pub garden, which sloped down to the river's edge. Frederica wore her hair down, loosely brushed, and was slender in boot-cut jeans and a hacking jacket. She lit a cigarette and exhaled smoke and smiled. She looked younger than she had the previous evening. Her eyes sparkled, but her nostrils were still pinkly edged.

'The first thing you need to know is that I'm not a fraud.'

Ruthie thought about saying that the suspicion hadn't occurred to her, but it would be a blatant and obvious lie. So she didn't say anything, merely nodding in response.

'I've exaggerated my gift. The gift is real enough. I feel the presence of the dead and sometimes believe they communicate with the living through me.'

Again, Ruthie restricted herself to a nod.

'I've never had any complaints from people trying to contact their loved ones on the other side. There is another side, you see, Ruthie, and as often as not the dead seek contact with the same ardour as the living.'

Ardour. In this context, the word seemed more than distasteful, almost obscene. 'Why do they?'

Frederica shrugged. She tapped ash into the circle of foil provided for the purpose on the table. She said, 'They do so because their deaths have been violent, or unexplained, or just abrupt, because they're premature. They do so because there's a need for closure.'

'And Martin Mear?'

She smiled. She looked up at the sky and then out over the river. She ground out her cigarette. She said, 'In my entire professional life, two fairly famous inhabitants of the spirit world have contacted me with a degree of consistency. They are the ballerina Juliet Devereaux and the romance writer Dorothy Harrington.'

'You made up Martin Mear?'

'I think last night proved pretty conclusively that I didn't make up Martin Mear.'

'But you fabricated contact with him?'

Frederica lit another cigarette. She said, 'I needed someone dark and glamorous. It's a precarious living. Dorothy Harrington wouldn't have got me the exposure, bless her. Martin Mear did.'

'It's interesting that you chose to present him so sympathetically.'

'He was sexy and enigmatic and the whole world has heard of him.'

'He's as much notorious as famous, though.'

'Making him out to be a good soul provoked interest. There'd have been no point, otherwise.'

'You might have been completely misrepresenting him.'

Frederica shrugged. She said, 'There's dark and light in everyone. My dad really did know him, really did provide the artwork for the first Ghost Legion record. He liked Martin, wouldn't have obliged like that if he hadn't.'

'But last night was the first contact with his spirit you'd regard as genuine?'

'It was. And he chose to expose us to the darkness.'

'Is that the reason you're telling me this? You aren't just telling me because you think I was kind to you last night.'

'I'm telling you because I think I'm obliged to. I think he's taken exception to the deception, if you will. I'm telling you because I suspect if I didn't do so, he'd pay me another visit and I wouldn't honestly relish that prospect.'

'Your secret's safe with me,' Ruthie said. 'I've no interest in exposing this. I'll just omit you completely from my research. My job's to verify facts, after all. It's only facts I'm being paid for. I'll assume you're giving up on Martin? On the pretence of Martin, I mean?'

Frederica didn't answer that question. She toyed with her cigarette packet, turning it like a fat playing card between her fingers. She said, 'He's extremely powerful, frighteningly so. There's more than darkness, there's some kind of turmoil there on a scale I sensed last night was nothing short of vast. You need to tread very carefully, Ruthie. This is quite something you've taken on.'

Saturdays were no different really to Paula Tort from any other day. The volume of work she had, the number of balls she juggled, the fact that she was where the buck stopped; all of this meant that she never really relaxed. That was how she liked things. She didn't delegate anything important. She employed capable people, but she made every single important business decision she faced.

It was years since she'd given any serious thought to this. She was ambitious and she'd proven in her character to be something of a perfectionist. But she had been thinking a lot recently about Martin. Her years with Martin, she thought, her place in his story, had been the spur that drove her business success from the outset.

She'd discussed it with April, only the other day. It was a big deal, breaking the silence of what seemed like a lifetime. It threatened to bring the sort of naked exposure that she thought made both of them understandably nervous.

She was in her studio, editing a fashion shoot, selecting the twelve pictures the editors would be sent and the four they would use for the spring women's-wear ad campaign. Except that her mind was half on Martin while the images flashed sequentially on the large screen in front of her.

Those days seemed a world distant from the present. People thought of it all as the apogee of depravity, the last word in decadence, rock stars as powerful as medieval kings and with fortunes and fawning retinues just as large, indulging their divine right to rule everything that surrounded them.

And it had been like that. There had been the drugs and the sex and the scary sensation-seeking that brought them into contact with all sorts of mystical shit. There'd been a swaggering, exotic, self-destructive sense of intoxication. But there'd also been a perverse sense of innocence back then, a quality that the modern world simply wouldn't comprehend. Martin had been as idealistic as he was corrupt, as purely artistic as he'd been morally and physically tainted. That was the truth, but it was a complicated truth she thought people now would never be able to appreciate.

She'd return the call made to her by Ruthie Gillespie. She'd meet the woman and answer the questions posed by Carter Melville's researcher. But she'd never get that across about the man she had loved. Martin would remain contradictory and somehow always teasingly beyond the focused clarity of objective truth. At least he would, taken out of his own time.

She watched the images wink and shutter seductively across the screen in her darkened studio. The photographer had done a good job. The shoot had been done in Thailand, not for the weather or the scenery, because it was a beach shoot and logistically, somewhere like the coast of Spain or Bahia California would have been far less complex and probably cheaper options.

The shoot had been done where it had because the photographer was exiled there, a fugitive from child-porn charges he didn't wish to face in a European court. He was a very good photographer and everyone, despite these allegations, still went to the expense of trekking out to South-East Asia to use him.

The fashion business was amoral like that. You ignored the prima-donna tantrums and the drug habits and the depravity and general weirdness because all that stuff went with the territory. You kept your own nose clean – in Paula's case literally – and you got on with things. The industry was what it was. And she was nostalgic sometimes for the brazen honesty and innocence of the world she'd shared with Martin Mear a lifetime ago. Though innocent, if she was totally honest, was an inexact word to describe any of it.

Her phone hummed in her pocket. It was April. She answered it saying, 'I was just thinking about you.'

'Carter Fucking Melville,' April said.

'Had no idea he possessed a middle name. All these years, bastard's been holding out on me.'

April laughed. She said, 'The whole thing's whipping up a shit-storm of memories.'

'Good and bad?'

'Almost totally good, until the end, anyway, but the weird thing is I can't control it. Some of this stuff I'm remembering for the first time since it happened. That's pretty freaky.'

'I'll tell you what's freaky,' Paula said. 'Freaky is realizing I'd have done none of this stuff I've done without your dad dying on us. I did it because I didn't want to be a footnote to Martin's story. The penny's only really just dropped. Does that sound callous?'

'It sounds normal, Paula. It's always seemed pretty obvious to me.'

'Really?'

'I did my degree in psychology, remember?'

'I should do, darling, I attended your congregation. I was very proud. I believe I cried.'

'What you did is normal. What's abnormal is doing it so well.'

'Thanks.'

'And it's a kind of compliment? Like you always knew Dad would end up a legend.'

That had been a given, Paula thought. She'd known that even before properly knowing him, when she'd seen his spare, sinewy silhouette under its halo of backlit hair stride onto centre-stage for the first time. She'd known that before he sang a single phrase or picked out a power chord on the white Stratocaster guitar slung low across his bared torso. She'd felt the force of him ripple through the tiered audience like a high-voltage surge. Few people possessed what Martin Mear had been gifted with, but Martin had possessed it in a strength that was off the scale.

'Do you still think we're doing the right thing?'

'Who knows?' April said. 'I want to do my dad justice. I think the time has probably come.'

'Amen to that,' Paula Tort said. But as their conversation ended, her phone was slippery in the grip of her palm with sweat.

Paula had checked out Ruthie Gillespie. She could have accepted Carter's recommendation at face value, but felt that face value and Carter Melville were terms uncomfortable with close proximity. And so she'd had the researcher checked out and discovered she was a sultry looking Goth novelist with an artfully indulged taste for ink.

She was from a port town named Ventnor on the Isle of Wight, where she still lived. She wrote for children and young adults and latterly for a more mature audience. She'd done her degree in history, so she was no stranger to thorough research. Ruthie G hadn't struck Paula as an obvious choice for the job, but she knew Carter worked on instinct and that his instinct had proven more often than not to be sound.

That said, she didn't think Ruthie's looks would exactly have been lost on Carter Melville. Carter Fucking Melville, as April had called him, which in his younger days, would have been an apt description.

Paula sighed and switched off the screen and scribbled a note on the pad on the arm of the chair she sat in about the shoot she had just viewed. It was wrong to judge people on their looks. Ideologically and politically, she believed that. She believed it personally too, the irony being that she had earned her fortune in an industry so vacuous that looks were the only criterion on which anyone was judged. Looks and age, she thought, thinking about the Thailand photographer and his dirty predilections and the fee he had just earned out of the company she ran for clicking his camera shutter on a beach.

She would be truthful with Ruthie G. There was no point in being otherwise. What she had to say would be influential in determining Martin's enduring legacy. She owed it to him, to herself, to April and even perhaps to Carter Fucking Melville to tell the truth. She would sell Ruthie short if she didn't and she had decided that she was predisposed to liking the young Goth writer.

There was only one experience she would not discuss. Since she had never discussed it with anyone, since it remained a secret almost from herself, she was confident it wouldn't come up. This particular episode had been endured anyway after Martin's demise, so she could fairly easily convince herself that it wasn't relevant to what would eventually be included in the piece being researched and then written about his all too short tenure on earth.

The grieving process after Martin's demise had been long and horrible to endure. His departure from her life had seemed to Paula like some rude affront to nature. And they had been inseparable for the last two years of that life, for the whole of the time she had known him. She had loved him deeply and would not deny, if challenged on the point, that she did so still. April Mear knew that about her, she was sure. It was an insight that didn't really require the degree in psychology Martin's daughter possessed.

So she had grieved for Martin. Then, after the shock and the accommodation of the loss, a couple of questions had occurred to Paula to which she could provide no answers. Those questions assumed the status over time of mysteries. They nagged at her and eventually, they seemed to her like a sort of taunt.

In an effort to solve them, she went back to a location important in Martin's life. She went looking for the clues that would give her answers. She travelled alone and told no one where she was going. It was an experience from which she considered afterwards she had barely escaped with her sanity. She was surprised, when she thought about it, that she had survived the episode at all. It hadn't answered her questions, either, only deepening the mysteries that had compelled her in the first place to go.

She wouldn't discuss this event with Ruthie G. It had happened after Martin's departure from life. Without Martin's absence, it would never have happened at all. It wasn't relevant, didn't fit into the chronology, the time-frame the researcher was concerned with. It could be regarded as an adventure. It could be seen as an ordeal.

It was an experience of which Paula, with her strong desire to rationalize, could still make no rational sense. She didn't like to think about it and couldn't see the value in sharing it with anyone.

'Not now, not ever,' she said aloud to the empty room she was in.

She'd give Ruthie G a call. She'd do it herself rather than have someone do it on her behalf. She knew her own diary. She'd have thought herself pitiful if she hadn't been fully aware of every engagement on her own busy schedule. The researcher had said that more than one long and exhaustive session would be necessary. She preferred a series of shorter interviews, she'd said in the message she'd left, saying, 'What I'm able to determine as fact will dictate the nature of the questions I ask from one interview to the next.'

It seemed a thorough and reasonable approach. She'd be speaking to the three of them in tandem. It would work fine for her and for April, they'd committed, after all. Terrible pun as it was, they both wanted the record put straight. She thought it a technique, though, that might test the patience of Terry Maloney, or Sir Terence, as he was now. She hadn't spoken to him or seen him in person for thirty years. But she remembered him and the man she remembered had never been known for his patience.

SIX

At five o'clock on Saturday afternoon, Frederica Daunt waited in a chair in her conservatory for darkness to descend. Her suitcase was packed and ready in the hallway by the front door. She was in the conservatory because that was the only place in the house she allowed herself to smoke. She had smoked pretty steadily since waking that morning and recalling the events of the previous night.

She could have smoked in the garden, but she'd had enough fresh air for one day during her meeting with the picturesque researcher being paid to investigate the somewhat troubled life of Martin Mear. It was Frederica's belief that kindly eyeful Ruthie Gillespie was going to have her work cut out. She didn't know the exact nature of the trouble Mear had got himself into but she expected it had to do with the subject that had fascinated him even as a teenager.

That subject had been magic, and not magic of the Paul Daniels/ Dynamo illusionist variety. When her father had first met Martin, he was a fifteen-year-old captivated by the possibilities of the occult. When her father had come up with the artwork for the *King Lud* record sleeve seven years later, he had been a young man about to be endowed with a fortune that would amply fund his fascination. Her dad had never doubted that Martin, in life, had taken this as far as it would go. In death, Frederica thought the previous evening had demonstrated that.

Her ticket was at the check-in desk at Heathrow and it was one way. She tended to winter in her Algarve villa. It wasn't quite winter yet, the weather wasn't vindictive and the trees were a glorious russet and gold and the river had looked beautiful and tranquil at Barnes earlier in the day. But the nights were closing in, weren't they? And there was such a thing as pragmatism, wasn't there?

She should not have indulged the deceit she had over Martin Mear. If his spirit had ignored it, it had done so perhaps out of gratitude. Her father had never been paid anything for the *King Lud* cover design. To have charged money for the work would have run counter to his hippie ideology. Her dad had believed art and profit irreconcilable.

The design still held up, hadn't dated, looked at once totally of its time and absolutely timeless. Its inspiration was those bearded images of Old Father Thames. He was portrayed in a full-face illustration on the sleeve as a mooring post, like the great bronze lions' head mooring posts stained green with age and the submergings of innumerable tides dotted along the river embankment. Like them, he had a mooring ring in the grip of his jaws. Like them, he had a mane of hair and look of weary stoicism in his ancient eyes.

Martin's spirit had remained grateful. And so it had tolerated Frederica's ongoing deception. But last night, with the researcher present, she had gone too far. She thought that when darkness fell tonight, and that moment was almost upon West London, there might be a repetition, or an escalation, and she would be forced now to flee her home and find some way in which to try to make recompense from a safe distance.

If nothing happened, she would simply cancel her ticket and unpack her case. She would do so with a long sigh of relief and a resolute promise to finally kick her smoking habit. She might even retire. Her work had made her comfortably off. The proceeds of her five-year-old divorce settlement still lay untouched in a very healthy deposit account. Intimacy with the dead had been cold and uncomfortable even before the antics of the previous night. It was a clammy sort of contact; dark, shivery, stained always by grief.

She had planned a little show. The buttons concealed under the table in the séance room would have reduced the temperature and generated a draught around their legs. There would have been the scent of Vetiver, which was the cologne she'd read Martin Mear had habitually worn. She'd mixed it with patchouli, which had been the signature scent of the heavy rock scene during his time. A ghostly wind would have moaned through the concealed speakers and the table would have rattled as she claimed contact with some skilful vocal projection.

Her gift was genuine, but it didn't always perform to order. She backed it up with a few tricks of the trade useful on those stubborn occasions when nothing manifested. She had got to use none of these though last night. Something had manifested, unexpectedly. She was still reeling mentally under the assaulting force of it. It had knocked her cold and ruptured her nasal membranes. It had brought on migraine and a buzzing that still pounded her eardrums. Mostly though it had terrified her, because she thought it only hinted at the real havoc Martin's antic spirit could provoke.

Shadows lengthened. She stubbed out her cigarette and lit another. She became aware that the birds that usually busily greeted the sunset were absent from her garden. She'd have heard them, faintly, through glass and she couldn't.

Rain rattled on the roof. Usually that was a cosy, comforting sound. Her conservatory was a warm, dry sanctuary from the weather. But this rain seemed frenzied, the drops spitting percussively like the mad skitter of drumsticks on a tautly stretched skin. She glanced up and saw of course that it wasn't raining at all. And it was then that out of her peripheral vision, Frederica saw there was a pale figure standing on her lawn.

She forced herself to look. He was tall and cloaked and had his head bowed. His long hair hung heavily in front of his face. Darkness had gathered about him, the last of the light leeching out of the lower extremities of the sky. It didn't obscure him, the darkness. He was detailed at the centre of it, as though some force at once attracted it and held it slightly at bay.

His fingers were very long, she saw. Then it occurred to her that it might be his fingernails only giving them the illusion of greater length. The nails continued to grow, didn't they, after death? Sometimes they grew for weeks in a coffin on the still hands of a motionless corpse.

She only became aware of how still the figure had been when he began to move. With slow deliberation he began to raise his head, the curtain of hair threatening to part and reveal his features as his head rose and straightened up.

Frederica fled. She ran through the conservatory and through her house to a deafening wail of sound, a screeching rumble distorting the air with the sheer strength of its volume, a violent, vicious storm of noise that hit her almost like a physical barrier to her progress towards the front door.

'Feedback,' she said to herself, numbly, when she was seated in the taxi she'd hailed at the kerb outside her house, with her suitcase on the floor beside her. 'He used feedback, didn't he, when he played the guitar?' She was deaf to her own question. She couldn't hear herself. She was in the outer suburbs, the dismal uniform reaches on the Heathrow route to the west of London, when she became aware that her ears were bleeding.

In Carter Melville's own words to Ruthie at their face-to-face meeting, 'Martin Mear *was* the fucking Legion.' Certainly it was true that he had written their songs. It was also true that he had performed the lead vocal and taken the lead guitar part. At the time of *King Lud*'s release, the claim made by Melville was literally true, because the character and sound of the band had been determined before Martin had recruited any personnel. But he did recruit band members and when they were assembled, they were widely considered the best in the business.

Drummers were traditionally half-insane in credible rock bands back then; a qualification taken seriously by the Who's Keith Moon and by John 'Bonzo' Bonham of Led Zeppelin. Both of those drummers could be said, if you were cynical, to have died in action. They were killed while still in their thirties by their own reckless hedonism.

The man behind the kit in Ghost Legion was Jason Ritchie. He was a Liverpudlian, the son of a docker and a school dinner lady. He'd been powerful through the arms and shoulders, as rock drummers tended to become. He'd had the obligatory mane of hair. He'd been heavily tattooed, decades before it became really fashionable among musicians like him to ink their skin. And though he'd outlived Martin, he'd done his best to live up to the tradition by drinking his liver into destruction before the remainder of his band mates perished. That had been in 1976, the year of punk, which Ruthie thought might and might not be a coincidence.

Ghost Legion's bassist was Patsy McCoy, who'd been in a rhythm and blues band with Terry Maloney when they'd still been at school in Dublin. A more talented musician than Terry, almost as soon as he joined the Legion he'd got his childhood friend the roadie job that would lead to far greater things for the future Sir Terence. McCoy was a solidly rhythmic player, but he was considered a great deal more than that.

There was something magical, the critics of the time said, when Ritchie and McCoy played together. They did a whole lot more than put down the beat. They swung and chugged and swaggered. It was alchemy. Patsy died when the converted Wiltshire barn he lived in caught fire in the summer of 1979. An accident investigator called to the scene as emergency crews damped down said that a cigarette smoked in bed was almost certainly the cause of the fatal blaze.

On keyboards and backing vocals, the Legion were lucky enough to land James Prentice. Prentice was an ex-public schoolboy and chorister, classically trained, Ruthie assumed the only member of the band ever able to read sheet music.

There was persistent speculation that if he hadn't actually co-written some of their material, then he had at least had an influential hand in arranging it. His living relatives had taken this claim to court twice, but had failed in both attempts to have a portion of the band's royalties diverted their way. James had not been able to contribute on either occasion to the argument. He had died at the wheel of his Porsche in a motorway crash in the spring of 1983, before either legal action was brought.

They weren't, in life, an acrimonious band. They got on with each other and they got on too with the bands they competed with. The egos back then had been gargantuan, but there'd been an ungrudging degree of mutual respect. Thus it was, 'Yeah, the Legion, they're hot, man, they're really fucking good. You've just got to live with it. Go see them. That's cool. Then afterwards come see us.'

Jagger had said that. Or he'd allegedly said it. It was unsubstantiated, like the claim that Jeff Beck had said Martin Mear was the best guitarist he'd heard since Hendrix, like the story that Paul Rodgers of Free envied only Martin Mear's set of lead singers' pipes. There was a whole lot of bull in the rock world and it mired honesty and slowed progress and frankly, sometimes it beggared belief.

By ten o'clock on Saturday evening, seated in front of her laptop, Ruthie Gillespie was developing a suspicion of her own about Martin Mear's early life, something that had never been speculated on or even publicly discussed. His father had been a farm labourer and his mother a domestic cleaner and both of them were long dead and he'd had no siblings. But he'd had an uncle, his mother's younger brother, who'd lived in Shadwell and worked as a shipping clerk in the London docks, back in the time when the Thames had still been a working river.

Ruthie strongly suspected that Martin must have gone to visit and stay regularly with his uncle Max. He'd been raised in Shaftesbury, studied hard at school, got excellent A levels and gone to Oxford as an undergraduate. But after three years of education in the west of England, his debut album had taken London as its theme.

You had to wonder why, if he had no personal experience of the capital. He had to have been there, didn't he? And not just on a day trip to some museum or gallery organized by his school. He had to have explored the city, to ever become as beguiled as he'd evidently been by its history and legends and landmarks that it became the subject of his first substantial and mature artistic endeavour.

His parents had been poor. He had relied on his paper round for pocket money. He had saved for and bought his first guitar himself, just like he'd saved for and bought the bike he pedalled to the hippie commune a few miles from his home where he joined jam sessions to practise playing his guitar in his teens. The only way he could have experienced London was if he stayed with his uncle Max and though Max Askew was long gone, Ruthie had discovered the address at which he'd lived until his death a few years after the death of his nephew.

Ruthie thought the London angle quite exciting. It wasn't yet proven, but it was as close as she had so far come to a fresh discovery. Verifying facts didn't deliver job satisfaction. Intuiting facts and then proving them when they'd been previously unknown did that.

It was at 10.35 pm and she was seriously thinking of calling it a day – and a night – when Carter Melville called her for a progress report. He'd done this the previous evening and she imagined it would become a regular thing, their habitual little phone ritual. If so it was another good reason for staying off the slosh. He wouldn't appreciate his pet researcher hiccupping and slurring through an account of her progress so far, losing her thread, repeating herself, brain drowning in Chablis. Or possibly something stronger.

'Can I ask you a question, Carter?'

'You don't ask, baby, you sure as damn don't get.'

'Did Martin ever discuss going to see his uncle Max in London?'

'Nope, never did.'

'Did he never mention his uncle Max to you?'

'Yeah, once, guy was named Max Askew and crewed in the war aboard one of the flotilla of little ships that got the beaten British army guys off the beach at Dunkirk. Martin thought that was very cool. I mean a cool experience to live through and all, with the German dive-bombers strafing the shit out of everything. Can't remember how it came up, but it did.'

The next question was a long shot, but still worth asking. 'Did he happen to say who it was Max Askew worked for?'

'Funny, I've got total recall on everything Mear-related until matters got galactic after the second album came out. It's after *Black Solstice* and the first really big American tour that things get blurry for me. Oxford, I remember like it was yesterday. And Max Askew was a college conversation.'

'Go on.'

'Max lived in Shadwell. He was a shipping clerk for an import and export outfit with a name that sounded French or maybe Belgian. I'll have it in a second. Yeah, the postcard just dropped through my door, Ruthie. Uncle Max worked for a firm called Martens and Degrue.'

Ruthie ended this conversation looking down out of the spare room window at the Hercules road railway arches. She was at eye-level with the passengers on the trains on the rails above, the numerous parallel lines in and out of the Waterloo terminus. She could see indifferent figures reduced by perspective seated in the carriages bathed in yellow light. She observed that it wasn't raining. The evening was fine. It was mild enough that she had the window open just a chink.

She got her coat and bag and exited the flat and walked the short distance to the Pineapple pub. She ordered a large vodka and tonic and took her drink and went and sat at one of the bench seats at the wooden tables outside on the street. She took a long swallow of her drink and then lit a cigarette and inhaled gratefully. There was a group of men at an adjacent table and she was aware of them noticing her but thankfully, none of them made any attempt at chat. She thought probably the expression on her face likely to discourage them from trying to flirt with her.

Martens and Degrue were a part of her personal history. They were why she had come originally to meet Michael Aldridge almost three years earlier on Wight. They were why she had subsequently come to meet and befriend Veronica Slade, in whose flat she was currently staying as an un-paying guest. They were the respectable face of the Jericho Society, a secretive cult that wasn't respectable at all. And the Jericho Society was the original reason Ruthie had become less than cynical personally on the subject of the occult.

She felt like calling Michael Aldridge. She felt like confiding this development in him. She felt like calling Veronica and telling her about it too. But she felt also that to do either of those things would be an unfair imposition. Neither of them was involved with this. She was, and voluntarily. It was a well-paid gig. It was her baby, she thought, taking another sip of her drink, thinking that Carter Melville's ghastly phraseology was dismayingly contagious.

Ruthie heard and felt the ice clack against her teeth as she raised and emptied her glass, her lips numb with cold and the warmth of the alcohol spreading through her chest and stomach. She looked at her wristwatch. She had time for another before last orders were called. She'd have another and then she'd go back and sleep on what she'd discovered. She didn't, suddenly, feel entirely comfortable with the thought of spending a second night alone at somewhere that wasn't home to her. But the Jericho Society had a long reach and she knew at heart that really, nowhere was beyond it.

She'd sleep on what she'd found out. She'd have a better idea of what strategy to take in the morning. Max Askew's employment might have nothing whatsoever to do with the dark reputation engendered by his nephew both in life and in death. It might be an innocent coincidence. Except that Ruthie didn't really believe very much in coincidence. More and more, to her, Michael's words about fate outside the Riverside Café were proving ominously prescient.

But the evening hadn't quite yet finished with Ruthie. She was twenty feet on from the pub, taking the short walk back to the flat, when her phone buzzed in her pocket and it was Frederica Daunt.

'Ruthie? I'm at Heathrow. I saw him, after sunset, in my garden.'

'Bloody hell.'

'You need to drop this.'

'You ran away?'

'Present tense, I'm running. Flight was delayed, so only about to board now. Had to call you, in the end. Had to tell you, you should leave this alone.'

Ruthie bit her lip, the phone tremoring slightly in her grip. She said, 'I need to ask you a question, Frederica. Have you ever heard of something called the Jericho Society?'

'Never, and this isn't the time for trivia quizzes, dear. You need to back off this one. It isn't remotely worth it.'

'You're shouting. You don't need to shout.'

'It's not deliberate. My hearing's been damaged. I can't hear myself. I'm going now. I sincerely hope we're speaking for the last time.'

She broke the connection.

Ruthie looked around at the night street, a car speedily whizzing by, lights lit in the Blake House flats behind the iron railings beside her, an eruption of laughter from outside the Pineapple to her rear. *I'm going nowhere*, she said to herself. *I'm not a quitter and never have been. I've taken on a job and mean to see it through.*

Besides, she thought, *I'm in the middle of a mystery here and mysteries are for solving.*

But the real reason she would carry on became clear to her in bed, just in the moment before fatigue claimed her and deep sleep descended. And it was nothing to do with unravelling old enigmas or with the substantial sum she stood to earn for doing so. The truth was that recent events had broken Ruthie's heart. She felt cleaved inside. A big part of her wanted to surrender to her feelings, to despair and just be broken. Doing what she was doing now was the only strategy she felt she had for avoiding that.

SEVEN

The flat Max Askew had lived in was in a post-war council block behind the now-fashionable wharves in which he'd worked. But even council blocks were highly desirable these days in that part of London. Most of the original tenants had bought in the 1980s and then sold and moved on she supposed in retirement to Essex and Kent. Max had lived at number 77 Proctor Court. It was unoccupied she discovered on Sunday morning, for sale. Estate agents worked weekends. She could go there posing as a potential buyer and get a feel for the place. There would be nothing of Max left there, Ruthie knew, but she could explore the locality, walk through the door and see the view out of the windows through the eyes of a teenage Martin Mear.

Estate agents. Bloody hell. As the wan sunlight of Sunday morning rose and Ruthie sipped her breakfast coffee, she pictured a young man in a tight suit and pointy shoes, the sort who talked about chillaxing and drove one of those Mini Coopers that looked like a steroid-fed version of the original. Estate agents were all essentially the same pushy, eager, superficial character. But he'd have the keys to the door of a place in which her subject had absorbed important influences. He'd have the power to unlock secrets.

At least, he might.

She was going to go to the residence where Martin's uncle Max had lived in Shadwell in the days when he worked for Martens and Degrue. She was determined.

She got a two o'clock appointment to view Max Askew's old flat, which suggested to Ruthie that the property wasn't quite the easy sell it should have been in that coveted location. There could be all sorts of reasons for that, though, and she'd keep an open mind until she'd seen the place personally.

She lavished £20 of Carter Melville's expenses money on a cab to Shadwell and her destination. Other than driving a Golf rather than a Mini, the estate agent was exactly as she'd pictured him in her mind. He was preening himself in a wing mirror when she approached him, parked outside a walk-up block with Proctor Court picked out helpfully in tiled mosaic above a communal archway entrance.

'Number 77's on the third floor,' he said, when they'd introduced themselves.

'I've got this thing,' Ruthie said, 'about viewing properties alone. I got the asking price and basic spec from the website. I'd like to take a look unaccompanied, if you don't mind?'

He shrugged. He held out a set of keys. He said, 'It's a vacant flat. No residents to tiptoe around, nothing valuable there to nick.'

'Charming.'

He had a nice smile. 'I was joking,' he said. 'Help yourself.'

'Thanks.' She took the keys from him.

'I'll wait for you here.'

He didn't seem particularly hopeful about the verdict. Maybe he was just pissed off at having to work when he could have been with his mates, in a pub outside Upton Park, getting nicely oiled prior to the afternoon's West Ham home game.

The entrance to number 77 was distinguished by a heavy bronze knocker. She thought this rather florid, mounted on the front door of a council flat. But the block wasn't typically utilitarian, like most of the social housing erected in inner London after the Second World War. There were a few arts and crafts movement nods and signatures in the brickwork and window frames.

The knocker reminded her of the cover of *King Lud*. But it wasn't a cast representation of Old Father Thames, was it? He was more magisterial. This was another folkloric character entirely. This was the Green Man, similarly bearded and wild-haired, but always with an antic grin and a look of mischievous glee in his eyes. The Green Man always looked ready to party. Ruthie didn't think she'd have liked his parties though and the thought of them made her shudder slightly. Paganism could be seriously dark. She let herself in.

The first thing she noticed was a smell, subtle but distinctly there and rather like the incense burned during the mass and benediction services celebrated in a Catholic church. She sniffed at the air and looked around, but could not readily determine where the odour was coming from. The flat was unfurnished and its wooden floors were bare. There was no fabric for a scent to cling to. The walls were painted rather than wallpapered, so there didn't seem to be anything in which a smell could really linger. It was curious.

The second thing she noticed was an absence of available light. The windows were quite large, even generous and their glass seemed spotlessly clean. But they didn't let much light in. The flat's interior was still and silent and dull; opaque, almost gloomy. And it seemed smaller than it should have. The rooms were not large, but there was a sense of confinement in all of them that she thought almost physically unpleasant. She felt a subtle, cramped sensation. The word for the place was dingy.

Ruthie noticed the design on the fireplace in the sitting room straight away. It was large and ornate, a heavy wooden construction rather grand-seeming for such a small dwelling, but quite in keeping with the arts and crafts touches she'd noticed on the stairwell and communal walkways of the block. It had been carved and then varnished. She ran a hand across it. She thought that there were many layers of varnish. They had obscured its grain and darkened the patina of the wood to something close to black.

Carved into the centre of this chest-high feature was a five-sided star with a circle around it. The circular groove touched the apex of each point. It was precisely done and prominently placed and Ruthie knew that it was a pentagram. She traced the design with the tip of her index finger. She didn't know precisely what it signified, but she knew that it was a symbol important to practitioners of the occult.

There was a slight tackiness to the wood. It was more than just a sweaty fingertip on paintwork. Her fingertip wasn't sweaty because the room was too chilly to provoke perspiration. There was something not quite gluey there, but a definite residue, unpleasant to the touch. It was as though the wood itself excreted something moist and very slightly sticky.

She made a fist and rapped her knuckles hard, once, against the wood. She was rewarded with a jolt of pain and a sound that seemed curiously dull. She stamped a heel on the bare boards under her feet and the impact, again, seemed muffled. She coughed, deliberately, and the cough seemed to her own ears to have the quality of a noise more remembered than spontaneously heard. It was odd. All of it was odd. And it was disconcerting. She remained still for a moment. She thought that the incense scent was growing in strength the longer she remained there.

She experienced a start, then, as though seeing someone appear suddenly behind her in a mirror. So vivid was the sensation that she turned swiftly around to confront whoever had stolen up on her. But there was nobody behind her. Just as there had been no mirror hung on the wall she'd faced to see them in. In the silence, from the parlour or lounge giving onto the sitting room from the open door to her left, she heard the distinct ticking of a clock she knew from examining it moments earlier that the room didn't possess. She could hear a sound too like a rusty pendulum swing.

The ticking got louder. It seemed somehow disapproving, reproachful. She imagined someone black-clad, swinging an incense burner in the parlour where she couldn't see them, yawing it back and forth to the rhythm of the clock that wasn't there, filling the air with a tainted, ceremonial smell. She thought she heard a dragged footstep, teasing and sly, but she knew there was no one in the room. There couldn't be. She'd only left it a moment earlier.

As calmly as she was able to, Ruthie turned and walked out of the flat. She locked the door securely behind her. She glanced at the Green Man knocker, which seemed to be grinning even more widely than it had at her original approach. That part, she knew, was her imagination, just as the feeling of a human presence had been her imagination. But she hadn't imagined the odour or the ticking clock and she certainly hadn't imagined the carving on the sitting-room fire surround. They'd all of them been real.

'How long's it been on the market?'

'On and off, for ever,' he said.

They were in a pub, the Prospect of Whitby, which had a prospect through the window only of a turgid, drizzly river.

She didn't resort to this tactic generally. It was specific to the circumstances. He was young and shallow and vain and probably enough of a chancer to see a pointed drinks invitation as the prelude to sex. Thinking with his dick didn't make a man blind, but it got in the way of him seeing straight. She didn't want evasion or the runaround, she just wanted clear and honest answers to questions she had no real business asking.

He sipped his lager. He fingered his wristwatch bracelet and then looked at the face of it. He did that a lot. The watch looked expensive. He was probably just concerned to get his money's worth out of what he'd bought.

'Original occupant died in 1978. The Court had been respectable but was on the way to becoming a sink estate back then and various homeless families were in and out of the property on short lets.'

'How short?'

'The shorter the better, apparently. No one liked it there, is the story.'

'Then what happened?'

'There was a mass buy out in '87. All the tenants got together and bought the block from the council. Kind of a class action, Margaret Thatcher's aspiring working class, fulfilling the Tory dream by investing in property ownership.'

'You're better educated than you look.'

'And you shouldn't make snap judgements about people.'

'What happened next?'

'They mostly refurbed. Some of them re-sold and moved on. That flat was never successfully reoccupied. It remains an asset worth a theoretical fraction of its market value to all of the block's freeholders. But an asset you can't realize is actually worthless.'

'How many times have you been in there?'

'Half a dozen? It merry-go-rounds from agent to agent, we take turns at putting it on, except it isn't exactly merry, is it? Everyone knows about it, nobody really says anything. Makes you look foolish, if you do.'

'What's the longest time you've spent in there?'

'Really starts to get to you after about twenty minutes.'

Ruthie nodded. She'd managed no more than eight or nine. She wondered how Frederica Daunt would cope if she visited Max Askew's old docklands flat. She thought the medium would probably light up like a Christmas tree. Or maybe her nose would bleed, like someone struck heavily by a blow to the face as it had in Chiswick on Friday night.

The estate agent's name was Malcolm Stuart. He told her he was a graduate of Birkbeck College, one of the more prestigious bits of the University of London, where he'd taken a degree in history. History didn't naturally suggest a career path, so he'd taken this job, because the only qualifications required were ownership of a suit and a driver's licence. He had those, along with his trophy watch.

'You know quite a lot about Proctor Court.'

He sipped his lager. 'I know quite a bit about this locale generally. Industrial decline in the Wapping area in the post-war period was the subject of my thesis. I distilled it down to eight thousand words, but there was a lot of source information.'

'Ever heard of a docks-based company called Martens and Degrue?'

'You never had any intention of buying 77 Proctor Court, with or without its peculiar atmosphere, did you, Ms Gillespie?'

'No, I didn't.'

'I knew that from the start. You develop an instinct for time-wasters, property voyeurs. Generally, they're a pain in the arse.'

'I'm sorry.'

'Tell me what your real interest is and I'll tell you what I know about that firm you're curious about.'

'Done.'

They shipped religious art and artefacts, he said. They'd had a bonded warehouse, which was long gone. They had been unpopular with the archbishop of the Catholic diocese, though the reason for this hadn't been made public. They'd been unpopular too on the docks, again for reasons that were obscure. Their employees were shunned among the wharves and in the ale houses and pie-and-mash and betting shops around them.

'So Max Askew wouldn't have been welcome here.'

Malcolm shrugged. 'He was white-collar so he wouldn't have drunk with the dockers and stevedores anyway. The Prospect wasn't full of locals with loft apartments and German tourist coach parties then. The wharves were rough and ready and the boozers crowded and volatile.'

'What do you think is wrong with that flat?'

He didn't answer her. Instead he said, 'My sister's a bit of a hippie. Second-generation, only twenty-three, but she goes to Glastonbury and believes all that stuff about ley lines and crop circles. She's heavily into Ghost Legion. She reckons there's an answer to the mystery of what happened to Martin Mear and it's all there on the second sides of the albums with no names.'

'What do you mean, the "mystery"?'

'She says he didn't die.'

'There was a funeral.'

'The box was empty. They dug it up a decade after his supposed death and it was full of bricks.'

'That's an urban myth.'

He smiled. He had an attractive smile. He was an attractive young man, despite the vanity. She'd got that bit right about him and everything else wrong.

'I don't take much notice of what my sister says. But her crowd believes it. They're all waiting for the Second Coming.'

'That's blasphemous.'

'The archbishop would certainly have thought so.'

'The same one that took exception to Martens and Degrue?'

'The very man,' he said. Then he frowned.

'What's the matter?'

'I'd like to ask you would you like another drink. But I think if I do you'll say no and it'll just make you leave that bit quicker than you would have otherwise.'

'I'm a good ten years older than you are, Malcolm.'

'I was also afraid you might say that.'

'And actually, I should be going.'

'You gave the office your mobile number when you made the appointment. I might be tempted to ring it.'

'Don't do that. But give me your number.'

He did. He said, 'You'll delete it the minute you get out of the pub.'

'I might,' she said, smiling. 'Then again, I might not.'

She stood. She began to button her coat. He glanced up at her and said, 'I think Martens and Degrue might have had some connection with Satanism.'

She sat back down again, heavily.

'Go on,' she said. 'You've got my full attention.'

'They pulled out of Shadwell in 1970. Max Askew would have retired by then, if my sums are right. Their offices were subsequently occupied by a firm of fruit importers that didn't hang about in their new premises for very long.'

'Shades of Proctor Court?'

'The fruit rotted in its crates with uncanny speed, is the story I heard. They were followed by a firm of cheese importers, but the cheese turned green with mould. It would happen overnight, apparently. Food didn't work.'

'Or it worked overtime,' Ruthie said.

'A rite of exorcism was performed in a warehouse building there at the beginning of 1971. It was done twice, apparently. The first time that didn't work, or take, or whatever the correct terminology is for something like that. It had to be done again.'

'And what do you make of that?'

'There was a bit of a craze for it, wasn't there, back in the '70s?'

'There was,' Ruthie said. 'But not until after the film came out, and *The Exorcist* wasn't released until 1973. Earlier than then it would have been highly unusual for anyone to request the rite and even more unusual for the Catholic or Anglican Church to act on the request.'

'Spoken like a professional researcher.'

'You're not a bad researcher yourself, by the sound of things.'

'Yeah,' he said. 'But I'm not paid to do it. Another drink? Go on.'

'One,' she said. 'Then I really am leaving.'

EIGHT

Ruthie had been listening quite intently to the Ghost Legion albums. They were steeped in religious and folkloric myth. Their lyrics were full of a dark and broody symbolism. That was true even of the first three, let alone the ones Malcolm Stuart's dippy sister had down as a kind of secret code. Listening to them had understandably made her highly suggestible to the weird.

She'd had his uncle Max Askew down as the character likely

to have most influenced Martin Mear's tastes and thinking before ever setting foot in his old abode. She'd convinced herself of it before seeing or hearing even a shred of evidence. Lots of people had a Green Man door knocker. It might even have been a present from his sister, Martin's mum. The Green Man was considered a good-luck talisman in rural England, and Shaftesbury was both rural and far enough west to be in England's pagan heartland.

The noises she thought she had heard from the parlour, the foot-scrape and clock ticking, had come from an adjacent flat or from outside. They'd been noises generated by a neighbour, pretty obviously.

That still left the pentagram. It still left Askew's sinister old employer, Martens and Degrue, who had antagonized the archbishop and provoked an exorcism at the offices they'd vacated in the aftermath of their unlamented departure. Ruthie knew from personal experience that Martens and Degrue were the public face of the Jericho Society. That experience had taken place on Wight and had involved Michael Aldridge. She'd learned two things from it. The first was that the Jericho Society was extremely bad news. The second was that it remained very much in business.

What else did rationalizing the oddities of Proctor Court leave? It left Frederica Daunt's bluntly ominous warning. It left the unsettling experience at the séance.

Frederica had reached the point where her Martin connection had morphed into personal hazard. That was the difference between their attitudes. Ruthie had twenty thousand good reasons to put up with a bit of weirdness. It hadn't so far harmed her health and she didn't think it would. Delving into Martin's life was a dark business because there'd been so much darkness in the man. But she'd known that when she took what Carter Melville called the gig, hadn't she? Friday night hadn't given her cold feet. She'd told Carter that truthfully. It had just made her more curious to discover the facts.

Something odd was going on that might evolve into inexplicable. But whatever it was, it wasn't about her. She couldn't really interpret anything that had happened as a warning not to pry. For the present, she thought she might as well just continue to discover what she could. If Martin Mear had harboured secrets, and she thought he had, he had also possessed a thrilling glamour. He'd been a massive star. He still was, still living in the minds of those who helped the Legion shift what Carter Melville claimed was five million units a year.

She wouldn't delete Malcolm Stuart's number from her phone. She wouldn't call him, obviously, but she wanted to recognise the number as his if he called her. He was a bit too young for her but he was nice and clever and interesting and though he wore the obligatory shiny suit and pointy shoes, she doubted the word 'chillax' existed in his vocabulary. She felt guilty about the deception. He'd enjoyed her company in the end, possibly a bit too much, but she'd been there under false pretences and he'd earned their little flirtation.

She needed to prepare for her encounter the following day with Paula Tort. She believed it would be a mistake at their first meeting to assault the woman with a long list of intrusive questions. Paula was media-savvy. She'd never spoken about her relationship with Martin, but she'd given plenty of interviews to the fashion and lifestyle press over the last two decades. In common with people like Ralph Lauren and Martha Stewart, she was a living advert for what she did.

Ruthie didn't want to put Paula on the defensive and didn't want to risk antagonism. She had decided that during their first meeting, she would simply listen and record. She'd have six or eight questions prepared as prompts if Paula got tongue-tied, but she thought that very unlikely to happen. This was a confident woman, a fluent and practised communicator. And the subject was one that couldn't have been closer to her heart. If she'd committed finally to discussing it, that could only be because she had plenty to say.

They were to meet at Paula's Mayfair atelier. Neutral ground might have been better, but there was something to be said, if you were intent on breaching years of secrecy, for doing it in your comfort zone, Ruthie supposed.

From the outside, Ruthie admired Paula Tort. She'd bought a suit and a coat from her diffusion range in a sale the previous January, but it was more than thinking she was a designer who created elegant clothes. She had come a long way since leaving her rural Californian home to follow the Stones on a West Coast tour. She'd begun adult life as a plaything for the rock stars of the period. She'd achieved an awful lot, from such an unpromising start, and she'd done it all herself. It was entirely down to her talent and will and ambition.

She didn't look like she'd had the obligatory face-lift, which was something else Ruthie admired. She looked pretty sensational, with her American thoroughbred bone structure, for a woman in her mid-sixties. But asked about cosmetic procedures in a clipping Ruthie had read from a *Vanity Fair* profile she'd said, 'Honey, I've earned every line on this face and some of them are priceless.'

It was a good soundbite and might have been scripted for her but Ruthie's instinct was that it hadn't been. It was defiant and slightly ironic and totally characteristic. She'd have an early night and in the morning do her hair and apply her make-up carefully and dress her best for Paula. She'd be a polite and scrupulously attentive listener. She'd make a good audience. She was greatly looking forward to it.

What she wasn't looking forward to was the trip she'd earlier told herself she would make to Brightstone Forest. She had committed in her mind to visiting the derelict mansion where in the late summer of '69 Martin Mear had written and recorded *King Lud*. She'd thought that an essential element of her research, exposing her to clues about his state of mind she wouldn't get anywhere else. It was the start of him, creatively. In a sense, it was the spot where Ghost Legion was born.

Ruthie didn't want to go back to the island. In a way that was ridiculous, because it was home. But home had associations she didn't feel she could deal with in her current state of mind. She hadn't so much left Ventnor as fled the place. Thank God for Veronica Slade. Thank God, so far at least, for Carter Melville.

When she got back from Shadwell to Lambeth, she called Michael Aldridge, unaware she was going to do it until the moment she did, unaware of what she was going to say until he answered the phone and she spoke awaiting the calm reassurance of his voice in response to what she said.

'There's a connection between Martin Mear and the Jericho Society.'

His end of the conversation contributed nothing but silence for a long moment. Then he said, 'You never were one to beat about the bush, Ruthie.'

'You remember that from our first meeting?'

'I remember everything about first meeting you. Not being able to look at you. Not being able to do it comfortably, at least.'

'You were married then.'

'I was.'

'Tell me what you think about what I've just told you.'

'During our last conversation, outside that cafe on the river, I said something about you and this job you've secured and fate. Or could it merely be coincidence?'

'Martin's uncle worked as an import/export clerk for Martens and Degrue at the Port of London when Martin was a child. I believe Martin was a pretty frequent visitor back then. And I don't believe at all in coincidence.'

'My unwitting involvement with the Jericho Society almost cost me my daughter. Not to mention my sanity. They're capable of things for which I can provide no rational explanation. You know that. You've seen it.'

'Warning me off, Mr A?'

Aldridge laughed. 'I know better than to try. Wilful is your middle name.'

'My middle name is May, after the month I was born in.'

He was silent. Then he said, 'Now I know something else about you I didn't know before.'

'And knowledge is power?'

'Be very careful. These people aren't just about secrecy and Satanic dabbling. They're powerful and completely ruthless.'

'And I don't intend to rain on their parade any more than I already have.'

'Which is substantially.'

'I've lived to tell the tale.'

'On the contrary. You've lived because you've kept it to yourself. It's my heartfelt wish that you go on living.'

'Heartfelt?'

'It was never just lust, Ruthie. I've had feelings for you since the afternoon we first met on the seafront at Ventnor and I think you knew that then and I'm sure you know it now.'

Should she tell him those feelings were reciprocated then and revived less than a fortnight ago? She didn't honestly think it was the moment. Instead she said, 'Take care, Mr A. If you like, I'll keep you in the loop.'

'Please' do,' he said. 'And Ruthie?'

'Yes?'

'You're the one right now who needs to take care.'

She could forget about Wight for the present, though. Over the next couple of days, it was the living and not the dead that were her direct concern, having Paula Tort and Terry Maloney to meet and talk to. They weren't phantoms, were they? Except that Ruthie didn't forget about Wight, or the house in Brightstone Forest, because after she'd spoken to Michael Aldridge it was still only six o'clock. She didn't want to spend the evening thinking about him and she didn't want to think about why she'd very recently become free to do that without guilt. Without guilt, she thought to herself, but with a sadness that felt in her recent loss much more akin to grief. She'd distract herself with a bit of research.

The Fischer house had been built in the 1920s. In pictures it looked much older. This was because it had been allowed to fall into dereliction, but also because the style in which it had been built was easily suggestive of a ruin. It was Gothic and constructed of massive stone blocks to soaring dimensions. There were high arched windows and an iron-studded oak front door as solid and substantial-looking as in a fortified castle's keep. There was a high six-sided tower with mullioned windows and the stone in the building's buttresses was everywhere carved and etched and embellished.

The mansion had been built for a German industrialist named Klaus Fischer. Ruthie could find scant reference to what he'd actually made, but he'd been industrious enough to prosper. The Fischer House was testament to that. He had also been something of a socialite. He had been friendly with people from Hollywood and some of the Paris expat crowd of the period. His acquaintances included a famous escapologist and a notorious duellist for whom he'd once apparently stood bail. He'd been a friend of the occult novelist Dennis Wheatley. He had also been an intimate, it was said, of the English magician Aleister Crowley.

Fischer threw extravagant parties. These must have been sufficiently remote from other Wight residents not to cause a nuisance, because his house really was isolated. But there was a suggestion that he was unpopular on the island. Ruthie thought that party guests arriving by luxury yacht and seaplanes putting down on their pontoons, the furs and jewels and retinues of staff and stately cars would likely have provoked a bit of local ire.

Or would they? Before the Crash of '29 and the Great Depression and the spread among the workers of a bit of Bolshevism, the English were completely accepting of the class system. No one questioned the right of the wealthy to privilege and excess. Perhaps something more personal to Fischer had upset the locals.

Klaus Fischer disappeared at the end of 1927. He just vanished, which was a far easier thing to do, Ruthie thought, in the first half of the previous century. Nobody then had a credit file. No one could be caught on CCTV. Finger-printing was the most reliable method of identification, but still far from definitive. And only known criminals had their fingerprints taken and filed and Fischer had been rich and apparently law-abiding, if not totally respectable.

It was odd, him disappearing like that. But no one had made much of it at the time publicly. The age had been celebrity-obsessed, but with the likes of Fay Wray and Jack Dempsey and Charlie Lindbergh, not with a corpulent German factory owner with a well-indulged appetite for cigars and cocktails. He'd partied without courting publicity beyond his own somewhat louche circle. And then he'd stopped and sold up and gone without a trail to follow. It had been abrupt, this departure from the demi-monde. But it had not provoked a single headline or retrospective news story. Or not one Ruthie could source.

He'd been a collector. He'd collected huge quantities of all kinds of arcane treasures, but religious artefacts had been a particular enthusiasm. He tended to buy at London and Continental European auction houses and he did so through sharp-eyed and well-schooled agents he retained.

Ruthie wondered if there was a connection between Klaus Fischer and Martens and Degrue. She thought it possible. But when she really thought about it, the likeliest way in which Martin Mear would have heard about the Fischer House would have been through the Crowley connection. Some of the big rock names of the period had been drawn to the legend of the self-styled Wickedest

Man in the World and Martin, from university days, had apparently been among them.

Ruthie yawned. She would have to be careful broaching this subject with Paula in the morning. Speculating on Martin's solitary sojourn on Wight, on the Fischer House and the Crowley connection could easily seem like prurience, or sensationalism.

She thought it relevant, though. She thought it likely to be more fertile ground when she came to speak to Terry Maloney on Tuesday afternoon. He'd sounded extremely relaxed on the phone. If he had his insights, and she had no doubt he did, she thought he'd sounded quite reconciled to having committed himself, at last, to sharing them.

Her phone rang. It was April Mear.

'Hope you don't mind being contacted on a Sunday evening.'

'I'm delighted you've taken the trouble.'

'I know you're seeing Paula tomorrow. Carter Melville told me you're seeing Sir Terence on Tuesday. I wondered if you'd have recovered sufficiently by Thursday to listen to some of my reminiscences about Dad.'

'Dad.' It was still difficult for Ruthie to see Martin Mear in any kind of mundane domestic role. It was imagining a medieval knight doing the washing up in full armour having swapped his steel gauntlets for a pair of rubber gloves. It didn't seem at all natural. The idea of him changing nappies or even pushing a child's swing seemed slightly surreal. He'd been a figure, at least on stage, cut out for curses and quests. Men who battled dragons atop mythic crags didn't readily do Mothercare.

'Thursday would be fantastic.'

'Are you a morning person?'

April Mear was fifty-four years old. She had the unlined face, at least in the few photographs Ruthie had sourced, of someone who had never really suffered the affliction of a single adult care. She'd didn't need a job. She'd never needed a job. There was a childlike quality to her sing-song voice, despite her being middle-aged. It occurred to Ruthie that her father's wealth had perhaps condemned April to a life so devoid of responsibility it had amounted to a permanent childhood. That would be another kind of curse, wouldn't it?

'I'm a morning person if you are,' Ruthie said, which hadn't always been true in her past but would do, for the present.

'Do you know the Riverside Café?'

'I do if you mean the one on the Promenade, the Kingston one.' Ruthie remembered that April Mear had a house in Kingston, only a mile or so distant from the Surbiton home of Michael Aldridge.

'If it's fine I'll meet you there at eleven o'clock.'

'And if it rains?'

'Then the coffee shop at John Lewis in Kingston proper. I like anonymous places. They're more comfortable, with strangers. If we get on, we'll stop being strangers and I'll be happy for you to come and speak to me again at home.'

One of your many homes, Ruthie thought, thinking that April meant the one with the panoramic view of the Thames. The others were in Cape Cod and the Bahamas. For their shared purpose, they were a less practical proposition.

'I'm looking forward to this experience,' April said.

'Then I hope you won't be disappointed,' Ruthie said.

'It's a terrible pun,' April said, 'but in some important ways, I feel the record needs to be put straight.'

NINE

Before she went to bed, Ruthie thought she'd view the disc Carter Melville had given her, with a whole sack-full of other research material, of the concert Ghost Legion had performed in Montreal in December 1972. This was the concert in which Martin was supposed to have levitated. It was inconclusive for two reasons. The first of these was the quantity of dry ice shrouding the lower half of the stage. The second was that Martin had never subsequently claimed to have done what most of the audience swore they'd seen happen.

Carter Melville had told her the levitation happened – or didn't – about forty minutes in. She searched for the spot, on Veronica's Blu-Ray player, rubbing her eyes with the hand not operating the remote, with finger and thumb. She was tired. She had only had a couple of vodkas in the afternoon with Malcolm Stuart and nothing alcoholic since, but the experience at the flat in Shadwell had been wearing on her nerves and stamina.

She found the footage she was looking for. Martin was backlit, centre-stage, his hair a riotous auburn halo cascading onto his shoulders. He wore hip-hugging blue jeans with a belt secured by a turquoise inlaid buckle and a denim shirt unbuttoned far enough to reveal his sculpted pectoral muscles. His skin looked pale and taut, as though he didn't tan, but that could have been the light, white and brilliant above the roiling, gaseous surface of the stage.

He was singing 'Siren Psalm', a song from the second of the nameless albums, the album the band's followers referred to simply as '2'. He reached the instrumental break, a long ethereal piano solo sometimes played live on Mellotron by keyboardist James Prentice.

Martin had been holding his stand-microphone between both hands. Now he released his grip on it and closed his eyes and raised his head and held his arms stretched out to either side in what a Christian Fundamentalist might take to be a parody of the crucified Redeemer. Several had, over the intervening decades, Carter had told her. Martin had been denounced from some thunderous pulpits since the Montreal performance all those years ago.

His shoulders swayed. He seemed to rise in height. The increase was subtle, but there. You could achieve it, Ruthie thought, by standing on tiptoe. But what happened next you really couldn't, as his whole body shunted right and left, back and forth, his posture stiff and vertical, his lower limbs motionless as far as the knee-high vapour opaquely concealing the stage floor.

His eyes opened. He came to a halt. The close-up camera caught sweat gathered like sparkling dew in the hair on his forehead, as though the movement just accomplished had been physically strenuous. He smiled a smile that seemed absurdly secretive given the spectacle he represented, up there in front of sixty thousand adoring fans. The volume fluctuated as the sound-man struggled to find a level to accommodate the roar his trick of weightlessness had provoked from the crowd. He was their God, the ovation suggested. And they had only then witnessed a miracle.

The keyboard interlude ended. Martin Mear seemed to remember the Stratocaster slung around his neck. He fingered the fret-board and bent a run of notes out of the instrument with uncanny speed.

The drums kicked in with a twist of his head and a spray of sweat in the direction of Jason Ritchie, enthroned on the high pyramid of his kit.

It had been suggested that what Martin was actually doing at Montreal was a kind of prototype moonwalking. That would have explained the weird absence of hip and upper-leg movement; the way he had seemed to be able to glide about the stage above his cloud of dry ice. With Michael Jackson and his unearthly choreography still a dozen years into the future, Ruthie thought the explanation absurd.

She had an observation of her own. She thought that she probably owed it to the unpleasant part of the afternoon she'd spent in Docklands. She watched the sequence again. She finished doing so unsure about whether Martin Mear had actually levitated or not. It was always possible someone had fitted castors to his boots to enable him to glide about the stage like that.

'Yeah, right,' she said to the screen, snorting into her glass of San Pellegrino and thinking that she really ought to go to bed.

She'd mapped in her mind the geometry of his movement. And you could claim all sorts of weird revisionist shit about Ghost Legion. And people like Malcolm Stuart's dippy sister did exactly that all the bloody time. But Ruthie was pretty sure that in his shunting this way and that, Martin had described the shape of a pentagram. And she thought the idea of his having done so with his feet trailing the floor and his arms out like Jesus more than a little disturbing.

Her phone rang again. She frowned and looked at her watch. It was 10.20 pm and felt like three in the morning and she needed a night's rest before Paula Tort. Her caller was Carter Melville.

'Is this going to be our evening ritual?'

'What does that mean?'

'You phoned me last night.'

'I'm entitled to phone you every night, weekends included, baby. Twenty large opens a wide window into your life. You'd find it expensive to slam it shut in my face.'

'Charmingly put.'

'I'm rightly famed for my tact and diplomacy.'

'Do you want anything specific?'

'I'm just touching base, honey.'

'I've been watching the Montreal footage.'

'Reach any conclusions?'

'It must have been shot originally on VHS. The digital quality has been enhanced for Blu-Ray. It's been cleaned up and the motion smoothed out and the colour enriched. But the original film was recorded before CGI was invented and if it's been tampered with, I'm buggered if I can see the joins.'

Melville was quiet. Then he said, 'You might want to ask Terry Maloney about that on Tuesday. Terry reckons he saw Martin do it again, on a terrace after a dinner in Montevideo. Said it was totally for real. Apparently, it was something Crowley could do, one of the old magician's party pieces, before he lost his mind and powers.'

'You believe that?'

'I believe drugs were ingested that night in Montevideo.' He laughed. 'It would have been a bigger miracle than levitation at a Legion party if they hadn't been.'

'So what Sir Terence saw was drug-induced?'

'He wasn't Sir Terence then, sweetheart. He was a completely different person, all of us were. Experience changes us. So do intoxicants. Memory is subjective. Best to ask him what it was he did or didn't see that night. But don't obsess over the occult thing.'

'The occult thing sustains the myth.'

'The music, baby, is what sustains the myth.'

'And magic seems to have inspired the music.'

'Now we're going around in circles.'

Geometry, Ruthie thought, thinking that she preferred circles to pentagrams. She decided that she would say nothing to Carter Melville about her Shadwell experience. She wouldn't be pushed into conclusions about Martin Mear. She wasn't a censor or a propagandist. He could have hired a public-relations specialist if all he wanted was airbrushing. Her job was finding out the truth and for better or worse, she intended eventually to deliver that.

'Paula giving you butterflies?'

'To some extent, yes,' Ruthie said. 'She's a formidable woman.'

'She's a pussycat,' Carter Melville said, registering the first statement he had made to her that she knew to be an outright lie. 'Goodnight, honey.'

'Sweet ones, Carter.'

TEN

They called it the Clamouring. Numerology figured large in Ghost Legion lore and Frederica Daunt thought that the Clamouring was probably the myth most pervasive among the many Legionaries convinced that the band's catalogue was capable of more ominous feats than merely providing background music.

This theory concerned the sixth track on the sixth and final album and the title of the track was 'Cease All Mourning', which was innocent enough in isolation, if a little clumsy and unpromising as song titles went. It wasn't alluring or intriguing, was it? Basically, it was an instruction to stop. It was a negative message. In the argot of the period in which the song was recorded, taken literally, its title was a downer, man . . .

But 'cease' was also the way the French pronounced their word for six, spelt exactly the same way in the French language as it was in English. The final album had been recorded largely in a chateau in the French Pyrenees. Sixth album, sixth and final track and a title providing, through a bit of linguistic trickery, the third 6 required to invoke the Number of the Beast. The hoary old Biblical 666; that terrifying cliché referred to when Apocalypse and Antichrist were the subjects under discussion; the number associated with the End of Days and Lucifer's final triumph over a God no longer Almighty.

Cease all mourning could also be interpreted as a prediction, meaning that soon there would no longer be a reason to grieve. Mourning required a death and believers were convinced that in the song, Martin had predicted his own. In telling his followers to stop mourning, he was also hinting at the song's power to restore him to life. That was where the theory behind the Clamouring really gathered its strength from.

Resurrection from the dead was a Christian concept demonstrated twice in the pages of the New Testament. Christ had brought Lazarus back from the dead. Then he had proven his divinity by returning from the dead himself.

Other faiths, though, ancient and more recent, had their own beliefs and rituals concerning a human defeat of death, a successful challenge to its cold finality. It was a common theme. It was a strong and persistent tenet of paganism from the Vikings to the Incas to faiths still practised in remote parts of rural Africa. It was a still-strong part of voodoo tradition in Haiti. There was the Gothic literary monolith of Mary Shelley's *Frankenstein*. And then of course, there was the role human resurrection had to play in magic.

Frederica lit another cigarette. She was seated on her terrace where it was dark but still warm and where she could smell the still-warm sea and watch it glitter shifting in moonlight beyond the olive grove between her villa and the beach. She could smell salt and olives and pine resin on the offshore breeze through the strong Portuguese tobacco slightly stinging her nostrils. Her nose still felt raw from its haemorrhage of Friday evening. She was awaiting a visitor, even though it was quite late to receive a guest. There were guests and guests, of course, but this one was living and in human guise and it was late for that variety; the only kind her shot nerves could at that moment pleasantly endure.

She sipped brandy from the heavy glass sharing the wooden table at which she sat with a white ashtray with lots of cigarette burns browned into it and the word *Cinzano* printed twice like the name of a ship a lifebelt came from on its rim. The brandy was cheap and local and tasted wonderful for being like nothing she would have surrendered space to in her drinks cabinet in her grand house in Chiswick.

Resurrection was the key to the Clamouring, unless the Clamouring was the key to resurrection. Either way, the theory was the same. The sixth song on the sixth Ghost Legion album, the one with the French pronunciation of 'six' playfully punned into its title, was said to be capable of returning Martin Mear to mortal life. That was what a lot of the Legionaries claimed, anyway.

The Number of the Beast was significant because returning someone deceased to life would be the devil's work. Their death had been God's doing. Only Satan possessed the power to bring someone back and thus defy His will. Martin returned would wear the number branded on his flesh. Otherwise, he'd be the same as he was before his mortal departure.

All that had to happen to accomplish this was for the song to be played, simultaneously, at a number of key places around the world. The problem was that no one could agree on the exact locations. And no one could agree the precise number of them. Synchronicity on that scale was difficult without such specifics. In fact, it was impossible. There was said to be a key, hidden somewhere. A key or maybe a formula. But nobody knew where. The problem with the Clamouring was that the ritual lacked a precise litany. There was no agreed script.

The song's lyrics didn't help. She thought about the opening four lines, which ran: *The sun will come back / The corn ear will flower / The lady will lack / For no bloom in her bower.* It was quite pretty in a cod-medieval sub-Tennyson sort of way, but it wasn't exactly detailed or emphatic. 'And that,' Frederica said out loud to herself; 'is because "Cease All Mourning" is an album filler and because the Clamouring is actually one big fanciful crock of shit.'

The brandy had emboldened her. The prospect of seeing her visitor had restored some of her courage and bolstered her resilience. She thought that she could hear his car approaching through the quiet of the night. She'd recognized the pitch of the engine. And she couldn't help smiling at the thought that after all these years, Sebastian Daunt was still driving the Mini Moke.

It suited the climate, of course and it was a mode of transport still popular on the French Riviera and his had only had to travel the ninety miles or so from his home in Spain. It was a sturdy, simple vehicle and it suited what she imagined still remained her father's image. He might not even drive the only Mini Moke in the coastal village he called home. He'd drive the only one, though, with a corn dolly dangling from its rear-view mirror.

A moment later his Moke's silhouette came into view. He killed his lights and then switched off the engine and she stood, waiting for her eyes to find him, recovering from the bright headlamp glare with spots on her retinas that took a moment to fade. When her focus returned he was still there, seated at the wheel, studying her, white-haired and extravagantly bearded, weirdly like the image of Old Father Thames he'd done for the cover of *King Lud*, dragged from the riverbed, brought to reluctant life.

He climbed out of his seat stiffly and walked towards her with a decided limp. She saw him inventory the spilling ashtray and half-empty brandy bottle on the table with a quick glance from eyes alert despite his years. He held out his arms and they embraced and she was the girl she'd been nearly half a century ago, sniffing back tears and inhaling the lost, familiar scent of him in the same half-hitched breath.

'You've been a very misguided girl, Freddie,' he muttered into her neck, kissing her cheek.

Make it all OK, Daddy, she wanted to say. But she was a grown-up now and so it was far too late for that and anyway, she didn't believe remotely that he could.

They went inside. She had earlier lit a fire. She'd had a wood-burning stove shipped from England not long after buying the villa because she liked the sight and smell of smouldering logs in the winter time and because collecting driftwood as fuel on the beach appealed to the thrifty side of her nature. It made the room look warm and homely. She had never held a séance here, had never communed with the dead. She shuddered, not cold, suddenly certain, however, that she had seen the inside of the Chiswick house for the last time. She would never willingly go back there.

Her visitor stood like someone waiting awkwardly for something to happen. He was deeply tanned and wore his abundant mane ponytailed by a leather thong. He was wearing a denim bib and brace and a faded collarless shirt and yellow Timberlands that looked like they hadn't left his feet in a hundred years. There were bangles on his thick wrists. Jet and moonstone inlay sparkled in the orange firelight.

'Sit down, Dad. I'll fetch you a drink.'

'I think you've had enough to drink.'

'I opened the brandy bottle when I arrived here last night. That was when most of the damage was done. I've only had the one tonight.'

'From what you told me on the phone, the serious damage was done in London.'

She got him a beer from the fridge in the kitchen and opened the bottle and poured it. She gave him the glass. He still hadn't sat down. He did so, with a wince of pain on a hardback chair. Arthritis had been the reason for his departure for Spain. It was the reason he'd given, anyway, twenty years earlier. She pulled out a chair opposite his and he sipped beer and rested his glass on the table between them.

'Is there anything I can do?'

'I don't know.'

'I'm not the only medium to have claimed contact from beyond with Martin Mear. He's like John Lennon and Michael Jackson and probably Elvis Presley too, in that regard.'

'He isn't like them at all and never was.'

'What do you mean?'

'People claim they've seen Elvis stacking shelves in branches of Walmart. Can you imagine anyone saying that about Martin?'

She smiled wanly. She said, 'He'd scare the customers away.'

'Alive or dead,' her father said.

'Will you tell me about him?'

'It's a bit late for that.'

'Will you tell me anyway?'

Sebastian Daunt reached for his beer glass and drained it and put it back down on the table with an emphatic thump. He said, 'Martin was fourteen when I met him. I was living at the commune where you were conceived. He was an adolescent with a gorgeous singing voice and a wonderful gift for playing the guitar. I was entranced by him, everyone was, practically spellbound, a pretty young folkie by the name of Julia Reed particularly so. But you know all this.'

'Tell me anyway.'

'He was a sweet-natured boy with dreams that seemed fantastical. Yet he fulfilled them, all of them. Have you ever wondered, Freddie, about the odds against his doing that?'

'He was marvellously talented. He was physically beautiful.'

Her father laughed. 'Lots of people are marvellously talented. Lots of people are beautiful. Or they were then, anyway, back in the '60s. They all had dreams. They didn't all become Martin Mear. They didn't all write songs that became global anthems and dream up the biggest rock band in the world.'

'What are you getting at?'

He was silent for a while. Then he said, 'What have your dead novelist and deceased ballet dancer had to say about events? How have your familiars reacted to Martin's comeback?'

'Only witches have familiars. I'm not a witch.'

'Answer the question.'

'I haven't attempted contact since what happened on Friday evening. I don't think I will ever again.'

'Then some good has come of all this.'

'Do you think Martin means to hurt me?'

'No, I don't. I don't think Martin's spirit or ghost or revenant or whatever gave a shit about your claims to be in contact with him. He would have thought it funny, frankly. What he took exception to was you trying to deceive this researcher person.'

'Ruthie Gillespie.'

'I think Martin has plans for Ruthie Gillespie, God help her.'

'Are you afraid of Martin Mear, Dad?'

This time the pause went on for so long that Frederica wondered had her father become hard of hearing since their last encounter. Then, eventually, he spoke.

'I never met a boy with a sweeter nature, like I've said. But he didn't just mature, Freddie, he changed. At some point, I think Martin struck some sort of bargain. That's why he became so blessed, is my opinion. He was never less than civil to me and could be kind and courteous and enormously stimulating company. But by the end, yes, I was frightened of him. I was afraid of what he became. I was even more afraid of the price I suspected he paid to become it.'

'I've been thinking about the Clamouring.'

'You should leave that kind of thinking to Ruthie Gillespie. I'm sure she's being well paid to ponder on all that stuff.'

'Do you think there's anything in it?'

Her father shook his head. 'Too haphazard, way too flaky, dreamed up by a Legion fan or maybe a bunch of them after too much dope or a bad batch of acid, is my take on that. It's the heavy rock version of a conspiracy theory. Look at Manson and Helter Skelter. Look at the bullshit people peddle about Jim Morrison and the Doors.'

'So he made no plans to re-join the living?'

'I didn't say that.'

'What do you think, Dad?'

He smiled at her. It wasn't a straightforward smile. It looked contingent, almost pained, to her. He said, 'Night driving has made me thirsty. And I'm not used to talking so much. Pour me another beer and I'll tell you what I think.'

ELEVEN

It was late and Malcolm Stuart had a full schedule for the following day. The property market had picked up to the point where the office veterans had stopped talking lyrically about the mini-boom at the beginning of the millennium. They'd even stopped waxing nostalgic about the boom proper at the start of the 1990s. The good times were emphatically back. He knew that the sensible thing to do would be to get some sound sleep before a hectic Monday.

He couldn't, though. He didn't know when he'd met a more attractive woman less aware of her own impact than Ruthie Gillespie had proven to be over a couple of enigmatic hours. There was a melancholy about her she carried like a weight and he was intrigued about where that burden had come from. She was slightly careworn and utterly stunning. He'd spent most of the late afternoon and evening wondering how he could overcome the obstacle of being a decade or so younger than she was.

And it was an obstacle. She had seemed to be single and straight, which meant that she was theoretically available. He had managed to establish that much about her during their conversation. But she didn't take him seriously as a suitor, or wouldn't, because she was in her mid-thirties and he had not long graduated from university. Calling her would be pointless. She'd be tactful, because she was courteous on top of all her other attributes. She'd be firm, though, because she knew her mind and the age difference would prevent him from being a credible romantic option.

He thought that he knew a way to impress her, despite this. He could help with at least one aspect of her research into Martin Mear. He'd done some oral-history recordings with a few of the old dock hands from Wapping and Shadwell. The recording themselves would not help, they were general reminiscences, the subjects of Martens and Degrue and their one-time clerk Max Askew had never come up. Why should they have?

He was thinking about one particular witness to the great days of the docks, however, and hoping that the man was still alive and that he had not succumbed to Alzheimer's or to a stroke or just the memory loss associated with old age. He'd interviewed this character at a sheltered housing block, in the pristine flat he occupied there, in Bethnal Green at the time he was researching his thesis.

And Ginger McCabe was a character. In his early eighties, ramrod-straight, the habitual wearer of a smart three-piece suit even indoors, even in his own home. In the 1960s he'd been a bare-knuckle boxing champion. He'd been an extra in a couple of British feature films, the kitchen-sink dramas shot in real locations in the days when the big stars had been Tom Courtney and Lawrence Harvey and Albert Finney. He'd had a small speaking part in the Stanley Kubrick film *Barry Lyndon*. He'd been on drinking terms with Oliver Reed and Anthony Newley.

Ginger had been a union activist, an organizer of strikes and a formidable human barricade against scab workers on any picket line back when the dockers were, with the miners, the most militant workers in the country when it came to protecting their hard-won rights. Malcolm thought that Ginger, with his perfect recall and his cockney rasp, would remember both Max Askew and the firm that had employed him until his retirement. He'd know all about the mysterious Martens and Degrue.

Malcolm still had Ginger McCabe's contact details. What he didn't have was a legitimate reason for questioning the old man about stuff that might provoke unpleasant memories. As Ruthie Gillespie had pointed out, an exorcism was an extreme measure at the time two had been performed in a Shadwell dockside warehouse all those years ago. Ginger would have been in his late thirties back then, wouldn't he, a big-shot on the quays, a union rep with keen eyes and his ear to the ground.

Things didn't generally go bump in Malcolm Stuart's night. He had never entertained the idea of the paranormal before taking his estate agent job. But since he'd taken the job, he'd encountered 77 Proctor Court and developed a perspective slightly different from the one he'd had before. This new outlook was somewhat less carefree and more cautious. It was less inclined to the bombastic certainties he'd held to back in his student days.

He'd gone back there, after saying goodbye to Ruthie outside the door of the pub. She'd raised the collar of her coat and smiled slightly wistfully and turned away from him and headed towards the tube. He'd had to leave his car where he'd parked it because the two pints of lager he'd drunk put him slightly over the limit if he got stopped and breath-tested. He'd parked where there were no restrictions on a Sunday so that aspect of things was OK.

He thought the two pints were probably the reason he went back. It was sufficient Dutch courage to get him over the Proctor Court threshold in daylight. Ruthie had been vague about whatever her experience had been once past Max Askew's old front door. It had been out of kilter in some subtle, disturbing way, but she hadn't heard a banshee wail or encountered a screaming demon. She would have said so, if she had.

Malcolm was wrong, though. The rain had strengthened while they chatted in the Prospect and he got to Proctor Court cold and damp-shouldered wearing the weight of his sodden raincoat like some sartorial defeat. His feet felt wet inside his shoes. They were almost wet enough to squelch. The stairwell echoed as he climbed the rain-slicked steps and when he reached the door and fumbled for the key a shiver wracked him more akin to dread than just a chill.

He stared at the Green Man door knocker and it stared back at him, gnarled and dripping, grinning and secretive, sly-eyed and antic and not welcoming at all. And through the frosted array of small glass panes above the knocker, he thought he saw a flicker of movement disturb the gloom within.

In Malcolm Stuart's stomach, dismay lurched into dread. He swallowed. The key was shaking in his fist. 'Sod it,' he whispered, turning away.

Now, he yawned and looked at his wristwatch. Home was a Hoxton studio flat he'd got on a two-year lease at a cut-rate rent care of a former colleague. It was small and secure and comfortable. It was warm and well-lit and he was sprawled on the sofa with Ellie Goulding turned down so low it was like she was whispering the songs personally to him. He would wait for lunchtime tomorrow and then give Ginger McCabe a call. He might even call him in the morning before work, aware of the habit the elderly had of rising earlier than they needed to.

It still bothered him that he had no legitimate reason to question the old man in this way, beyond trying to access information that would aid his bid to be taken seriously as a romantic proposition by Ruthie Gillespie. Against that, though, was the fact that Ginger liked to reminisce. He was proud of his own fairly flamboyant history as one of the district's faces.

'It was my manor,' he would say with an indignant flush, slapping a big fist into a still meaty palm for emphasis.

Malcolm would take him for a drink. It wasn't a dry academic exercise, this. He'd buy him a few beers and make a social event of it. And if it looked like trying to recall Max Askew and Martens and Degrue was distressing him in any way, he'd simply change the subject, move on to something else, like the time Ginger drank Richard Harris under the table on a film set; or the time he fought the Irish King of the Gypsies to a bloodied standstill in an Epsom meadow on Derby Day.

He looked at his watch again. It was almost eleven o'clock. He was pleased now he had a plan of sorts in place. More of a scheme than a plan, but he felt he had to do something. He couldn't just let Ms Gillespie slip out of his life carelessly, without some attempt to influence matters to the contrary.

He met a lot of women. It was inevitable in his line of work. They tended to be ambitious and forceful, of a type, on the up, acquisitive and slightly flashy and a bit vacuous and almost inevitably blonde. Ruthie was raven-haired and clever and serious and though she'd turned practically every male head in the pub on their arrival at the Prospect, she'd been completely unaware of the fact. She was probably out of his league, but he had to try, didn't he?

He thought about his sister. He knew that Ursula would still be up. She'd been christened Bernadette, but had become Ursula at art school when, in common with most of her friends, she'd been more creative working on herself than on her courses. She'd still be up because Goths were essentially nocturnal creatures.

She wasn't quite a Goth. She wasn't quite a hippie, either, which is how he'd described her in the pub to Ruthie. She was somewhere between the two. She didn't drink cider in cemeteries or make Whitby Bay pilgrimages but she mostly wore black and a great deal of mascara and her lipstick was always red. She read a huge amount of horror fiction and of course she listened to Martin

Mears' old band and banged on about him never having actually died to anyone who'd listen.

He called her. She answered at the tenth ring. He said, 'Tell me about Ghost Legion.'

She said, 'It's a pretty huge subject, Mal. Heavy, too, for a Sunday night.'

'I'm a captive audience,' he said.

On the Portuguese coast, it was very late and Frederica Daunt was either on the cusp of drunkenness or the cusp of sobriety, depending upon a person's outlook. Her father was seated in the armchair opposite hers on the other side of the wood-burner. There was a slight smell of salt and tar from the driftwood she gathered from the shore to fuel her fires and to her this mingled scent had a nostalgic quality. Or that could just have been her father's company, she thought, slightly dozily. She hadn't enjoyed that for a long time and his presence was largely something she associated with her childhood.

Now, she looked at her dad and something in his expression made her say, 'What?'

'I think you might have imagined the figure in the garden. I think it might have been only a projection. I suspect you saw it because you expected to.'

Frederica thought about this. She said, 'I wouldn't have expected to see his fingernails as grotesquely long as they were. As though they'd grown in his coffin after his death. That was a detail too far.'

Sebastian Daunt raised an eyebrow. There was a beer bottle beaded with moisture in his right fist. In the firelight, the bottle looked bejewelled. He took a sip and said, 'That happens in life. It's a detail your subconscious provided. You'd been dwelling on the subject of Martin. Flight was already on your mind. You needed a tipping point and your imagination cooperated in providing one. You need him to look scary and so he did.'

'It's a seductive theory,' Frederica said.

'Really?'

'Of course. It would be reassuring to think that's what happened. It's less disturbing than the alternative.'

'So give it some consideration.'

'It doesn't explain what happened at the séance. There was a witness to that. Or maybe more accurately a participant.' Frederica realized she was still fairly sober. 'Participant' was a minefield of a word to someone pissed.

Sebastian reached for the rattan table in front of him and his daughter's phone. He'd earlier in the evening used it to source a picture of Ruthie Gillespie. It was a press-shot taken at some reception or launch of something and used as publicity material by her publisher. She looked happy, clutching a champagne flute. She looked exotic in an evening dress with her precise black fringe and crimson smile and elaborately inked arms.

Sebastian studied the image, suppressing a slight smile. He said, 'An author of stories about elves and curses written for children.'

'She's a respected researcher.'

'One with a florid imagination.'

'I saw what I saw.'

'I wouldn't call Ruthie Gillespie to the stand with anything approaching confidence.'

'That's unfair. Yes, she's on the picturesque side.'

'Picturesque is one word for it.'

'She's also intelligent and shrewd. And when I was shaken and bleeding she was kind to me. She was cool-headed. She took control.'

Her father merely shrugged.

'I saw what I saw, Dad.' There was an edge to Frederica's voice, suddenly. A touch of steel: 'I heard what I heard. We both did. It was him. One way or another, Clamouring or no Clamouring, he's back. Maybe I did imagine what I thought I saw in the garden the following evening. I was alone and frightened and pretty suggestible, I suppose. But Martin Mear is back and I don't find that thought terribly relaxing.'

'You should turn in, love. We both should.'

'I'm reluctant to sleep.'

'That's just silly.'

'I'm frightened of what I might dream about.'

Sebastian sipped more beer and turned his gaze to the fire. It was fading now, diminishing; the feeble orange of a small sun extinguishing the world it had faithfully enabled. Carefully, he said, 'Martin was a keeper of secrets. I wouldn't pretend to have known the half of what he thought or much at all about any dark stuff he got up to privately after the Legion went global. But if anyone could cheat death, he'd be my candidate.'

'I'm not seeing your point here.'

'Assume he's done this by some occult means. The preparation would be elaborate and the effort enormous. He wouldn't do it just to put the wind up a medium, not even one as high-profile as you've been over the last few years. He'd have an agenda. It would be serious and ambitious and he wouldn't be sidetracked or distracted.'

'You're just telling me what you think I want to hear.'

Sebastian frowned. He said, 'What I'm doing is applying logic to a supposition that beggars sane belief. But if Martin's really back, he's got bigger fish to fry than you, Freddie.'

Frederica peered through the wood-burner's soot-smeared door. She said, 'Our fire's gone out.'

Gently, her father said, 'A good moment for us both to admit that we're tired and need some rest. Is the bed in the spare room made up?'

'Of course it is, Dad. I don't see much of you. Doesn't mean I don't always live in hope.'

Malcolm Stuart called Ginger McCabe at a quarter to nine on Monday morning, forty-five minutes before he was due to be at his desk, making the call on his mobile from a Costa coffee boutique not far from Shadwell underground station. The street outside was cobbled and slick with rain and rain streaked the window through which he watched the wet stones reflect the headlamps of cars passing streakily by. Ginger answered on the third ring.

'Mr McCabe?'

'Who wants him?'

'It's Malcolm.'

There was a pause. 'Remind me.'

'Malcolm the student?'

'Don't do that upspeak thing, Malcolm the student. Drives me potty the way all you young people do that. Anyway, I've got you now. Social history. What can I do for you that I haven't already done?'

'There's a company I want to talk to you about. Bloke worked for them I'm hoping you might remember.'

There was another pause. Then, 'This pan have a handle?'

'Max Askew. He lived in Shadwell, at an address at Proctor Court.'

'He did indeed, Malcolm the Student.'

'And he worked for—'

'I know very well who he worked for and if I were you I'd avoid mention of the name on an open phone line.'

'Isn't that being a bit you know, paranoid?'

'It might be. And it might only be taking a sensible precaution. Come and see me tonight. Don't come alone.'

'What does that mean?'

'You'll be accompanied, Malcolm the student. Mr Chivas and Mr Regal are coming with you. Seven o'clock.'

TWELVE

(Transcript of Paula Tort interview session 16 October)

I'm going to tell you something about him no one else knows. No one alive knows it, anyway. As far as I'm aware, I'm the only person to whom Martin ever confided this particular detail about his life.

He would do that, you see. It was one of the principal things about his character. I don't know if he deliberately followed that maxim which suggests you divide and conquer, but certainly he divided. Everyone, even those closest to him, got their own individual Martin. He was never quite the same person to any two people. He was an incredibly devoted father to April; but I didn't witness that side of him. He was supposedly pretty debauched with the boys in the band but I only have hearsay where that's concerned. I never saw it personally. The version I got of Martin seemed wonderfully complete, but it was mine alone.

People who can present themselves in that way sometimes have something wrong with them, something like Asperger's syndrome, leaving them emotionally detached. It wasn't like that with him, though. I think it was a mathematical skill. He was brilliant at mathematics. That was why music came so easily to him. He understood the chromatic scale immediately. He taught himself to read and write music when he was still a child. He divided himself up and the part of him I got was dedicated to me alone. I knew how precious it was, even before knowing how short-lived it would be.

But I was going to tell you a secret, wasn't I? I was going to confide something and it's this. He endured an experience once that took away his fear of death. He came so close to dying that the terror of it perished in him. He said there was nothing mystical or sinister about the process. It was dark, he said, but only as dark as you would expect it to be.

You've seen what he looked like? The first time I ever saw him was on stage and he looked like a god, like Thor or Parsifal, something epic and Wagnerian about his features and his musculature. I've been in this business for thirty years. That's a lot of catwalk shows, a lot of ad campaigns, hundreds of hours of castings and model portfolios from every corner of the world and I've never once seen a man as physically beautiful as Martin Mear was when he strode into that spotlight that night in Berlin.

Men didn't go to the gym back then. You had to be Arnie or you had to be Ali to go to the gym back in the 1970s. Either that or you were gay. It certainly wasn't something rock stars did. They tended to be thin; pre-pubescent thin was the voguish look, not like now. Some of them looked like girls who'd somehow eluded puberty. Bowie looked a bit like that, before he became Ziggy Stardust. Jagger and Marc Bolan, before he bloated, looked that way.

When Martin was twelve, he began to help his dad with the supplementary work his dad had taken on digging graves. His dad was dying of asbestosis, though nobody knew that then. Martin and his mother put the persistent cough down to tobacco and the damp West Country weather. But asbestosis was killing Martin's dad and he could hardly get through his farm chores, let alone the added toil of shifting six feet of earth with a hand-held spade.

Martin did it, or he did the lion's share of it, while his dad wheezed and watched gratefully and talked about the weather and the prospects of the harvest and probably the life and death of the person whose coffin they were digging their hole for. It was a small community, close-knit, everyone knowing everyone else.

The earth was heavy and reluctant and the digging made Martin strong. And his father got sicker and the pretence that he was doing the work was abandoned as he was forced to leave their cottage less and less. And one rainy afternoon in December, when Martin was fourteen, the grave he'd almost finished digging alone collapsed on him. Its walls buckled and sagged and fell in on him and he was buried under the black weight of the soil's immensity.

So great was the weight of it, he said, it pushed him down and pressed on him so that he couldn't move his chest to breathe, had there been air to breathe, which there wasn't. For a moment in the blind, suffocating silence, he thought he was dead. Then he thought with certainty that he would die, crushed. Then he gathered himself and set about digging himself out, with his hands, while he still retained the strength to struggle to live.

He never knew how he survived that experience. He always suspected afterwards that he shouldn't have. As near-death experiences go, I suppose there's none so vivid as being buried alive in a pit you've dug for someone already cold and mourned and awaiting their interment in their coffin. Martin escaped the grave and thought he'd also, in some significant way, cheated it. I think that experience informs a lot of the songs he wrote. Death preoccupied him because he thought very seriously that he'd outlived his own.

His father was near to death by the time of Martin's graveyard ordeal. He said for that reason, he never mentioned it to him. He didn't want his father's conscience burdened, as it would have been, by having a boy do a man's work to supplement the family's sparse income. And after his father's death, he never mentioned it to his mother, either. I was the first person he told and I was the last and now I've told you.

Do you want to know something else? I'll tell you anyway, my dear. April is going to be proven right about this, there is something liberating about setting the record straight. In the lazy liner notes and Ghost Legion album reviews I'm always referenced as a groupie. Actually, I'm referred to as a legendary groupie, as though my talent for getting laid defined me, like it was a full-time occupation requiring boat-loads of rock bands coming ashore on a daily basis.

I never sought to make a sexual conquest of Martin Mear. It wasn't like I needed to cross him off my list. There was no list. By '71 on that German tour I was making a good living designing stage costumes for some of the biggest acts in the industry. I was in West Berlin researching the leather scene. There was a shoe designer I knew there who made Martin's boots. He always wore these engineer-type boots and she had a spare ticket. I went to their gig out of curiosity and he saw me from the stage.

The rest, as they say, is history. But most of it's speculation and rumour, because no one knows the real history except me and I've never told anyone until now. And I've never minded the hype and distortion, or even the outright fabrications, if I'm honest. I've always had my memories and they've remained unsullied and absolutely clear. They're also very dear to me, which has made sharing them hard. If there's a part of me liberated by this process, there's another part of me that feels I'm giving too much away.

You could have privacy back then. Fame carried a price, Lennon was right about that and God knows John paid it, but beyond the reach of the autograph-hunters bothering him in restaurants and hotel lobbies it was possible for Martin to have a private life in a manner that no longer exists. Everyone now has a movie camera in their phone. The curious world is a mobilized army of citizen reporters. In the early 1970s it was completely different. I don't think Martin would have been all that impressed by Facebook and Twitter and social media generally. He performed on the stage and people paid to watch and listen. That was the deal. The rest of the time was entirely his own. I think he liked it that way. In fact, I know he did. And now you can switch off your tape machine. I've told you enough for today.

Ruthie Gillespie was a habitual early riser. She had woken at 6 am and brewed a pot of coffee and taken it out to drink in the cool darkness of Veronica's small back garden where she had smoked two cigarettes pondering on how nervous she was already about the interview with Paula Tort scheduled for noon.

Ruthie was nervous for two reasons. She was a researcher when she wasn't writing fiction but wasn't a reporter or features writer and considered interviewing a journalistic skill she couldn't to any great degree really claim to possess. She'd done her research. The rest was down to hope, more than it was down to expectation or interview technique.

The second, slightly vaguer reason for the butterflies of trepidation fluttering in Ruthie's stomach as dawn broke was the Max Askew revelation. He'd worked for Martens and Degrue. Martens and Degrue were the acceptable face of the Jericho Society. Ruthie had endured personal experience of this mysterious and always menacing cult and consequently felt staying free of their tentacles an extremely sensible thing to do.

Michael Aldridge had warned her about pressing on further. He'd done so explicitly. And he'd done so because he had her welfare at heart, whether things evolved romantically between them or whether they didn't. He was a good, sober, sensible man and he didn't want her endangering her safety for Carter Melville's temptingly lavish fee.

Ruthie wondered if the fee was lavish only as a consequence of the risk. Did Melville know about Max Askew's dubious employers? Ruthie didn't think he would. He'd barely remembered the name of Martin's uncle. And Melville struck her as a man who would place self-preservation high on his list of personal priorities. He wouldn't deliberately shine a light on something not only dark, but innately hostile.

'And secretive,' Ruthie murmured out loud. 'If he knew anything at all about them, he'd know how secretive they are and the steps they'll take to stay that way.'

After coffee in the garden there was the domestic whirlwind of Veronica going from a pyjama-clad mumble to a svelte and feted fine-art expert in about five minutes flat before she slammed the front door on the way to Lambeth North underground and her daily commute to the auction house where she worked.

After that, the hours delivering Ruthie's noon appointment dragged. The nerves got no better. She successfully avoided smoking any more than she already had. She showered and dressed demurely – or at least as demurely as she felt capable of dressing. She put on the black Paula Tort diffusion number she'd scored in the sales. And when a quarter to eleven finally came around she tested her tape machine and packed her notebook and two Uni Ball pens and put on her coat and walked the distance to Paula's Sloane Street atelier through wan October sunshine and the kaleidoscopic crunch beneath her feet on the pavements of fallen, un-swept leaves.

Ruthie felt the first real thrill of achievement, with that opening interview recorded, she'd felt since taking on the project. Being right about Martin Mear's inspirational visits to stay with his Uncle Max had proven a discovery with too ominous repercussions for her to regard it as an unmitigated triumph. But Paula's story about Martin being buried alive was a dream revelation, the sort of story that would have Legionaries listening to the catalogue afresh to learn whether the experience had informed any of their idol's song lyrics. It was a thematic earthquake, a cataclysm of experience and destiny. He'd been served up a slice of immortality when not yet out of his teens. What had it done to him in terms of belief and faith? An ordeal like that would surely make a boy feel singled out for something extraordinary.

These thoughts occurred as Ruthie sat on one of a set of wicker chairs, sharing a table with Paula in the perfectly manicured garden at the back of her building, drinking Earl Grey tea with a woman who seemed in no hurry for her to leave.

'I'm grateful to you.'

'Why?'

Paula hesitated. Then she said, 'I was able to go back just now without the attendant grief. Remembering those times is usually a bittersweet experience. Not today.'

'It sounds as though the two of you made the most of your time together.'

'I suppose that's true. But there's never enough time, Ruthie. As you'll discover.'

Ruthie looked down to the rim of her cup and sipped tea.

'If you haven't already.'

'You're very astute.'

'And you've bandaged the wound. But the bleeding hasn't really stopped. Was he worth it?'

'I thought so.'

'The past tense sometimes hurts, doesn't it?'

Ruthie looked at the woman looking back at her. At the subtly layered and coloured hair framing her face. At the black leather jacket that contrasted so pleasingly with those blonde tresses. At the man's Rolex Explorer ticking expensively on her wrist. Her right wrist, in the American manner. It wasn't hard to feel inadequate in the company of such a woman. It wasn't a push to feel clumsy and inept and altogether a bit of a failure at life.

'I know what you're thinking, Ruthie. Let me tell you something. That dress you're wearing is five seasons old and you totally pull it off. And I've looked you up and don't think you're lacking either in the talent department.'

Ruthie thought Paula Tort a woman so perceptive she made Frederica Daunt seem like someone blindly groping along a cul-de-sac. She said, 'We should talk about you. It's what I'm being paid for.'

'We've talked enough about me for today.'

'I can't really argue with that.'

'Will this whole project be London-based?'

Ruthie thought about the concert footage from Montreal. She thought about the party in Montevideo where Martin had apparently repeated the trick and levitated, as Aleister Crowley was said to have been able to do. She remembered that Crowley had been a guest at Klaus Fischer's parties on Wight before Fischer's sudden vanishing in 1927. Before the trail had gone abruptly and completely cold on Klaus Fischer.

'I plan to visit that ruin in Brightstone Forest,' she said. 'I want to see the place where Martin got the inspiration for *King Lud*, to experience it first hand for myself. It's where everything began.'

Two things happened before Ruthie had quite finished voicing this thought. The first was that the cup convulsed in Paula's grip, spilling some of its pale contents onto the clipped grass under their feet. The second was that the skin on Paula's face paled to a death-mask tightness.

'That's a bad idea,' she said.

'Why is it?'

'The Fischer mansion isn't a benign place, Ruthie. It's . . . malignant.'

'You've been there?'

'It's not a subject I wish to discuss.'

'You have, haven't you? My God. You've been there.'

'I'm tired. I'm tired and all talked out. We'll talk again. But now I think it's really time you left.'

THIRTEEN

Ginger McCabe looked no different to Malcolm Stuart's eye when the octogenarian ex-docker opened his door at 7 pm prompt on Monday evening in Bethnal Green. The suit was pale grey with a subtle green overcheck and the tie had an equestrian motif and so was probably from Hermès. There was a white rose buttonhole in the left lapel of the suit, its petals fresh-looking, the bloom probably bought at a stall at the flower market on Columbia Road.

The old man nodded appreciatively at the bottle tucked in the crook of his visitor's right arm and then looked around Malcolm both to right and left as if to check that he hadn't been tailed there. Malcolm thought this a little dramatic, but then remembered that Ginger had several film cameos to his name as well as a past connection with their stars. Such men had a way of seeing their lives as an ongoing drama, even perhaps in retirement.

They settled themselves in what Ginger called his parlour. There were many framed photographs on its walls and on top of the upright piano occupying half the length of one wall. Most of them had been shot in black and white, mostly with flash. Examining these was a vital part of the ritual of an encounter at his home with Ginger. Malcolm had first done this eighteen months earlier, interviewing the man for his dissertation. But it was a necessary rite and so he did it again; seeing Ginger share an evening-suited moment with Henry Cooper and Nosher Powell; seeing him with an avuncular arm around an elderly Fred Astaire. John Wayne. Burton, Niven, Diana Rigg. The Bobbies, Moore and Charlton. Peter Sellers, of course. Shirley Eaton looking gorgeous. Eastwood improbably fresh-faced.

'You knew everyone, Ginger.'

'A slight exaggeration, Malcolm. Only slight, mind. No complaints at all. It's been an interesting life.'

They were two scotches apiece and twenty minutes of small-talk in when Ginger McCabe began the story of his encounter with

Martens and Degrue. He did so without preamble. He drank his Chivas neat and didn't pour singles either, but seemed completely cogent when he began his story. His voice was steady and his words precise and apparently carefully chosen. Malcolm Stuart did wonder whether alcohol was colouring the story slightly. The old man's tone suggested it wasn't. Though Malcolm did consider that Ginger had needed a couple of stiff ones to make him comfortable with this particular recollection.

It took him back to the spring of 1968. He'd been a shop steward in the Transport and General Workers' Union (TGWU) and that had been then one of the more powerful and influential unions representing workers on the docks.

Union membership was pretty much mandatory back then and almost everyone was in and that went for Martens and Degrue as much as it did for any company employing workers at the quayside.

'So they were pretty normal, then,' Malcolm said.

'No, Malcolm, they weren't normal at all,' Ginger said. 'And don't interrupt me again.'

Ginger was thirty-five that year and in his physical prime and supplementing his docker's pay with stunt and film-extra work and with the odd unlicensed boxing bout as well. He had become a well-known and well-respected figure on the wharves in an industry rightly renowned for its camaraderie. Dockers worked and drank together. It was shoulder-to-shoulder night and day. They all lived in the same neighbourhoods and shared their class, their values and their politics.

Or most of them did. There were exceptions. Martens and Degrue were one of those.

Regional Secretary Mick Maddigan charged Ginger with the mission at his office in Tabernacle Street in Bermondsey as a dray cart unloaded clattering barrels of beer and stout on the cobbles outside. They were piled on the pavement, above the street cellar door of the neighbouring pub. It was a hot day in May. In some of London's green spaces and on some of the old bomb-sites too white cherry blossom was a feathery explosion in the branches of trees. Donovan was singing something jingly-jangly on the transistor radio in its punched leather case atop a grey metal filing cabinet. Maddigan lit a cigarette with a Swan Vesta from a packet of John Player Specials on his desk. Ginger was grateful for the scent of tobacco. The weather was unseasonably hot and the smoke reduced the sour tang of Mick's body odour. Mick was a big man and he sweated in the toiling heat.

'Hardly anyone wore deodorant back then,' Ginger told Malcolm Stuart. 'Hardly anyone knew about it. Christ, the stench in the high summer on buses. At the cinema.'

'You must have been used to it.'

'You endured it, which is not at all the same thing.'

'They're a problem, Ginger,' Mick Maddigan said.

'I'd call them more of an anomaly.'

'Oh, they pay their dues. It's the lack of representation. They don't even turn up at the AGMs.'

'What's their voting record like?'

'Non-existent. It's total lip-service, they're in the union but not of it, in only because they have to be, end of.'

'They're toeing the line.'

'Barely.'

'They're foreign, aren't they? Foreign ownership?'

'Belgian. If they're not Flemish.'

'Well then.'

'Spoken like a scab, Ginger.'

'Just playing devil's advocate, Mick.'

Mick Maddigan stubbed out his cigarette in a large rubber-tyred ashtray, glass with the Michelin Man embossed on its side. He exhaled smoke at the turning blades of his ceiling fan. He said, 'Go and talk to them. Give them a bit of encouragement to get more involved in the body that champions their rights as workers.'

'Do you have a contact?'

'Surprise them, Ginger.'

Ginger McCabe thought about this. 'My reception might not be altogether warm.'

'Why I've picked you for the task, son. Horses for courses. You can handle yourself.'

'Know any names? Every pan has a handle, Mick.'

Mick Maddigan frowned. 'Max Askew. Import/export clerk. Loner. Spends words like a miser spending his last pocketful of pennies. You'd be wise to find someone a bit more loquacious.'

'What does that mean?'

'Talkative, like your film-star chum.'

'Burton? O'Toole?'

'I was thinking the Irish feller.'

'Richard Harris.'

'You're priceless, you are, Ginger. Good luck.'

'Thanks.'

'And Ginger?'

'Mick?'

'Take care.'

Ginger McCabe went to the Martens and Degrue warehouse building on the Thursday of that week. He went there unannounced, as Mick Maddigan had said he should. Before setting off, he invested fourpence in a call from a phone box alerting Mick's secretary to the fact of his going. That was his insurance policy. There was camaraderie on the docks, but it was neither completely consistent nor universally felt. There were occasional brawls. There were thefts and there was intimidation. Violence was fairly common, because the wages were high and where there's money among working men there's greed, and there's competition when it comes to earning that money.

It wasn't only a warehouse building. That much was obvious just approaching its exterior. It was very substantial and extremely well appointed, Portland stone with veined marble lintels and sills and an elaborately engraved bronze relief greening sedately on the closed door of the vast main entrance. There was no getting around to the lading side of the business facing the river. A high brick wall shouldered the Martens and Degrue edifice to either side. Getting over it would have been climbing a cliff. Ginger had no alternative but to press the ivory buzzer set into the granite door-frame. After a pause of about thirty seconds, it was opened by a liveried man who more resembled a butler than any sort of stevedore Ginger had ever encountered.

He flashed his union credentials and explained the purpose of his visit.

The liveried man merely raised an eyebrow and then said, 'Please wait in the vestibule.'

The vestibule was more marble, this time a black and white

pattern on the floor and green and veined in wall tiles. There was a staircase leading to an upper floor with a polished brass handrail rising through its centre. Commerce was present, if muffled, from somewhere at the back of the building in what sounded to Ginger's knowledgeable ears like packing cases being hammered together, or possibly just being hammered shut, their contents checked off against an inventory, or import licence or just a bill of lading.

Ginger McCabe knew the business Martens and Degrue were involved in. They imported and exported art, most of it religiously themed. It was the sort of business that required a lot of paperwork and careful handling at either end. And evidently it was very profitable. He associated the sort of opulence surrounding him now with companies like Tate and Lyle and ICI and Shell, the great powerhouses of international industry. He hadn't thought for a moment there could be this sort of money in icons from Imperial Russia or pious Italian statuary.

'You live and learn,' he said out loud, whispering into the gloom, aware of a slight echo reverberating through the cool, quiet stillness of the space he was in. He didn't much like it there. He felt nervous. It wasn't the nervousness he felt before a boxing bout or even at a film audition. Opponents were solid and usually predictable. Film directors were men with capricious natures and big egos. In the prize ring or the rehearsal room, you took the rough with the smooth. This was different. This was a sort of queasy trepidation Ginger thought quite unaccountable.

After a few minutes, a man in a suit appeared and introduced himself as Peter Clore. Ginger judged Clore to be around ten years his junior in age, but the man was so overweight, it was impossible to gauge this accurately. He was the size of the pianist Oscar Peterson; the size of the film director Orson Welles. He had an air about him of authority. He was management, though, and what Ginger was after was some sort of engagement not with Martens and Degrue's bosses, but with someone from the shop floor.

As if reading his thoughts, Peter Clore said, 'You can use my office for your meeting, Mr McCabe. I think that's how we can best facilitate matters. I'll get you seated and comfortable, organize some refreshments for you and we can fetch Max Askew to come and have a little chat with you about work and conditions here. You can do that confidentially. No eavesdropping.'

'Max Askew is a clerk,' Ginger said.

'Yes. And a very competent clerk.'

'He's white-collar.'

'He's also a fully paid-up member of your union. Carries his card proudly. He's the nearest thing the staff here have to a shop steward. He negotiates pay and conditions and overtime terms here on behalf of a contented workforce.'

'He's never attended a single AGM.'

Clore raised an eyebrow. 'That's between you and him,' he said. 'Now would you prefer tea or coffee? Or there's wine, or beer? We can probably run to a single malt, if you'd prefer something stronger.'

'The good old days,' Malcolm Stuart said.

'This wasn't one of those,' Ginger McCabe said. 'And that, Malcolm the student, is the last interruption I'll tolerate.'

Peter Clore left the room into which he'd ushered their visitor as soon as Ginger was served his coffee. He closed the door firmly behind him. And Ginger looked at the object that had claimed his attention the moment he entered, a large frame mounted on the wall opposite the single window, presumably hung there to benefit from the spread of natural light, but covered by a velvet curtain fitted to the frame to conceal entirely what was represented there.

The frame was ornate and rectangular, longer than it was wide, suggesting the dimensions of a portrait rather than a landscape. There was a pull invitingly placed to one side of the upper reach of the curtain and Ginger knew that a tug on that would reveal what the velvet concealed. He was still seated, still drinking his excellent coffee, still speculating on the subject matter of the picture when there was a light tap at the door and Max Askew walked in.

Askew was slightly over average height and slim. He was blond haired and blue eyed and Ginger McCabe judged not too far off retirement age. He had a slightly nasal local accent and an arrestingly honest gaze when speaking or when spoken to. His argument was that his firm's workforce were exceptionally well treated and paid. He was adamant that the union members among them were loyal to the organization, though. He said that something like docks-wide work to rule or strike action would receive 100 per cent member support, but that no one in almost thirty-five years of service had been given any cause to complain specifically about the firm employing him and them. He promised to attend that year's AGM.

'It'll be my last,' he said, rising from where he'd sat to leave the room. 'I'm almost ready for that gold watch with the bit of engraving on the case back.'

'It'll be your first and last,' Ginger McCabe said. 'And it's a promise we'll hold you to.'

Max Askew left the room. Ginger noticed for the first time that the sedate ticking of a wall-mounted wooden-cased clock punctuated the silence. Involuntarily, he looked at the velvet curtain concealing whatever image lay behind it. Then almost without any conscious decision, he strode over to it and tugged the cord and revealed what it had masked.

Now, recalling this moment five decades later, he asked Malcolm Stuart a question.

'Would you happen to know what's meant by the Sacred Heart of Jesus?'

'Yes,' Malcolm said, 'I would. It's a painted representation of Christ usually found in Catholic churches. Sometimes I think also in prayer books. Christ's heart is revealed in the image, wrapped in thorns like the crown of thorns at the crucifixion. And with flames emerging from the top of it. It's an image that's meant to represent the way Christ suffered during his time on earth for mankind.'

'Very good, Malcolm the student.'

'I dated a Catholic girl in my first year at uni. She still went to mass every now and then. I went with her once out of curiosity. Statues, bells, candles, the works. So this painting was one of those?'

'In every particular,' Ginger McCabe said, 'except for one detail, which concerned the head. This particular Sacred Heart of Jesus had the horned head of a goat.'

'Christ.'

'Yes. Though not entirely. The eyes in that long head were almond-shaped and painted with a feral gleam and the goat head was grinning, slyly, narrow carious teeth above a coarse brush of beard.'

'Then what?'

'Then I heard footsteps approach along the parquet outside. Leather, steel-tipped heels, Peter Clore's shoes. No mistake. I remembered their hardwood clack. I pulled the drapes closed and walked back across the room as he entered it.'

'Do you think he knew what you'd done?'

Ginger was silent for a long moment. He looked down at his empty glass and gestured at the Chivas bottle. Malcolm refilled for them both and Ginger nodded thanks and then drank his whisky down in a swallow with a slight tremor in the hand holding the glass.

'What I think, is that they wanted me to do it. What I think, is that I was set up. It was a demonstration of their arrogance, their boastfulness. You can't touch us, they were saying. We're rich and we're up to no good and you can't do a bloody thing about it because our pockets are deeper and our morals more corrupt than you can possibly imagine. They were laughing at me. And why wouldn't they, if they thought they could sneer at God?'

'Bloody hell.'

'There's more. The image was beautifully painted. So skilful was it that I'd looked for the painter's name. And he'd signed it, bold as brass in the bottom right-hand corner. The name meant nothing to me but a fortnight later I was on set with Harris.'

'Richard Harris?'

'Dickie played the Roaring Boy, all that Brendan Behan nonsense in the pub. But it was a sham, really. He wasn't even a Dubliner. He was from a wealthy Limerick family. And when he wasn't threatening to fight Ollie Reed in a charity bout at the Albert Hall, he wrote poetry. And he collected art. The name Arthur Sedley-Barrett meant nothing to me. But it meant something to Harris and I expect it means something to a clever lad like you.'

'I know the prices he fetches at auction.'

'Supply and demand, Malcolm. Sedley-Barrett's been dead fifty years. He ain't painting no more, is he?'

'He was the most eminent British painter of the twentieth century. He was called that even in his lifetime.'

'And that lot could commission him. Unless they just twisted his arm. Makes you wonder, doesn't it?'

'What happened after?'

'The following year, Martens and Degrue shut up shop. They vacated the premises in '69. They may have opened up for business elsewhere but if they did, they did so very discreetly because I never heard anything about it. Word was that building remained an unhappy place. It was never successfully occupied again despite the shenanigans you already know about with the fellers wearing dog collars and sprinkling holy water.'

Malcolm said, 'On two separate occasions?'

Ginger nodded. 'Didn't work, apparently. Place was demolished in '71 during the night. If I'd been on that demo crew I'd have wanted to do it in daylight. And I didn't scare easily back then.'

'You said it was a big building.'

'Dynamite or TNT. Blown to smithereens.'

'And that's everything?'

'Heard Peter Clore set up a marine-salvage business in Pompey. He might have and he might not, never bothered to verify that. Max Askew retired the year after I met him. And he never did make it to that AGM.'

Malcolm poured them another whisky apiece. The Chivas bottle was slightly over half empty and to him, looked a bit like he felt.

'What's tickled your interest in ancient history?'

'I've met someone researching the rock star Martin Mear. Askew was Mear's uncle and she thinks Martin was a regular visitor to 77 Proctor Court as a child.'

'I've a grandson who's got every record that man ever made,' Ginger said. 'He's fanatical about Ghost Legion, our Denny. Always trying to convince me that Martin's coming back.'

Malcolm didn't reply to this. His mind was on the movement behind the glass panes in the front door of Askew's old flat when he put the key in the lock on his most recent, abortive visit to the address.

'She a looker, this rock-music researcher? Or are you helping out only as a consequence of the goodness of your heart?'

Malcolm just blinked, feeling a bit drunk now, looking at the whisky bottle.

'No reply needed, son. I know the answer to that question without you having to tell it me.'

'I'll tell you a bit about her, Mr McCabe.'

'Ginger to you, son.'

'I'll tell you a bit about her, Ginger. And you can tell me whether I'm being a fool.'

FOURTEEN

Getting out the Ouija board late on Monday evening was Sebastian Daunt's idea. He'd enjoyed a convivial dinner accompanied by slightly too much wine with his daughter. It might have been nostalgia that prompted him. Later, he wasn't sure. Certainly they'd played in the commune where Frederica had grown up often enough. In a way, those Ouija sessions had been her apprenticeship in matters speculative and spiritual. Electricity had been sporadic and largely battery powered among the commune's ramshackle dwellings. There had been no television and its members had consequently to find other means of entertaining themselves, sometimes esoteric.

Or it could simply have been boredom. Sebastian was a man still with a restless sort of energy that could descend into listlessness without some sort of creative challenge to fulfil. At Frederica's villa, he was deprived of his potter's wheel and clay. He was denuded of his easel and canvases and oil paints. He was denied even his sketch book and the sticks of charcoal used to create the images that filled its pages. He had responded to the urgency of his daughter's summons by hastily packing a single overnight bag. He was materially incomplete as a consequence. He'd had to cadge a spare toothbrush from her only that morning.

Frederica was on the terrace when he opened the door from her sitting room and came out and suggested it. She was smoking a cigarette and contemplating her night view of the sea. Stars twinkled in the vastness of the sky above the Atlantic and moonlight quivered, jittery on the surface of the ocean.

'We should take a turn with the board,' he said.

'Really, Dad? Maybe we should just leave well alone.'

'Martin Mear died owing me a huge debt of gratitude for the *King Lud* cover. That album made his fortune and I was never paid a penny. If he's out there, or up there . . .'

'Or down there,' Frederica said.

'Wherever he is, if he's anywhere, he isn't going to harm my daughter. Not while I'm alive, anyway.'

'There's a comforting thought.'

'I'm in pretty good shape.'

'I'm delighted to hear it. But is the board really the healthy option?'

'Healthier than standing out here staring at the stars and chain-smoking.'

And that settled it. Asked later, Frederica would have said guilt obliged her into it. She was embarrassed at indulging a filthy habit of which she knew he disapproved in front of her father.

Frederica retrieved the board, blew off the coating of dust covering its box lid and laid everything out on her kitchen table. They put their forefingers on the planchette with a shot glass brim-filled with brandy for each of them poured by Sebastian and placed at their left elbows. Frederica had left on a single kitchen light, burning a low-wattage bulb. She asked the space around them the inevitable question and with a force that made Frederica gasp audibly, the planchette slid to 'Yes.'

'Bingo,' Sebastian said, or rather whispered, a stunned quality to his utterance of the single word. The planchette had moved emphatically. He knew he hadn't pushed it and didn't think his daughter had either. She just didn't seem in the mood for fakery. Anything but.

'Hello,' was the planchette's next destination. It paused there for a moment. Then it slid under their fingers to the number 7. It was moving with a speed and sureness, a sort of antic energy that left the father and daughter trying to harness its alleged power slightly spellbound. Next, and with no hesitation, it spelled out M-A-Y. Then it was back to the number 7. It finally paused. And then it slid to goodbye and they felt the planchette grow inert under their fingertips with an abrupt and total absence of life.

Frederica withdrew her hand from the board and picked up her shot glass, downing its contents in a single gulp. 'Short and to the point,' she said.

'But to what point?' her father said.

'I don't know. It was a message politely delivered. I sensed no hostility or threat. It was even courteous, wasn't it?'

'Except that it makes no sense.'

'Two sevens and the word May, which is the fifth month of the year.'

'Except we're in the middle of October.'

'It's a sort of code,' Frederica said.

'It makes no sense.'

'No, Dad,' she said, after a moment. 'It makes no sense to us. It will make perfect sense to someone.'

'It's after midnight,' her father said. 'We should both turn in, Freddie.'

'I might not be able to sleep for a while yet.'

'I'm sorry. Mightily bad idea,' he said, staring at the board.

'We've both had our share of those,' Frederica said. 'But I don't think it actually was. Someone was trying to communicate something to us and it might be important. It's not fear that will prevent me from sleeping, it's intrigue.'

She put the Ouija contents back into their box and put the lid back on and took the box to where she kept it, locked away and out of sight.

Ruthie Gillespie awoke on Tuesday morning to a text message from Sir Terence Maloney apologizing for having to postpone their interview planned for that afternoon. He regretted the short notice, but something unavoidable had come up and needed dealing with. What that was, he didn't say. The rest of the morning passed uneventfully. She took the call from Detective Constable Mark Sorley at noon. He got straight to the point.

'Malcolm Stuart didn't show up for his first appointment at eight-thirty this morning. He isn't at home either. This is an extremely punctilious young man. You were among his recent appointments and I'm wondering if you can shed any light.'

'He's not shacked up with me, officer. Am I a suspect?'

'We want to know where he is, how he is and what's happened to make him abandon his routine without explanation. You seem to have come into his professional life very abruptly. It's anomalous, from my perspective. Where are you?'

'North Lambeth. Just off Lambeth Bridge Road. I don't honestly think I could tell you anything of value.'

But between Ruthie ending that conversation and the detective constable's arrival at Veronica's door shortly after 2 pm, she spoke to Frederica Daunt for twenty minutes on the phone. And Frederica told her about the Ouija board session of the previous evening. And so by the time Ruthie opened the door to the DC, she suspected she had the information to tell him all he needed to know. She also suspected it to be extremely bad news.

Frederica called, she said, just to touch base. She sounded bright and cheerful, much more positive than she'd been after the ordeal of the Friday evening séance. She was out of the country, she was in the company of her father and no one was terrorizing her from beyond the grave. She was extremely interested to hear about Ruthie's meeting with Paula Tort. And since Paula had spoken on the record, Ruthie was happy to share the information. All except for the part about the ruined mansion in Brightstone Forest on Wight. The Fischer House part of the interview, Ruthie regarded as confidential.

Frederica talked about her most recent struggle to quit smoking and Ruthie listened with the genuine sympathy of a fellow sufferer. And then, prompted probably by association, she mentioned the Ouija session and the short, strange assemblage of letters and numbers the planchette had picked out.

'Inexplicable,' she said.

'Not to me,' Ruthie said, suddenly certain that she would need a cigarette before the arrival of the detective constable, wondering would she be able to stop at one.

She told Frederica about Malcolm Stuart and Max Askew and her theory about *King Lud* and 77 Proctor Court. She said, 'And May is my middle name. After the month in which I was born.'

'How would Malcolm Stuart have known that?'

'You have to register with an estate agent before you can view a property. They tightened the rules a few years after Suzy Lamplugh. I did that using my passport. My full name's there on the inside back page.'

'This sounds ominous, Ruthie.'

'There's a police detective on his way to see me. I'll suggest he go on to Proctor Court.'

'He's too late. What reason will you give him?'

'Intuition. He'll check it out because he's got no leads.'

'I hope I'm wrong, Ruthie.'

Ruthie sniffed. 'I don't think you are. Just as you say, Malcolm's polite, courteous. He's not at all typical of the breed. A sweet young man, gentle and clever.'

'I might be wrong,' Frederica repeated.

'But you're not,' Ruthie said.

After her conversation with Frederica concluded, Ruthie made herself tea and sat and sipped it in Veronica's garden, wishing it was a glass of something more potent, knowing that the last thing required was alcohol on her breath or fogging her brain when she needed to persuade a detective to do something for which she'd only be able to claim a morbid hunch as justification. She tried for a hopelessly distracted hour to transcribe her interview of the previous day from her voice recorder to her laptop screen. She saw that she'd missed a call at 1.15 pm from Carter Melville. Carter Fucking Melville, as Paula Tort habitually called him. She wondered why he hadn't called late the previous night, as what had seemed to be becoming his habit.

DC Sorley arrived. He was smartly dressed and seemed implausibly young. He was slim and dark haired with an intense gaze emanating from intelligent grey eyes.

'There's a property you should check out, one he showed me around.'

'On what basis?'

'On the basis that if you think I'm worth following up, you have no concrete leads.'

Sorley took a notebook from the pocket of his jacket. He said, 'Where is this address?'

Ruthie told him.

'Why would he be there?'

'Why would he be anywhere except where he's supposed to be? But he's not where he's supposed to be. It's worth checking out.'

Sorley was simultaneously peering through the garden window and fishing a phone from his pocket. He nodded, 'What's phone reception like out there?'

'Pretty good.'

'Stay here. I'll call this in. Where were you last night?'

'Do I need an alibi?'

'Not yet. You're the children's author, aren't you?'

'Young adult, mostly.'

'Yeah. My little sister reads you. Would you be prepared to sign something?'

'A statement?'

'An autograph.'

'You're not taking this seriously enough. It doesn't have a happy outcome.'

'I'll call in the lead, Ms Gillespie. You wait here.'

Ruthie waited for his return craving nicotine and feeling increasingly miserable. She trusted her intuition and felt that something had gone very wrong for Malcolm Stuart in a way profoundly final. She didn't wait for the detective's return. She put ice in a glass and poured him a glass of Diet Coke from a bottle in the fridge and joined him outside so she could smoke. He accepted his drink with a nod and joined her at the garden table. Diet Coke: not ideal for October but the weather was mild and dry and it was quicker to prepare than coffee or tea. She lit a cigarette.

'What was your interest in 77 Proctor Court? You're based on Wight, aren't you?'

'It was occupied by a relative of someone I'm being paid to research. I think my subject visited the place quite often as a child.'

'So you posed as a buyer?'

'Only at first. I went for a drink with Malcolm Stuart after my viewing. I was truthful with him.'

'Was he angry, resentful?'

'He was philosophical. He told me it was a difficult sell.'

'So he'd developed an emotional relationship with the property?'

'I wouldn't put it that strongly, officer.'

'If it was a waste of his time, he'd resent it.'

'Maybe. He didn't resent me.'

After about twenty more minutes of verbal back and forth, Sorley saw an incoming call on his phone and excused himself and walked through to the street outside to take it in privacy. He came back through the flat and into the garden shortly after looking grimly serious.

'There's a fatality at 77 Proctor Court. It looks like a straightforward suicide. He'd hanged himself. ID and description a match, I'm afraid.'

'He didn't kill himself.'

'An inquest will determine whether he did or he didn't.'

'Detective Constable? He didn't kill himself.'

'The front door was locked. There are two sets of keys. He had one set and the second was with the block's caretaker. That's how we gained entry. He locked himself in, Ms Gillespie. His set of keys to the flat were found a few minutes ago in his pocket.'

'He didn't kill himself.'

'You've said that three times now. It runs counter to the available evidence. Putting yourself in the frame?'

'I have an alibi. Or I will when Veronica gets in. She owns this place. We were both here all of last night. And there's a senior Met police officer can give me a character reference. Commander Patrick Lassiter happens to be a good friend of mine.'

'That sounds highly unlikely.'

'It's nevertheless true.'

'I'd like you to stay put,' DC Sorley said. 'You're here for the duration of this research job?'

'Yes. The reason Malcolm Stuart didn't kill himself is because he had plans for his future life. One of them involved me, or he hoped it did. He gave me his number to phone him if I changed my mind and decided to meet him sometime for a drink.'

'He must already have had your number.'

'Which he wouldn't use because he didn't want to pressure me. It was my decision to make.'

'Had you made it?'

'He was too young for me,' Ruthie said. 'And it's too soon after a rather bruising experience.'

'So this job you're doing is a sort of exile from yourself?'

'That's an astute way of putting it.'

'I'm paid to be astute. Doesn't look like it's going to be much help to poor Mr Stuart, though.'

'What's your sister's name?'

'Alice. Her favourite is *The Spire Under the Sea*.'

'There's a copy here, in Veronica's bookcase. I'll pinch it and sign it for her if you like.'

'Good coming from bad?'

'Not really.'

The detective left a short time later. 'Thanks for the Coke,' he said, exiting through the front door.

After the DC had gone, Ruthie remembered the last time she'd spoken to Commander Patrick Lassiter. He'd called her out of the blue one afternoon about a month earlier. He was the best friend Professor Philip Fortescue possessed. And so to her, the call came as a surprise.

'Don't tell me you want my help with a case, Patsy.'

'Just calling for a catch-up,' he said.

'I thought Phil got you, like with a divorce.'

'Not the way I operate,' Patsy Lassiter said.

'Wouldn't it be less complicated?'

'Sometimes, friendships have to be persevered with. Sometimes, that's the quality that makes them worth having.'

At her end, Ruthie closed her eyes and smiled. It was wonderful to hear his voice, which cleaved her too, dragging the past with such painful clarity back into the present. She'd allowed herself to forget just quite how fondly she felt for this man.

'You should come and visit, Ruthie,' he said. 'I know Helena would love to see you.'

'I will,' she said, knowing, as she knew he did too, that she never would.

He cleared his throat. He said, 'How's that gift you've got?'

'What gift would that be, Patsy?'

'The one for getting into trouble.'

'It's more of an instinct than a gift,' she said. 'I've sort of curtailed it. Why do you ask?'

'Because I'm only ever a phone call away, Ruthie. Because I'll always pick up. And because I'll always have your back.'

FIFTEEN

Making Alice Sorley's day didn't do the same or anything similar for Ruthie Gillespie. She felt wretched. She hadn't put the noose around his neck, but she felt that had she never met Malcolm Stuart, he wouldn't now be dead. She felt uneasy about continuing with her research into the life and myth of Martin Mear, uncomfortable about the cloying way in which those two elements combined so inextricably. She felt that fate was linking her to Frederica Daunt and her father too in a way that seemed ominous. And Sebastian Daunt had known Martin in life. She couldn't bring herself to return Carter Melville's call. 'Carter Fucking Melville,' she said aloud to Veronica's still and empty sitting room. She wouldn't begin to know what to say to him.

She left the flat, locking the door behind her, and walked the five-minute distance to the river and the foot of Lambeth Bridge. There was a cafe on a short pier to the right of the bridge where Veronica had told her they made excellent coffee. They sold sandwiches and pastries too. It was after lunch and she hadn't eaten but Ruthie couldn't face any of it. She sat on a walled stretch of manicured grass and smoked a cigarette, watching the water course by in those rippling patches where the river wasn't slack. It was sunny in a pale, gentle sort of way. It was windless and benign and a day young Malcolm Stuart hadn't lived to see.

Ruthie called Michael Aldridge. She did it just to hear a sympathetic voice. She told him about what had happened. Or she told him as much as she knew, because she felt there were large and important unanswered questions about this particular turn of events. Michael listened in silence.

Eventually he said, 'You're blaming yourself. It's in your tone, Ruthie. You sound as guilty as sin about something that can't possibly be your fault. Think about it logically.'

'About which bit? About how I learned about it via a bloody Ouija board?'

'You're upset.'

'Of course I'm bloody upset.'

'There's traffic noise. Where are you?'

'South side of Lambeth Bridge.'

'Are you wearing a coat?'

'What kind of question is that?'

'A practical one. Stay put. I'll be there in forty minutes.'

'You're at work.'

'I'm the boss. I can delegate. Sit tight.'

'Thank you.'

'There might be strings.'

Despite herself, she smiled. His voice, his humour. 'There are always strings,' she said.

'What have you got on your feet?'

'Black Doc Marten's. Black jeans. A black pullover under a black wool coat. I like black.'

'Perfect,' he said

They took the fast train from Waterloo to Surbiton. They walked down to the Riverside Café and Michael persuaded Ruthie to eat a tuna melt ciabatta washed down with a can of Orangina. She felt better with her belly full, hollow only when her thoughts turned to 77 Proctor Court. She could imagine few bleaker places in which to end your life than Max Askew's strangely unstill Shadwell flat.

They walked along Kingston Riverside to Kingston Bridge and then crossed the bridge to the towpath on the other side. Michael told her that the towpath led to Hampton Court and that the distance was about three and a half miles.

'All flat,' he said.

'Is this where you do your running?'

'It is, but we're not running today and we're getting the last ferry back and that will be before dark.'

'Where is this going?'

'I told you, Ruthie. Hampton Court.'

She punched his shoulder. 'You know what I mean.'

'It goes only as far as you want it to,' he said. 'There are no strings. I've got no shortage of faults. But crassness isn't one of them.'

The sun had begun its autumnal descent by then and the riverbank was abundant with wildlife. There were rabbits and squirrels. Ruthie saw a heron. Murderously territorial parakeets squawked, a vivid green in the trees above them. There was an urban myth about how they'd got to south-west London when they were essentially birds of paradise, but Ruthie couldn't remember what it was.

'Jimi Hendrix owned a breeding pair when he lived in London,' Michael said, reading her mind. 'The story is, he let them go.'

Rowing eights practised on the river coached by a man with a megaphone and a boat on floats in an accent Ruthie thought honed at public school. The water flowed serenely by, travelling in the opposite direction from the one in which they walked. They passed an island Michael told her was named Raven's Ait. Shortly after, a pheasant exploded out of the undergrowth to their right and hustled off the way they'd come. The odd mountain biker passed them. They saw no other walkers. The ground was pale orange clay, potholed, under their feet.

'Boots holding up?'

'Better than their wearer. How far have we come?'

He pointed to a huge water-pumping station building on the bank opposite. It was Victorian, she thought, stone soot-stained by the coal fires of earlier decades and constructed to resemble a fortress.

'That marks the halfway point,' he said. A little further on, he offered her his arm without comment and without comment, she took it.

Hiking wasn't really Ruthie's thing and by the time they got to Hampton Court, it was almost time for the last ferry to take them back. She looked at the Tudor facade, flushed by the sunset, its centuries-old brickwork almost blood-red, its chimneypots a haphazard cluster of silhouettes against the darkening sky.

'Do you think when things become that old, they're indifferent to the world, Michael?'

'I think when things become that old, they're like querulous elderly people, requiring a great deal of care and attention and blithely ungrateful for it. But then I'm an architect and I've specialized in restoration. You're a romantic.'

'I'm not a romantic.'

'I think you are.'

They were silent for a moment. Michael said, 'What went wrong, Ruthie? With your maritime scholar; with Phil Fortescue?'

She thought about this. She said, 'It was wonderful. It really was. And then suddenly it wasn't. Suddenly it was nothing at all.'

'Why wasn't it?'

'He never got over the death of his wife. Eventually I realized that sustaining the grief was his way of keeping her alive. The only way he could, really. That penny dropped with an almighty thud.'

'I'm sorry to ask.'

'I didn't have to answer. And you've been very kind to me today.'

They walked back from where the ferry dropped them to the Waggon and Horses pub in Surbiton. It was shortly after 7 pm by then. Michael ordered food for them and bought drinks while Ruthie found somewhere quiet for them to sit and took off her coat. She took her phone out of her pocket and saw that she'd missed two further calls from Carter Melville and that Veronica had sent her a text which read: *Saw the detective's card on the mantelpiece. You OK Hon?*

She texted back that she was. She knew she wasn't, but she also knew that things could be a great deal worse. She smiled thanks as Michael Aldridge handed her a large gin and tonic and then sat down opposite her. She sipped from her drink and said, 'What about you?'

'I'm not involved with anyone. Haven't been since the business on Wight with Ashdown Hall. Not since my marriage imploded.'

'It was an imperfect match.'

He laughed. 'You can say that again.'

'Once is enough.'

He sipped beer and held her eyes frankly in a way that made her realize he'd spent the whole day so far with her avoiding doing that. He said, 'The truth is that I fell for you the moment I sat down to talk to you outside the Minghella Ice Cream Parlour on Ventnor seafront almost three years ago. I saw you and I heard your voice and I was utterly captivated. But I was also spoken for. And by the time I was free, you were with your scholar of the sea.'

'Bad timing,' Ruthie said.

'The worst. Will you persist with this research work?'

'I don't honestly know. What do you think?'

'I gave you the reference that you say got you the job. I'd hate to have you on my conscience.'

'It shouldn't be intrinsically dangerous.'

'Someone's been scared so badly they've fled the country,' Michael said. 'And now someone has died. And the Jericho Society is always extremely bad news. Why are you smiling?'

'Without the Jericho Society, we'd never have met.'

'What's the next step?'

'I've an interview with Martin Mear's daughter on Thursday and another to schedule with his pet roadie from back in the day. I want to go to one of the festivals die-hard Legion fans organize where they rehearse this bonkers ritual they call the Clamouring. I want to get a sense of who they are and sample the atmosphere. There's one coming up on Sunday at a stone circle in Wiltshire.'

'So you'll carry on?'

'I want to know what or who killed Malcolm Stuart.'

'Probably depression.'

'It absolutely wasn't,' Ruthie said.

Her phone rang. She'd hung her coat over her chair. She fished it out of her coat pocket expecting to see Carter Melville's name on the display. But it wasn't him, it was instead her London agent. 'Excuse me,' she said.

She went outside. She wondered what Eileen Masterson could possibly want. She was a good agent, calm and loyal and supportive, but Ruthie wasn't working on anything worthy of Eileen's attention currently. And it was eight o'clock in the evening.

'I'm working late, running on New York time, talking to an American publisher where it's three in the afternoon.'

'What's this to do with me?' Ruthie said.

'Nothing. Not directly. But I'm in the office, where I've just taken a call from a very persistent man named George McCabe. Ginger to his friends, he informs me. He wants to see you and he doesn't want to wait. 9 am tomorrow morning, he says. Claimed to be an old actor. So I googled him before calling you and he's exactly who he says he is. Colourful career. I'll text you his contact details and address.'

'Did he tell you what it was about?'

'That's for your ears only, darling. In person.'

Ruthie couldn't imagine what a veteran actor could possibly want with her. Since she was outside the pub, she lit a cigarette and pondered on it. Once or twice she'd been approached by younger industry people trying to get film rights to one of her stories without paying an option fee, but this sounded completely different from that. That was cheeky. This sounded somehow ominous. She smoked and paced and considered, and then she decided with a shrug that she could do nothing that might enable her to learn anything now and might as well forget about it until the morning.

Back inside the pub, Michael had bought them fresh drinks. They talked and drank and then quite close to closing time he said, 'I'd very much like you to stay with me tonight.'

'No strings, you said.'

'Not to do anything. I don't think you should be alone. Sometimes a bit of human warmth is welcome and valuable. It's comforting. I think this qualifies as one of those times.'

'Human warmth?'

'Yes.'

'So this isn't a gender-specific offer, Michael? You'd as willingly cuddle up to a man?'

'You can tease all you want, Ruthie. And I've been honest about my feelings towards you. But this is a suggestion sincerely made for entirely the right reasons.'

Ruthie rose and grabbed her coat.

'So it's a no,' Michael Aldridge said, quietly.

'Phone reception isn't great in here. I'm going outside to text Veronica not to expect me back tonight. I need to do it before she turns in, worrying. Then I'm coming back inside and we're having one for the road. I hope you're as fastidious as I am about clean laundry, Michael. Dirty sheets are gross.'

In the event, Ruthie awoke early the next morning unable to think of very much they hadn't done. But since she'd instigated most of it, she didn't think she had any great cause for complaint.

'I might have been a bit forward last night,' she said to his sleeping back.

He stirred and turned to face her. He said, 'I was afraid to wake up in case I was just dreaming.'

'I don't normally do one-night stands, Michael.'

'An excellent principle. One I very much hope you stick with.'

'Really?'

'I've been wooing you for three years, on and off.'

'Mostly off.'

He raised a hand to stroke her hair and kissed her. 'Good morning, Ruthie.'

'Good morning, Mr A.'

SIXTEEN

The mostly black-and-white photographs on the walls of Ginger McCabe's parlour made of it a rogues' gallery of mid-to-late-twentieth-century celebrity. Ginger had anticipated the selfie by half a century. The man himself looked less flamboyant today than he did in the framed images, sharing space with dead film stars and long-retired sportsmen. He was over six feet tall and broad and had a boxer's emphatically flattened nose. He looked extremely fit for his age in a charcoal three-piece suit. He also looked more than subdued. He looked sorrowful.

'Only met the lad twice, miss, but he was a very amenable boy,' he said. 'Respectful of his elders. Appreciative of tradition. A good listener. It's a terrible shame.'

'How did you find out?'

'Copper came round. Irish moniker.'

'Sorley.'

'That's the feller. I was a diary entry in Malcolm's phone. Last person to see him alive, allegedly.'

'I doubt that,' Ruthie said.

'Foul play?'

'He wasn't suicidal.'

'No, miss, he wasn't. But he did leave here half-cut.'

'You told him something that made him go back there. Will you tell it to me, Ginger?'

'Not here,' he said, looking around, grimacing. 'I need fresh air, revisiting that particular story.'

They walked to the river. Then they walked along the river and Ginger recounted his story about Max Askew's broken union promise and the picture hung behind a velvet curtain on Peter Clore's office wall at the Martens and Degrue building first contaminated and afterwards dynamited into oblivion.

He finished his story. They'd found a bench. Ruthie took out her cigarettes and lit one with a pink Bic lighter.

'Haven't had one of those for over fifty years,' Ginger said.

'Do you ever miss it?'

'Only after meals.'

'Still?'

'And when I have a pint, obviously.'

'Obviously,' Ruthie said.

'Do you believe in atmospheres, Ruthie?'

'You mean like at Proctor Court?'

'Never been to Proctor Court. Hospitals, hospices, sometimes churches and funeral parlours. Cemeteries. Old houses, sometimes. Seaside guest houses of the seedier variety. There's a reason they demolished the place Fred and Rose West lived in.'

'Some of the victims were under their garden,' Ruthie said. She'd sourced an archive photo of Klaus Fischer's mansion on Wight before it became a ruin. He stood before the main entrance in broadcloth suiting and spats. It flashed suddenly into her mind and she shivered.

'Some places feel diseased,' Ginger said. 'As though the evil things thought about and done there are contagious.'

'The place where Max Askew worked was like that?'

Ginger nodded slowly. 'The place where he lived too, according to Malcolm.'

'I went there. He took me there but I went in alone. It felt funny; sort of cold and restless at the same time. Like something squirming, almost. Hard to describe in words.'

'Words don't get close,' Ginger said. 'They're feelings we had before words were ever thought of and first voiced. They're ancient feelings. They're the oldest part of us.'

'Why did you want to see me today, Ginger?'

He was silent for a long time before answering. Then he said, 'I wanted to warn you. The inquest will say Malcolm Stuart died by his own hand. But we both know he didn't. He came to me to ask about Max Askew to learn something he could pass on to you. He just wanted an excuse to see you again. If that was enough to get him killed, you're probably in a lot of trouble. I don't think Martin Mear is a healthy subject to be researching.'

'What did you tell DC Sorley?'

'Nothing to make him change what passes for his mind. He's one of those young coppers who thinks everyone over the age of forty senile.'

Ruthie smiled. 'You're a long way off senile.'

'Senile or punch-drunk,' Ginger said. 'I met Martin Mear, once. I didn't tell Malcolm that, but I did. He didn't much resemble his Uncle Max, I can tell you. Max Askew you'd have trouble picking out in an identity parade. His nephew was charismatic, a human klieg light, lighting up the room, making it glow around him. It was at a wrap party for a movie I was in. They'd used a couple of Ghost Legion songs on the soundtrack and the whole band was there, all dead now, bless 'em.'

'Which strikes me as odd. Or it would if I were an actuary.'

That made Ginger McCabe chuckle. 'You don't much resemble an actuary, miss.'

'What was he like, Martin? At the party?'

'He was making stuff disappear. Coins, wristwatches, wallets, all this women's tomfoolery.'

'Tomfoolery?'

'Jewellery.'

'Oh.'

'The director's Rolex came off his arm and somehow Martin got it onto mine. Director wasn't happy about that but pretended to be amused. Martin was a big star, after all. I couldn't see how it was done. Couldn't see the join at all, if you get my drift. Told him it was a bloody good trick.'

'What did he say?'

'He was smiling but he had this detachment, this look in his eyes. Could've been drugs, don't think it was. Like someone amused by something secret they're not going to amuse you by sharing. He told me I was mistaken. Said there was no need for trickery.'

'How did he strike you?'

'A lot of people were intimidated by me back then. I haven't always been an old man. I was a bruiser, one who looked like a bruiser. When you fight for prize-money you develop an instinct about people. You become a sort of connoisseur of fear. There was no fear in that man, not an ounce of it.'

'He was buried alive digging a grave as a teenager,' Ruthie said. 'The fact that it didn't become his tomb apparently had a big effect on him.'

'We're none of us immortal, Ruthie,' Ginger McCabe said. 'And sometimes fear's your friend.'

She got back from Bethnal Green to Veronica's flat at noon. A large sleek grey car idled at the kerb. Ruthie, indifferent to cars, didn't know the make, but it was an ostentatious vehicle. There was a liveried chauffeur at the wheel and Carter Melville sat in the rear, with an open laptop across his knees and a phone secured by his shoulder to his ear. He said something into the phone on seeing her and allowed the phone to drop onto the leather upholstery next to him.

He pushed a button and the window next to him swiftly rolled down.

'Get in.'

She did.

'The dirty stop-out finally gets home,' he said.

'I'm sorry I didn't answer your calls.'

'Where were you last night?'

'Unfinished business.'

'Presumably he has a name?'

'Private unfinished business.'

'How I know you weren't home is your flat-mate was when I arrived. She was just leaving for work. Cute chick, Veronica. Good manners. Invited me to wait for you inside. But small rooms give me claustrophobia.'

'You've been here for three hours?'

'And you don't have the remotest idea of what three hours of my time is worth.'

'Why are you here at all?'

'Max Askew. Proctor Court. A young estate agent, an ex-estate agent when they found him, discovered there yesterday afternoon. It made the late edition of the *Standard*. And you weren't picking up your calls. I'm employing you, which means I have a duty of care. Just like you have a responsibility to respond when I try to contact you.'

'I've already said I'm sorry.'

'It's a question of priorities. Nothing comes in front of me. Savvy?'

'Yes.'

'Put your seatbelt on. We're going on a little trip.'

'I'd like to put fresh clothes on, if you don't mind.'

'They're yesterday's threads?'

'And this morning I cleaned my teeth with a borrowed toothbrush.'

'Which suggests last night was a spontaneous thing. Interesting,' he said, grinning. He stopped short of a wink, which Ruthie thought just as well. Had Carter Melville winked at that moment, she would have told him precisely where he could stick his job.

Carter did plenty of talking on their journey, but none of it to her, which Ruthie considered a blessing. Instead he was involved in what she supposed was deal-making. There was lots of ball-breaking type terminology and much discussion of bottom lines. He spoke to several people, but it was impossible to keep track because he called everyone 'baby', seemingly regardless of their gender. Ruthie spent the journey wondering whether Carter Fucking Melville was an unwitting self-caricature or a man striving hard to live up to his own myth. By the time they reached their destination she'd decided he was both, simultaneously.

They rolled conspicuously through the dreary wastes of south Wimbledon and pulled up outside a large building in a heavily guarded storage facility. Melville unlocked an outer door with a key produced from his own pocket. He gestured for Ruthie to follow him through it. His chauffeur stayed in the car.

About ten feet beyond the front entrance, a wall obstructed their progress to the full height and width of the building's interior. This wall had a metal security door cemented into its centre. To the right of the door was a number pad. Melville entered an eight-digit code far too dexterously for Ruthie to have observed the number sequence. She wouldn't have remembered an eight-digit number anyway.

The door unlocked and Melville stepped through it and switched on an interior light. Ruthie stepped through the door following Carter's beckoning arm and he closed it behind her.

'Temperature and humidity control,' he said. She nodded. He'd whispered the words, as if in some place of worship. Looking around, Ruthie could fully understand this, for she saw that they had entered a shrine.

It was a shrine to Martin Mear and it seemed to her both pristine and complete. She saw his guitars first, racked vertically on a stand. From left to right they were the Yamaha FG acoustic on which he'd composed *King Lud*; the oxblood-red Gibson Les Paul he'd first used as the Legion's strutting axe-man and the white Fender Stratocaster Eric Clapton had given him as a birthday present in the summer of 1971. He'd mostly used the Strat on the three nameless albums Legionaries claimed would orchestrate the Clamouring. Though on 'Cease All Mourning', he'd famously used the Gibson.

Ruthie shivered. She had just seen the cloak among a display of hung stage clothes Martin had worn in Montreal when he'd apparently levitated in front of his adoring, spellbound audience. There was a story it had belonged once to Aleister Crowley, for which it was one of her tasks to try to establish provenance.

Martin Mear had been a collector of weaponry. He'd had a sword belonging to Napoleon Bonaparte and a pair of duelling pistols Lord Byron had once owned. A cutlass wielded once by the pirate Blackbeard. A bayonet last fixed in the Zulu War at the battle of Rorke's Drift. There was modern as well as antique stuff, though. The shotguns and semi-automatic rifles and racked revolvers and automatic pistols looked far more deadly than they did decommissioned.

There were several motorcycles. There was even a car. It was a purple E-Type Jaguar convertible with purple leather seats.

'Martin pimped his ride before the TV show was ever thought of,' Carter Melville said from behind Ruthie.

'Why did you bring me here?'

'It's hard to separate man and myth. I thought that seeing his things up close and personal might help that process.'

'The problem being that it's pretty mythic stuff.'

'The release date of the box set is December 15.'

'Just in time for Christmas.'

'This lot, most of it, goes on show at the V and A to coincide with that.'

'Like the Bowie exhibition?'

'It'll be bigger than the Bowie exhibition. Trust me.'

She bit her lip on the cliché that she would trust him really no further than she could throw him.

There was some esoteric stuff. There was a pack of Tarot cards and a pair of ivory dice and a set of black rosary beads with a large crucifix, a bronze Christ writhing nailed to it. There was a crystal ball and a bleached willow fork she thought probably for water divining. There was a staff of the sort Morris sets clatter together in West Country summers on English village greens or outside Cornish pubs. A pair of the bells on leather pads they buckle around their knees.

'Is all this yours?'

'Of course not. Most of it was bequeathed to Paula and the rest pretty much to April. April still wears her daddy's wristwatch. I'm curating, is all.'

Something in a small glass display case on a table-top caught Ruthie's eye. She went over for a closer look. It was cream coloured, faded and hand-torn. It was about an inch square and had smudged ink fading on it in letters too small and indistinct to properly make out. Ruthie picked up the case for a closer look, squinted at the artefact inside.

'What's this?'

'It's Martin's return ferry ticket to Wight, when he went there to compose *King Lud*. He'd have had the Yamaha six-string strapped to his back and his head filled with dreams.'

'And chords. And lyrics.'

'They didn't come to him until he got there.'

Ruthie didn't say anything. She'd remembered Paula Tort's warning about the Fischer House, convinced looking at Martin's old ferry ticket that after his death she had indeed gone there herself. She could smell Carter Melville's aroma from behind her, his signature scents; hair tonic, expensive cologne, the pungency of smoked cigars. He was much more in the moment to her than the ghost of a dead rock star was.

'In a way that's the most important single item in this room,' Carter said. 'Peacock Blue by then was ancient history. Tallow Pale was behind him too and the path was clear and the Legion lay ahead. There's a real sense in which what you're holding in your hand is Martin Mear's birth certificate.'

SEVENTEEN

(Transcript of April Mear interview session 19 October)

He was my dad. I didn't see him every day and won't pretend I did, though I wish I had. He was famous, obviously, and the band was something of a treadmill. They toured and the tours were lengthy and often in far-away places. Pre-internet and MTV you toured to promote every new album. No promo videos. No YouTube. The Legion didn't even release singles. That was just the way the industry worked back then. The top bands were very industrious. The tours were arduous and the gigs were marathons.

So I didn't see my dad sometimes for weeks on end. But when I did, he was wholly there. Nothing intervened or interfered or competed. There were no distractions or interruptions. He gave me 100 per cent of his attention. And he was wonderfully normal. No ego. No black moods. No mystique. All the bullshit associated with his legend was totally absent.

We'd go on camping trips he always called our expeditions. Or he'd rent a cottage in rural Wales or the Highlands of Scotland. That was at the time of the Troubles in Northern Ireland, but we still went to the South, to County Clare for a week in a fisherman's or crofter's cottage. To the Wexford coast. The more remote the better. He was quite courteous when Ghost Legion fans recognized and approached him, but he didn't like it. Or at least, he didn't like it happening when he was with me.

I asked him about it once, when we were in a bothy halfway up a Scottish mountain. We'd sheltered there after our tent became waterlogged and collapsed. My dad had lit a fire and heated us broth and it was quite cosy really, watching the lightning through the window, listening to the rumble of thunder above us. My dad had placed a plaid rug around my shoulders and had made a sort of turban for my wet hair with our one dry towel. I asked him why he was so attracted to the wilderness, though I might not then have been aware it was called that.

He replied by quoting some lines from Shelley. My dad loved poetry, everyone from Dryden to Philip Larkin. Shelley and Tennyson were his favourites. And Eliot, they were his top three. He said: *I love all waste/ And solitary places; where we taste/ The pleasure of believing what we see/ Is boundless, as we wish our souls to be.*

It's from *Julian and Maddalo*, which is really about Byron and Shelley and their friendship during their self-imposed exile together in Italy. I wouldn't have known that then either, but the words stayed with me. It was the one occasion in my entire life when I got a glimpse of my dad's power as a performer. He quoted four lines. I could have sat there with the soundtrack of that thunderstorm and listened to him recite another thousand. He always had the charisma, the presence. And the looks and the physique, obviously.

But just for a moment I'd seen and heard him perform and the power of it matched the elemental stuff booming above us and giving us strobed flashes of the wet crags around us. It was an immense gift he possessed. Truly immense. It was almost scary.

He saw the look of nervousness or trepidation or maybe just of awe on my face and remorse and something close I think to self-disgust flickered over his features because he never, ever wanted to be anything other than authentic with me. He wanted me to get the part of him no one else did, the piece of him reserved solely for his daughter. He really didn't want to waste time with me trotting out the act. He just hugged me then and untied the towel turban and began to dry my hair with it very gently. He was always gentle. He never physically chastised me. He never even raised his voice.

Some people will tell you that my dad was enigmatic. Some people will tell you he was basically shy. I think that's Carter Melville's take on him, and Carter knew him pretty well and also in fairness for a lot longer than I did. But I think the truth is more paradoxical and less obvious than that. I think my dad was basically a very private person. He was thoughtful and articulate and unbelievably well read. If he had an interest in the esoteric, he never discussed it with the child I was and I never saw a shred of evidence.

Like I've said, he never shouted. He laughed at silly things, banana-skin moments. He really liked old Laurel and Hardy films. The silent, slapstick ones. He thought Garbo the most beautiful woman ever to appear on celluloid. May was his favourite month. He liked that line from Chaucer about the squire, 'He was as fresh as is the month of May.' He said if he ever wrote a single line of a song with that gleaming clarity of that one, he'd die a happy man.

But he didn't really talk about death. At least, not to me. He was knowledgeable enough and interested enough to answer most questions posed by the slightly precocious child his daughter was and on the rare occasions he didn't know the answer, he'd find it out and report it back.

I never saw him smoke or pop a pill. I never saw him drink anything more potent than Diet Coke. If he was critical of my mother for putting me in an orphanage, he never let it show in my presence. What else can I tell you? I didn't know him for anything like long enough. And he was everything to me.

* * *

April Mear reached for the glass of water on the table between them and Ruthie observed that her hand shook slightly lifting it, the surface tremoring. She didn't turn off her tape machine. She'd noticed the wristwatch straight away. She liked watches and April's heirloom was conspicuous. It was an Omega Speedmaster Professional, the moon watch bought by NASA for their Apollo astronauts on their voyages into space. It was too big really for April's wrist, but still looked very cool to Ruthie on its vintage bracelet.

She gestured at the watch. 'That was your father's, wasn't it?'

'Someone gave it to him. Someone from Omega, or maybe one of the NASA people or maybe even an astronaut. He met lots of different people.'

'It must be very precious to you.'

'Carter Melville wants me to loan it for the exhibition. I'm frightened it could get lost.'

'More likely stolen,' Ruthie said.

'I'm not materialistic. I don't drive a fancy car or bedeck myself with diamonds.'

'Which presumably you could.'

April held out her wrist. 'This is priceless to me.'

'Do you listen to the records?'

'Only the acoustic numbers. They're sung in something closest to his speaking voice.'

'You make him sound misunderstood.'

'He's deliberately misunderstood. It's like the old newspaper guys used to say. If it's a choice between the truth and the legend, print the legend.'

'Today's the first time you've spoken about this stuff?'

'On the record, to a stranger, yes.'

'But you and Paula have talked?'

April smiled. 'Paula has the reputation in the fashion industry for being a real ball-breaker. She's another misnomer victim.'

'You and she have a lot in common.'

'How did you find her?'

'I liked her, April. No vanity. No bullshit.'

'And she liked you. And so do I.'

'I'm being well remunerated.'

April smiled again, this one more complex than the last. 'Not really why you're doing it. Paula thinks you've had your heart recently broken.'

'As I told her to her face, she's perceptive. But my heart's on the mend.'

'You needed a distraction.'

'I needed an escape. But I intend to do a good job. I intend to earn what Carter Melville pays me.'

'He'll see to it that you do,' April said. She looked around. They were in a quiet corner of a coffee shop in the Kingston branch of John Lewis. They had a view of the river below them. Or April Mear did. Facing her, Ruthie Gillespie had her back to the water.

'We'll do the next one at my home,' April said. 'We won't have to murmur there like spies.'

'Thank you.'

'You can switch the recorder off now. No more revelations for today.'

'Do you find the process tiring?'

'What's tiring, Ruthie, is processing the grief. No one gets over losing their father as young as I did.'

'I can imagine.'

'No, you can't. Have you heard of Otto von Bismarck?'

'Prussian aristocrat, became Chancellor, unified Germany.'

'Very good.'

'I took my degree in history,' Ruthie said.

'Bismarck said that the only true immortality is posthumous fame. And he was right. His fame keeps my father alive for everyone but the people who loved him. It doesn't remotely work for us.'

Ginger McCabe spent the early part of Thursday afternoon mulling over the death of Malcolm Stuart. He was over eighty and his womanizing days were a warm and misty recollection somewhat distorted both by nostalgia and exaggeration. But he thought Malcolm had been right on the money with the picturesque researcher. She was a looker who behaved as though she didn't know she was. She was a stunner, but she was very approachable. It was a winning combination in a woman. And it was rare.

He couldn't work out what it was he might have said to Malcolm to send the lad back to Proctor Court. He'd told his Martens and

Degrue story to Malcolm and then he'd repeated it verbatim to Ruthie Gillespie and he still couldn't determine what the trigger had been or when he'd unknowingly pulled it. Ginger woke from his post-lunch nap mulling over the whole mysterious business and then decided he'd go and take a look at Proctor Court for himself. Just from the outside, though he knew a bit about by-passing locks from his own largely misspent East End youth.

He arrived outside the block at a quarter to five. It was still light and the sunsets that close to the river could be spectacular in late October. But it was a grey sort of day, one of those autumnal London days that never really seems to get going in terms of light; bland, undistinguished, damp and pewter-tinted. He climbed the steps up the stone stairwell to Max Askew's front door remembering the man. He'd been blond, blue-eyed, unremarkable. He'd been as undistinguished as the day was, quite difficult to describe. He'd been a liar, because his pledge to attend that long-ago union AGM had been deliberately insincere. And he'd disappeared after his retirement, slipped into obscurity in the same vague way his employer had gone, just vanishing, without fanfare or even any sort of notice.

Ginger knew that most men of his vintage struggled with more than one or two flights of steps. But he was a vigorous man for his age. He was still fairly agile and his wind was good. He thought of himself as similar really to a cared-for vintage car, old, but regularly serviced. He still attended his old gym three times a week. His days of skipping over a heavy leather rope were behind him, but he still did a bit of round-shadow and he was still capable of three or four rounds on the heavy bag. So he got to Max Askew's door breathing normally, his heart thudding away at a respectable sixty beats a minute.

The upper third of the door was paned glazing, nine little square lozenges of frosted glass above an over-large Green Man knocker, bronze and truly greened over time and grinning evilly. It seemed melodramatic to Ginger McCabe to think that way but think it he did, standing there as a light rain began to fall from a sky turned gunmetal now and the raindrops hitting the brittle leaves of the pavement trees lining the block with a sound like a ghost ordering the world to hush.

Ginger shivered. It wasn't cold. He was wearing a Crombie

overcoat over a three-piece suit and there was a woollen scarf around his neck and he had just climbed three flights of stairs. But he shivered anyway. Proctor Court was entirely still and but for that whisper of rain, all was silent. The Green Man grinned and glared, the knocker redundant, for of course, no one was home. For a mad moment, Ginger thought about using it anyway, as a sort of dare with himself, just to see what doing so would summon, or conjure. But he didn't, because at that moment something caught his eye, entering his peripheral vision from the right, from the street.

Where a grey Morris Minor had come to a halt at the kerb. Which prompted Ginger to think that you didn't see those too often these days. Not in that condition you didn't, because this example was weirdly pristine, the coachwork and split windscreen gleaming as though with a factory finish. Ginger had time to wonder how the car lustred so in the falling rain before the driver wound his window down and the bland features of Max Askew arranged themselves into a smile and Askew waved at him before driving serenely on. Max Askew, aged not a day.

Ginger McCabe collected himself. He was not a man easily spooked. He could not remember enduring the feeling he felt now since an afternoon more than fifty years earlier, catching a glimpse of a painting in a building on the Shadwell docks.

He went for a much needed drink. He got to the Prospect of Whitby at six-thirty. The Prospect was a historic pub and rightly famed for its perfectly preserved decor. It was also a horrible tourist trap usually full of German and Japanese coach parties taking endless selfies sipping token pints; but Ginger remained badly shaken even after the twenty-minute walk to the pub and he needed a stiff one and beggars couldn't really be choosers, could they?

After two large White & Mackay whiskies and a pint of Guinness he felt much better. Not quite yet his old self, but getting there. Ginger McCabe had ridden a lot of hurtful punches in his time and he'd taken a fair few right on the chin, but he'd never been off his feet and he'd never taken a standing count either.

Three doubles in, he began to rationalize what he'd seen.

He'd been suggestible, was all. He'd had to revisit his Martens and Degrue story not once but twice, after an interval of half a century. Malcolm Stuart's death had been grisly, sad, shocking and suspicious. The Green Man door knocker had been right out of a Hammer Horror movie. And Ginger had featured briefly in a couple of those. He'd played a grave robber in one, a phantom horseman in another. The Morris Minor had been real. It was a collectable car but hardly unique, you could bid for them on eBay. It hadn't been Max Askew at the wheel. It had just been a blond young chap, a car enthusiast, waving from the wheel, full of neighbourly joys on a dismal day.

Ginger liked this version of events. They emboldened him. Or maybe the drink did that, or a combination of alcohol and positive thinking. He'd got his swagger back, or at least he'd get his swagger back when he got up from the table he sat at near the pub's picture window overlooking the river. He'd go and look at whatever now occupied the spot where Martens and Degrue's baleful old building had been before someone public spirited – probably the Port Authority – had had it blown to smithereens at the start of the 1970s. He'd lorded it, had Ginger, back in the day on the docks. He'd go back there. It was no distance. He'd do a bit of gloating.

Getting to his feet and weaving through the throng was trickier than he thought it would be and Ginger realized that he was actually a bit pissed. He'd always had a strong head for drink, but you had to make allowances for age and he'd eaten nothing since a light lunch prior to his afternoon siesta. Then he'd had a shock, hadn't he?

It was fully dark when he got outside. Breathing fresh air wobbled him a bit further, but then his oxygenated lungs cleared his head and he set off at a determined lick, a big, dapper, distinguished-looking man with a prosperous air and a purposeful stride.

The river's edge was even more sobering, when he got there. The commerce was gone, the bustle absent, the sights and importantly the smells of the docks nothing more than a cherished memory soon not to be even that. Wharves and warehouse buildings were now luxury flats. Ginger breathed in the dank Thames odour remembering when the spot he stood on had smelled of hemp rope and fruit cases and baled tobacco. It was almost completely quiet. All he was aware of hearing above distant traffic noise was the gentle lapping of water. He went to look.

As he toppled down, before he hit, Ginger McCabe had time

to think the job expertly done. Two simultaneous knees buckling his, the single, firm, flat-handed push to coincide with it between his shoulder blades. A generous target. He had a broad back. Two men? One, if he really knew what he was doing. Ginger surfaced gasping at the cold, thinking he did.

He mumbled a useless prayer he was in slack water as the current took him and the weight of what he wore dragged him under to travel its length unseen.

EIGHTEEN

Veronica Slade was the possessor of a Ph.D. in the history of art. She held a job at one of London's most venerable and most esteemed auction houses. She worked in Mayfair and was a frequent business traveller. Her job involved authentication and establishing provenance and evaluating the worth of artefacts before they went under the hammer in the sales room. She was highly respected and generously paid. She owed her friendship with Ruthie Gillespie to Michael Aldridge.

Veronica's firm had come into possession of a goblet of dubious provenance that proved to have been not just a goblet, but a ceremonial chalice once owned by the Jericho Society. It had been at the centre of their rituals and they badly wanted it back. She linked the chalice to a long-demolished building on Wight on property now owned by Aldridge. She cold-called him and he agreed to meet her. At their face-to-face, he told her truthfully that no one knew more about this sinister cult than Ruthie Gillespie did. Their temple on Wight had been reduced to rubble in the time of Ruthie's grandfather, who'd had a hand in that event. Aldridge had been the victim of a Jericho Society conspiracy from which Ruthie had basically saved him. His marriage had not survived the fallout from that, but Michael believed he owed Ruthie his daughter Mollie's life.

Veronica travelled to Wight to meet Ruthie. And Ruthie helped Veronica extricate herself from a situation that had seemed to her both deadly and inescapable. She did this partly out of a natural inclination to help those in distress. She was motivated also by an energetic hatred of everything the Jericho Society represented. And there was the fact that from the moment they met, Ruthie Gillespie and Veronica Slade established that strong bond of friendship which sometimes occurs only when people are opposites as characters.

On Friday morning, Veronica phoned in sick to work. This was a lie. She wasn't sick. She made the call because at 8.45 am, Ruthie was seated in her garden, weeping and already halfway through a bottle of white wine. Chablis, probably, she thought. Though Ruthie would drink Sauvignon Blanc or Blanc de Blanc at a stretch. This looked like a stretch. Veronica thought that today, turpentine might very well do the job.

Veronica went outside. She'd dressed for work before abandoning her schedule and her heels sank into the well-tended turf of her neat little lawn. Ruthie looked a mess. Up close, her eyes were raw and she reeked of booze and tobacco. Her glass was almost empty. Her ashtray already teemed. Veronica moved the chair opposite where Ruthie sat closer to her and sat down beside her and put an arm around her and kissed her on the cheek. She hugged Ruthie hard and Ruthie sobbed and hugged her back.

'What happened?'

'Somebody died.'

'I know. The boy.'

'Not him, someone else. Because of him. Because of me. An old man. Kind. Courtly. Found in the Thames in the early hours at Greenwich. It was on the news. The regional news. He was quite well known. I mean, he'd been quite well known, in his day.'

'Accident?' Veronica said. 'Suicide?'

Ruthie shook her head. 'He and the boy had something in common. An address.'

'And this is all to do with Martin Mear?'

'I think so, yes.'

'Maybe you need to leave that alone.'

'Probably. Except I signed a contract.'

'With someone litigious?'

Ruthie sniffed. 'I'd think very.'

Veronica was silent. Then she said. 'On Tuesday night, you slept with Michael Aldridge, didn't you?'

'Yes.'

'How was that?'

'Wonderful.'

'Planning to see him again?'

'He has his daughter, Mollie, for the weekend. I'm seeing him on Monday night.'

'I know you, Ruthie. When you've sobered up and slept, you'll feel inclined to visit this address, wherever it is. But you're not going back there. Not without Michael Aldridge holding your hand. Promise me?'

'I promise.'

Veronica stood.

'Where are you going?'

'On a mission of mercy. Eggs, bacon, mushrooms, black pudding, that kind of thing. Orange juice, freshly squeezed. Hot buttered toast. I'm going to feed you and then you're going back to bed. Even in your world, darling, wine before noon is a bit extreme.'

By four o'clock on Friday afternoon, Ruthie felt slightly parched but completely sober after a few extra hours of sleep and what she thought of as a good cry. She considered it entirely possible that Ginger McCabe had met with a mishap. He'd been spotted early on Thursday evening by a film buff who'd recognized him in the Prospect of Whitby, drinking alone and liberally. He was a man elderly by any standards and drink affected the elderly more potently than it did the young. He'd gone into the river fully clothed. The police were saying there were no suspicious circumstances. The post-mortem would confirm that he was intoxicated at the time of his falling into the river. He was a classic accident victim.

Except that Ruthie didn't believe in coincidence and two people had died in under a week and there was a connection between them and it was Max Askew or it was Proctor Court, where Max Askew had lived.

Ginger had been a thorn in the side of Martens and Degrue in the 1960s, but he'd been no more really than a minor irritant. They'd dealt with him with a combination of brazen contempt from Peter Clore and patronizing dishonesty from Askew himself.

Basically, they'd just brushed him off and he'd not been in a position to do anything significant about it. If they'd threatened him, he'd probably have been sufficiently brave and headstrong to do something about it physically, to retaliate with his educated fists. But that hadn't happened. He would have told her if it had. His experience with Martens and Degrue had been strange and strangely incomplete, but that was often how life happened. Life wasn't the same as a feature film with everything neatly tied up in an emphatic ending. Life was what John Lennon said it was; what happens when you're making other plans.

If Ginger's death had been deliberately contrived, it wasn't the settling of an old score. It was about what was happening now. And it involved Max Askew or his old flat at Proctor Court or maybe both.

Ruthie called Carter Melville.

'Baby. How was April?'

'Forthcoming. Sweet, actually. Rather poignant. She still misses him.'

'So would you, if you'd known him like I did. A day doesn't go by I don't miss Martin.'

'He was a contradictory man, Carter.'

'All of us are, baby. Different people to everyone who knows us. All that existential bullshit.'

Ruthie thought bullshit was precisely what it was.

'What's next?'

'Some Legionaries are planning a Clamouring rehearsal at a stone circle in Dorset on Sunday afternoon. You OK with me hiring a car?'

'Invited or gatecrashing?'

'Anyone can turn up.'

'They're a bit dark, some of them. It's a ghoulish agenda.'

Ruthie said, 'Is that a warning?'

'People with extreme beliefs can be paranoid is all, hon. But the car's totally cool. Expense anything you need. Hotels, flights, no one makes an omelette and all that.'

'Can't really imagine you making an omelette, Carter.'

'But I'm capable of a figure of speech.'

'No argument there.'

'Baby?'

'Carter?'

'Book a nice hotel for Sunday night in Devon.'

'Dorset.'

'Whatever. And watch your back.'

'Generally?'

'And specifically,' he said. 'Watch your back.'

After her conversation with Carter Melville concluded, Ruthie deliberated over calling Frederica Daunt. She thought she might profit from Frederica getting out her Ouija board again. She might get some clue as to whether malice had been involved in the death of Ginger McCabe. Or she might just trigger some jeopardy risking the wellbeing of Frederica and her father. She didn't think Ouija boards inherently magical or evil. She thought if they were anything at all they were catalysts. As such, though, they could be dangerous.

She decided against it, because she thought the risk likely to outweigh the reward. She was still mindful of how badly wrong the séance had gone, still able to remember Frederica shrieking over the phone as her damaged ears bled in the taxi as she fled for the airport the following day.

Ruthie was alone in Veronica's flat, contemplating all this. Veronica tended to spend weekends with her French farmer boyfriend. She was a person who valued routine. Ruthie's routine had involved her cottage in Ventnor, her sea-scholar boyfriend and her word count when writing. All that remained of all that was the cottage. She couldn't really imagine writing fiction again. It was a life of surprises, as the old song went, and some of them weren't very nice.

She was seated by the window in her guest bedroom with a view of the street outside. Friday afternoon was lulling its way into Friday evening and she had no immediate plans. There was a car parked opposite, an old Morris Minor, grey coachwork, split windscreen, mint condition. A man leaned against it, smoking. He had blond hair and a bland expression and he wore a tweed jacket with leather patches stitched to the elbows. He glanced up, perhaps sensing her scrutinizing him and his expression was too distant or just too noncommittal for Ruthie to read. Then he blew smoke at the sky and got into the car and it trundled away.

Her phone rang. She saw with no surprise whatsoever that it was Frederica Daunt.

'What are you up to?'

'Just sitting here trying not to smoke.'

'With you on that one. Daddy disapproves.'

'Your father still there?'

'He's babysitting. He says he'll leave when he thinks it safe for him to leave. He'll probably be here till Christmas.'

'Well. It's a family time.'

'You sound upset.'

'Someone died. Two people. I didn't know either well, but both were nice and I feel to blame.'

Frederica was quiet. Then she said, 'Are you to blame?'

'One of them tried to warn me. Warn me off, really. Martin Mear might have been involved with some very unsavoury people. I think it likely, actually. They're Satanists. They're secretive and absolutely serious.'

'Do you want to tell me about the two people who died?'

'Is that wise?'

Carefully, Frederica said, 'It isn't like googling someone, Ruthie. It isn't straightforward and it's far from unequivocal. But you can learn things. And sometimes the things you learn are quite valuable.'

'I think one of them has communicated with you already, through the Ouija board. The name you got is mine. I'm Ruthie May. The numbers you gave me were where he was found.'

'I see. Tell me about the other one.'

'You can google him,' Ruthie said. 'He was once quite famous.'

At eight o'clock, she went to the pub. The Pineapple was only a five-minute walk from Veronica's flat. Going to the pub wasn't the same as going to the dogs and she'd resolved only to have a couple of drinks before turning in for the night. It was a mild evening and she sat at one of the vacant bench seats attached to the tables outside. If she was hassled, she'd just drink up and leave. But she didn't think she would be. The pub was close to Kennington Police Station and quite a few off-duty officers drank there at the end of their shifts. That tended to give the place a bit of decorum, better manners than would otherwise have been the case.

She decided she would toss a coin over future involvement with the Martin Mear box-set project. The heads or tails wouldn't be definitive, but it was a good way of gauging how she actually felt about continuing with it. Either she'd feel disappointed or she'd be relieved. But she wouldn't honestly know which of those it was until the coin fell flat and still.

'Heads I carry on, tails I pack it up and go home,' she said aloud.

It was tails. She felt a tinge of anti-climax and then the overwhelming certainty that she couldn't go home. Not yet, she couldn't. She had unfinished business with Michael Aldridge. She had unfinished business with Paula Tort and April Mear and Sir Terence Maloney and Carter Fucking Melville. She would hire a car in the morning and drive to the Dorset village near the stone circle earmarked for Sunday's Legion-inspired ritual. She would get to the heart of the enigma that was Martin. She would solve his mystery. She had a proven knack for doing that.

She looked up and saw the split-screen Morris Minor parked a little way down Hercules Road. She couldn't tell at the distance whether there was anyone at the wheel. She wasn't headed in that direction and it didn't matter anyway. She finished up her second drink, got up from where she sat as planned and buttoned her coat for the short walk home. When she got to the door, with her key in the lock, her phone rang. And Frederica Daunt's number showed on the display.

NINETEEN

The circle of standing stones was five miles to the south of Shaftesbury, on private land owned by a farmer named Edward Coyle. Coyle was a committed Ghost Legion fan who Ruthie thought privately might well deserve to be committed. He maintained a Ghost Legion fan-site on the internet. He seemed to credit Martin Mear with the status of a prophet, if not some kind of deity. Some of what he claimed struck Ruthie just as classic conspiracy theorizing.

The salient facts about Martin Mear's death were scarce and becoming increasingly difficult to verify. 1975 was a long time ago and the people directly concerned with the event sometimes misremembered and in some cases had died. He was believed to have been killed by electrocution while rehearsing for a concert in Morocco. There was heavy rain, a leaky roof and miles of exposed power cables used to generate noise on a stage. But the location had been remote and the weather sultry and once pronounced dead, he was buried without a post-mortem. There wasn't a death certificate. No one had thought to photograph his corpse. His grave had gone unmarked.

There had been attempts over the years to locate the grave with a view to disinterring his remains and re-burying them with suitable ceremony in a suitably lavish tomb. But Paula Tort had been extremely hostile to this idea. Paula had not been the main beneficiary of Martin's will, that had been his daughter, April. But Paula Tort built her business in the years following Martin's demise. She had extremely deep pockets and a talent for getting what she wanted – or didn't want – done. She wanted Martin spared the indignity of exhumation. She'd apparently been with him on that fatal day in Morocco but if she knew where he was buried, she wasn't saying.

According to Edward Coyle's fan-site, Martin had been murdered.

'Well of course he was murdered,' Ruthie said to herself, puffing away against the rules at the wheel of her hire car, door windows optimistically open a chink, a bottle of Febreze ready for action later on the front passenger seat.

A disparate group had conspired to kill him because he undermined the American values they so treasured. The group included then President Richard Nixon, NATO General Alexander Haig and Evangelist Billy Graham.

'And probably Elvis Presley,' Ruthie said, to her audience of no one. 'Elvis wouldn't have liked the competition.'

Ruthie thought Edward Coyle an object lesson in what happens when fandom turns into obsession. She thought that she might explain her research brief to him and get a few outrageous Mear-related quotes. It would add colour to the essay and surely fans who'd become fanatics had their place in a world as excessive and distorted as the world of heavy rock. Idolatry and delusion weren't terribly far apart. In fact, she thought, idolatry was a sort of delusion.

The significant thing about Edward Coyle in practical terms was that everyone was welcome at the event he was staging. You didn't even need to think that the Clamouring would work, or would ever really be enacted on a sufficiently epic scale to have a chance of working. You just had to be a sincere liker of Ghost Legion's music. And speeding along a blessedly uncluttered A303, listening to them on the car's hi-fi system, Ruthie realized that somewhat to her surprise, she'd become very much that now.

She was staying in Shaftesbury, in Bell Street, in a cottage with a wood-burner and a pretty garden she'd found on AirBnB for not very much of Carter Melville's expenses money. She'd booked it for two nights and had arranged to collect the keys from a Mrs Hughes, a volunteer staffing the public library on the opposite side of the road. The cottage was charming and cosy with only one real problem, which was the thatched roof. Thatch meant spiders and autumn was the season for them and Ruthie didn't like spiders at all. So she'd gathered some conkers from under the horse-chestnut trees in Archbishop's Park before setting off. They were in a paper bag in her travel case in the boot.

She parked in the Silver Band car park, which was free, and walked the short distance to the library and then on to where she was staying. She made herself a cup of tea. She checked her phone for messages and saw that the reception wasn't great. She unpacked and fired up her laptop and re-read the stuff on Edward Coyle's fan-site; not the mad stuff, just the stuff about the timetable for tomorrow's event at his circle of stones. Then she read an independent history of the stone circle. But before she did any of that, she took out her conkers and left them in little trails under the doors and windows, wishing she'd known conkers were a spider deterrent for many years longer than she had.

Ruthie shopped for wine and other essentials at the Co-op branch she'd been told she'd find at the end of the road. Then she lit the wood-burner. And then she pondered on her strange conversation of the previous evening with Frederica Daunt.

Frederica hadn't dusted down her Ouija board again. She'd succumbed to the heat of Portugal's apparent Indian summer and taken a siesta. She'd dreamed of an angry man. The anger was in the man's tone and gesticulation. His features were nondescript and bland. She said he was a man it would be difficult to pick out at an identity parade or to photofit even with the new computer software police forces used.

'What was he angry about?'

'I've no idea.'

'How was he dressed?'

'Like a geography teacher,' Frederica said, 'the sort that taught me, anyway. Tweed jacket with leather patches on the elbows.'

'I've seen him,' Ruthie said. 'I saw his parked car tonight.'

'I don't think he's real, Ruthie. Not in the way that you would understand the word. If you see him again, on no account engage with him. Act as though he isn't there, as though he doesn't exist. Engaging is very dangerous.'

'Thanks.'

'I'm sorry.'

'No, I mean it, Frederica.'

There was a silence. Then, 'My friends call me Freddie.'

'Goodnight, Freddie.'

'Goodnight, Ruthie. And take care.'

The stones were Neolithic. The site had been erected five thousand years ago, for what purpose nobody knew. There were twenty-four stones in total and they'd been quarried in Derbyshire. The circle they formed was geometrically precise. They were each about sixteen feet high, but six of those feet were their foundation, buried firmly in the ground. They each weighed around ten tons. Quite a feat logistically for a Bronze Age tribe. Unless the tribes had come together to achieve the feat collectively. And a feat dwarfed by Stonehenge, where some of the sarsens weighed forty tons and had somehow been transported to Wiltshire from a quarry in Wales.

Sheep kept the grass neatly clipped at Edward Coyle's stone circle. The stones themselves were granite and rose like gaunt enigmas from the ground. The weather forecast was good and there was to be a side-show of festival-type entertainment. A fire-eater and a team of acrobats were billed. There were to be beer and cider tents and stalls selling food. Profit wasn't the motive – Coyle owned five thousand acres of prime arable Dorset farmland. Paying proper tribute was the motive. Around a thousand people were expected to attend and they would come from all over the world.

Just after nine o'clock on Saturday evening, Michael Aldridge called her. Ruthie went into the garden to speak to him, where the signal was slightly stronger.

'How's your week turning out?'

'Eventful.'

'Why does that sound so ominous?'

'I've got no proof anything's ominous, Michael. I've just got a feeling that the truth about Martin Mear is going to turn out to be really weird. How's your gorgeous daughter?'

'Fast asleep, as of five minutes ago.'

'You're an architect,' Ruthie said.

'Guilty as charged.'

'And you do restoration work, old houses.'

'Grand old houses,' Michael said.

'Have you ever been in one that's haunted?'

'Where's this going, Ruthie?'

'There's something odd about that address I told you about in Shadwell. Would you come there with me on Monday afternoon?'

'If the alternative is you going there alone, then yes.'

'What are you like with locks?'

'I know how to get through them,' he said.

'Then we're in business.'

'Breaking and entering on a Monday afternoon,' he said. 'Probably a routine assignment for you. Probably just your way of staying young.'

It was a comfort to hear his voice. She hadn't realized how tense she'd felt ever since Frederica Daunt's warning of the previous evening until relaxing now, smiling to herself, listening to Michael's words. She was alone in a strange place in a quite remote part of the country. And all she had for protection was her conkers for the spiders. She remembered the concern in Carter Melville's tone when he'd told her to watch her back. Both generally and specifically, he'd said. There were things people knew that she wasn't being told and the deception was deliberate and she knew that now. She was sure of it.

'The address you're talking about belonged to the man who worked for Martens and Degrue, didn't it, Ruthie?'

'Proctor Court,' she said. 'I think there's something there. I need to find it.'

'We both know who Martens and Degrue are really.'

'That's my point.'

'Where are you?'

'You wouldn't believe me.'

'Try me,' he said.

'I'm in Dorset. The Legionaries have these warm-ups for the big event when they orchestrate the Clamouring and bring Martin Mear back to life.'

'Jesus.'

'Not quite, but the same principle, I suppose,' Ruthie said.

'Except occult, or pagan, rather than Christian.'

'I suppose. I'll have a clearer picture this time tomorrow. I'm going to try to speak to the lunatic responsible for organizing it. They're doing it at a stone circle.'

'Course they are,' he said. 'And it's Dorset, so there'll be cider involved. The Wurzels. Maybe Mumford & Sons.'

'Ghost Legion only,' she said. 'And they take it extremely seriously. People attend religiously.'

'Sacrilegiously.'

'That too, I suppose.'

He didn't say anything. Then he said, 'I wish you were here.'

'And I wish you were here, Michael. But you're on Mollie-time.'

'No hot date then?'

'I've got one of those on Monday,' she said.

'What's the plan for the rest of this evening?'

'A bit of exercise,' she said.

'Really?'

'Wrestling the top off a bottle of Sauvignon Blanc.'

TWENTY

There were probably five hundred people gathered at the site when Ruthie got there on a bright Sunday shortly before noon. She followed cardboard signs attached to wooden posts along a lane that petered into a track before opening out into a meadow become temporary car park. From there she could see a trail of people headed for a low hill. She assumed that the standing stones would be on the other side of it. Cake stalls and tightrope walkers might be OK, but Coyle evidently didn't want vehicles ruining the mood anywhere within sight of his ceremony.

She studied the cars. She was no one's idea of a petrol-head, but she thought the vehicles might provide a first insight into the socio-economic status and also into the age of the Legionaries. And there were a few real classics sprinkled among them. She saw a Bristol, a Jensen, several MGs and a smattering of original VW Beetles. There were at least three E-type Jags. There were a couple of Triumph Stags, some wire-wheeled Morgans and a beautiful old Sunbeam Rapier. Audis and Saabs from more recent years proliferated. There were several Harley Davidson motorcycles and a disproportionately high number of Land Rover Defenders, even for the West of England.

People straggled over the hill brow in small clusters, in conversation, some of them gesticulating, none of them paying any undue attention to her. She was attired in black jeans and a black pullover under a black wool coat. Her boots were black Doc Marten's and only a red silk scarf worn around her neck broke the monochromatic Goth rulebook. Most people there, when she summitted the hill and saw what lay on the other side, were dressed the way people had dressed at festivals in the early 1970s. There were Afghan coats and what looked like authentic WW2 flying jackets. There was a lot of denim and a lot of hair and the crowd were split roughly seventy–thirty, she thought, in favour of men.

The atmosphere was quite subdued. Ruthie, who had a natural distrust of the outdoors, didn't do festivals and never had, but she thought there would have been more excitement, more of an anticipatory buzz at one of those. She thought that probably this was a reflection of the fact that the headline act here were all of them deceased. And that statistical anomaly struck her again. She didn't know the odds against there being no survivors into their seventies of the four members of Ghost Legion, but she knew there were several very pickled rock gods still breathing. Still, for that matter, performing.

She saw a man approaching her like someone swimming against the tide. He wore a battered brown leather coat like an aviator from Baron Manfred von Richthofen's Flying Circus in about 1917. He had on cavalry boots and jodhpurs. The coat was unbuttoned and open to reveal a mint-condition vintage Ghost Legion tour T-shirt probably worth close to a grand on eBay. He was smiling at her, beaming in a way that made her think she must have met and then forgotten him at some point in her past. She smiled back, mortified, desperately trying to remember. He stopped in front of her and thrust out his hand and she felt obliged to shake it.

'Edward Coyle,' he said, 'Eddie to you.'

'Ruthie Gillespie.'

'I know. I got the press release. Oh, it's all embargoed until the week of the actual release and Carter's a bugger for protocol, but I know you're doing the research for the book in the box-set goodies. My daughter's thrilled. She's your biggest fan.'

The boots and the coat were antique and the jodhpurs beautifully tailored. He was probably wearing a couple of thousand pounds' worth of clothing. As if to emphasize the point, he pushed his sleeve back to look at his wristwatch and she caught a glimpse of a Tudor Black Bay. She'd described this man as a lunatic to Michael Aldridge the previous night, but he'd have been the most flamboyantly dressed in the asylum by a mile. He was evidently a prosperous lunatic with rather distinctive taste.

'Do you own the Sunbeam in the car park?'

Eddie Coyle grimaced. 'Defender, I'm afraid. Bit cliched, but what can you do? Most of my driving's off road.'

'How long have you been a Ghost Legion fan?'

The grimace became a wide grin. 'For ever,' he said.

Which Ruthie knew was an exaggeration. It had to be because the man standing in front of her couldn't have been over forty.

'You're on first-name terms with Carter Melville?'

'No biggy. Carter's hot on protocol but doesn't do formality at all. Unless your experience has been different to mine and he calls you Ms Gillespie, which I somehow doubt.'

'Can I take up a few minutes of your time, Eddie?'

Coyle looked again at his wristwatch. 'Things to do, Ruthie, people to see. Maybe after the fireworks?'

'Literally fireworks?'

He grinned again and winked. 'You'll see,' he said.

More and more people were arriving. And Ruthie noticed that the sky was darkening. Rain hadn't looked likely earlier, but it was beginning to now. She saw that the refreshment tents were firmly shut and she hadn't seen a single acrobatic tumble or a solitary tongue of bellowed flame. The food stalls had not yet opened. There was no smell of hog roast or burger meat on air untainted by fried onions or the sickly drift from a waffle iron. There were to be no preliminaries, she realized. The business end of things came first. The fun and games would follow the solemn ceremony.

People were forming a circle of their own around the stones. In some places, they were tiered three-deep. Ruthie estimated there had to be at least a thousand people there, each holding the hands of their neighbour, most with their eyes closed, some wearing beatific smiles, no one actually touching the stones in the circle they surrounded.

Ruthie became aware that a drone was sounding, somewhere. People were starting to hum. A noise grew from the back of a thousand throats and became a note and then a hummed song. She recognized the melody. It was 'Cease All Mourning', the sixth and final song on the sixth Ghost Legion album. It was noon and the sun had disappeared behind a low, stretched veil of thickening grey. Someone poked Ruthie hard in the back as her prompt to join the singing and she stumbled forward and almost fell and for the first time had the inkling that the afternoon might not go well as the first fat raindrop hit in front of her right ear and dribbled down her cheek.

People had started stamping. They stamped in unison to the rhythm of the song they hummed and the single collision of a thousand feet boomed like thunder and the earth shook under them. Then the sky flickered and spat a zig-zag of fire and Ruthie looked up into the deluge and saw that there was a storm raging right above them, lightning tearing bright, antic paths through the gloom and thunder in a creeping barrage loud enough to make her ears hurt and her skull shake.

Something was solidifying at the centre of the stones. Something was etching itself into life, darker than the murky gloom surrounding it. It was a dark shape and it looked human as it unfolded and rose there.

Someone screamed. There was a surge to either side of and behind Ruthie as people broke ranks and rushed towards the figure at the centre of the circle and she was pushed awkwardly forward and tried to break her fall with her hands as her head descended towards the stone in front of her, accelerating with her own unbalanced weight and pitch of momentum, only half succeeding so that her head hit the stone hard and for a star-filled, black moment of pain she thought she might lose consciousness.

She lay on the ground. She was winded as well as dazed. Feet had trampled over her back, possibly shod in cowboy boots judging by the pain. It didn't feel like concussion in her head, it felt like waking with the worst hangover she had ever experienced except innocent of any drinking binge to trigger it. She lay there and became aware that the rain had stopped and that the sun was warming her palely through her wet coat. Someone helped her to her feet and she clung to the stone that had hurt her for balance for a moment. She put her hand to her head and it came away bloody. She saw a silhouette approaching her out of the light and it was Eddie Coyle.

He looked concerned and when he spoke, his tone was kind. 'Come with me,' he said. 'Let's get you cleaned up and patched up. Carter Melville will have my bloody guts for garters.'

'What just happened?' Ruthie said. Her voice was a stranger's; weak, shaky, disembodied.

'That rather depends,' Coyle said.

'On what?'

'On one's perspective,' he said.

Her teeth felt bruised. That wasn't medically possible she knew, but she had bitten down hard on nothing and heard them squeak when she collided with the stone. Maybe tender was a better word. She was ruefully aware that a human jaw against ten tons of granite was a genuinely one-sided contest.

There was a first-aid station rather shrewdly placed strategically, Ruthie thought, between the cider and the beer tents. Both were open now and both were very busy. The air smelled of hot dogs and hand-rolled tobacco and patchouli oil. She was cleaned up by a very solicitous St John's Ambulance volunteer while Eddie Coyle watched with what she thought was a rather sardonic expression. She underwent a thorough test before the medic finally conceded she wasn't concussed. Outside, the mood was raucous, celebratory. They'd been vindicated, hadn't they? They had come here hoping for some sign or portent and their god had responded by coming among them, summoned back by his most mysterious and celebrated song.

That was what had happened on the face of it. But as Frederica Daunt had demonstrated to Ruthie, these things could be embellished or even faked entirely. A thousand people had gathered willing it; a thousand suggestible souls. A legion of wishful thinkers with a single shared desire to have fulfilled. What had really happened? On the solitary occasion Ruthie had been cajoled into attending a cricket match, the players had come off for bad light. She thought at noon around that stone circle, it had become conveniently gloomy. A cricket umpire would certainly have offered batsmen there the light.

She walked in silence beside Eddie Coyle until he came to a halt. They walked past the now incandescent fire-eater and past the human triangle of wobbling acrobats and through scores of people looking now slightly the worse for drink. And they reached the thick trunk of a fallen tree Ruthie realized made a natural bench as Coyle stretched a long leg over it and he sat down.

'I hope there are some designated drivers among this lot,' Ruthie said.

'Most of them are fairly law abiding. Can I get you something to eat?'

'My teeth are too sore to eat.'

'I'm genuinely sorry about what happened to you.'

'You told me to expect fireworks. I didn't think they'd be going off in my head.'

'I'm sorry.'

'What happened,' Ruthie said, 'when they got to him?'

Coyle shook his head. 'They never get to him. It's a vision, or an illusion. It has no substance. When you get to it, it's gone.'

'Like a mirage?'

'Good analogy. I've only seen it happen twice, though. And I've attended these gatherings all over the world.'

'You seem quite a rational man,' Ruthie said.

Coyle frowned. 'In view of what?'

'The conspiracy theory stuff on your website.'

He laughed at that. He said, 'That's a double-bluff, Ruthie. That's my early warning system. It attracts the cranks so I can weed them out so they can be ostracized by the respectable Legionaries.'

'Isn't that an oxymoron?'

'Is it? You didn't find today's evidence compelling?'

'It was certainly entertaining. And puzzling. And dramatic. I enjoyed the part of it I spent vertical.'

'It's a very powerful ceremony. That's a very powerful song.'

'When did you get into Ghost Legion?'

'At St Martin's studying for my degree in fine art. Sebastian Daunt taught for a term there. He did a lecture on the cover design for *King Lud*. I was sufficiently intrigued to listen to the music. And I was hooked straight away.'

'You're an artist?'

'I'm a landowner, Ruthie. I inherited as the eldest child. Money doesn't necessarily make people happy, but it does sort of insulate you. I'm rich enough not to have to worry about what people think of me.'

'And you think Martin Mear's coming back?'

'More than that,' Coyle said. 'I think there's a sense in which he never went away.'

Ruthie left shortly after this conversation concluded. She sensed that Eddie Coyle was impatient to join in with the fun, the celebration. He'd hosted the event after all, he'd gone to the trouble of making a kind of carnival of things. He'd paid for the catering and the entertainment and he'd be left presumably to do the cleaning up. She had six rural miles to drive and much thinking to try to do and didn't want to wrap a hire car around a roadside tree after a couple of rash glasses of fermented apple juice. Coffee and Nurofen were what she needed. It was still only two o'clock in the afternoon.

On the short journey back to Shaftesbury and the Bell Street cottage, she was able to some extent to rationalize what she'd seen. Rain could be sown in the sky from an aircraft. The Russians had perfected the technology in the 1960s. It required the right formulation of chemicals and there was an airfield close by, at Compton Abbas. And the figure at the centre of the stone circle could have been a projection, or a hologram. Or he could have been flesh and blood and come up from a trapdoor concealed by sods of earth. If you could hire acrobats and fire-eaters, you could hire illusionists. And some of them were these days very accomplished.

It occurred to her then that she could have been deliberately hurt, by someone wishing to distract or divert her or actually stun her, to prevent her from examining matters with a level of clarity that would prove them bogus. Was that paranoid thinking? Eddie Coyle, friendly, ebullient Eddie Coyle, had been vigilantly looking out for her. Only two people had known she was going there. One of those was Michael Aldridge, who had no connection whatsoever to Coyle. The other was Carter Melville.

Or Coyle could have just put two and two together. To get full access to his website you had to register and thus identify yourself. Ruthie's name had come up as one of those people intrigued enough to want to know details about the time and exact location of the ritual she'd just witnessed. Coyle knew her name because his daughter was a fan of her fiction. At least, he'd said she was. And she'd been named specifically in the Melville Enterprises press release alerting interested parties to the imminent launch of the Martin Mear box-set.

What Ruthie couldn't come up with was a motive for faking what she'd just witnessed. Unless Eddie Coyle just delighted in fooling gullible Ghost Legion fans, she couldn't think of anything that was plausible. Perpetuating Martin's myth?

He'd said he was a wealthy man. What if that was a lie? What if Carter Melville was paying Eddie Coyle to big up the Ghost Legion mystique just as a marketing ploy? Except that seemed a bit far-fetched. His admiration for Martin had seemed genuine. And he said though he'd attended events like the one he'd just hosted all over the world, he claimed to have experienced something like what she'd just witnessed only once before. It was a modest return for a trickster or conman.

From the Silver Band car park, Ruthie called Frederica Daunt.

'Did your dad ever lecture at St Martin's School of Art?'

'I don't know. But he's here. I'll ask him.'

'Ask him does he remember a student there by the name of Edward Coyle.'

Frederica called her back less than five minutes later. 'Dad remembers him well. Eddie apparently badgered him into signing his *King Lud* album sleeve. Talented student, but born with a silver spoon, apparently. Only thing he applied himself to was listening to Ghost Legion. Fanatically, Dad says.'

Early on Monday morning, before handing the keys back to the volunteer librarian, before the library opened, as dawn broke, Ruthie drove back to the site of what she'd seen and heard and endured the previous afternoon. She parked her hire car in a now empty meadow and walked over the hill and down to the stone circle. The stones themselves had a poised look about them, their shadows lengthy in the ascending sun. The tents and stalls and she assumed their attendant litter had all been taken away. She walked to the centre of the stones and examined the ground. She had the circle to herself. The sheep that grazed there must be penned somewhere, she thought. She tested the ground with her full weight and discovered nothing hollow sounding, no trapdoor. No place of trickery and concealment.

She looked around. She could see her breath in the dawn chill. No birds broke the silence with song. Everything seemed very still, almost petrified. And she didn't feel alone there. She felt observed, as though the victim of some deliberate and infinitely subtle intimidation. It filled her mind with thoughts of running away and finding a refuge where she could hide unseen in safety. She wasn't sure, though that such places really existed. She walked back to the car, trailing dew. She sat at the wheel and smoked a cigarette and consoled herself with the thought that before day was out, she'd be at his home with Michael Aldridge. Or she would if they got out of the Proctor Court flat unscathed.

TWENTY-ONE

She met him outside the underground station. He was attired quite formally, in a suit and tie under the raincoat he wore. That was fawn-coloured and single-breasted with concealed buttons.

'This is as close to fancy dress as I ever want to get,' he said. 'If someone sees us, and someone will, they need to assume I'm an estate agent. You, they'll remember. You're having another look, which is the most natural thing in the world.'

'Not there it's not. I doubt anyone ever has a second look.'

'We just need them not to call the police, Ruthie.'

'Where did you learn your burglary skills?'

'I work with high-end people. Carpenters, engravers, guilders, locksmiths. You learn some tricks of the trade. A sixty-year-old council-fitted mortise lock is not a difficult mechanism to pick. I can do the Yale with a credit card.'

'And there's me thinking you're an honest man.'

'I was. You've led me astray.'

'You're more fun than you used to be.'

'I don't think we'll be having much fun when we get to Proctor Court.'

'You are though.'

'When we first met I was in an unhappy marriage,' he said, 'though I didn't realize that then. And I was in danger of losing my daughter. It's largely thanks to what you found out for me then that I didn't. And I'm immensely grateful.'

'That why you're here?'

'There's more to it than gratitude. Always was. You know that.'

'Doesn't mean I've got tired of hearing it.'

'You're more insecure than you look, Ruthie.'

'And right now, I'm also scared.'

'Sure you want to do this?'

'There's something there. I'm sure of that. I need to find it.'

Together, they walked the route to Proctor Court. Ruthie appraised Michael. He looked fitter than most of the estate agents she'd seen outside their offices, having a fag break or talking on their mobiles. His suit was a better fit and the fabric wasn't shiny and his shoes weren't pointy enough. He'd put product in his hair and combed it straight back from his forehead to give him a more businesslike, commercial character. It was a detail that made her smile. She didn't think he was a man with much personal vanity and she liked that.

He got them through the door in seconds. He did it very coolly, she thought. But then it was a door at that moment he had never previously been through.

The smell hit her straight away. That churchy scent of charcoal burning incense. And there was something else, which Ruthie thought might be candle tallow. That and something else again, sourer.

'Sulphur,' Michael said, closing the door behind them, wrinkling his nose.

'It gets worse,' Ruthie said, aware of the grey, furtive quality of the interior light. Though light was an exaggeration. Murk was better, as though the windows were opaque with years of grime, which they weren't. When they walked into the sitting room, the window possessed a dull, lustreless sheen.

Ruthie looked around. There was no noise in the flat. No ticking, absent clock with a phantom pendulum swinging invisibly from side to side in its non-existent case. There was no noise from above, none from below and none from the street. It was as though the world had become stilled around them, she thought, as though they were the only people still extant and alive.

'We need to get on with it and then get out,' Michael said. 'This place is intolerable.'

Ruthie nodded.

They checked the kitchen cupboards and the bathroom cabinets. They looked behind all the radiators. Michael stood on tiptoes and ran a hand along windowsills. All he got, was dust.

'There's nothing here,' Ruthie said. She sounded crestfallen. 'I was sure, but I was wrong.'

Michael was staring at the bare floorboards. He said, 'One of these has been taken up and put back again.'

'How do you know?'

'I specialize in restoration and I've worked with some of the best chippies in the business.' He nodded at a floorboard. It was unvarnished and around four feet long and looked to Ruthie exactly as they all did.

'Not seeing it, Mr A.'

He was sweating, she saw. There were beads of sweat at the hairline on his brow and he'd grown pale and his skin had a waxy pallor. It wasn't hot or muggy. It was October. It was this place they were in.

He said, 'The grain is different, Ruthie. It's been put back the wrong way round. It's a snug fit, but I'll be very surprised if it's nailed down. It's concealing a hiding place.'

There was a noise then, a sort of feathery thump. It was loud enough to make both of them jump. Ruthie said, 'What was that?'

'I don't know. But it came from inside the wall. I think we need to be quick.'

Michael got down on his hands and knees and tried to get some play into the board by pushing it. It shifted just a fraction, but it was enough for him to reverse his position and prise the timber out with his fingertips. Sweat was running down the sides of his face in salty rivulets and his facial skin looked almost translucent, like that of a resting corpse. Ruthie wondered if she looked as bad as she felt. From the direction of the sitting room, she thought she heard a clock begin to tick.

There was only one item in the shallow rectangular space Michael Aldridge revealed. It was a bundle of postcards; old, cracked, faded and tied with a criss-cross of black ribbon like a small gift. Ruthie reached for it and put it into her bag. Michael replaced the floorboard, she presumed the right way round.

'Let's get out of here,' she said.

Michael relocked the door. They walked in silence to the Prospect of Whitby pub. Ruthie felt no feeling of triumph or even of satisfaction. She sensed she was about to discover something both secret and significant. But she had an ominous feeling it would deepen rather than solve the mysteries she was grappling with.

Michael got them drinks and they found a quiet table. Then Ruthie took the postcards from her pocket and untied the ribbon and put the postcards face-up on the table. There were seven of them and they all showed the same picture. Some of them had cracked glaze from age and handling. The picture on each was black and white and it was the Statue of Liberty.

Ruthie turned the postcards over. They were all addressed in handwriting to Max Askew and they'd all been written by the same hand. They'd been franked and the franking dated them. They'd been sent at six-monthly intervals from July 1975 until July '78. Not one of them had been sent from New York, but their sender had been to lots of other places. They each bore the same freehand legend. It read: Liberty is sweet. And they all carried the same signature and the name was Martin Mear's.

'He didn't die in 1975,' Michael said.

'And he didn't stop sending them because he died in 1978,' Ruthie said. 'I'm guessing that's when Uncle Max checked out.'

'So he was alive, and he was taunting him.'

Ruthie said, 'Any other conclusions?'

'What was the name of your estate agent?'

'Malcolm Stuart.'

'I think Malcolm Stuart might well have killed himself. I felt utterly wretched in there, almost overwhelmed by despondency. A deep sense of wretchedness and futility overcame me. I only saw the disparity in the wood grain of the floor because I couldn't raise my head to look around. It was like nothing I've ever felt in my life. Without you there, I might not have got out again.'

'The place guards itself.'

'Yes, it does, vehemently.'

'Where would he have got a rope?'

'He could have used his tie, Ruthie. He could have used his belt.'

'And he could have been murdered. Let's talk about something else.'

'Martin Mear successfully faked his own death.'

'To escape something.'

'Liberty is sweet,' Michael said. 'Do you think he's living still?'

'If he is,' Ruthie said, 'I'll find him. I've got one or two questions need answering. And if he's still breathing, he's the man in the know.'

'Where would you begin to look?'

'I've got one or two ideas.'

'Are you going to share this with Carter Melville?'

'I don't trust Carter Melville to know that I know. April and Paula believe Martin died in 1975 unless they're both consummate actresses who put on the performances of their lives just for me. I don't think they are and I don't think they did.'

'You're on Melville's payroll.'

'You think there's a pressing moral obligation here, Mr A?'

'I think there are two unexplained deaths linked to what you're working on. And now you've exposed a secret that's been kept for more than forty years.'

'On the plus side, there's us,' Ruthie said. 'And you exposed the secret. I'd never have noticed the grain in the board.'

'Us is important to me, Ruthie. You're important to me. Don't you think it might be wise just to walk away?'

Ruthie sipped from her drink and spoke carefully. 'If someone wanted to hurt me, they've had ample opportunity. They could have done it over the weekend.'

'You were hurt over the weekend. You've got the headwound to prove it.'

'I mean deliberately and fatally. In and around Shaftesbury, I was alone for a lot of the time.'

'Has it occurred to you that you might be being played?'

'It has, Michael. The tone of those postcards is defiant, taunting. It's as though Martin Mear had escaped the orbit of his Uncle Max. If he did, it might explain why he hasn't come up for air.'

'And Uncle Max worked for Martens and Degrue, which is the acceptable face of the Jericho Society. And they never forget and they never forgive.'

'And there's always a price to pay,' Ruthie said.

'And if he is still around, maybe they're going to let you do the hard work of finding him for them.'

'Come on,' Ruthie said, grabbing her coat from where she'd hung it on the back of her chair. 'I don't like this part of the world very much any more.'

'Where are we going?'

'Carter Melville is treating us to a cab ride to the Waggon and Horses and then he's buying us dinner. And then we're going to your place.'

'I do like a woman who knows her own mind.'

'It's not really my mind I'm thinking about.'

They were seated in a taxi twenty minutes later when the number Ruthie knew belonged to Sir Terence Maloney came up on her phone. He was calling personally, he explained. He said he felt obliged to extend that courtesy since he was phoning to say that regretfully, he was no longer prepared to say anything on or off the record about his association with Ghost Legion or his friendship with the late Martin Mear. It was all a very long time ago, water under the bridge, the sort of tedious, cliched war stories familiar to anyone who knew anything about the rock business in the days of its pomp. Nothing new, he said, nothing revelatory, nothing he felt the slightest inclination to revisit. Carter had caught him at a weak moment. He'd agreed to participate in haste. On reflection, it wasn't something for which he had the necessary enthusiasm.

Sir Terence ended the call and Ruthie reported what he'd said verbatim back to Michael. Michael took a moment to digest the information and then asked, 'How did he sound?'

'Honestly?' Ruthie said. 'He sounded terrified.'

The second call came as they were getting out of the taxi and Ruthie took it standing in the rain on the Waggon's gravel forecourt. It was Frederica Daunt and she was speaking so quietly that Ruthie had to strain to hear her. She guessed that Freddie's father hadn't left yet and she didn't want him to overhear her.

'You remember I told you it's not all fakery?'

'I know it's not all fakery. I know what happened with the Ouija board.'

'There was a death on the docks last week. A recent acquaintance of yours?'

'Yes, there was.'

'It wasn't an accident, Ruthie. It was murder. And it was professionally done.'

'I think Martin Mear might still be alive, Freddie.'

'Except I didn't imagine what happened at that Friday evening séance, and neither did you.'

'There were four members of Ghost Legion,' Ruthie said. 'Jason Ritchie drank himself to death. That's cut and dried. But Patsy McCoy burned to death in a house fire and James Prentice died at the wheel of his Porsche. What if they weren't accidents? What if we summoned an indignant ghost who isn't Martin at all?'

'Who would your money be on?'

'Prentice. He harboured a grudge over song-writing credits he claimed were his due. Since his death, family members have tried to sue Martin's estate on several occasions, never with any success. I don't think he died an admirer of his band's old front-man.'

Ruthie pressed the phone as close as she could to her ear. Frederica Daunt's voice was a whisper now in the strengthening rain, almost drowned out by the passing traffic noise. 'Why would anyone kill off Ghost Legion?'

'Revenge,' Ruthie said. 'Martin was involved with a cult. He got out of their clutches. They were very aggrieved by that and they went after his old bandmates because they couldn't find him.'

'You have a vivid imagination, Ruthie.'

'I do. And I can't prove any of this. Doesn't stop me thinking I'm right about it though.'

'Do you think I'm in danger?'

'I think you and your dad should sit tight. Don't do anything to draw attention to yourselves. Your dad is going to be on their radar, because they know all about Martin's history. They have no compunction, but if you don't antagonize or obstruct them, why would they harm you?'

'And if James Prentice pays me another visit?'

'I don't have the answer to that.'

TWENTY-TWO

Ruthie got back to Lambeth early on Tuesday morning on what she'd already decided would be a decisive day. She was back in time to share a pot of coffee with Veronica Slade. Their chat, before Veronica left for work, was sobering,

'When they wanted their chalice back, one of them confronted me, in a graveyard. It was after the funeral of my boss, whose apparent suicide they'd recently engineered. He told me they could do the practical stuff, like that. Or they could do the esoteric stuff.'

'Such as?'

'He was quite specific, Ruthie. You have a brain scan and you're perfectly healthy and then six weeks later the neurologist tells you you've a tumour the size of a grapefruit pressing against your frontal lobe. But you kind of know that by then because by then, it's blinded you.'

'Movers and shakers,' Ruthie said.

'It isn't funny.'

'No, Veronica. It's anything but.'

'What's next?'

'Wight. This morning. Back tomorrow evening, if everything goes according to plan.'

Veronica said, 'Does anything ever? Go according to plan?'

'No,' Ruthie said.

She called Carter Melville.

'He told me. He called me right after he called you. Bummer, baby.'

'He's frightened.'

'Stage fright?'

'A bit more than that.'

'Probably a karmic thing. Maybe he thinks his pals at the Garrick Club will blackball old Sir Terry if he starts waxing nostalgic about his freebasing days.'

'It's not a catastrophe. I'm getting good stuff from Paula and April.'

'Good to hear. And sometimes you gotta let go.'

'I suppose.'

'What's next?'

'I'm going back to where it all began.'

'Russian dolls, Ruthie baby.'

'What does that mean?'

'No one ever figured Martin out,' Carter Melville said.

She packed her overnight bag and locked Veronica's door behind her and went to the cashpoint at the NatWest branch on Westminster Bridge Road and took out £200. Then she walked to Waterloo Station and bought a return ticket for Portsmouth Harbour. She worked on her laptop on the route to Pompey and bought a return ticket at the Wight ferry terminal. She spent the crossing on the deck, watching Pompey recede into the distance, passing the sullen mass of the Solent sea forts, then watching the detail of the island gain in complexity as she approached Fishbourne Harbour, her heart heavy with recollection, her mind bittersweet remembering her lost scholar of the sea and the cherished times they'd shared together.

A taxi dropped her outside her cottage in Ventnor at 2 pm and Ruthie went inside where everything was both familiar and strange, as though all of her belongings had been swapped for stage props cunningly identical to everything they'd replaced. She was a different person from who she'd been the last time she'd been there and she knew it. And she knew it was because of Michael Aldridge and didn't know whether to be angry about that or simply grateful to him. She felt torn.

* * *

'Like the song,' she said aloud. And her own voice in the dusty stillness of her neglected home sounded strange to her.

She could go directly to the dogs. There were two chilled bottles of Chablis sitting in her fridge. There was the Spyglass Inn, no more than five minutes away. There was a pack of cigarettes still in their cellophane in the pocket of her coat. But she wouldn't do that. She had plans for the following morning she needed to leave unhindered. She'd had a sandwich for lunch aboard the ferry. She'd order dinner later at the Spyglass. But before that, she'd take a long walk at the edge of the sea to think about things generally. To try not to reminisce too much. To ponder on the obstacle to romance a wilful twelve-year-old girl might be. And to think hard about the veiled warning Paula Tort had given her concerning what she intended to do at first light tomorrow.

Martin Mear had written *King Lud* at Klaus Fischer's derelict mansion in Brightstone Forest. He'd had a couple of false starts with his earlier almost schoolboy bands, but that had been the start of Ghost Legion. He'd themed the album around London and London's mythic history, stuff gleaned presumably on those occasions when he'd stayed at Proctor Court with his Uncle Max. When he'd written the album, he recruited the three musicians who would perform it. And he'd got Sebastian Daunt to do the cover artwork and the rest was rock history.

How much had the Jericho Society had to do with Martin's success? Had Max Askew initiated him into its dark rites and ancient secrets? Had *King Lud* been successful because of a deal done with the devil? Did Martin owe his talent in the first place to some satanic bargain struck because above all else he craved success? Why had he composed it where he had? Maybe that had been the suggestion of Uncle Max, or the dictate of Uncle Max, who knew the location had a residual magic of its own, its own potent, talismanic power. If so, that would point to a connection between Max Askew and Klaus Fischer. Except that Askew could not have been much more than a child when Fischer disappeared in 1927.

Likelier that Klaus Fischer had been a member of the Jericho Society himself. An influential member, someone with considerable occult power of his own. There was no way of knowing that for certain, but it seemed likelier than not. German industrialists did not build mansions on Wight without motive. And there had been a temple on the island then, the Jericho Redoubt. Ruthie had discovered that three years earlier doing her research for Michael Aldridge. 1927 had been the year of its deliberate destruction in an arson attack.

On the seashore a mile to the west of Ventnor, she called Frederica Daunt. 'Is your dad still around?'

'I told you, he's practically taken root.'

'Do you think he'd agree to speak to me?'

'On the record? I doubt it, Ruthie.'

'Confidentially, then?'

'Possibly.'

'Would you ask him?'

'He isn't here,' Frederica said. 'He's popped into town for supplies at the wheel of his relic of a car. And he doesn't carry a mobile. Says they give you cancer.'

'Everything gives you cancer.'

'What do you want to ask him?'

'I want to know whether the *King Lud* experience changed Martin's character. It seems mysterious and significant. Crossing the Rubicon or burning his bridges. There seems to have been something irrevocable about it.'

'I can tell you that,' Frederica said, 'Because Dad told me the night he arrived here. He said writing that album changed Martin completely. And not at all for the better. He said it corrupted him. Between the two of us, Dad became afraid of Martin.'

Ruthie ate dinner at the Spyglass wondering only half in jest whether she ought to make a will. She felt glad she was doing what she was doing the following morning in daylight, but nervous truthfully about doing it at all. Derelict buildings were hazardous places at the best of times and this one had a dubious history.

She drank most of a bottle of wine with her meal. She got back to the cottage chilled, the cottage cold, wondering whether it was worth the effort of lighting a fire in her wood-burner when she knew she'd turn in before another hour was up.

She took off her coat and rubbed her hands together and knelt before the fireplace and screwed sheets of newspaper into the grate and put kindling on top of that and a log on top of the kindling.

She spent three matches before the paper caught. She sat watching the flames curl and expand and strengthen in a blossoming of sudden orange heat. And as the fire gently began warming her, Ruthie burst into tears.

Everything there reminded her of the man she'd shared the place so often with before their break-up in the summer. Every stick of furniture, every item of crockery, even the floor under her feet spoke to her of Phil. It was why she'd fled the place for Veronica's. She supposed it was grief for something lost. She supposed it would pass eventually and she'd felt lucky at other moments to have re-met Michael Aldridge. But now, here, she was hurting. And there was no point pretending otherwise.

Ruthie closed the wood-burner's glass door and latched it safely shut. She made and drank a small cup of Earl Grey tea. Then she climbed the stairs wearily to her bedroom and got undressed in darkness. She slid between sheets that felt both cold and slightly damp in a bed she'd come to consider too wide for one occupant. She listened for a while as the fabric of the cottage groaned and stretched with the heat spreading from beneath her. She listened for noises from beyond her walls, but the night was quiet. She tried to concentrate on the mysteries confronting her, but found concentration hard to come by. Eventually, she cried herself to sleep.

It was foggy when Ruthie awoke. Looking through her bedroom window out to where it lay, she couldn't see the sea. She was in a grey, groping, insulated world extending only an arm's length in every direction. She got out her black Pashley bicycle – originally pastel-blue, but Ruthie was Ruthie – and pumped the tyres firm. She drank a pot of coffee and dressed sturdily and set off.

It was a Wednesday morning out of season and it was early and the coastal road that led to Blackgang Chine and Brightstone Forest beyond it was quiet. Fog made the world silent but for the odd discordant, disembodied noise. The swish of her tyres on tarmac under her turning pedals was her steady soundtrack as she rode. Her mind was empty of conscious thought and her mood was serene. Almost fifty years earlier, a youthful Martin Mear had shown up at her destination and over the course of a few days determined his fate and secured his fortune. Had it been a deal done with the devil? If so, there might be some scattered, remaining clues concerning the bargain struck.

She was disappointed with herself. She felt she'd been self-indulgent the previous evening. Her relationship with Phil Fortescue had existed only under the delusion that he had let go completely of his love for his dead wife. But his moving on had been merely a lie of which Phil had convinced himself before convincing her. Michael Aldridge was a sincere, gentle, honest man deserving of love and loyalty. She hadn't slept with him out of pity or compassion and she'd been confident she'd been moving on herself. The previous evening, though, had sown its seed of doubt.

It took her forty minutes to reach the forest. She chained her bike to a tree at a spot not far from the road she thought she would remember even in the fog, which was even thicker here than it had been in Ventnor on her departure from home.

There must have been an access road once, she thought, back in the days before conservation laws and civic planning permission and green belts, when toffs with the sort of fortune Klaus Fischer had boasted were a law entirely unto themselves. But ninety years of dereliction and neglect had seen that obliterated by nature. The only way to get to his mansion was through the wood. And it was tricky going, laborious in the thick blanket of salt-smelling fog that had stolen in from the sea in the night and now draped and smothered the island.

The forest seemed denuded of wildlife. She didn't hear a single rustle in the undergrowth or a solitary note of birdsong. The hush was palpable, the silence so pressing it was almost a sound in itself. The walk seemed interminable. She wondered about her orientation, knowing that right-handed people tended to lead with the dominant foot when walking blind, eventually in large anti-clockwise circles. She adjusted every hundred paces to prevent this, to make her progress a straight line to where she knew her destination lay.

The forest cleared about her all at once. The trees didn't thin, she just left them behind her as abruptly as the curtain opening on a stage. And in front of her, like some phantom prop, she saw through the fog the ghost of a building; its windows blind, black sockets, its turrets faint clusters and its mass uncertain despite the size of it, rippling slightly through the grey, like some dangerously incomplete illusion.

Earth turned to weedy gravel under her feet and she sensed rather than saw that she was on a broad sweep of drive. She pictured the liveried chauffeurs of Klaus Fischer's guests; Daimlers and Rolls-Royces and Bugattis; the odd majestic Mercedes Benz. Bentleys, Packards, Delages, their dinner-plate headlamps yellow orbs out here as the dissolution and the darkness reigned within.

The main entrance door was breached, buckled and cleaved as though some rough beast had shattered it, intruding. Ruthie walked up the broad flight of stone steps that led to it and took a deep breath and shuddered once and then entered the Fischer House, feeling like the solitary gatecrasher at some long-forgotten ball.

The vestibule was vast. And the fog had intruded. It roiled to a height of about four feet and concealed the floor, which was hard and slippery and Ruthie assumed to be made of marble. The wood-panelled walls were mildewed in diseased splotches. At a point thirty feet from the front door, and directly opposite it, a central staircase rose to the upper floors. Bits of its balustrades were missing. Its once lush carpet was rotting and slime-covered. Its runners must have gleamed once, chrome now barnacled with rust where they weren't missing entirely. The steps didn't look to Ruthie like they could be trusted to take her weight.

There were chandeliers suspended on chains from the ceiling. There were six of them, their intricate crystal dulled by time and neglect. Their chains had rusted, and frayed snakes of cloth-sheathed wiring coiled around their length. Where the chains were anchored to the ceiling, weight had long rendered the plasterwork to spiders' webs of cracks. Each of the chandeliers looked like it might at any moment come crashing down, exploding into hurtled shards of glass invisible under the fog. It seemed wisest not to walk directly underneath them.

She walked past the staircase to its left and on through a large door, pillared and architraved to either side and above, closed but not locked, high and heavy and stiff on its hinges when she pushed at its once-polished oak surface.

The room beyond was baronial. The fog had not penetrated this far into the building and the floor was intricate parquet, soft and sodden with decades of water penetration, a hardwood bog, mushy under her feet as she progressed further into the Fischer House. The furniture had all long gone, but there were sconces set at intervals high on the walls and the pitch-dipped torches that had once illuminated this great hall's evenings still resided in them damp now, redundant.

There was an old gramophone player abandoned in one corner, like some material non-sequitur amid the general emptiness, its horn rising and swelling like some silent rebuke. Around it lay shattered records; brittle, shellac 78s that would have sounded scratched and reedy on the primitive machine they were meant for even when brand new and gleaming out of their paper sleeves. Ruthie could imagine the handle of the machine abruptly turning itself, music blossoming out of the horn to breach the silence, a decades-dead operatic tenor summoned for one last, reluctant encore. Unless jazz had been Klaus Fischer's thing; loud piano, frenzied clarinet. Ruthie shivered. She sensed that across the lost decades, the house was communicating with her. It wasn't in the least friendly. But it was amused.

Ruthie had crossed the room to another door. She had decided she would explore only the ground floor. She wouldn't risk the stairs to the upper floors and shuddered afresh at the thought that there might be a lift. Imagine getting into the lift, she thought. Imagine closing yourself inside its musty confinement. Imagine its ancient machinery, clanking through old force of habit into weary life.

There would be a cellar, too. She could imagine a dim catacomb down there, harbouring obscure and silent secrets. But she had a suspicion, a sort of presentiment, that if she discovered and descended the cellar steps, she might find herself in a dark stone labyrinth she might never be able to grope her way back out of.

She walked into another room. This one was smaller, possibly a smoking room, and there was a bathroom off it and from the bathroom, Ruthie was aware of two things. One of these was almost expected and the other an unpleasant surprise. A tap dripped persistently, percussively, she thought, against tarnished porcelain. And she could smell tobacco, so strong she thought it probably a pre-war blend and almost certainly Turkish.

Ruthie held her breath aware that the moment had the still expectancy of dawning horror, a sort of slow-motion dread that made her motionless as her skin pinpricked into gooseflesh. Then, unmistakably, she heard someone speak. The sound came from inside the bathroom's yawning open door.

'Marvellous,' a male voice said, fruity and lisping. And absolutely clear and undeniable. And Ruthie shrank, recoiling at the sound, fear thrilling through her like some rude invasive force.

TWENTY-THREE

There was a Fred Astaire patter of shoe-leather on linoleum; an antic, joyful sound that signalled excitement and filled Ruthie Gillespie with terror. Her own feet felt leaden, immovable, literally petrified. A stiff black shape skittered through the bathroom door and wheeled across the floor in front of her. It became still and was a top hat, the black silk lining coarse with ancient grease she saw, the sheen long absent from its black, moth-eaten exterior.

'Tine to make whoopee,' the voice from inside the bathroom said, and Ruthie knew that the voice, with its tone of antique pastiche, belonged to someone from the distant past, from the time when the Fischer House revelled and thrilled, from a decade of debauchery and from someone long dead, reluctant to be forgotten despite that.

'Who'd have thought it, after all this time,' the voice said. 'Happy days are here again.'

Strong hands gripped Ruthie's shoulders and she was wheeled about, gasping. And she was staring into the face of Paula Tort, wide-eyed, turning her head slowly from side to side in a way that firmly signalled for her not to speak. Ruthie saw that Paula had a large crucifix on a leather thong looped around her neck, Christ writhing on her chest. She took her hands from Ruthie's shoulders and one of them held something and Ruthie saw it was the rosary she'd seen among Martin Mear's assembled possessions in the storage facility in Wimbledon to which Carter Melville had taken her. She slipped this over Ruthie's head.

'Bother,' said the voice from the bathroom. 'Neither of you is any fun at all.' Petulant, amused, menacing.

Paula put her right hand in the small of Ruthie's back and pushed her firmly in the direction she'd come. She didn't hurry, as though hurrying would be a mistake, a tactic that might encourage pursuit. She just strode purposefully through the door, over the baronial mush of the rotten parquet, past the spoiled and reeking carpet of the great staircase, out of the main entrance and onto the sweep of weedy gravel, where Ruthie saw that the fog was reluctantly lifting. She remembered then it was only the morning. Inside the Fischer House she realized it had felt like some dark and eternal night.

They walked through the forest in silence. Ruthie came slowly back to herself. Dread and shock receded. She began to notice small details; how purposeful Paula looked in her jeans and leather jacket with her hair unbrushed and her face devoid of make-up. How the forest seemed to awaken, stirring with sound and movement now as they progressed through it. How it transmuted from the lustreless, fog-bound monochrome of earlier into a riot of autumnal colour now under pale sunshine.

Paula's black Porsche was parked beside Ruthie's black Pashley bicycle and Ruthie thought how symbolic that juxtaposition was of two lives lived in absurd contrast.

'Get in,' Paula said.

Ruthie did.

Paula started the engine.

'You saved my life.'

'Maybe not your life,' Paula said, 'certainly your sanity.'

'How did—'

Paula lifted a vertical forefinger to her lips. She said, 'Full disclosure, honey. But not until we're well away from here.'

Ruthie was aware of the rosary she wore, the weight of its cross between her breasts, the feel of the beads encircling her neck, the talismanic strangeness of it. Organized religion wasn't her thing at all. She closed her eyes. She felt numb and weary. She shut out the visible world and beside her, Paula drove.

'I spoke to Carter Melville right after you did. He told me you were going back to the beginning. I figured that meant only one thing, one place, to someone with a mind the way yours works. So I followed you.

'Then this morning, I missed you. I didn't figure you for an early riser.'

'Why not?'

'You've got a sort of nocturnal look.'

'Looks can be deceiving.'

'And you've recently had your heart broken and so probably you're not sleeping great. I should have factored that in. What time did you set off?'

'First light.'

'I missed you by half an hour. But I knew where you were going and I got there just in time.'

'I think you're incredibly brave.'

'Or incredibly dumb.'

'Because you've been there before, haven't you, Paula?'

They were in the lounge at the Hamborough, where Paula Tort had booked a room the previous night. It was off-season and so they had the lounge to themselves. They had been served coffee, though Ruthie felt like drinking something far stronger. But it was still only half-past ten in the morning and Paula's hard-rock past was a long way behind her.

'I went for the same reason you did. Only with me, it was personal. It was where the Martin I knew was born and I wanted to see his birthplace.'

'What happened this morning?'

'I can't explain it, Ruthie,' Paula said. 'I think bad things were done there a long time ago using potent magic. It's a place that sort of revels in its malignant past. The present intrudes there and the place gets provoked.'

'And that resident?'

Paula shuddered. 'Not real, I don't think.'

'So the Fischer House is haunted?'

'If there are ghosts anywhere, honey, it's there.'

Ruthie said, 'They don't seem to have bothered Martin.'

Carefully, Paula said, 'Martin had a kind of protection.'

'Because he was part of the Jericho Society?'

'My, what a clever girl you're turning out to be.'

'I've had a run-in with them in the past.'

Paula sipped coffee. 'And you're still around. More lives than a cat.'

Full disclosure, Paula Tort had said. Ruthie took the ribbon-tied pile of Proctor Court postcards from her pocket and put it on the table between them. Paula picked up the bundle and untied the ribbon and read each of the cards. And Ruthie studied her expression, doing it.

'You faked his death.'

'I helped engineer his escape,' Paula said, trying and failing to clear with her fingers the tears now trickling freely down her face.

Ruthie offered her a paper napkin from their table and she took it and dabbed at her eyes.

'Is he still alive?'

'I don't know.'

'How can you bear that?'

'We were saving his soul. That was the deal. I knew I'd never see him again. It's why my grief is real, Ruthie. And still raw.'

'Does April know?'

'April can't know. She'd try to find him.'

'She'd never forgive you.'

Paula let out a snot-filled bark of laughter. She said, 'In her position, neither would I.'

Ruthie thought that this was as close as the woman ever came to losing her famous composure. Glacial, was the word most often used describing Paula Tort. Except she hadn't been that at the Fischer House, or at the wheel of her car. And she wasn't glacial now.

Paula nodded at the postcards. 'This your world exclusive?'

'It's our secret, if you want it to remain that. I'm a human being and I owe you big time.'

'Who else knows?'

'A man I trust.'

'Not Carter Melville, then.'

'Never Carter Melville,' Ruthie said. She had remembered it was Wednesday. She said, 'What would you be doing now, if you weren't here with me?'

Paula looked at her wristwatch. It was a Cartier, probably white gold, Ruthie thought. She said, 'We'd still be in conference. Christmas is still huge in retail and I've two collections to create for early January. Maybe a spin class at lunch time or hot yoga or Pilates. Your body starts to cheat unless you take yourself by surprise.'

'I'll take your word for that.'

'So I tend to vary things. I had a meeting scheduled for this afternoon with the architecture firm responsible for the new flagship store scheduled to open in May next year. And after that I was going to brief the photographer shooting the diffusion menswear range for the spring catalogue.'

'Just an average day, then.'

'Pretty much.'

'One I've sabotaged.'

'I had to come,' Paula said.

'You could probably still make the noon ferry.'

'I'm doing no such thing,' Paula said. 'I've never needed a drink more in my life. And something tells me you know better than most would where we can get one.'

Ruthie picked up the pile of postcards. She hesitated and then handed them to Paula. 'Find a safe place for these,' she said. 'I'd suggest the bottom of the Solent on your ferry ride back to the mainland.'

'Thank you. Where are we headed?'

'The Spyglass Inn is five minutes away,' Ruthie said. 'Panoramic sea views. And I'm buying.'

They walked down the hill to the Spyglass. The day had cleared and there was no wind. The sea stretched calmly in subdued, English light.

'Who's the guy you showed the postcards?'

'He was with me when I found them.'

'I'm guessing you found them at Proctor Court.'

'He's a man named Michael Aldridge.'

'Aldridge the architect?'

Ruthie stopped walking. 'Are Aldridge Associates doing your flagship store?'

'No. A few years ago I bought a Jacobean manor house in Sussex.'

'As you do,' Ruthie said. They'd resumed walking.

'Aldridge was recommended as a specialist in restoration,' Paula said. 'Kind of cute, in an understated sort of way. You involved with him?'

'You cut to the chase, don't you, Paula?'

'Always have. Too late to stop now.'

'Anyway, the answer is yes. Tentatively.'

'Tentative won't do it, hon,' Paula said. 'Tentative will get you nowhere.'

They'd arrived at the pub. They ordered drinks and found a vacant table outside, where Ruthie could sit and smoke in the wan sunshine. 'A bad habit,' she said, taking her pink Bic lighter from her pocket.

'I had a lot worse,' Paula said.

'What was it really like?'

'Utterly crazy,' Paula said. 'We were making up a life as we went along that no one had lived before. It's impossible to describe because it was so insane. Sometimes it was wonderful. It wasn't always, but it was most of the time. And I'd have been dead decades ago if it hadn't stopped when it did.'

Something had happened, Ruthie realized. They were no longer interviewer and subject. They were something more. Ruthie felt indebted to Paula Tort, but there was more to it than that. There was a chasm between them in age and experience and status. But there was suddenly also a closeness. Paula reinforced this notion, saying what she said next.

'It's a huge relief to me to be able to share that secret with someone I'm able to trust, Ruthie. And God help me, I do trust you.'

'I get the impression you and April are close.'

'As close as we can be.'

'Sir Terence Maloney was scheduled to talk to me. Then he postponed. Then he cancelled altogether. Have you any idea why he would do that?'

Paula gulped vodka and tonic. There was a tremor Ruthie noticed in her hand, picking up her glass. 'I can theorize,' she said.

Martin had been corrupted by his Uncle Max. The Jericho Society was dynastic and Max Askew had no heir. So he had inducted Martin, sharing the rites and beliefs and secrets, seducing him with the promise of what belonging could bring in terms of worldly success and power and prosperity.

And Martin Mear got those things. He attained his rewards. But instead of remaining loyal to what had enabled all that, he faked his death to escape it and then renounced it from beyond his apparent grave. He didn't merely defy the man who had indoctrinated him as a child, he taunted him. It was more than a betrayal. And they never forgave. And they never forgot. And there was always a price to pay.

'Bad news for Uncle Max,' Ruthie said, remembering the passive neutrality on the face of the man at the wheel of the split-screen Morris Minor, with his bland features and his leather-patched tweed.

Bad news for the surviving members of Ghost Legion, Paula said. Not for Jason Ritchie, intent on drinking himself to death. But she believed both Patsy McCoy in '79 and James Prentice in '83 had met with intentional rather than accidental ends. They wanted to destroy what remained of Martin's life-work. They wanted to send him a message. They wanted to silence forever the people in whom Martin might have confided about the cult to which he'd once belonged.

'They didn't kill you,' Ruthie said.

'They dismissed me as a groupie,' Paula said. 'In today's language, I was arm-candy. And even if I was more than that, what rock star in the '70s ever confided anything in their old lady?'

'But Terry Maloney knew.'

'To anyone outside the band, Terry was just a roadie. To the inner circle, he was so much more. He was a part of the inner circle. He was probably the person Martin trusted most.'

'I'd say that was you,' Ruthie said.

'OK. The man Martin trusted most.'

'Not Carter Melville?'

'Never Carter Melville,' Paula said.

Terry going public about the trusted fixer he really was in the Ghost Legion era might make him the same sort of vulnerable target McCoy and Prentice had been. It made him much more likely to have been a party to Martin's secret. It practically made him a member of the band. And the Jericho Society were intent on destroying Martin's artistic legacy.

'Because they never forget and they never forgive,' Ruthie said. 'Yet Carter Melville is still in the best of health.'

'Which kind of makes you wonder,' Paula said.

'Because he's the gatekeeper, or the engine, or the master of ceremonies or whatever metaphor you want to use. Sir Terence is a merchant banker, a respected figure in the City, these days. That's what got him his gong. More than anyone, Carter Melville is Ghost Legion now.'

Paula didn't comment.

Ruthie said, 'Unless you count Eddie Coyle.'

Paula remained silent. Then she belched audibly. Then she said, 'He's just a fucking idiot.'

Which made both women laugh.

Matters got a bit bleary after that. They ate lunch at the pub and then drank and chatted until 6 pm when they wobbled their way arm-in-arm for ballast to the Bistro in Pier Street. After dinner, they went back to Ruthie's cottage, where Paula was shown up to the spare bedroom.

'I used to be able to do this,' she said.

'I need to pick up my bike,' Ruthie said.

'Your bike can wait, hon.'

In her own room, Ruthie peeled off her clothes and climbed into bed and was asleep in seconds. Her night wasn't, though, untroubled. She dreamed of a death's head in a top hat and a monocle, crooning music-hall ditties through chattering teeth.

TWENTY-FOUR

Ruthie returned to the mainland on the noon ferry on Thursday sufficiently rested not to be feeling any ill-effects from her shared session with Paula the previous day. Before leaving, Paula gave her a lift in her Porsche to the edge of Brightstone Forest to retrieve her bike. Ruthie pedalled back more or less oblivious to the spectacular coastal charms of her scenic route. The island had been a tolerable place for her in the company of Paula. Alone, she still found it all but unendurable. The memories were too fresh, the wounds too raw. She had no doubt whatsoever that Paula was right and that tentative wouldn't do it with Michael Aldridge. But tentative was how she honestly felt.

Carter Melville called her on the ferry. He asked her about her visit to the Fischer House and she told him it had been uneventful. She told him about the old gramophone player and the shellac records lying brittle and shattered around it. She thought the symbolism interesting on two counts. Fischer's mansion had once been a place of debauched parties raucously celebrated, very rock and roll for their time. And the gramophone was the elderly ancestor of what Martin's records had been played on in the time of his own pomp.

'It's a nice detail,' Carter agreed.

She didn't tell him about the owner of the plummy voice inhabiting the bathroom off Klaus Fischer's smoking room. She didn't tell him about the intervention of Paula Tort.

'Was there a brand name on that gramophone?'

'His Master's Voice.'

'The little black and white dog logo. Did you take a photo?'

'Yes. On my phone.'

'They're HMV now,' Carter said, chuckling. 'They just put in a humungous order for the Legion box-set.'

His master's voice. Suddenly Ruthie thought she knew what had happened when Martin had been there composing *King Lud.* She could picture it, she could hear it. *He had protection.*

Ruthie got back to Veronica Slade's flat just before five o'clock. She tried to make some notes about structure, to plan the shape of what she intended to write, to outline a thematic narrative. She could just write chronologically. Which would be straightforward enough. Or she could begin by deconstructing the mythology to reveal the man more truthfully than had ever been done before.

As she saw it, her problems were two-fold. Carter Melville had called Martin Mear a Russian doll of a man, layer upon layer revealed until almost nothing was left. Paula Tort had described someone who carefully compartmentalized himself, so that everyone got someone different. To some extent, April Mear had borne this out, painting a verbal portrait of a kind and dedicated father with a strong inclination for isolating himself from the world. Yet he was also the consummate showman, able to dominate an audience of thousands with his potent projection of talent and sheer charisma. It didn't add up at all. Tightening the focus seemed to Ruthie all but impossible.

The second, insurmountable problem was the dishonesty. Ruthie wasn't going to betray her promise to Paula and reveal the fact that Martin's death had been faked. She had anyway surrendered her proof of that. And she wasn't prepared to go public on the Jericho Society and Martin's involvement with and eventual rejection of that. They were tenacious about their secrecy. They were spiteful and they were deadly.

The chalice that had come into the possession of Veronica's auction house had originally been used by the Jericho Society in ceremonies at their Boston temple on the Eastern Seaboard of the United States. Its owner had been the descendent of a G-man involved in the FBI raid on that in the 1920s. The temple had been bulldozed to rubble, the ground sown with salt and their sacrament performed by two powerful exorcists from the Boston Diocese. The rubble had been dumped in the harbour. But the chalice had been looted from the temple first.

Now, the chalice resided in the trophy room at Quantico. And the FBI were newly aware that the Jericho Society were still active. That was a situation for which Ruthie Gillespie, Veronica Slade and Michael Aldridge all bore partial responsibility. They could be blamed. It would be extremely unwise for Ruthie to draw their attention to her. Except, she thought, she was probably already on their radar. Why hadn't they at the very least intimidated her, frightened her off? She was growing more and more convinced that there could be only one reason for that. They believed Martin was still alive, somewhere. And they believed the access she had to the people in his life could give her the necessary clues as to his whereabouts. She might lead them to him and in so doing, provide them with a useful service.

And if she did so, where would that leave her? She'd be a witness they'd need to silence in the way they'd already silenced Malcolm Stuart and Ginger McCabe. She'd die as she slept in her burning cottage in the manner of Patsy McCoy. Like James Prentice, she'd have a car accident. Or she'd just get knocked off her Pashley bike in a fatal hit and run on one of Wight's lonelier roads when she finally discovered in herself the gumption to go home.

Her phone rang. It was Eddie Coyle. 'We're staging a bigger event on Sunday.'

'My forehead's healing quite nicely, thank you.'

'Carter Melville thinks you should attend.'

'I spoke to him this morning, Eddie. He would have mentioned it.'

'He's only just learned about it from me.'

'Another Neolithic site?'

'Remote spot on the Portuguese coast. So remote that my accommodation there's a forest hunting lodge. Sleeps ten and there's a berth for you if you want it.'

'How many of these do you honestly think I should do? I'm not like one of those people with a compulsion to see *The Sound of Music* or *Les Misérables* every night for a year.'

'I'll bet you've got every record the Cure ever made, though.'

'What's that to do with anything?'

'This one's going to be huge,' Eddie Coyle said, 'maybe the final precursor to the actual event.'

'Then you'd be wise to wear your wellies and cagoule,' Ruthie said. 'It'll probably piss down.'

Portugal was where Frederica Daunt and her father were. If Sebastian would agree to talk to her, she could kill two birds with one stone. The air fare wouldn't be an issue, if Carter wanted her in Portugal anyway.

'I'll think about it,' she said, touching the spot, bruised and scabbing, just below her hairline tenderly.

'Splendid, Ruthie. Let me know if you need a ride from the airport. I'll sort something.'

She called Frederica Daunt. 'I'm in Portugal on Sunday. Would your dad agree to speak to me on Monday?'

'Off the record, yes.'

'Fantastic.'

'Stay the night. We'll have a few drinks and I'll break out the Ouija board.'

'That's a terrible idea.'

'I'm joking, Ruthie. Where's your sense of humour?'

'I've hidden it under a bushel for the duration.'

'What's a bushel?'

'I've never been quite sure.'

'The duration of what?'

'This job I'm supposed to be doing.'

It was seven o'clock before Ruthie remembered that Veronica would be home late. She had some sort of event to attend concerning one of the few living artists regularly to feature in the sales room of her auction house. Champagne and canapes and probably quite a bit of gossip and name-dropping. There were aspects of her job Veronica was quietly contemptuous about, but she was well paid and her position was a prestigious one. She was closer career-wise to Paula's black Porsche than she was to Ruthie's black Pashley bicycle.

Ruthie debated how much to tell Veronica about what had gone on at Klaus Fischer's house and afterwards. It was a question of how much comfort she'd gain from confiding in her friend, versus the jeopardy the knowledge might put Veronica in as someone party to something secret. Ruthie already had one Fischer House confidante in Paula Tort. She thought she'd spare Veronica anything that might in the future endanger her.

At 8 pm Ruthie opened a bottle of Chablis. She sat in the darkness in the garden to drink it. Though in reality it was never that dark in this part of London, there was too much ambient light from the streets and surrounding buildings. She'd briefly entertained the idea of going and sitting outside the Pineapple just to be surrounded by other people, but she didn't want to risk seeing the split-screen Morris Minor float past, its small engine singing, a featureless man under a blond swatch of hair eyeing her incuriously as he drove by in a curious parallel world extinct, she knew, sixty years ago.

Michael Aldridge called her at nine o'clock. He said, 'How busy are you over the weekend?'

She remembered that he didn't have Mollie. This weekend was her mum's. *Tentative*, Ruthie thought. She said, 'You've got tomorrow evening and all of Saturday, Mr A.'

'And Saturday night?'

'Early start Sunday. Catching a flight.'

'I can give you a lift to the airport.'

'That would be nice.'

'Anywhere exotic?'

'The Algarve,' she said.

'Nice this time of the year.'

'It's just for a couple of days. And it's work.' If the lunacy of the Clamouring could be described as work.

'What have you been up to since Tuesday morning?'

She would tell Michael everything, she decided. He already knew the big secret, that Martin Mear had faked his death. There would be no betrayal of Paula, Ruthie didn't think, in appraising him of the rest. Paula was right about Michael. Tentative wasn't going to do it. She had to be committed for anything to have a chance of working. Besides, he was her ally. He was on her side. He was one of only three people she completely trusted in all this. April Mear might yet make that number four. But Michael's was the name at the top of the list.

'You didn't tell me you'd met Paula Tort.'

'You didn't ask,' he said.

'Not good enough, Mr A.'

'She was looking to have a pile restored out in deepest Sussex. She'd been told it was Jacobean, but that wasn't the full story. Rarely is, with large old houses. Parts of it were Tudor and some of it was older than that. The original rectangular tower was probably built at the time of the Plantagenet kings and the chapel in the grounds was Norman.'

'It had its own chapel?'

'Extensive grounds, loads of character, even a lake.'

'Blimey.'

'The interior required a lot of work. But the shell was intact,' Michael said. 'So no problem with water penetration. I told her it would be a very expensive commitment and she should take her time making a decision.'

'Very noble.'

'I try to be fair.'

'She's a good-looking woman.'

'She certainly is. But she's a bit mature for me, Ruthie. If that's what you're thinking.'

'You made an impression.'

'Which is flattering,' he said, 'but the only person I want to make an impression on is you.'

'You'll have your opportunity to do that tomorrow evening.'

'And I intend to take it,' he said.

Ruthie went back inside after this conversation concluded. She brushed her teeth and drank a glass of water and was about to hit the sack when Veronica came in.

'Good evening?'

'I've just seen the cutest little car,' Veronica said, unbuttoning her coat, face flushed from the champagne she'd drunk. 'Parked at the end of the road. Drove off, just as I turned the corner. Old Morris Minor in fabulous condition. Split windscreen and everything. I know cars aren't your thing, darling, but this little beauty ticked all the boxes.'

Ruthie met Michael Aldridge at Surbiton station at seven o'clock on Friday evening. They walked the route to the Waggon and Horses. She told him in precise detail about her visit to Klaus Fischer's ruined, not quite uninhabited mansion. She told him about her rescue literally at the hands of Paula Tort. He listened in silence, his face unreadable. When she'd finished, he said, 'What do you know about Klaus Fischer?'

'Not much. He disappeared in 1927. The same year the Jericho Redoubt outside Ventnor was destroyed in an arson attack.'

'Do you think Fischer was a Jericho Society acolyte?'

'He had an interest in the occult,' Ruthie said. 'Aleister Crowley was a guest at his parties. Martin Mear probably learned about the existence of the Fischer House from his Uncle Max during his occult grooming. The truthful answer is that I don't know.' She sipped from her drink. 'Have you ever come across anything like my experience? You've been in a lot of old buildings.'

Michael thought about this. Eventually he said, 'It's a matter of contamination, I think. Can bricks and mortar become diseased, pestilent? Most people who've visited Bergen-Belsen would probably say yes. But very few people will admit to having seen a ghost.'

'I didn't see a ghost,' Ruthie said. 'It might just have been a sense memory.'

'Chucking top hats around?'

'Whatever it was deliberately scared me,' she said.

'Don't you just want to walk away from all this?'

Ruthie pondered that. Then she sat back in her chair and said, 'I think Martin Mear's still alive. I think I know where to find him. I don't think I'll stop till I do.'

'Someone's killing people, Ruthie.'

'And I think I know who that is. But knowing it and proving it are quite different.'

* * *

On Saturday they went to Hampton Court. The weather remained benign, autumnal, the trees gorgeously coloured on the towpath on the other side of the river from where they waited for the ferry turning. They ate breakfast at the Riverside Café before getting on the boat.

'You do this all the time, with Mollie, don't you?' Ruthie said.

Michael nodded. 'It's become a bit of a ritual,' he said. 'It's a nice change to do it in the company of someone grown-up.'

'What's the biggest difference?'

'I won't struggle to get you out of the gift shop.'

'Don't bet on it,' she said.

They toured the Tudor buildings. Ruthie paused in the Whispering Gallery but didn't sense its rumoured ghosts. They saw the room in which a hundred pikemen slept nightly to protect the king when Henry the serial monogamist sat heavily on England's throne. They walked through the gardens and risked the famous maze. They ate lunch at the Tiltyard Café.

'You're still hurting, aren't you?'

It wasn't even a question, really. 'I'm sorry,' Ruthie said.

'Don't be,' Michael said. 'These things take time.'

'Will you give me time?'

'I don't really think it's mine to give. But the answer's yes.'

TWENTY-FIVE

Eddie Coyle met her personally at Arrivals at Faro airport after an uneventful flight at four in the afternoon. The location of the gathering was about two hours by car, he said. His ride was a soft-top Jeep, the choice of a Land Rover man gone reluctantly Continental. He was decked out like a squire, or maybe a member of the rural rock band Jethro Tull in the mid-1970s. Ruthie hadn't even known you could still get leather waistcoats. And she thought corduroy trousers probably a bit warm for Portugal in October.

He had the top rolled down, so Ruthie felt less guilty than she would have otherwise about smoking in the front passenger seat.

Flying wasn't something she enjoyed and she felt entitled to a post-flight cigarette to calm her nerves.

Coyle didn't say much on the journey. He seemed a less confident man playing away from home, unless he was just preoccupied with thoughts of the spectacle to come. Ruthie speculated on the pyrotechnics of the ritual. This was a bigger event, he'd said, a much more serious deal. Maybe it would provoke hailstones the size of tennis balls or rain frogs. Likelier sardines, she thought. Sardines were very popular on the coast of Portugal.

'We're not going straight to the site,' he said. 'I've organized a beach barbecue as dinner for a few of my English Legionary friends. We'll eat and then go on. It's another thirty minutes on along the sand. Thus the four-wheel-drive. Quite a remote spot, as I think I've already told you.'

'And the attendance will reflect that?'

Coyle laughed. 'Not at all,' he said. 'This is a very committed group of people. The ink suggests otherwise, but are you a prudish person, Ruthie?'

'Why should my morals concern you?'

'They don't, directly. It's just that some of tonight's attendees are likely to be naked. And some of them are likely to be uninhibited too.'

'I thought Portugal was a Catholic country,' Ruthie said.

'The location's more or less incidental,' Coyle said. 'The Clamouring is essentially a pagan ceremony. In Catholic terms, it would count as blasphemous.'

'Why's that?'

'We believers are expecting big things ultimately from Martin Mear. Well, actually one big thing. But coming back from the dead is a trick only Christ has successfully performed in the past. He did it with Lazarus and then took a personal turn.'

'Allegedly.'

'Cynic,' Coyle said.

And Ruthie realized that now they were nearing their destination, he was getting some of his bounce back. And she wondered if she was an unwitting guest at her first ever orgy. She hoped not. She wasn't about to participate. And she didn't think she'd get off on watching either.

There were a dozen of Eddie Coyle's guests at the barbecue

and Ruthie thought that all of them were likelier to look better in their clothes. There were nine men and three women. Half a dozen – including one of the woman – were bikers. The rest looked like academics, except for a very chic couple she judged to be in the Paula Tort class of affluence.

She remembered Paula's words concerning Eddie Coyle then, *He's a fucking idiot.* And she smiled to herself. She was eating bread and cheese, keeping things light, and drinking only cola, keeping things sober. Everyone else was drinking wine or beer and some of them shipping quite a lot of it. One of the bikers had lit a *Withnail and I*-sized spliff. It smelled strong, probably packed she thought with lethal Amsterdam skunk. It reminded her that drugs and the occult had always gone hand in hand. And that reminded her of the debauched tone and rich Turkish tobacco scent emanating from an empty bathroom at the derelict Fischer House and despite the southern European warmth of the oncoming evening, Ruthie shivered.

The barbecue wrapped up and they set off in a convoy of two Jeeps and four powerful motorcycles with what Ruthie judged to be no one completely sober at the wheel. She was glad that the soft sand they travelled over restricted their speed and happier to be on a beach that she would have been on a Continental road. The sun was setting and it set quickly in Portugal. She couldn't help thinking that the pagan rite she was about to witness was little more than an excuse for a piss-up attended by a bunch of hedonists with a taste for mysticism. She'd noticed one of bikers wore a horned Viking helmet.

The atmosphere, when they reached the site, was very different from what it had been at the stone circle in Dorset. There, everything had been serious and no one had been drunk. Here there was a restlessness to the mood of a much bigger crowd. There was a circle, but it comprised nine enormous bonfires built on the sand. There was an effigy mounted at the top of each but the bonfires had been lit before their arrival and the flames were too fierce to make out who the burning figures were meant to resemble.

There would be no communal singing either, Ruthie realized, noticing a huge pair of Marshall speakers rigged on a platform erected behind the bonfire furthest from the sea. They crackled and squawked with feedback at a volume that made her flinch.

Ash burned the back of her throat. Smoke made her eyes smart and she knew that she was sweating. The radiant heat from the bonfires was fierce and the crowd dense, jostling, volatile and maybe even dangerous. The opening chord of 'Cease All Mourning' thundered through cinder-filled air and a huge triumphant cheer went up and people all around her started wrestling themselves out of their clothes.

Someone grabbed at her breasts from behind her and Ruthie wrenched herself effortfully free and turned and it was the biker in the horned helmet, his eyes glazed and his lips foam-flecked as though he'd taken a draught of poison or just become deranged. He'd grabbed her roughly and hard. She felt a flare of pain from the bruises on her back inflicted when she'd been trampled at her last Clamouring event. She tried to get out of the circle, stepping over and around coupling bodies, already grunting and thrusting urgently.

Someone grabbed her hand and it was Eddie Coyle. 'We're getting out of here,' he shouted over the music vibrating through them. 'This is going wrong.'

Stronger than he looked and sobered by events, he pulled her through the throng to where they'd parked the Jeep.

'My God,' Ruthie said, risking a glance back. 'Look at that.' She pointed. By moon and firelight, half a dozen figures seemed to be standing, rigid and unsinking on the surface of the sea. Each of them was naked. And they all had their arms raised, as if beseeching the heavens.

Eddie Coyle confirmed to Ruthie that the Viking-helmeted biker wasn't staying with him at the rented hunting lodge. 'No one's staying, it's just us,' he said, 'and your tits are perfectly safe, darling, with me.'

He drove slowly, sand swapped for scrub now in the headlamp beams, their progress on an upward incline, the odd sapling a spindly hint at the forest they would enter before they reached their shelter. Ruthie wasn't in truth paying much attention to the terrain. Her reeling mind was struggling to make sense of what she'd seen.

If she didn't take it at face value, then it was trickery. Skilled illusionists such as David Blaine or Dynamo could pull off that sort of stunt convincingly. But what would be the point? She thought she knew the answer to that question. The point was reinforcing Martin Mear's mystique. It was helping that mystique grow. It was about enhancing a legend that helped shift five million units a year. It was about money, about profit, about guaranteeing a bottom line. And for that reason, the person most likely to be behind the smoke and mirrors was Carter Melville.

Was the man sitting next to her in on it? She thought that he probably was. Which made him not quite the idiot Paula Tort dismissed him as. He'd told her he was rich, but that didn't mean he wasn't also greedy and Carter Melville paid well above the going rate.

'Penny for them,' Eddie Coyle said.

'How often does it go wrong like that?'

'There's a sense that we're reaching the end-game,' he said. 'It's encouraged a bit of hysteria and slightly altered the demographic. So we're getting die-hard Legionaries but also sensation-seekers and an element of what back in the day was called the lunatic fringe. I don't think synthetic drugs exactly enhance matters. When a crowd reaches a tipping point it becomes a mob. There was a contagious quality to the rutting back there. Didn't you feel that?'

'I wasn't even tempted to take off my coat. The bloke who groped me looked deranged.'

'I'd like to apologize for him.'

'Some friend.'

'More an acquaintance. Nobody's searched. Nobody's vetted or drug-tested. No one's asked for a character reference. You get the odd bad apple.'

'Back there you had a barrel full,' Ruthie said.

'Most of it looked consensual to me.'

Ruthie touched her sore forehead. 'On the whole, I preferred Dorset,' she said.

'Are you up for a drink?'

'Are you suggesting a date?'

'You're the wrong gender for me, darling,' Coyle said.

'Oh. But you said you had a daughter.'

'Youthful aberration.'

'I see.'

'Frankly, your tits could be in Fort Knox for all the danger they're in from me. What I'm suggesting is a drink at the lodge, which has a well-stocked bar for when the hunters want to wax nostalgic in the evening about all the wildlife they've butchered during the day.'

'I think a drink is an excellent idea,' Ruthie said, failing to add that she almost always thought that.

'Would you do me a favour, Ruthie?'

'Out of gratitude for letting me keep my bra on?'

'I'm serious,' he said.

'I will if I can.'

'Don't let on to Carter about what an unholy mess tonight became. He doesn't react well to any kind of negativity around Martin and Martin's legend.'

Ruthie said, 'You want it whitewashed?'

'I'd just be grateful if you could tone it down,' Coyle said.

'I'll confine myself to a description of that sea stunt,' Ruthie said.

'It wasn't a stunt,' Coyle said.

'And I'm really looking forward to that drink.'

After breakfast the following morning, Eddie Coyle insisted on driving Ruthie the seventy miles to Frederica Daunt's villa. She said she was more than content with a lift to the nearest place she could rent a hire car, but he was adamant. It was as much a gesture of contrition, she thought, as it was a bid to guarantee her silence concerning the ceremony on the beach of the previous night. She accepted because though she thought of herself as resilient, being groped had been one of her more unpleasant adult experiences. It could have been worse, but it was still a nasty violation.

She knew she had the right place as she waved Eddie off because a Mini Moke was parked outside it and Ruthie remembered Frederica's choice description of the vehicle her father drove. They must have been looking out for her because Frederica opened the door before she got there and danced down the short flight of wooden steps and opened her arms and embraced her, hugging her hard. 'Feels like it's been years,' she said.

It had been a little over a fortnight. But it felt a lot longer to Ruthie too.

She looked past Frederica to where a man now stood in her doorway. He had grey hair and a white beard and his skin was deeply tanned. He was wearing combats and one of those canvas jerkins fishermen were partial to, with ammo-pouch pockets everywhere. He had bunches of gap-year bangles on the wrists of both bared arms. He didn't wear a wristwatch. And there was only one person he could really be. He came down the steps, openly scrutinizing her. It was like waiting for a verdict.

'So you're the spectre haunting Martin Mear,' he said.

'More stalking than haunting,' she said.

'I think he'd have been flattered,' Sebastian said.

'Oh? Why?'

'Because you're suitably picturesque, my dear. Martin valued beauty and brains in equal measure.'

'You don't know I'm smart.'

'Freddie says you're as sharp as a knife and I trust my daughter's judgement in all matters except the consumption of tobacco.'

Ruthie pulled a face. 'Is that going to be an issue?'

'Probably not, now there are two of you to gang up on me,' he said.

He wore flip-flops and when he turned his head, she saw he wore his hair in an abundant ponytail. He'd already proven himself physically vain and at least borderline sexist but he had to be over eighty and Ruthie liked him. There was something noble about someone who'd spent his entire life being so resolutely nonconformist as this man evidently was.

'That was Edward Coyle at the wheel of the car you just got out of,' he said. 'The hair-style has changed, but he still attires himself like someone out of Thomas Hardy.'

'Or Jethro Tull,' Ruthie said.

That made Sebastian Daunt laugh. 'On the cover of *The Heavy Horses*,' he said.

'You a Tull fan, Sebastian?'

'Probably as keen on them as you are on Twisted Sister. What were you doing with him?'

'He's one of the Legionaries' star turns. He's a big cog in the Clamouring.'

'That nonsense.'

'There was an event last night, seventy miles south of here, on the coast. It very quickly became heavy nonsense.'

'Come inside,' Frederica said. 'I'll make us some lunch. It's really good to see you, Ruthie.'

'In one piece, you mean?'

'I've spent the last fortnight worrying about both of us. I won't lie about that.'

'Shouldn't lie about anything,' her father said. 'Tell one, you end up telling a hundred.'

Ruthie felt encouraged by his saying that. Carter Melville had kept things back from her she sensed, and Paula Tort had been forthright but still not entirely truthful in their formal interview. Sebastian was speaking off the record, which meant he could do so without repercussions. She thought the Martin Mear he'd tell her about as close to the man as anyone living could describe.

After their lunch, Sebastian Daunt slept for an hour, as he explained to Ruthie beforehand had been his regular habit for the last decade of his life. 'You slow reluctantly. But you can rage against the dying of the light all you want, you still slow. Age is a bitch, Ruthie. I'll nap and then we'll talk.'

Ruthie spent that hour seated on Frederica's balcony, shaded from the strong autumn sunshine by a table parasol, bringing her up to speed on where she'd got in the pursuit of her research, omitting some detail but telling her most of it, aware that Freddie had ways of finding things out unavailable to most people.

'I came into contact with three versions of Martin,' Sebastian Daunt said. 'The first was the sweet boy who came to the commune to learn to play the guitar, to lose his virginity and to become a father far too young. The second Martin, the one I found dark and intimidating, arrived shortly after the success of *King Lud*. The third Martin was mellow and seemed to have achieved a measure of serenity and I didn't know him for anything like long enough, because that Martin died prematurely.

'My own relationship with the man was complex. I played a significant part in the success of Ghost Legion's first album, which Martin actually composed and wrote and played and sang on solo, using a four-track tape machine. He was literally a one-man band. The cover art, according to the A&R men and the marketeers and the proprietors back then of record shops, suited the mood of the music with an almost uncanny aptness and played an iconic part in defining the future character of the Legion, the band's perception in the minds of the press and wider public.

'*King Lud* was the template, yet I honestly think Martin came to hate that album. I was on a car journey with him once, can't remember where to or where from, and one of its tracks began to play on the radio. He grimaced and went pale and quite rigid. And then he reached out and turned it off. *Black Solstice* and *Exiled Souls* are better records, because by then James Prentice was on board and the band had discovered their groove. And the three albums with no names are peerless. But *King Lud* was where it all began and yet if he could have, I think he would have disowned it completely.

'He wouldn't even discuss it. Martin didn't do many interviews. I think there's the one carried by *Rolling Stone* and the televised one with Joan Bakewell and that's pretty much it. Extraordinary really for someone so famous. But Martin was never a one for Lennon-style soundbites. This was way before the internet and even promo videos were still in their infancy because MTV was still a good decade away. Anyway, every journalist knew back then that if they ever got the chance to interview Martin, mention of *King Lud* would conclude matters very abruptly.

'So there you go, Ruthie. A complex character. Quite a contradictory sort of man in some respects. A mesmeric performer, a devoted father and according to Paul Tort, a faithful lover. But not a man anyone knew everything about, partly because he was private but also because he was fundamentally unknowable.'

'A keeper of secrets?'

'I strongly suspect he had some of those. And suspect too that they were big ones.'

'Thank you,' Ruthie said. He had confirmed something she'd already strongly suspected. She switched off her tape machine.

'This is all strictly off the record. Terrible pun but I want nothing to do with Melville's ghastly commercial circus.'

'I'm a researcher, Sebastian. I'm not a clown.'

'No offence intended. Would you like a drink, Ruthie? All this talk has made me thirsty. I'm going to have a beer. I assume you're staying here tonight?'

'No offence taken. Carter Melville is a ring-master, right down to the red frock-coat and the whip. I'm staying at Frederica's invitation until tomorrow. And white wine, if you have some.'

It was four in the afternoon. They joined Frederica in the kitchen where the three of them drank and ate tapas she'd prepared. Ruthie could not later have said at what time it was decided that they should get out the Ouija board. She thought they must have shipped quite a lot of alcohol for it to have seemed a good idea. She thought that the wisdom of age might have intervened in other circumstances, that Sebastian Daunt might at least have sounded a note of caution. But he was tired after his Martin Mear recollections and a bit lager-befuddled and so he just went with the flow.

They did it there in the kitchen, by candlelight. They did it at an old oak table far too sturdy to shiver or tilt under the joint pressure of their fingertips. Ruthie tested it with a knee and reckoned it probably weighed a quarter of a ton. A bodybuilder couldn't have shifted it.

Ruthie liked candles in the same way that she liked incense burners and joss sticks and songs sung by Siouxsie and the Banshees. But these were tallow candles and smelled strongly of animal fat and made her feel queasy and bilious after all the wine she'd drunk.

Sitting with them around the table, she could smell beer on Sebastian Daunt's breath and tobacco on the breath of his spirit medium daughter. These scents mingled into an aroma very similar to that Ruthie remembered from pubs before the smoking ban. She'd been twenty-three when the ban had come into force. She'd known several people who had died since then. She really didn't want to commune now with any of them. Why on earth was she doing this?

They each put a forefinger on the planchette, which moved indeterminately about the board. It felt slightly slick with her own sweat to Ruthie, touching it as lightly as possible so as not to dictate the direction of its movement even subconsciously.

There was noise in the kitchen. But it had reduced to their shallow breathing, the hiss of tallow burning against wicks, the mouse-squeak of the planchette on polished board. It didn't seem to be working and Ruthie was about to voice that thought in a tactful murmur when something about the room shifted. Suddenly it was full of the heady reek of Vetiver cologne and Havana cigars and brilliantine. There was a loud swell of accordion music, mushy and imprecise. Ruthie's finger recoiled and Sebastian muttered something she didn't catch and she became aware that Frederica was staring at her with someone else's eyes out of a face tilted in an attitude of cold contempt.

The voice that emerged from her wasn't hers either. It was a man's voice, the nicotined baritone of someone corpulently male, strongly accented, the words grunted out like heavy blows.

'Most unwise to meddle, Fräulein,' it said. 'Impertinent to trespass, which you barely got away with. Foolish to persist, don't you consider?'

Ruthie didn't say anything. You didn't engage. That's what Frederica had told her; Frederica, who was at that moment absent from her body and the room, inhabited by someone else, long dead. Squatting, rude and imperious.

The mouth opened and a laugh emerged from it, a fat man's laugh, high and girlish and in horrible contrast to its speaking voice.

'Cat got your tongue, Ruthie?'

It knew her name. Probably it knew everything and she knew who it was. It was Klaus Fischer, into whose domain she had stumbled without its owner's consent. She stayed silent, her skin coarse with gooseflesh under her shirt, aware that Sebastian Daunt was shaking next to her, not sure how much of this ordeal they were sharing an old man's heart could endure.

The candles extinguished themselves.

A stench of corruption, a strong smell of human ordure blossomed over all the other smells in a sensory cocktail that seemed stifling and unbreathable. And Ruthie forced herself to her feet gagging and groped by the kitchen door for the light switch.

When the lights came on, Frederica's head had slumped forward, her chin on her chest, a string of drool hanging from her lower lip.

'Help me with her,' her father said. And together they carried her to the sitting-room sofa. She seemed physically relaxed now, just sleeping deeply. Ruthie put a blanket over her and wiped her mouth with a clean tea towel.

'Has anything like this happened before?'

'Are you out of your fucking mind, woman? Do you think I'd risk something like that happening again to my own daughter if

I'd witnessed it before? I've never seen anything like that in my life. Have you?'

'No,' Ruthie said.

Frederica's eyes snapped open then. And she screamed.

TWENTY-SIX

Sebastian Daunt drove Ruthie Gillespie to Faro airport the following morning at the wheel of the Mini Moke. They were silent until they got there. Then he turned to her and said, 'There's more to tell you than I told you yesterday.'

'I know there is.'

'Do you think my daughter's going to be OK?'

'Has she told you about the Chiswick séance?'

'Only the bare bones.'

'We think James Prentice came calling,' Ruthie said. 'He put on quite a show, if it was him. It left Freddie much more beaten up than last night did. I don't think it was anywhere near as gruelling. I think it was actually worse for the two of us than it was for her.'

'James Prentice had a royalties beef with Martin. He died an angry and bitter man. That dude last night was Klaus Fischer. You'd been to his house and he didn't like it.'

'He didn't seem to mind Martin squatting there.'

'Martin was into some serious occult shit. So by all accounts was Fischer,' Sebastian said. 'Maybe Fischer admired Martin. Maybe he even got an invitation.'

Ruthie said, 'Why don't you tell me what you didn't tell me yesterday?'

'Because it's going to sound crazy.'

'I doubt that.'

'OK,' Sebastian said. 'The old mansion when Martin got there in the late '60s was devoid of furniture except for two items. One was in the cellar and it was a full-size snooker table. Martin told me there was a big black stain on the baize. Organic matter degrades over time, but Martin figured it was blood-spill. And there was a lot of it. He thought something might have been sacrificed there at one time in a ritual. The victim could have been anything from a chicken to a child.'

'Chickens don't bleed hugely,' Ruthie said.

'No, they don't.'

'What was the other item?'

'You may have seen that yourself. It was an old gramophone player with a winding handle and a horn. His Master's Voice, white dog logo enamelled on its side.'

'Black and white dog. I did see that,' Ruthie said. 'It was broken.'

'It was all busted to shit even back then. Didn't stop Martin hearing it.'

'The song cycle from *King Lud*?'

'Just the tunes. He dreamed the lyrics, sleeping there on his camp-bed during the night. Wrote them up in the morning, he told me. But he heard the tunes, coming out of that gramophone horn, one every day for seven days, until they stopped.'

'How did he engineer that?'

'Don't know the specifics. Never wanted to know.'

'Why do you think he eventually told you the truth; that *King Lud* was gifted to him?'

'That I do know, Ruthie,' Sebastian Daunt said. 'That was repentance.'

'Repentance for what?'

'Whatever it was he did to be gifted *King Lud*.'

The sun was shining quite brightly and of course, the car was roofless. In this merciless light, Ruthie noticed that Sebastian's ponytailed hair didn't quite look so abundant as it did indoors. There were dark shadows under his eyes and a scrawny quality to the skin of his neck, as though through sudden, recent, unplanned weight-loss.

He smiled ruefully at her. 'Six months,' he said. 'Maybe a little longer if I take things easy. Which I will. I'm in no rush.'

'I'm so sorry.'

'It's been a full life.'

'Does Frederica know?'

'Frederica has a random gift from which family seem to be immune. Gift apart, you're a much more intuitive woman than she's ever been.'

'Your relationship with Martin was basically paternal, like a father to him after his own father died.'

'He first learned guitar from me. I was more John Martyn than Clapton, but it was a start.'

'You loved him, didn't you?'

'The good book got that bit right, Ruthie. A father always loves the prodigal.'

Ruthie spent most of the duration of the return flight trying not to think about the hazards of occupying an aluminium tube six miles above the earth for almost four hours. She knew that statistically flying was probably the safest form of travelling. She was helped more in truth by the large gin and tonic she drank before boarding and the two she sipped at demurely strapped in her seat on both occasions the trolley came around. What she tried to concentrate on was her research conclusions so far.

She didn't believe anything she had witnessed at either of the two Clamouring events she'd attended anything but bogus. They had contrasted widely because the demographic had been so widely different. The Dorset event had been very middle-aged and middle-class; Morgan Roadster and Sunbeam Rapier owners of classic cars and New Age hipsters drawn because they were searching for a new faith and a new Messiah to lead it. There had been a definite quasi-religious feel to the ceremony at the circle of standing stones.

Portugal had been much more sybaritic; hard-core cultists frenzied into orgy by drink and drugs and the intoxication of believing something both occult and blasphemous might be about to manifest in their presence.

Both events had been pagan. Both had brought forth apparent miracles. But Ruthie thought them just slick tricks orchestrated by the man who stood to profit most from broadening Martin Mear's constituency of fans and encouraging their commitment to their idol. Carter Melville had invented the Clamouring motivated by the oldest of impulses – the desire to make money. And Eddie Coyle was in on it. Even if the Clamouring events occasionally got out of control, it was in his interest financially to spread the word, to make it seem if not plausible then at least convincing. He'd told Ruthie himself that the walking on water she'd seen was no mere theatrical contrivance. He was lying because that's exactly what it had to have been.

She thought Frederica Daunt's psychic gift genuine at least some of the time. For the previous evening's events and sensations to have all been faked required a lot of preparation and Sebastian Daunt's complicity. He generally disapproved of his daughter's spirit-medium antics, at least when he was sober. He wouldn't have contrived with his daughter to fool her with no real motive. Plus they hadn't known she'd been to Klaus Fischer's house. It was a detail she hadn't shared. And the idea that Paula Tort might have told them was laughable. Paula didn't do gossip.

Ruthie wasn't sure what to make of the gramophone story. It was the kind of thing a bombed-out rocker might imagine in the grip of LSD or on a booze and Quaaludes binge. But Martin Mear had been initiated into the Jericho Society and to them, his Master's voice was something specific and real and never lightly invoked. Sebastian had said Martin became repentant. Maybe he really had had something to be repentant about.

She'd been right in what she'd said at Faro airport, seated beside Sebastian in his parked-up Mini Moke. The Klaus Fischer interlude had been worse for them than it had for Frederica because she hadn't really been present for it. A glass of brandy and a cigarette on the terrace in the fresh air and she'd been fine, after she woke up properly and got back her bearings. But Fischer had warned Ruthie off. And sitting there in her British Airways seat, she wondered at the wisdom of persisting with this. £20,000 was a lot of money, but she couldn't spend a penny of it dead. Two people had already died. Michael Aldridge, a sensible man, had told her to give it up.

Carter. Carter Melville. Carter Fucking Melville.

'You think he's alive,' she said aloud to no one. 'The people closest to him are telling me things they'd never in a million years share with you. You think I can lead you to him and until I do that, I'm probably safe.'

Ruthie didn't like the 'probably' in that sentence very much. But it was a question of degrees. The man in the business suit in the seat next to hers didn't look as though he'd enjoyed any of it. He continued to stare at his in-flight magazine, but the perfume ad on its double-page-spread apparently claiming his rapt attention just wasn't as arresting as his glare made it look.

'Rehearsing a play,' she said to him with a smile and he smiled back, looking less than fully convinced.

Maybe she should write a play. It was possible that wrestling with a new form would help unblock her. Or she might sit there in front of an empty screen, searching her blank mind for lines of dialogue that just didn't wish to be voiced. She didn't think it worth the risk. It would be painful and humiliating and would give rise to the panicky conclusion that she might never write creatively again.

Michael Aldridge was in the arrivals hall to greet her. That was a surprise and it was a pleasant one. She shook her head though and tapped her wristwatch in mock admonishment as he took the travel bag from her hand and he kissed her.

'It's four o'clock on a Tuesday afternoon and you've an office to run.'

'I'm delegating.'

'Skiving, is what you're doing.'

'They work better when I'm not there. They're always telling me to take up golf. My car's a more relaxed ride than the Heathrow Express. And instinct tells me Portugal wasn't relaxed at all.'

'Bang on.'

'Want to talk about it?'

'Yes, if only to get it all straight in my mind. I have a noon meeting with the man employing me tomorrow and very little of substance to share with him.'

'You knew at the outset Martin Mear was a secretive man.'

'He compartmentalized his life. And he covered his tracks, Michael.'

'North Lambeth or Surbiton?'

'The latter'

'Thank you. My reward for skiving?'

'Skiving is its own reward. I didn't sleep well last night and I don't want to sleep alone tonight, is the truth. And you're lovely company and I feel safe with you.'

They were on the M4 when a brown panel van rattled past them at speed, Martens and Degrue coach painted onto its side in white italic script, Michael's car rocking on its suspension with the draught created by the mass and velocity of the vehicle overtaking it. The co-driver glanced down at them as it passed and he made a comment to his colleague as he looked. Michael Aldridge kept his own speed steady and his expression neutral and Ruthie was about to ask him had he seen it as the van shrank into the distance in the lane outside theirs.

'Of course I saw it,' he said. 'I saw it a mile or so back in my wing mirror.'

'Coincidence?'

'You don't think so,' he said.

'What then? A warning?'

'Tell me about Portugal.'

So Ruthie did. When she'd finished, he was silent, pondering.

Then he said, 'They like people to know nothing about them. But they like the few people who do know about them to think they're omnipresent and omnipotent too. I don't think that was a warning of anything specific. I think it was just them flexing their muscles.'

'We know where you live,' Ruthie said.

'Exactly that.'

'I'm tired, Michael.'

'And hungry?'

'Very.'

'Let's go for the hat-trick,' he said. 'Cold?'

'No. Not with you sitting beside me.'

'We'll have an early dinner at the Waggon and just turn in,' he said.

'I don't think I deserve you.'

'But happily, that's not your decision to make.'

Traffic was heavy and a lane ahead of them blocked by an accident and what should have been a forty-minute journey took an hour longer than that. Ruthie spent that last hour fast asleep and woke feeling revived, just as Michael parked on his spot on the drive outside his flat. They walked straight to the pub and bought drinks and ordered food. When it arrived, Ruthie was ravenous and the conversation was sparse until she'd cleared her plate.

She looked around the pub. Most of the patrons were threes and fours of men having a pint before making the commute home. She thought maybe academic and admin staff from the Kingston University building just down the road. Or maybe from the crown court, which was opposite that. Normal people leading conventional lives to an established routine. It even described the man in whose company she ate. It didn't at all though describe her in her present role or disposition. She wondered was she slipping into depression. Ruthie had once, naively, thought herself immune to that.

'What are you thinking?' Michael asked.

'I'm wondering whether I'll ever write again. I mean write fiction. The other stuff I can do by rote.'

'Do you need to be happy to write?'

She shook her head. 'It's more that writing makes me happy. But I need to be rooted and contented or it doesn't come.'

'Leave it alone, Ruthie. Give up and go home.'

She shook her head again. 'I won't be scared off by a bloody panel van. I'll find Martin Mear, then I'll go home. And you can come and visit when I do.'

'Find him symbolically? Or do you mean literally?'

'Find him and speak to him,' she said. 'He's got some explaining to do.'

TWENTY-SEVEN

The following morning, on no more than a hunch, Ruthie Gillespie rose early and switched on Michael's desktop computer. She'd asked him for his password just before they descended into sleep the previous night and he'd mumbled, 'Rosebud.' It was easy to remember if you'd seen the movie *Citizen Kane* and Ruthie had.

She wanted to know where Klaus Fischer had been educated. She thought probably Heidelberg, maybe the Sorbonne, possibly the London School of Economics. That had been founded in 1895 and Fischer had been forty-six in 1927 when he disappeared, so it was plausible he could have been a student there at about the turn of the century. Did industrialists become such after studying economics? When Ruthie thought about it, chemistry was probably just as likely. But he'd been an anglophile, the owner of a house in Mayfair, a hunting lodge near Dartmoor and a mansion on Wight. Had he been educated in England?

She discovered that he had. Using Michael's computer and doing a Google image search she found a formal study of eight students seated at dinner in evening wear. Klaus Fischer was the cold-eyed, corpulent, swarthy young man pictured third from left. He looked uneasy at being photographed, as though trapped or compromised.

'Still a student, and already plenty to hide,' she said aloud.

The caption hand-written in ink faded to bronze under the photograph was copperplate and easily legible. Fischer's alma mater had been University College, Oxford. The caption failed to provide any information on what course he'd been studying. And if the group or the dinner they were attending had any special significance, the caption wasn't saying.

She was seated in Michael's study, at his desk. The door opened and he came in and kissed the back of her neck and slid a fresh cup of coffee in front of her. He said, 'You remembered Rosebud.'

'In *Citizen Kane*, Rosebud is the name of the sled Charles Foster Kane had as a child, before he became a newspaper magnate monster. It's his last word, uttered on his death-bed.'

'I knew that, Ruthie.'

'Orson Welles based Kane on the real-life media tycoon William Randolph Hearst. Hearst had a mistress named Marion Davies. Rosebud was his pet name for a part of her anatomy of which he was particularly fond.'

'That, I didn't know.'

'You might want to change your password.'

'And I might not. I'll never forget it now.'

They shared the journey aboard the fast train from Surbiton and parted at Waterloo Station. Ruthie walked the ten-minute distance to Veronica's flat from there and resumed her research quite confident of the links she thought she might now discover.

According to his Wikipedia entry, Rhodes Scholar Carter Melville had taken first-class honours in PPE at University College, Oxford. Ruthie was too fastidious a researcher to think the online encyclopaedia an infallible source. But she thought this information probably spot-on.

There was going to be an archivist, she thought, at University

College. The colleges competed these days both for prestigious students and the high fees they brought with them and the endowments that sometimes followed from wealthy families either grateful or just star-struck by all that august tradition their precious son or daughter had just become a part of. Peddling that tradition would be the archivist's principal job. Once, that would simply have been keeping an accurate record. But times and values had changed.

She waited until ten-thirty rolled around before calling the college. She made more coffee and smoked a cigarette in Veronica's garden to pass the time and contemplate on what she'd already learned. She was finding out more, but it was incremental and a bit like the mental version of what it had been physically to find a route out of the maze at Hampton Court. Lots of dead ends and false trails. Time-consuming distractions such as the Clamouring had proven to be. The ceremonies were redundant. Martin wasn't coming back. He wasn't coming back, because he had never gone away.

Her thoughts turned to Frederica, who she liked. And to Frederica's father, who she thought she liked even more. In six months or so, Frederica would enter a season of grief. It would be hard and bitter and lonely and irrevocable. Ruthie wondered what it would be like for Sebastian to be reunited with the prodigal one last time before death claimed him.

'It would mean the world to him,' she said aloud, aware that this talking to herself lark was getting totally out of hand.

The University College archivist turned out to be a woman named Dora Steel. It wasn't an encouraging omen, but she sounded friendly and intrigued by what Ruthie was engaged in until she mentioned its link with the Fischer House. When she did that, Dora did indeed turn steely.

'Not one of our greatest successes,' she said.

'So you've heard of him?'

'He became quite notorious. There was some sort of scandal or disturbance. I honestly don't have any detail on that. He seems generally to have been an insalubrious character. Some sort of character flaw. He was sent down halfway through his second year. So obviously he didn't complete his degree.'

Ruthie said, 'Can you tell me any more?'

Dora Steel was silent. Then she said, 'Look, I was a researcher too, before I landed this job, so I'm not unsympathetic and I do appreciate what you've told me about the Fischer House and the *King Lud* album. I mean I get the significance. But honestly? I can only help you if you don't cite me as the source. Understood?'

'You have my promise on that,' Ruthie said. Her eyes were closed and she was smiling as she said it. These were the bits that made the work worthwhile and there'd been precious few of them so far.

'He was a member of some sort of secret society. It was so secret that the college authorities were never able to discover its name, despite stringent efforts. And these were people with very sharp minds. And they exerted considerable pressure. But the feeling seems to have been that breaching this cult's secrecy was a greater threat to its members than any formal punishment the university could mete out.'

'How were they discovered?'

'There's no account of that,' Dora Steel said. 'I'm guessing Fischer might though have been personally culpable. He was weirdly contradictory, secretive and flamboyant at the same time. But he was vulgarly wealthy and of course twenty is hardly a mature age in a man.'

'What do you mean by vulgarly wealthy?'

'Splashy opulence. Even then, how many undergraduates do you think owned a Mercedes Benz and retained a chauffeur?'

'Fischer did that?'

'Indeed he did, Ms Gillespie.'

A thought occurred to Ruthie. She said, 'Do you by any chance have the name of the chauffeur?'

'It's not to hand. I'll see if I can find out for you.'

Dora Steel called Ruthie back fifteen minutes later. She said, 'Klaus Fischer's chauffeur had to register for a pass to enter college grounds to pick up his charge. He was a man named Terence Askew.'

It was eleven o'clock on Wednesday morning and Ruthie had a meeting scheduled with Carter Melville at twelve.

'Ruthie, baby,' he said. 'What gives?'

She gave him a truncated account of what she'd been doing.

She said she'd got some great material from Wight that would establish an atmospheric tone from the outset. She reprised what Paula and April had told her and mentioned the Shelley poem with its line about loving all waste and solitary places. She said that since Martin had so successfully compartmentalized his life, it was difficult to provide a coherent linear narrative.

'He's a jigsaw puzzle to which I'll never have all the pieces.'

Carter Melville snapped his fingers and pointed at her breasts. 'Great line, baby. Going to use it?'

'I don't know Martin Mear at all.'

'You're getting to know Martin better than anyone.'

'Except you. And April Mear and Paula Tort and Eddie Coyle and Sebastian Daunt.'

'And Uncle Tom Cobbley and all,' Melville said. 'We none of us knew anything other than the fraction of himself he chose to show us. I get your jigsaw analogy. But, hon, you're getting a more complete picture than anyone's ever gotten before.'

'Should a Rhodes Scholar really be saying gotten?'

'An American Rhodes Scholar? Damn right.'

'Did you know Klaus Fischer attended the same university as you and Martin?'

Melville steepled his fingers and blinked. 'Don't recall seeing him there.'

'It's a coincidence. If it is, actually, a coincidence.'

'What the hell does that mean?'

'You tell me.'

'I'll tell you this, honey,' Melville said, pointing at her cleavage again, 'Restrict your conspiracy theorizing to the Clamouring and you won't entirely be wasting your time. That stuff intrigues people. It embellishes the legend. It keeps Martin today's news if not even tomorrow's. It's Mystic Meg with balls.'

'It's a crock,' Ruthie said.

And Melville grinned. 'That boarding-school language, Ruthie?'

'How do you know I went to boarding school?'

'Relax. It was on your CV, which I took the trouble to read.'

Ruthie had moments earlier been about to ask him whether Martin Mear's uncle and Klaus Fischer's chauffeur having the same surname was another coincidence. But something had stopped her. Now, she opened the briefcase on her lap and took out a folder full of notes.

'This is my progress so far,' she said. 'Facts, testimony, contemporary critical appraisal of Ghost Legion, the transcripts of the Joan Bakewell interview and the one he did with Norman Mailer for *Rolling Stone*. All the plausible theories, as comprehensive an account of the circumstances of his death as I've been able to put together. And two first-hand Clamouring Experience reports.'

'You're gold dust, baby,' Melville said, waving it away. 'Outline your essay plan and email it to me. This is a bitch of a gig I'm trusting you with. Don't make me regret it.'

Ruthie smiled tightly and got up to go.

Outside on the street, she wanted to find a Costa branch where she could switch on her laptop and do a bit of research. Then she changed her mind about that. Much of Soho had succumbed to luxury flat developments and boutique coffee shops. But central London was still encouragingly full of alluringly old-fashioned pubs and the Carter Fucking Melville Experience had made her feel like something stronger just then than a flat white. She didn't like being drooled over and she liked being played even less.

About the responsibility of penning the box-set's definitive Martin Mear essay she felt a bit numbed, curiously neutral, compromised by being obliged by circumstance to say less than she already knew or strongly suspected about Ghost Legion's founder and the eventual fate of his band members. The real story simply couldn't be substantiated and would therefore never be told. And its last chapter, Ruthie felt, had anyway yet to be written.

She found a double-fronted pub with a pillared porch and mullioned windows and went in. It had a low ceiling and horse brasses behind the bar and a thankful absence of piped music and gurgling fruit machines. She ordered a large glass of house white which when she sipped it was as surprisingly good as it was staggeringly expensive. She found a vacant table and got out her laptop. And a few seconds later she'd learned that there were approximately 8,211 people with the surname Askew in the UK. That was around 130 out of every million people in the country. Askew was the UK's 1,309th most common surname overall. How far, she wondered, was the long arm of coincidence permitted to stretch?

The origin of the name was Saxon and Danish. An 'acksheugh'

was an area of hilly land covered with oaks. Or there was Aschau, a town on the bend of a Danish river in Sleswick. Askew in Danish meant crooked.

'They got that bit right,' she said, attracting a sharp glance from a florid-faced man in a pinstripe suit. Someone better able than her to pay London's surreal pub prices, she thought, switching off her laptop and putting it away, concentrating fully on enjoying her drink.

The Jericho Society membership was dynastic. Terence Askew had been either Max Askew's father or his grandfather. Max had been childless, so had inducted his nephew. Martin Mear had met Carter Melville at the same university that Klaus Fischer had attended more than sixty years earlier. What had dictated that choice for either man? Whose idea had it been for Martin to travel to Fischer's derelict mansion on Wight to hear his Master's voice?

Ruthie Gillespie had previous with the Jericho Society. She'd helped outwit them twice. The first occasion had involved Michael Aldridge and the second Veronica Slade. She strongly suspected that they knew she had achieved at least one of these feats. They knew her capabilities and Michael was right, she'd always been the person who was going to be picked to do this particular job.

Outside on the street again she called Jackie Tibbs, the schoolfriend from Ventnor who'd tipped her off about the gig.

'How did you come to work for Melville Enterprises in the first place?'

'I was headhunted, two months ago. They offered me a salary I couldn't realistically turn down.'

'Was it really just the kindness of your heart, thinking of me for the Ghost Legion thing?'

The silence on the other end of the line was to Ruthie very eloquent. And also, she thought, quite chilling.

'It's true that I'd heard you were in a bit of a trough, Ruthie. I'd heard you were drinking quite a lot.'

'Which isn't really answering the question, is it?'

The voice on the other end of the line was a whisper now. 'Mr Melville put out a memo, asking could any of us think of someone literate with a fairly comprehensive knowledge of the music industry, maybe someone passionate about a particular genre, who could do a research job. They had to have the availability to start right away. There was a finder's fee of a thousand pounds. I naturally thought of you.'

'Naturally,' Ruthie said.

She called Frederica Daunt. Frederica answered, her voice tremulous, broken.

'You've had the conversation with your father?'

'This morning.'

'I'm so sorry, Freddie.'

'I'm not giving up on him. There's a clinic in Germany. I'll have plenty of money for the treatment from the sale of the Chiswick house. I'll happily spend every penny.'

Ruthie didn't say anything. There was nothing to say.

'Why have you called?'

'To ask a favour.'

Frederica laughed. It was a shrill sound. 'There's only one kind of favour you'd ever ask of me.'

'Maybe another time,' Ruthie said.

'No time like the present, Ruthie. I learned that from my dad this morning.'

'My recent acquaintance, Ginger McCabe?'

'The old man whose death wasn't accidental.'

'I need to know where and when he went into the water. I need the exact time, the precise location.'

Frederica was silent. Then she said, 'No guarantees. But I'll try this evening,'

'Thank you,' Ruthie said.

TWENTY-EIGHT

Ruthie Gillespie spent Wednesday evening in her Lambeth flat with Veronica Slade. Veronica opened a bottle of wine and they ate dinner and Ruthie brought her up to speed on events of the previous few days and her theories concerning them.

When she'd finished, Veronica said, 'Anything else?'

'Yes. As our meeting concluded today Carter Melville presented me with a corporate Amex card. Has my name on it and everything.'

'A credit card is basically a tracking device.'

'Only if you use it,' Ruthie said.

'Do you think you're being followed?'

'I wouldn't be surprised. But that just might be me being paranoid. Or egotistical.'

'Your ego isn't that big. Anyway we could find out,' Veronica said. 'Work's pretty dead until December. I could take tomorrow off. We could both travel to somewhere completely unrelated to what you're doing. Except your tail wouldn't know it was unrelated and would be obliged to follow. He follows you and I follow him. Simple.'

'Unless it's a she. If anyone's following me at all.'

'Where should we take them?'

'Lewes is nice.'

'Brighton's more interesting.'

'I'm not up to Brighton,' Ruthie said. 'I spent quite a few weekends there with Phil.'

'Michael Aldridge not doing it for you?'

'He is and he isn't,' Ruthie said. 'I think it's just that the heart works to its own timetable.'

'Spoken like a writer,' Veronica said.

'Yes, well I used to be one of those.'

'You still are, love.'

After dinner and in the company of a second bottle of white, they watched the notorious Montreal concert footage together; the event at which it was claimed Martin Mear had levitated from the stage. The quality, transposed to Blu-Ray and viewed on Veronica's high-definition flat-screen, was superb. But it still looked inconclusive to Ruthie. The quantity of dry ice on the stage just made it so. It was too densely billowing to properly see his booted feet.

When they'd watched it twice, Veronica said, 'Unless he invented moon-walking a decade before Michael Jackson started doing it, my money says he's off the floor.'

'He describes the shape of a pentagram,' Ruthie said.

Veronica sipped wine. She didn't look completely sober. But she didn't drink much, didn't drink every night and held down a high-pressure job. She said, 'I think there was probably an actual pentagram painted onto the stage.'

'Probably in goat's blood,' Ruthie said. She was thinking of the painting Ginger McCabe had glimpsed at Martens and Degrue's warehouse on the Shadwell dockside. Then she thought of the stamping feet and human hum of the Clamouring event she'd witnessed at the circle of standing stones in Dorset. She touched the scab, a hard ridge healing reluctantly at her hairline, where a bruise lay underneath it. All the people who'd attended that event would think this footage genuine. The pervert thug with the Viking helmet who had groped her breasts would believe it too. Martin as a deity would permit that kind of thing of his true believers. He might even approve.

'I think the significant thing is the direction in which he's moving,' Veronica said.

Ruthie said, 'I think the significant thing is that his feet appear to be trailing the ground by an impossible distance.'

'I'm serious, Ruthie. I don't know a great deal about the occult, but I do know acolytes of black magic refer to it as the Left-Hand Path.'

'And Martin's moving to his right,' Ruthie said. 'He's tracing the pentagram in a clockwise direction.'

'Like he's trying to undo something,' Veronica said. 'Whether he's off the floor or he's not, that little dance is recompense.'

'Bloody hell, it is too. I never thought of that.'

After the Dora Steel revelations of the morning, after enduring the Carter Melville Experience and afterwards learning how she'd been lured into his orbit, after studying the concert footage with Veronica, Ruthie felt all in. She climbed the stairs to the guest bedroom wearily. As she did so, an incoming email signal pinged in the phone in her hand. She read it in bed. It was from Frederica Daunt and it was a precise time and a precise dockside location picked out on a Google Maps image. She texted her sincere thanks and descended through velvet veils of fading consciousness into a blissful sleep.

The rail journey to Lewes involved a change at Clapham Junction. But they took the train because they could travel to Waterloo Station separately. Then they could travel on in separate carriages. Over breakfast, Ruthie had sketched out a map of the route she'd take to the various locations she'd visit once there. She had the advantage of knowing the Sussex market town they were headed to, which Veronica didn't.

It was a question for Veronica of waiting until Ruthie was out of sight and only then following, gaining on her and identifying her tail from behind and then trying to sneak a look at his or her face somehow, without being spotted herself. She'd told Ruthie she was confident she could do it. She was fit and athletic and Ruthie's progress walking anywhere was on the slow side of serene. She had excellent eyesight. She was naturally observant as a function of her career. She'd said over breakfast that more than anything, it was a case of wearing the right shoes. It was Jimmy Choos and pencil skirts and a rope of pearls for the office. For today, though, it was jeans and trainers.

Veronica had plaited her hair and crammed it under a watch cap. She had on a leather biker jacket and was totally devoid today of make-up. She wore dark glasses and when she'd looked in the full-length mirror before leaving home five minutes after Ruthie had that morning, hadn't looked very much like herself at all. Apart from the outfit, she was about four inches shorter than she habitually tended to be. She spotted Ruthie, about 300 metres ahead of her, heading as she'd said she would for the Costa coffee shop on Cliffe High Street. It had chairs and tables on the pedestrianized street outside, just this side of the bridge that crosses the River Ouse.

Ruthie would sit at one of the pavement tables and drink her regular flat white and anyone studying her while she did so would be in plain sight and easy to spot. There weren't that many pedestrians about at eleven in the morning in this prosperous little town. The weather was mild and dry, but it was a long way out of the tourist season.

There was a busker squatting against the wall by the cafe entrance playing something tuneless on a penny whistle. There were a couple of customers whose tethered dogs stopped them drinking their beverages inside. There were a couple of kids who Veronica thought should probably have been at school, since it was far too quiet for half-term. There was a group of vagrants drinking cans of Special Brew and K Cider on a bench on the other side of the road, but she saw no one who looked as though they might have followed Ruthie Gillespie there from inner London that morning.

Veronica watched Ruthie light a cigarette like she hadn't a single care in the world. Unlike Veronica, Ruthie had travelled there very much as herself; glossy black bob, red lipstick, black coat, jeans and Doc Marten boots. Here, she looked even more conspicuous than she generally did. Lewes tended towards the florid, wardrobe-wise; a lot of the checks and overchecks and plaid and ginghams Veronica associated with the beaus and hipsters of Brighton. Some of the clothing she saw had a quite Dickensian character. Some of it was vaguely rural in a way that evoked the Bloomsbury Group. She'd read that Virginia Woolf had drowned herself not far from here. The prosperous residents of Lewes had a self-conscious stylishness about them.

Two things happened then almost simultaneously. Ruthie scrabbled out her cigarette in the ashtray on her table and took a final sip of coffee and got to her feet and went into the Costa branch, Veronica assumed to use the loo. Coffee was a diuretic. And public loos tended to be unpleasantly dirty places. And then a blond man with indeterminate features strode past the point at which she stood in the direction of the High Street proper, back up the hill the way she and Ruthie ahead of her had come.

Veronica turned. There was something familiar about the man. And she saw the brown leather patches sewn onto the elbows of his tweed jacket and knew it was the driver of the vintage Morris Minor. The mint condition Morris Minor, she reminded herself, the one that had parked a few evenings earlier at the end of her own road. She'd hadn't described him to Ruthie. Had she done so, she'd have said he looked like a secondary school teacher from an earlier decade. Sociology, or maybe geography.

Veronica looked back to the Costa branch, but there was no sign of Ruthie emerging. Maybe she was in a queue at the counter. She didn't want to lose this potential lead. She began to follow the man, trying to match his pace, keeping her distance, close to the windows and awnings of shops because should he turn unexpectedly they provided at least a measure of concealment.

He didn't look terribly intimidating to her. He was a slight man, narrow-shouldered and she thought no more than about five feet eight in height. His trousers flapped loosely around skinny legs. He had the bantam physique she thought of another era, one that predated the general prevalence of junk food and sugary soft drinks. The days when men didn't snack on crisps and chocolate because a two pack a day Woodbines habit killed their appetite and stopped their taste buds from functioning.

He seemed to know where he was going. His pace was steady and unhurried but he didn't dawdle to window-shop and he kept looking straight ahead, as if sure of his goal. When he got to the top of the hill, to the elaborate Lewes landmark of the bronze war memorial, he turned sharp right and out of sight.

There was no sign of him when Veronica reached the spot. He had vanished. She thought there was only one place to which he could have gone, though, and that was an antiques market directly in front of her. A vintage car stood outside it, a Jaguar from the pre-war era. The building itself was mid-Victorian and austere, cloaked still in the grainy soot from the period before the Clean Air Act presumably put an end to the coal fires of Lewes back in the late 1950s.

She smiled to herself at the irony of it. Touring the rooms and stalls of an antiques market wasn't how she'd planned to spend her day off when the bloody things surrounded her at work on a daily basis. But a woman had to do what a woman had to do. She didn't intend to confront this man, but she wanted a closer look at him and some clue if she could get one about precisely what he was up to.

She went inside. There was a reception desk to her left and beyond that a warren of display cases crammed with the curios of past eras. Her first thought was that the people of this part of Sussex had owned an enormous quantity of stuff. They had been inordinately fond of carved wooden candlesticks and pocket watches. There were toy locomotives and cars made from pressed tin. There were old leather footballs preserved over decades by faithful applications of dubbin. There were pairs of boxing gloves and cricket bats that looked old enough to be Edwardian. Some skilful taxidermist had preserved a large tarantula, which made Veronica shudder despite it being behind glass and dead.

Right at the back of the gallery, there was a coloured bead curtain obscuring the entrance to somewhere. Through it, she could hear a classic single being played. It was The Beatles. It was 'Eight Days a Week'. It sounded scratchy with surface noise, like vinyl under the tone-arm of a record player. Veronica could smell cafe smells through the curtain, but couldn't see anything. She could smell coffee and potatoes baking and chili con carne and curiously, also cigarette smoke. That was surely against the law? Did the antique arcade cafes of Lewes possess some special dispensation?

She didn't think so. Affluent bits of Sussex were as much victim of the curse of health and safety as anywhere was.

She went through the curtain and from wood under her feet, to the slippery smoothness of a linoleum floor. The smells and the music swelled in intensity. There were no other customers. There was no one either behind the zinc counter to serve her. Not that she wanted to eat anything, with that bitter pall of smoke making the air in the cafe hazy and opaque.

The Beatles were playing on a Dansette portable, an antique in itself, Veronica knew, who was surprised you could still get the styluses for their head-shells. She noticed a discarded cigarette packet on a table, red and white livery and empty when she picked it up, the brand Embassy No. 6. She'd never smoked in her life, but she was fairly sure that these days the packets were anonymous, uniform, dull. And they had gruesome pictures on them underscored by dire health warnings, didn't they? The tables were all identical, Formica topped with a lurid starburst pattern. The chairs pulled up to them were plastic and modular with spindly metal white-painted legs.

The Beatles record clicked, trapped in a single groove she supposed by a scratch on the vinyl, or a bit of fluff trapped against the stylus. Whatever it was had marooned the phrase 'Eight days', which now repeated, Lennon and McCartney's ageless harmony endlessly echoing through time, trapped in isolation and monotony and somehow, completely disembodied and sounding weirdly inhuman.

Eight days. Eight days. Eight days . . .

It was then that she noticed the Pirelli calendar tacked to one wall. A Bardot-esque woman draped in a bikini lay across the bonnet of a vintage Porsche, a cigarillo clamped between her bared teeth. According to the calendar, they were in March of 1965.

Veronica swallowed, suddenly and coldly sure that the split-screen Morris Minor wasn't, with its showroom-sheen, an immaculate collectible at all. It was actually a brand-new car, bought probably on hire-purchase, for a price quoted in pounds, shillings and pence. But that impossible certainty was interrupted then by a voice, drifting out from someone somewhere unseen, from the back of an alcove behind the counter, behind the Perspex display cases with their smoke-scented custard slices and tarts with smeared toppings of raspberry jam and glaze-cherry-topped cream buns.

'I'm sorry to have kept you,' the voice said, male and blandly classless. 'I'll be with you in no time at all.'

I'm sorry to have kept you.

It felt to Veronica that no time at all was exactly where she was. On rubber legs, on smooth linoleum, she backed the way she'd come through the bead curtain, turning only when she was three feet beyond its fingering reach and back among the solid baubles of Lewes' verifiable antique past.

She paused at the reception desk. She thought about asking casually about the period cafe at the other end of the gallery. But her mouth was too dry for her to be able to articulate the words and she was too fearful anyway of the answer she would get.

Veronica turned right outside the antiques emporium when she should have turned left and left again to get back down the hill to Cliffe High Street and the Costa Coffee branch. She had reached the spacious car park of the Tesco superstore before she came to herself and went in and bought a can of Diet Coke to quench her thirst and drank it down and fumbled out her phone and called Ruthie.

'Where are you?'

'Tesco's car park.'

'Stay there. It's five minutes away from here. I'll come and get you.'

'Something weird happened, Ruthie. After I saw the Morris Minor guy.'

'Right. Then it's the White Hart bar for a stiffener,' Ruthie said, 'and you can tell me all about it there.'

A fire burned brightly in the big grate in the lounge of the White Hart Hotel. They took their drinks to chairs where it would warm them. It was still quiet, just before noon, after the breakfast stragglers, too early for the lunchtime clientele.

'I doubt it any longer exists,' Veronica said.

'I doubt it ever existed,' Ruthie said. 'What you've described is one of the milk bars opened in London by George Walker in the 1960s. He was the tycoon brother of the champion boxer Billy Walker. I think Billy's prize-purses were where George's capital originally came from. But George sited them in the West End of London. They were part of the swinging London scene. They just wouldn't have worked somewhere this staid and provincial.'

'How do you know this stuff?'

'Studied twentieth-century British history at uni,' Ruthie said. 'The 60s were the end of the age of austerity. And I know that antiques market. There's no cafe there. What you saw was something Max Askew remembered from his life.'

'It seemed pretty real to me.'

'You haven't described windows. You haven't described a view.'

'Oh my God.'

'Because there wasn't one, was there?'

Veronica gulped brandy and coughed. Ruthie was drinking only tonic water but had insisted her friend self-medicate with the classic remedy for shock.

'Look, I'll go back and check,' Ruthie said. 'They could have built a film-set there, I suppose. It could have been set up for a period drama.'

'Can Max Askew hurt us?'

Ruthie was silent. Then she said, 'Frederica Daunt said not to engage. I think I've stirred the memory of Max Askew by going to Proctor Court. His memory and his memories too. But he isn't real.'

'So I hallucinated it all?'

'Something a bit stronger than that,' Ruthie said. 'I think it's called a scent memory. There are places where sane people claim to have heard and seen things that aren't actually there.'

Veronica looked around, at the eighteenth-century fireplace and hung portraiture on the panelled walls. At the Chippendale chairs and antique tables with their elderly cut-glass vases filled with autumnal blooms. 'It probably happens here.'

Ruthie shrugged. 'All the time,' she said.

'But you're not actually being followed. Not by anyone real, or living.'

'No, I'm not. Not yet, anyway. That will come when I get closer than I am now to the truth.'

'I think you think you already know the truth.'

Ruthie said, 'Without evidence there is no truth. Without solid proof, everything's just speculation.'

'By which you mean bullshit,' Veronica said. She drained her glass. The hand holding it still shook slightly.

'If we're calling a spade a spade.'

Her phone rang. She saw without real surprise that her caller was Sir Terence Maloney.

'It's time we talked,' he said.
'High time,' she said. 'Tomorrow?'
'The Garrick Club at 11 am. Be punctual.'
'I'm always punctual.'

TWENTY-NINE

Ruthie dressed for her encounter with Sir Terence in a black pencil skirt and black jacket over a silk ivory shirt. The jacket and skirt had been bought separately but were of the same finely woven woollen cloth and so looked to the casual eye like a suit. She looked in the mirror thinking that this was as demure as she ever got. She would have dressed exactly like this for a court appearance if she were the one in the dock. Bail allowing, of course. All her ink was covered and she wouldn't wear lipstick or perfume. She looked demure, but she felt equipped today for a combat role. It was, she considered, the right mentality for the coming confrontation.

That Thursday morning, the weather had finally broken. Fallen leaves gusted against Veronica's windows, and rain pattered incessantly on the glass. The temperature had plunged by a good – or perhaps bad – ten degrees. Carter Fucking Melville's money would pay for the cab she intended to take into town, though she wouldn't use the Amex card made out in her name. There'd been something confidential, maybe even clandestine about Sir Terence Maloney's tone. And she wasn't going to run into Melville at the Garrick. He was exactly the sort of aspiring member unanimously blackballed.

She'd shared breakfast with Veronica, who had been remorseful about their misadventure of the previous day. It had been her idea, after all. It had been one of those wine-fuelled schemes that had still seemed attractive the morning after and so they'd gone through with it and the outcome for Veronica had been grim and chilling. She'd been forcefully reminded that the world was a more complex and ambivalent place than she'd ever personally wished it to be.

'We learned something from it,' Ruthie said to her, who had

gone back to the antiques arcade where of course, there'd been no sign of any 1960s era milk bar. Not so much as a relic.

'I've learned something,' Veronica said, 'which is not to meddle.'

And Ruthie nodded, knowing resignedly that meddling seemed these days to be what her life mostly comprised.

Now, her cab beeped in summons at the kerb. She put on her coat and picked up the bag containing her tape machine and her notebook and pens and locked the door behind her.

Sir Terence had organized a private room for their audience. A sherry decanter stood on a card table at his elbow, but he was drinking from a cup and there was a tray of coffee-related items atop a trolley under the window against one wall. He rose to greet her and shook her hand quite formally. His grip was firm but not bone-breakingly so. He looked like he did in most of the photographs she'd studied of him; physically fit in a superbly cut suit she knew he'd had hand-tailored by Anderson & Shepherd of Savile Row. He wore his wavy grey hair rather long for a businessman, but it looked good on him. He was well over six feet tall and looked a decade younger than his calendar age, tanned and appraising her with amused grey eyes she knew in his past had witnessed some terrible excesses.

He poured coffee for her and she sat opposite him, in the chair facing his. 'Ask away,' he said.

'He was fond of Sebastian Daunt and he loved Paula Tort faithfully. But would it be fair to say that you were Martin Mear's best friend?'

'I was a humble roadie.'

'You were a bit more than that. A lot more.'

'And Martin had three bandmates,' Sir Terence said.

'More in the nature of employees than anything else,' Ruthie said. 'And he clashed with James Prentice.'

'Often when people clash it's because of their closeness. Passions running high.'

Ruthie shook her head slowly. 'I'm not buying it,' she said. 'You were the best friend he had in the world.'

Sir Terence frowned. He sipped coffee and then placed his cup and saucer carefully on the card table beside him. He said, 'Where is this going?'

'I don't know precisely, Sir Terence. But I do know you fly a light plane.'

'Man's entitled to a hobby.'

'Except that your plane is equipped with pontoons.'

'Not considered a crime in aviation circles.'

'And good for landing somewhere remote surrounded by sea water.'

'Your point being?'

'I reckon you spend a lot on aviation fuel,' she said.

He shrugged. 'I can afford it.'

'And I think the flight logs you're obliged to keep are completely bogus. Martin Mear is alive, but he isn't totally self-sufficient. The place he's hiding isn't altogether self-sustaining for a human resident. It's remote. It's inhospitable. From time to time he needs supplies. You're his supplier.'

That earned a burst of laughter. 'It's a bloody long time since I was Martin Mear's fetcher and carrier, darling. Are you saying once a roadie, always a roadie? Because if you are that's absurd. I know you're a novelist. But that's not a licence to involve me in your outlandish flights of fancy. Martin is dead. He's been dead a long time. And I wouldn't waste my time flying a ghost supplies of anything.'

'You're thinking Paula cracked. But Paula didn't crack. She didn't need to. I uncovered evidence of my own. I know for certain that Martin didn't die in Morocco in 1975.'

Sir Terence stared at her. He still seemed amused. He said, 'How is that proof Martin Mear is still alive?'

'You're the proof, Sir Terence. Summoning me here today is the proof. You think the closer I get to Martin, the more imperilled your best and oldest friend becomes. I'm only here because you want to know how close I am to finding him.'

'You're nowhere near as clever as you think you are, Ms Gillespie.'

'I don't think I'm clever at all.'

'Any woman who willingly gets into bed with Carter Melville—'

'Charming phraseology.'

'I'm quite serious,' Sir Terence said. 'He's an extremely ruthless and dangerous man.'

'I know that,' Ruthie said. 'I think he's something to do with the Jericho Society. I think he wants me to lead him to Martin so they can take their revenge on him for walking away from them. For defying them. Nobody does that without them exacting a price.'

Sir Terence Maloney had gone pale. Under his tan, his skin had a taut sickly look, suddenly. He had taken his eyes away from Ruthie and was staring through the window at London's gunmetal air. At the falling rain.

He said, 'You shouldn't even mention them by name.'

'Like Voldemort?'

'This isn't funny. How did you hear about them?'

'I came across them a couple of years ago,' Ruthie said. 'I think Carter Melville knows I did. He knew I'd find out about Martin's Uncle Max, that I'd understand the significance when I did.'

'You're playing with fire.'

'And you're not?'

'Martin is my friend.'

'Present tense?'

'This conversation's over,' Sir Terence Maloney said.

Outside the club's ornate entrance, Ruthie raised the collar of her buttoned coat against the rain. It was teeming now, and she did not possess an umbrella. She crossed King Street and walked along Bedford Street to the Strand. She turned right and then crossed for Villiers Street, the bulk of Charing Cross Station to her right, ramshackle shops in a faded parade to her left, the road descending as it ran down towards the Embankment. Her immediate destination was the Victoria Palace Gardens, where she could shelter under a tree and smoke the cigarette she craved. Then she'd walk over Waterloo Bridge towards her temporary home in Lambeth.

She had gambled with Sir Terence and considered that she'd won but felt no sense of triumph or even of vindication. She felt that he'd confirmed her suspicions with his denials. Martin Mear might well love all waste and solitary places, as his melancholy daughter had insisted he did, but as another poet had written in an earlier century, no man is an island.

Her audience with the esteemed businessman had actually reminded her of something more recent, a song lyric written back in the decade when he'd still been hauling amps and tuning guitars and brokering Ghost Legion's drugs deals; and it was the line from the Eagles anthem *Hotel California*, about being able to check out any time you like but never being able to leave. That one had come out three or four years after Martin's apparent death and burial. But she'd have bet money he'd have heard it and thought it would resonate very strongly with him if he had.

Ruthie had another task to perform in London that Thursday but knew with a heavy heart that it would have to wait for dark before she could carry it out in a meaningful way. It was now only just after noon. She had a long and nervous wait until then. But the somnolent rhythm of the rain dripping through the trees was calming, the hiss of impact on rigid, autumnal leaves a hypnotic backdrop, nature making sweet music in dismal light in the subdued heart of the city.

Michael Aldridge called her as she smoked her cigarette in her imperfect, leaky shelter. She didn't pick up the call. She thought she might cry if she tried to speak to him just then. Her voice might break and she might sob, the phone trembling in her uncertain grip. She would call him later, when her self-possession had more fully returned to her than was currently the case. She liked to hear the kindness in his voice. It would be in pleasant contrast to the derision and contempt with which Sir Terence Maloney had greeted her. But she didn't condemn Sir Terence at all for that. She thought fear and loyalty in equal measure had prompted his scornful denials. The loyalty was an admirable quality. And Ruthie knew his fear to be fully justified.

She would go back to the home that wasn't her home and would try to calm the butterflies spreading wings in her stomach suddenly at the thought of the evening to come. She would take a shower and wash her rain-drenched hair and dry out and try to warm herself. She would try to fool herself that she could find the appetite to eat something. Her efforts to try to forget Phil Fortescue by relocating and doing something different to earn a crust were, she had to admit to herself, at least to some extent working. Just not in a way she would have expected or wanted them to.

Ruthie walked back through the rain to Veronica's flat over Westminster Bridge. She arrived there at 1 pm. She ate scrambled egg on toast and drank a cup of Earl Grey tea. She powered up her laptop and prepared for the sorrowful ritual of opening a Word document and staring emptily at blankness for an awkward and painful period of time as her redundant fingers drummed an absent tattoo on the wood of the desk in front of the keyboard. Instead, on this occasion, without rhyme, reason or preamble, the words tumbled out of her mind and onto the page.

She wrote solidly for three hours, saved what she'd written and looked at the word-count. There were just under 2,000 of them and when she read them back, they made complete sense and began a coherent story. She pressed save again and closed the file and went out into the garden to call Michael Aldridge feeling almost stunned with relief. She was no longer blocked. Her mind had found the key to a door that had been locked to her. It had done so without her knowledge and it was a delightful surprise. The rain had stopped.

'I'd very much like to see you tonight,' he said.

She remembered it was his weekend to have Mollie.

'There's something I need to do first in town,' she said.

'I hope to God it doesn't involve Proctor Court, Ruthie.'

'Close,' she said, 'but no cigar, Mr A.'

'Call me as soon as you've finished?'

'I will.'

She'd picked up on the concern for her in his voice. He was worried on her behalf, but would never make the mistake of trying to tell her what to do. Only men who were insecure or jealous did that and he manifested neither failing. At least with her, he didn't. She wasn't so rose-tinted as to think he might not have been different with his former wife. Maybe he had been but if he had, he was proof now that people could wilfully change.

Ruthie decided when she got to Shadwell as dusk descended to do it exactly as Ginger McCabe had, with a drink in the Prospect of Whitby beforehand. She honestly needed to do that, to steady her nerves before seeing the spot where Ginger had gone into the water. Unlike what the film buff who had spotted him in the pub said he'd done though, she confined herself to just the one gin and tonic. Her hand when she picked the drink up off the bar was encouragingly steady, really.

She thought she knew what had taken Ginger to the edge of the water in that precise spot. He'd recounted his strange story about his solitary visit to Martens and Degrue's dockside building in the 1960s. He'd told her about it on the Tuesday morning of their single face-to-face encounter. He'd told her about its subsequent demolition.

Blown to kingdom come had been his expression, his tone gleeful even fifty-odd years after the snub he'd endured there. *Dynamited, unless they used TNT.*

Ruthie suspected that something had spooked Ginger. She didn't know and never would know precisely what had done that. But whatever it was, it had been connected to Martens and Degrue. Which meant it had been connected to the Jericho Society. Maybe he had gone back to the spot just for the reassurance of seeing all trace of that baleful place vanished from the earth; from the docks, a place where Ginger had habitually walked with a swagger, where he'd been a face and a hard man both and earned the respect of his peers. She would never know. But Ruthie could speculate.

The feeling that she was being followed wasn't immediate. It was subtle, ambiguous, almost incremental. It was the rhythmic tapping of iron on stone, as though from a cane or stick, someone who laboured in their progress, the chink of a metal ferrule striking home with every second step.

Except that when she turned to look, the tapping stopped. And there was no one visible behind her. The streets were dark, street-lighting scant, few people walking the pavements, the rain cleared now, the air cold enough without cloud cover for Ruthie to be able to see each billowed breath plainly when she exhaled.

After each pause, every time she resumed walking towards her destination, after a few steps the tapping noise would also begin again. It was as though she generated it herself. She wondered if it did not actually resonate through Shadwell's gloomy thoroughfares; perhaps it began and ended only in her own head. That percussive echo of her own progress might actually exist only between her ears. In plainer language, she was merely imagining it. Except that Ruthie knew bloody well she wasn't.

Eventually she got to where she was going. She felt the chill of the night river envelope her like a ghost's embrace and she shivered. All trace of commerce had vanished through recent decades. There were sumptuous vestibules and bored concierges behind hotel-sized desks. The dockside buildings were luxury flats. She walked between them, past stern signage warning against trespass, seeing on the corners of the buildings what she'd been looking for, watching as their motion sensors picked her up and they stirred into life, precisely aimed at her like curious, gimlet-eyed, perching metal birds.

She was at the quayside. She could hear water lap and gurgle against masonry twenty feet beneath her feet. She could see a thin sliver of moonlight, a reflection from the sky, ripple glimmering out near the far bank. This was a wide, deep stretch of river, braided with current, colossal and cold.

Ruthie heard music then, something antic and scratchy, vintage jazz, she thought, someone hardy enough for an open window in one of the opulent apartments to her rear. And she smelled brilliantine and brandy, as though sweetish on breath and then the pungent exhalation of a cigar. And the tapping, which had stopped, resumed now, much closer and more rapid than it had seemed to her before. Louder, nearing her.

She had what she needed. She did not need to linger at the spot. She turned and walked back rapidly in the direction she had come with her eyes held rigidly forward, trying to block out sound, barely even breathing until she reached the warm and welcoming yellow light of Shadwell Underground Station and the safe refuge of a westward-bound train. In under an hour, she'd be in the company of Michael Aldridge. And it would only be 8.30 or so by then and they'd have the whole evening. *Close but no cigar*, she'd said to him. Except there had been a cigar, a fat and reeking Havana at that. Even aboard her underground train, surrounded by indifferent week-night travellers, her skin was coarse still under her clothing with gooseflesh. There were times, Ruthie knew, when a person was wiser to say nothing at all.

THIRTY

They went to the Waggon and Horses, where Michael Aldridge said, 'Is this routine becoming tedious?'

'Is it tedious for you?'

That made him laugh. 'One on one with the most beguiling woman I've ever met? I'm bored to distraction.'

'I like the routine,' Ruthie said. 'It's at odds with everything else in my life just now. It's a comfort. Do you think we have a chance?'

He looked down at the table between them. He rubbed at the circle of condensation revealed on the wood when he'd picked up his beer glass to take a sip. He said, 'I remember what you said about one-night stands. But my fear is that you'll go back to Ventnor and think of this as a holiday romance. You'll relegate it to the past.'

'I'm not on holiday.'

'You know what I mean.'

'Well,' she said, smiling, 'we'll know soon enough.'

'What does that mean?'

'On the way here, I called Carter Melville. Carter Fucking Melville, to give him his full title. I requested and got a meeting with him tomorrow morning. Actually, I demanded it. Then over this weekend I'm planning a trip. And then I'll be done, I think. I'll go back home to Ventnor. And I wish you were coming with me.'

'I think I can manage a few days,' Michael said. 'All of next week if you like.'

'What about work?'

'I keep telling you, Ruthie. I'm the boss. It's Aldridge Associates. The associates can survive a week without me.'

'That would be lovely,' Ruthie said.

'Don't deprive me of the detail,' Michael said. 'Tell me what you're up to.'

'Not here,' Ruthie said. 'Too many prying eyes and ears. That can be your bedtime story.'

They ate dinner at the pub. Ruthie was quite surprised she had any appetite after the Shadwell experience, something she wasn't going to describe in any unnecessary detail to Michael. She might have imagined it, though she didn't think she had. She had entered Klaus Fischer's derelict mansion and the dereliction hadn't quite been as complete as she had supposed it would be.

Since then, on two occasions, in two separate countries, a price had been exacted of her for doing so. And on the first occasion, she'd also been delivered a warning. Could the indignant ghost of Klaus Fischer hurt her? She didn't think so. She thought the two deaths so far deliberately inflicted, achieved by someone all too human. Ruthie had been given ample cause in her life to have a healthy belief in events that didn't conform to logic, in phenomena that weren't easily explicable or at all straightforward. But most mischief was done by people, not phantoms. And the motives were a squalid assortment of greed, fear, lust and revenge. And panic, she thought, which had prompted the death of poor Ginger McCabe. That particular capital offence had been committed with indecent haste.

They left the pub well before closing time. They shared an urgent need to get the physical stuff accomplished before Ruthie was ready to elaborate on her plans. Afterwards, lying entwined, regaining their breath, she realized as he tenderly kissed her on the mouth that it had suddenly and quite overwhelmingly become more than physical. The human heart was resilient. It could also be sometimes surprising.

'I began writing again today,' she said, speaking into the bedroom darkness. 'I mean stuff of my own, not just commissioned notes about Martin Mear and Ghost Legion.'

'You've been blocked?'

'For a while, yes. I think I'm unblocked now because of you.'

'That's quite a compliment.'

'Yes, Mr A. It is.'

They lay silently for a while. And then Ruthie outlined her scheme. Michael didn't interrupt or ask for clarification, he just listened as she explained her reasoning and subsequent intentions until she'd finished.

'How dangerous is all this?'

'That really depends on how my meeting concludes tomorrow with Carter Melville.'

'Assuming it goes as you expect it to?'

'Then I'll be in less danger on Sunday evening than I am now.'

'I pick Mollie up from school tomorrow afternoon,' Michael said. 'I take her back to her mum on the Sussex coast on Sunday evening. Will you be back by then?'

'God willing,' Ruthie said.

'Do you believe in God, Ruthie?'

'Only under duress,' she said.

He was quiet again, thinking, she supposed. Then he said, 'What's your guiding principle in all this?'

'That's an easy one to answer, Mr A. Better the Devil you know.'

'Know thine enemy?'

'That one too.'

He was quiet again. Minutes ticked by. She thought of the morning, in the rain after the storm that Sir Terence Maloney had proven to be, how close she'd been then to tears. Now, she thought Michael Aldridge was probably asleep. So she whispered what she said to him next. She said, 'How tired are you?'

'Not tired enough,' he said.

She reached for him. 'I was hoping you'd say that.'

Ruthie hired a car an hour after her meeting with Carter Melville concluded the following day. She hired a nippy two-seater, a mile-eater of a vehicle that would go fast without consuming a huge quantity of fuel. She wouldn't do it on a single tank, but she wanted to get the driving done with as little drama and as few stops as possible.

She remembered her last car trip north, in the driving seat of Phil Fortescue's Fiat Coupe, him a nervous passenger in the seat beside her at the beginning of the summer just passed. She did so with a wrench of loss and absence in her stomach that felt like a betrayal of Michael Aldridge. It wasn't that, though. It was just that what she had said to Veronica was true. The heart healed to its own timetable. Her feelings for Michael were strengthening. Her feelings for Phil hadn't weakened as much or as quickly as she'd hoped they would.

She'd booked a B&B room at a country pub just the other side of Carlisle. She'd paid for that and for the car hire with Carter Melville's money. She was quite confident now that she wouldn't be followed but had used her own debit card rather than the corporate Amex card he'd given her. The events of the past couple of weeks had encouraged a certain caution in Ruthie Gillespie. And though she expected not to be followed, that was only by anyone living. She didn't expect to see a Martens and Degrue liveried panel van flash past her on the motorway. If she saw Max Askew's split-screen Morris Minor in her rear-view though, she didn't think she'd be at all surprised. That she even half expected, like she half expected a Ghost Legion anthem to leak out of the car stereo's speakers without her having to trouble to turn the system on. There was a saying, wasn't there, one she hadn't referenced the previous evening with Michael, but one she thought nevertheless probably true. *The Devil has all the best tunes.*

There were tricks like those indulged by Eddie Coyle and his clever and clandestine band of technicians at the Clamouring events that kept Martin Mear's brand current with new-agers and conspiracy theorists and biker gangs and vogueish academics and the heaviest of heavy rockers. There were the tricks the mind played on people who were tired or in the grip of psychotropic drugs or just over-imaginative. And there was the other stuff, the strange and bizarre stuff that ambushed and dismayed you and paralysed you with terror because you simply couldn't process it in any rational way.

The car duly ate the miles. To try to keep herself calm, Ruthie turned her thoughts to the story she'd unexpectedly begun the previous day. She tried to map out some of its progress in her mind. And to her own relief, she discovered that she knew quite firmly and clearly the direction in which she would take it. She'd found her lost fictive voice again and was grateful for that.

She thought about Frederica Daunt and her dying father, Sebastian, and Frederica's self-imposed exile in Portugal. She didn't think the expensive alternative therapies in Germany would work in prolonging his life. The cancer had a firm hold on him. People talked – mostly in obituaries – about fighting the disease. But that was a meaningless cliché. No one was equipped with the weaponry to fight it once it got a firm grip on its victim. She thought that Sebastian would die and that his death would achieve only one positive outcome. Frederica would in her grief lose her enthusiasm for communicating with unrestful spirits. She would be finished as a medium and it would be a blessed relief for her. She'd struck Ruthie as quite a lonely woman. She could only redress that by existing more among the living than she had.

Afternoon turned to evening and Ruthie Gillespie drove. It was six o'clock before she saw her first road sign signalling a Scottish rather than an English destination ahead of her. She reached Carlisle and her B&B shortly before seven, weary and stiff, eyes tired from their forced alertness on the road. She took her bag out of the boot and smoked a cigarette in the pub's car park and went in and ordered a bottle of Chablis and a chicken casserole. She was aware of the humdrum nature of her actions in the momentous face of what she planned to try to do the following day.

What had brought her to this? Fate, she thought, recalling that meeting outside the cafe on Queen's promenade with Michael

Aldridge not quite a month ago. She'd brought her laptop with her with the intention of writing herself to sleep and drinking nothing stronger than tonic water. But she knew she had neither the concentration nor the stamina to conjure fiction tonight. She needed to sleep on the eve of what was likely to be the most difficult day of her life. A couple of glasses of wine and she knew she'd be slumbering deeply by nine o'clock at the latest.

She was in bed and about to close her eyes when she heard the ping of an incoming text. It was from Michael. It read: *Thinking of you. Stay safe. Much love x*. Ruthie closed her eyes smiling and went straight to sleep.

She checked out of the B&B immediately after breakfast at first light on Saturday morning. She had a drive and then a walk ahead of her. The weather was capricious in Scotland and in the Highlands could be severe. She'd packed the right clothing and her hiking boots but hoped the walk wouldn't be too arduous. She'd been strong and fit and her endurance had been good on the cadet-force exercises at boarding school. But that had been almost twenty years ago. She did the Tennyson trail a few times every summer on Wight. But the Scottish mountains were a more formidable proposition, glowering and wind-scoured and remote. And it wasn't summer, was it? It was a long way north at the end of October.

Ruthie eventually ran out of road what she estimated was about eight miles short of her destination. There was still a track of sorts, but it was so bumpy she thought she risked breaking an axle if she persisted along it at the wheel. And it looked anyway like it would peter into nothing in another few hundred yards. She could see the rectangular ruin ahead that was all that was left of the farmhouse to which it once must have led. She had a map, a compass and her mobile phone, fully charged, if she got into distress. 'Difficulties' was the euphemism most often used by mountain-rescue volunteers when townies bit off more than they could chew in the wilderness.

She thought that with caution and a bit of luck she could avoid the natural hazards. It was the unnatural ones she was honestly more concerned about.

'If everything goes tits up, there's a one-man tent in my rucksack,' she said aloud to the rocks, the heather, the strengthening rain descending from flurries of lead-coloured cloud. Which bit of defiant rhetoric didn't comfort her in the slightest.

She heard a wolf-howl then, a feral, barren echo of a sound that scraped out her stomach and made her teeth clench with foreboding and wish she was at the wheel of Eddie Coyle's Land Rover Defender with the sturdy doors locked and the heater warming her as she rattled effortlessly over the ground.

There are bound to be safeguards, Ruthie, she told herself. *There are deterrents, the closer you approach. He'll have taken precautions. He hasn't gone undiscovered this long by accident.*

There were no wolves in Scotland. Maybe there were at a zoo somewhere, but there were none in the wild. No wolves and no bears. Her surrounding might appear desolate, but this was still the UK, not the Australian Outback or the Rocky Mountains in bloody Colorado.

What if the howl had come from wild dogs? Unwanted pets dumped in the wilderness. Dobermans and Rottweilers and Alsatians and pit bulls reverted to nature and hunting in a pack? Would that be any easier to confront than a wolf? It was, she knew, what she was supposed to think. They were the commonsensical fears that would turn someone back or make them veer off out hiking in a less hazardous direction. But Ruthie didn't have the luxury of that option. She had a precise destination in mind. And she didn't know when she had felt more alone in her life.

She became aware of the smell of decay about half a mile further on. It was strong and strengthening with every step. It was a corrupt stench making her eyes water and her nostrils smart when she came upon its cause. It was a dead sheep, its belly erupted now, burst with the gasses of decomposition, its innards purplish and black with decay and the carcass seeming to tremble and shift with movement the closer she got. It was maggots, she realized, thousands of them, palely squirming and feasting in an infestation that made the wool of the animal's coat writhe. Ruthie was a foot away from this obscenity when a large rat, its coat slick with the slime of rot, burst out of the sheep's exposed stomach, tugging at some intestinal morsel with its teeth.

Ruthie screamed. It was a sound that withered swiftly in the surrounding silence, the stone and heather vacancy of the empty landscape, the vast indifferent sky above her. She felt small, solitary, cruelly exposed. She felt honestly lost. But she pressed on. She knew that she would not be deterred. She walked on from the stinking thing now at her back. She swallowed bile. She heard a single keening bark of sardonic laughter. She didn't imagine it. She thought she knew from whom it had come. It didn't matter. He couldn't hurt her. If he could, he'd have done it at his leisure in his not quite derelict home.

She passed a tarn, or pond, its surface pewter, reflecting the grey, wind-harried sky. Its surface rippled, she thought with the gusting breeze, but then it bubbled, and she knew something substantial would imminently breach from its depths.

It was an eel, she thought, confronted by its wide slit of a mouth and dead-eyed stare when they emerged. But then it slithered onto the shore and she reasoned that despite its smooth, scale-less skin, it was a snake, bigger than any she thought native to the British Isles and moving quite rapidly towards her.

Ruthie didn't change direction. She ran past the reptile, moving faster, much faster than she'd ever have imagined she could shift, fuelled by a high-octane cocktail of determination and terror. And she saw the snake rear up as she passed it, maybe surprised by her movement, because it didn't strike. But she didn't slow. She ran on until her lungs felt confined in her chest by a hoop of iron, steadily tightening. She ran until exhaustion forced her to stop. And when she could run no further she did stop and turned, gasping, her head bowed and her hands on her knees. And she saw that nothing visible had followed her.

Her ordeal wasn't quite over. She had to negotiate a patch of gorse between two high rock outcrops. Through seemed easier and more practical than around. Then her right foot got stuck and when she tried to pull it free and it wouldn't come she looked down and saw that the gnarled fingers of a human hand had snagged her ankle, pushing up the hem of her jeans, barking her shin and trapping her. It took a panicky moment for the reality to make itself plain in a rough lattice of small, sinewy branches into which her own weight had thrust her. And she was able then to disentangle herself without further damage to her leg or her dignity.

The land flattened out after that. Eventually, she came to a loch. She'd been wrong in her island theory. Sir Terence Maloney's pontooned plane wasn't thus equipped for a landing at sea. It was for putting down here. And on the far bank of the loch, Ruthie saw the house to which April Mear's father had taken her as a child. Not a bothy, nothing so public for so private a man. Not somewhere he might be obliged to share with some random stranger. Not a refuge marked on Ordnance Survey maps for the use of grateful travellers but somewhere he owned, bought probably from the descendants of the crofter who built it, paid for in cash and acquired through his old roadie intermediary so no one could put a name to its owner's face.

Just a theory. But the evidence was stacking up. And there was more of it in the thin column of peat smoke rising from the chimney into a rainy sky.

Ruthie thought suddenly about all the varied elements that had delivered her to this moment. She thought of Phil Fortescue's obstinate grief and Veronica Slade's endlessly tactful kindness; of Frederica Daunt's impulsive warmth and coldly uncertain gift. She thought of Max Askew's shabby, vapid ghost and the courteous dreamer she'd briefly known in Malcolm Stuart. She thought of Ginger McCabe's dapper pride and Paula Tort's less than icy hauteur and the abiding gentle sadness of April Mear and the malign hints Klaus Fischer's angry spirit still insinuated into the world. Eddie Coyle's epic sleight-of-hand. Carter Fucking Melville's dark agenda. She thought of Michael Aldridge and the enduring love she still didn't really believe she deserved to receive from him.

A long and complex litany of names and places, people and events and contrasting motivations would be pulled together into clear focus in the person she believed she was about to confront. Everything had rippled out from the splash Martin Mear had made in life and then allegedly in death. Ruthie felt a slight weariness, but she also felt quite calm. This moment she had reached was, after all, much more about him, at its conclusion, than it was about her.

It was a simple place when she got there, granite, slate-roofed, whitewashed. But the twin windows to either side of the door were shuttered. The building was blind, unless there was a peephole in the door. It was blind to her, though, from the outside. And so she stood there feeling suddenly naked for a charged instant until she heard the rasp of bolts being drawn back and the door opened inward on a gaunt man with a shotgun broken over his right forearm. The weapon had two barrels.

Ruthie expected him to snap the barrels shut, to ready the gun for firing. But he didn't do that. Instead he smiled at her and in the low murmur of a voice that sounded not much used, said, 'The polite thing to do would be to knock.'

THIRTY-ONE

It was warm in the shelter of the cottage. The place was spartanly furnished, lit by gas lanterns he turned off after opening the shutters. He wore a full beard and had shaved his head, so he didn't look very much at first glance like the leonine Martin Mear of the early 1970s. He was limber when he moved, had the sinewy build of a fell runner and eyes the flecked green of the sea in a storm. His eyes held hers with fierce directness. But the extraordinary thing about him was his presence. The sheer physicality of the man radiated off him. He charged the air in a way that made her expect it to crackle with energy. Ruthie didn't think charisma anywhere near an adequate word.

She had to drag her gaze away from him to study the cottage interior. It required an actual effort of will. The space she was in was contradictory, ordered and precise, but busy with the accoutrements of a remote, rural life.

Some of it was the stuff of sustenance. A fishing rod rested in a corner above a woven basket filled with lures and hooks and coils of line. There was a serious looking archery bow and beside it, a quiver full of arrows. There was a large bone-handled bowie knife in a leather sheath. To the right of an old enamel cooker, game had been hung. There was a red grouse and a mountain hare, still with their feathers and fur.

Some of it, though, was recreational. A coil of rope and climbing boots and a helmet hung from hooks, along with a powerful-looking pair of binoculars and a belt full of carabiners. He had snow shoes and a pair of ice-skates. There was a folded kite, poignant because she thought of them essentially as children's toys, not the plaything of a mature exile from his rightful life. It would go high, she thought, plied on the Highland winds.

A floor-to-ceiling bookcase dominated the rear wall, its shelves crammed, almost overflowing. Pinned to the walls there were frameless charcoal sketches she thought he'd probably done himself. Wildlife was the theme; a sea-eagle, a kingfisher, a falcon, an otter, a salmon depicted mid-leap. Ruthie thought these studies probably what the binoculars were for.

'All mod cons,' she said, 'sort of. Bankrolled by Sir Terence?'

'I died a wealthy man, but live on in a kind of penury.'

'Sounds like a line from Eliot.'

'Nope. I'd know, if it was.'

Ruthie hesitated and then took off her jacket and he appraised her. Neither of them had sat down. The light through the un-shuttered windows had a pale uncertainty that bled the room of shadows. Her eyes were lured back to him, her focus strongly pulled, dragged, like magnetism tuned to work on an aesthetic level. He was a sensory assault, making her feel slightly giddy. She thought that in sunlight he would look like an ageing god.

'I never imagined my death sentence would come quite so exotically wrapped,' he said.

'I'm not your death sentence, Mr Mear.'

'Martin, please. And you'll be Ruthie Gillespie.'

'You heard about me from Sir Terence?'

'He figured you were looking in the wrong places. Didn't stop him warning me.'

'April led me to you,' Ruthie said.

'Ah,' he said.

'Those lines from Shelley. All waste and solitary places.'

He looked out of the window, out of both windows, at a vista he no longer thought of as innocent. 'Not solitary for much longer, Ruthie. They'll have followed you.'

'The Jericho Society?'

He shook his head. His smile then was heartbreaking, she thought. He said, 'There's always a price to pay. They never write off a debt. They never forget. There's no forgiveness.'

'They're not coming,' Ruthie said.

'I'm intrigued to know why you think that. You can tell me, if there's time.' He glanced over at the table on which his gun now lay, inert and lethal. He went over to a cupboard and took a leather bandolier of cartridges out of it and put that next to the gun. He thought he was going down, but wasn't resigned to going quietly. He had the determination to fight. It was there in the detachment of his glance and the set of his jaw. He sniffed the air, as if he could scent impending intrusion. There was no loudening rumble of off-roader engine, no drone of an outboard amplifying with the approach of a boat on the loch, no closing tread of a party of professional killers on foot. And to Ruthie, the man in front of her looked far more predator than prey.

'Do you have any coffee, Martin?'

He smiled at her, a bit distractedly. 'A last request? You're not one of them. They'll kill you too, for which I'm sorrier than I can say. I'll take as many of them down as I can, and I can shoot, Ruthie. And have no compunction where they're concerned, but I'm a single gun.'

'They're not coming,' Ruthie said. Then she said, 'Hope that coffee's not instant.'

'Blue Mountain Jamaican, care of Sir Terry. One of the hermit's little luxuries,' Martin said. His speaking voice was deliberately quiet. It was a melodic voice, but he had no interest himself in hearing it. He was very alert now, to noise, to intrusion. She observed how his hands flexed convulsively at what he still believed was to come. He was ready for the confrontation, resigned to conflict. He was brave and absolutely determined to sell his life as dearly as possible.

'You loathe them, don't you?'

'Loathing and shame in equal measure, Ruthie. Most of a lifetime of both.'

'You need to let go of the shame.'

'I made even Sebastian Daunt afraid of me.'

'Not at the end. At the end, he loved you.'

Martin Mear scanned the view through his windows; the wilderness under its gunmetal-grey sky, the smudged horizon. Ruthie looked and swallowed at the vastness of it, at the way she'd come, approaching this place. And behind his home, the emptiness rose and loomed, on an epic, inhuman scale. Then he turned to her. 'There's a rear door. Stay out of their sightline and you might have chance if I can pin them down, hold them off for long enough.'

'They're not coming.'

'I know them, Ruthie. I was born to this shit, remember? So, I know that they are. They got you, because you were the kind of person Paula and my girl would open up to. They thought you'd be given the clues. How did they?'

'I've got previous with them,' Ruthie said. 'Two past encounters.'

'Terry sussed it straight away, that you were the lure.'

Ruthie didn't say anything.

'Shit, Ruthie. I should have died when I was fourteen. Everything since that day has been a weird kind of encore. You're young, with a lifetime in front of you, and you might still be able to get away. I'm begging you, if that's what it takes.'

'They're not coming,' Ruthie said again. 'Make me a mug of coffee, Martin, and I'll tell you exactly what I've done to stop them.'

Ruthie had done it only the previous morning, at her scheduled meeting with Carter Melville. She'd done it heartily sick of being played, aware that a reversal of roles in their relationship felt more than overdue to her.

'Baby,' he said. 'You called this one. I've had to shuffle my schedule. Make it worth my while.'

She sensed that for the first time there was a hint of vulnerability about him. He didn't know what she wanted there and wasn't a man who welcomed surprises. He looked more marooned than moored behind his aircraft-carrier flight-deck of a desk. She looked at the trophies lined up on the shelves at his back, at the industry plaudits framed on his walls. And she thought that in the uncompromising autumnal light through his room-length window, they looked a bit tawdry and cheap.

'I think I know why you sent me firstly in the direction of Frederica Daunt in Chiswick on that rainy Friday night about a hundred years ago,' she said.

'Go on.'

'It was a test. You wanted to know if I was easily scared. I passed the test. It's more a sort of stubbornness than actual courage, but the fact is that I'm not easily frightened. I wouldn't be here now, if I was.'

'You're speaking in riddles, Ruthie.'

'Then I'll make it very plain. I think you killed Malcolm Stuart. I don't think you planned to, but it became necessary. It was bad timing. He went back to Proctor Court half-cut after sharing a bottle of whisky with Ginger McCabe and you were there planting the postcards Martin Mear sent to taunt Max Askew. You were doing that for me to find them.'

'You've a lurid imagination, Ruthie. How would I come into possession of Max Askew's postcards?'

'Because the cult you belong to is dynastic and hierarchical. Max Askew was a foot-soldier. He'd have felt obliged to hand over the postcards, if not to you back then, I suspect to your father.'

'I don't belong to any cult.'

'Of course I can't prove you killed Malcolm.'

'That's a relief.'

'You're not entitled to sarcasm.'

Melville glanced at his wristwatch. 'This conversation's going nowhere,' he said.

'On the contrary, Carter, it's going to Shadwell, where I can prove you killed Ginger McCabe.'

Under the nicotine gloss of his sunbed tan, Carter Melville turned pale. 'How can you do that, Ruthie?'

'The event was filmed. I've got the footage.'

'You're bluffing.'

'The whole area's crawling with CCTV cameras and they've all got motion sensors.'

'You're still bluffing.'

'How do I know the exact location? How do I know he went into the water at precisely 7.16 pm? It's because there's a time-code on the video, you fucking murdering jerk.'

'You're quite fuckable yourself, Ruthie, in a low-rent, shop-soiled sort of way. Is that how you got the video? Or was it just a blow-job?'

'I got lucky, Carter. A luxury apartment building, a concierge with a little sister who reads my books. He swapped the video from that night for a couple of signed hardbacks. They hadn't even looked at it. No crime had been committed that night, after all. Ginger McCabe's death was an accident.'

'I still don't get how you knew where to look.'

'Malcolm Stuart had reminded Ginger of Max Askew and Martens and Degrue. He saw something sacrilegious there, decades ago. He went back to the scene of the crime. It's what people do.'

Carter Melville sat silently, sucking his teeth.

Ruthie said, 'Why did you kill him?'

'Are you wearing a wire, Ruthie?'

'I don't need to wear a wire, hon. Not when I've got the video.'

'I was at Martens and Degrue all those years ago when he visited. I was working there in the Easter vacation from university at Oxford. I was the flunky there served him his coffee that day. In a few weeks, my name and picture are going to be everywhere when we launch the box set. Archive shots of me back then with Martin. I didn't want the old guy remembering something I'd rather keep confidential.'

'I think you enjoyed it,' Ruthie said, kicking at the hide rug with its bullet holes, splayed across his office floor. 'You stalked an old man like prey.'

'And you're giving the video to the police?'

Ruthie shook her head. 'Won't bring Ginger back, will it? No, Mr Melville. It's my belief you're very high up in this cult to which you say you don't belong. Maybe right at the top of the food chain. Anything unfortunate happens to me, the video goes straight to a senior Met Police detective. Check him out, he's Commander Patrick Lassiter. He's very much the real deal. And shop-soiled or otherwise, Patsy's quite fond of me.'

'That's all you want?'

She shook her head. 'That's the least of it, hon. You let bygones be bygones with Martin Mear. I very much doubt he has any interest any longer in performing, or even very much in being Martin Mear again, frankly. But when I find him, he'll probably want rather badly to see April and Paula. You and your people will leave him and them alone.'

'I don't like blackmail,' Carter Melville said.

'I put Patsy Lassiter on your case, Carter, and you'll die in a high-security prison cell. And where I'm concerned, Patsy's never further than a phone call away. So, my advice to you, is suck it up.'

THIRTY-TWO

The smile on Martin Mear's face when Ruthie finished her account was much more open and less conflicted than the one he'd worn earlier. He said, 'Where's the video now, Ruthie?'

'There is no video,' she said. 'I mean, there might be. I got the exact time and location of Ginger McCabe's murder by less conventional means than CCTV. But Carter thinks it exists and that's all that matters.'

He laughed. 'You're a piece of work.'

'I'll take that as a compliment.'

'This big guy from the Met another of your bluffs?'

'He's my ex-boyfriend's best mate. We were on an expedition together. Something happened that caused him to come apart quite badly. I got to him first, helped put him back together.'

'Strong at the broken places,' Martin said.

'That's Hemingway, isn't it? April said you were a big reader.'

'More poetry than prose. Is he, your police chief? Strong at the broken places?'

'Yes, he is. But it isn't that, really. Sometimes you just like people and they like you back. There's a rapport, it's human nature. It's chemistry.'

There were tears in Martin's eyes, tears tracking the contours of his cheeks, disappearing into the unruly salt and pepper of his beard. 'I don't know what to say to you. How to thank you,' he said. 'There are no adequate words.'

'If they'd got you, would the Clamouring have brought you back?'

He sniffed. He said, 'The Clamouring was always a crock.'

'Did you really levitate in Montreal?'

'The evidence is inconclusive.'

'That's a politician's answer.'

'The honest answer is that I don't know,' he said. 'I believed I could, but I was pretty drugged up that night in Montreal. They were weird times. I made some very uncool decisions. What these days you term judgement calls.'

'You've paid a hefty price.'

'Just paying my dues. Nothing to the price Paula and April have paid. And they did nothing wrong.'

Ruthie nodded towards the gun. 'Would you have shot me?'

'People change, Ruthie. They mellow out. At one time I was wild. But I can't remember a version of me would ever have pointed a gun at you and pulled the trigger.'

She thought that a more honest answer than the one he'd given about Montreal. She said, 'Carter Melville?'

'Carter finished the job at Oxford my uncle began on me as a kid.'

'And at Klaus Fischer's mansion in Brightstone Forest, you heard your Master's voice?'

Martin Mear nodded slowly. 'Man, did I ever. It took Paula to teach a corrupted soul how to know right from wrong.'

'I think you knew it already,' Ruthie said. 'Your daughter's the living proof.'

Martin Mear didn't react to that. Ruthie asked, 'Why is *King Lud* about London?'

'I think because that's where the seed was sown by my Uncle Max. He worked on the river at Shadwell. But that recording was heavily influenced. Crazy, spellbound, not much to do with me. Not with the conscious part.'

'It set the Legion template.'

'And probably cost me any hope I had of salvation. Is Sebastian Daunt still breathing?'

'Frail,' Ruthie said, 'dying. His daughter's a medium, held a séance a fortnight ago, thought she'd summoned you. I was there. Didn't feel like smoke and mirrors. I think it might actually have been James Prentice.'

'James could be very bad news,' Martin said, 'could be one angry motherfucker. He was the cat that mostly trashed the hotel rooms. Pissed Terry off big-time.'

'I've heard he died angry with you.'

Martin shook his head. 'Not true,' he said, 'we never had a beef. His family's stories are a courtroom con. Terry kept me briefed on the cases. James was a hot arranger, but I did all the writing. And we had this groove together, musically. And a shared interest in the occult. Though mine came from bloodline and his was just personal enthusiasm. We were always going in opposite directions with that.'

'Could James perform sleight of hand?'

Martin nodded. 'Saw him do things a couple of times. Wouldn't really call it conjuring, though. Esoterically, James was extremely creative.'

'What does that mean?'

'He was the one always thought the Clamouring could work. So, if I'm wrong and it ever does, he's the one "Cease All Mourning" will be bringing back. Maybe not in the best of shape.'

'I had a bit of trouble getting here,' Ruthie said.

Martin Mear laughed, 'Natural deterrents?'

'They didn't seem very natural.'

'And they didn't deter you.'

'That your doing?'

'Simple stuff,' he said. 'Tricks.'

She remembered then what he'd done on a film set, when poor dead Ginger McCabe had found himself wearing the director's Rolex. Martin Mear's definition of trickery differed from most people's in the crucial regard that it wasn't trickery at all.

He said, 'What happens next?'

'Do you have a vehicle?'

'Old Defender,' he said. 'Hidden, camouflaged, a mile from here. Looks like shit but they go on trucking for ever.'

'I'd like a lift back to my car,' Ruthie said. 'But if that's a general question, I'd say what happens next is up to you. How big a wheel is Carter Melville?'

'Very,' Martin said. 'His grand-daddy founded the Society's Maine Chapter after fleeing Europe in 1927 and changing his name legally from Fischer. Carter's the main event, the headline act, destined for it from birth. A divine right to misrule.'

'And if he values his freedom, he'll leave you alone. It might take a while for that penny to drop, but what happens from now on is your choice. How does that make you feel?'

Martin Mear sniffed and wiped tears from his eyes with shaking fingers. His voice shook too when he answered her, saying, 'Honestly? Like I've been born again.'

There was a silence between them. Ruthie broke it by saying, 'Tell me about the Jericho Society.'

'You're better off not knowing,' he said.

'That was certainly true before yesterday morning,' Ruthie said. 'I don't think it is any longer.'

'When I was seven years old, I learned that Santa Claus didn't exist. Got the glad tidings from an older boy at school. I was pretty cut up and then in the Christmas holidays went to stay with my Uncle Max. And he told me that there was someone much better than Santa, someone who didn't confine his generosity to just the one day a year. But that it was give and take, a two-way street. That was the start of it for me.'

'Except that Santa is a fairy tale and not a cult.'

Martin said, 'What do you know about Deism? About Theism?'

'I took my degree in history, Martin. I don't know much at all about theology.'

He said, 'The Societé Jericho was founded in the French Revolutionary Terror. Deism is believing that God made the world and then washed his hands of it. Theism is a belief in an interventionist Creator. That short-fused, bearded guy from the Old Testament who flooded the world in a sulk and only saved Mr and Mrs Noah and their kids and their boatload of assorted beasts.'

'Among other incidences of plague and pestilence,' Ruthie said, 'and the burning of whole cities he'd taken exception to with pillars of fire.'

'Scorched earth, more than just burning,' Martin said. 'When the old guy pulled that move, everything breathing perished.'

'So basically, you weren't Satanists? You just believe in the vengeful God of the Old Testament?'

'It isn't that simple or innocent,' Martin said.

'Tell me.'

'The Societé Jericho was no more than a flag of convenience. It was a bid for legitimacy at a time and in a place when pretty much any tin-pot creed was tolerated just so long as it wasn't Catholicism. The French revolutionaries held a pagan Festival of the Supreme Being back then, just to piss off the Church.'

'I know about that,' Ruthie said. 'It was organized by the Jacobin Joseph Fouché, the Executioner of Lyons, the man who became head of Bonaparte's secret police.'

Martin nodded. He said, 'Not a cool dude. And the main man in forcing the society to flee France eventually for America. But that's not the issue. The reality is that the cult into which I was born predates Christianity by millennia.'

'Jesus.'

Martin shook his head. 'Jesus hadn't even been thought of. This stuff goes way back.'

'How far?'

'To the time when the most seriously enchanted place in the Western world was a large and intricate stone construction in the west of England, in Wiltshire. There's still a bit of it left.'

'Stonehenge is four thousand years old.'

'More like five,' Martin said.

'You're saying this goes all the way back to the druids. It's why *King Lud* plays out the way it does thematically. That song where the Roman invaders die in their sleep? It's a tribute, isn't it?'

'It's an act of fealty,' Martin said.

'So you're a slave to this cult?'

'Was. You're basically a believer in a merciless god.'

'But one that can be bribed?'

'Humoured,' Martin said. 'Flattered. Cajoled.'

'Antic and cruel. Mischievous and sybaritic.'

Martin laughed. He said, 'You've just described Mick and Keith.'

'I've just described the Green Man,' Ruthie said, 'for whom your uncle had a soft spot.'

'Yeah, he was a big fan of that guy too.'

Ruthie pondered. She was thinking about the druids and standing water, about the amphibious reptile she'd seen emerge from that tarn. It hadn't been real. She'd seen the thing she'd most feared seeing. She said, 'The druids went in for human sacrifice. Have you—'

'No,' Martin said. 'Though I believe it was done one time at the Fischer House. Very bad karma in the cellar there. Strange stain on a snooker table. Kind of a weird aftermath thing too, like a premonition in reverse.'

'Paula told me.'

'Really?'

'Really.'

'I guess that makes you one of those women other women trust.'

'Are Carter Melville's hands stained with sacrificial blood?'

'The honest answer is I don't know, Ruthie. All I do know is I never would have vouched for Carter, even before I extricated myself from all that ominous, poisonous shit.' He looked at her, levelly. And he said, 'Given how high up Carter is in the hierarchy, you'd be pretty dumb to bet against it.'

'Do you remember a man named Ginger McCabe? You once played a conjuring trick on him.'

'I do, and I did, but it wasn't really conjuring.'

'He told me you had no fear.'

'Then he got me very wrong.'

'He once saw a blasphemous painting at Martens and Degrue. The signature was Arthur Sedley-Barrett's.'

Martin raised an eyebrow. He said, 'It could have been Bacon's signature or Lucien Freud's. Go back a few centuries and Fuseli could have painted what he saw. Or Caravaggio. They have deep pockets and persuasive ways.'

'How influential are they,' Ruthie said, 'how powerful?'

'You want personal or political?'

'How about both?'

'I don't know whether they've thrived, or they've declined. I've been what's nowadays called off-message for a long time. My instinct is that they're doing OK. There'll always be greed and people with an appetite for badness. It didn't take all that long back in the day for Woodstock to turn into Altamont.'

'Personally?'

'I've served a life term, Ruthie. Do the crime, do the time. No complaints. But I've been deprived of the people I love, and it's been worse for them and for forty years I've thought I'd die this way. Figured we all would. Die, lonely and alone.'

'But now you've been born again.'

'When I opened the door to this cottage and saw you standing in front of it, I thought everything was over. Finished, right there and then. But it's only now starting. Thanks to you.'

'All told,' Ruthie said, 'I think it's only what you deserve, Martin.'

There was a guitar leaning against the wall by the cottage door. It was acoustic, and the lacquered varnish of the body was worn away in patches with use. This instrument seemed more poised than recumbent where he'd leant it, to Ruthie. As though it was only waiting patiently for its moment as this scene between the two of them played out. He saw her looking at it and went across and picked it up. He put its strap over his shoulder and gripped the neck with his left hand and strummed the strings with his right thumb. The sound resonated with loud clarity between stone walls. The instrument sounded perfectly tuned. Martin Mear cleared his throat with a cough.

'Any requests, before we leave, Ruthie?' he said. 'You might have to forgive a little rustiness. It's a very long time since I last got to play to an audience.'

She wanted to cry, when he said that. Instead, she went across and he put the guitar back down and she hugged him, and he hugged her hard in return. She held on until the sobs stopped shaking him.

THIRTY-THREE

Eddie Coyle was extremely pleased with the way the rehearsal went. They weren't going to call the installation at the V&A a Clamouring event, but that's what it was in all but name. Six sumptuously high-end belt-driven Rega turntables, each equipped with an SME tone arm and an Ortofon cartridge, all wired to play 'Cease All Mourning' simultaneously as the punters filed past the artefacts so painstakingly gathered together by Carter Melville for the forthcoming exhibition celebrating Martin Mear's enigmatic life and splendidly inglorious times.

Krell integrated amplifiers. Martin Logan electrostatic speakers. No-expense-spared kit, which Carter would gain a large dose of very public kudos from, in donating it all to a list of strategically chosen inner-city schools and orphanages once the exhibition wrapped up at the end of January. He could afford the gesture, Eddie thought. The show was a sell-out. Ghost Legion dead were an even bigger draw than they'd been alive. Ticket sales had earned four and a half mill and counting. Merchandise might bring the eventual profit up to around the six million pounds mark.

Carter was talking about touring the exhibition. New York, Barcelona, Paris, Milan – maybe Rio and Beijing. It would keep Eddie a busy man throughout next year, he thought. And his contribution was flawless, the synchronicity perfect, the overall effect with 800 watts of power produced by each of the Krells almost overwhelming in its weight and detail, the width and depth of its soundstage, the energy and clarity and sheer, brutal melodic force. Music could move you. And it could remind even Eddie Coyle afresh of just how good a band the Legion had been; of the energy and drive they'd possessed, their unstoppable, hypnotic, relentless propulsion. Man, they'd fucking *rocked.*

Afterwards, after the adrenal rush and precise calibration of setting up and triggering everything just right, after the triumphant glow of getting it all absolutely perfectly on time, on song, on the nail – Eddie needed a drink to calm himself down, a liquid sedative self-administered somewhere quiet where he could reflect on his achievement in anonymity. The opening chord of the song reverberated through his mind. He couldn't get it out of his mind. Martin had originated that chord, had come up with it, so the legend insisted, at a recording session at the studio on Eel Pie Island in the middle of the Thames at four o'clock in the morning.

Martin had played it and James Prentice had named it. *Christened* it, if that wasn't sacrilegious, because Prentice had dubbed it the Lucifer Chord. The nice, well-spoken, expensively educated and delightfully cooperative staff at the V&A probably didn't know that and weren't going to hear it from Eddie Coyle, but he believed the story to be true. Lots of the stories about the Legion were fanciful and some were utter bullshit, but that one had about it the ring of authenticity.

The chord itself had been played on a red sunburst solid-bodied Gibson Les Paul guitar given to Martin by the man himself. Usually, Martin had played a white Fender Stratocaster, but he'd played the arguably more resonant and tuneful Les Paul recording 'Cease All Mourning' and the guitar had recently been valued by Christie's at £800,000. It was proof to Eddie that the Legion's excesses hadn't died with them. But the vial of pure Colombian product in the breast pocket of his jacket was also proof of that. He was part of the Legion himself, he considered, one of the band's rightful heirs, privy to the secrets, first-class ticket aboard the gravy train, front-row seats for the only show in town really worth seeing.

In the street between the V&A and the Kensington pub that was his destination, Eddie called Carter Melville. It was eight o'clock in the evening. Darkness had fallen, but it wasn't late. He wanted Carter to know how well the rehearsal had gone. But Carter's phone went straight to messages, which it had been doing now for a couple of days. That was a bit disappointing and a bit frustrating too, but it wasn't unprecedented and didn't really ring alarm bells.

On a whim, he rang Ruthie Gillespie. 'I've perfected a rendition of the Clamouring,' he said to her. 'The synchronicity is fucking awesome. You need to hear it. It's got to be referenced in the essay you're writing. Just as a piece of performance art it's honest to God flawless.'

'Except I'm no longer writing the piece, Eddie,' she said. 'I'm off the project. No hard feelings. But I'm done with it.'

Eddie Coyle took a moment to process this. He said, 'I lied to you, darling. Biker guy who grabbed your tits is one of my best buddies. We were at school together.'

'I knew you were lying,' she said.

'I'd like to apologize sincerely for his abysmal taste in women.'

'Goodbye, Eddie,' Ruthie said. 'It's been a blast.'

Eddie Coyle felt a bit hollow after that. But he wasn't going to let a vacuous goth bitch like Ruthie Gillespie rain on his parade. He'd just enjoyed one of the most creatively fulfilling experiences of his entire life. His status now was, as he'd just implied, surely that of performance artist. The Lucifer Chord was still reverberating around the echo chamber of his head. He reached the pub and ordered a bottle of champagne at the bar and then pondered on how discreet he'd need to be to get away with a fat line in the toilets. Not very, he didn't think. It wasn't the sort of pub that employed bouncers on its doors. The clientele was more an affluent trickle than an uncouth flood.

Carter had said he was paying the Gillespie bitch twenty large for the think-piece on the Legion. Eddie didn't really understand how she could readily walk away from that. But then it occurred to him of course that she hadn't walked away. She wasn't up to the job was all, and Carter had fired her. It was probably why he wasn't taking calls, he was looking for a short-notice replacement to write a crucial element of his pet project. It was a tall order. Eddie could help with that by texting him a couple of likely names.

The champagne went down quickly and well. He'd order another bottle when he got to his hotel suite. It was a boutique place, pricey but worth it. And he was expensing the cost of it entirely justifiably to Melville Enterprises.

He wasn't the wealthy man he'd told the Gillespie bitch he was. His father, a louche figure at Mayfair's blackjack tables back in the day, had dribbled away most of the family money gambling. The country house was grand, but heavily mortgaged. The land surrounding it, he'd had to lease out. But the exhibition, his part in it, stood to make Eddie so financially secure, he might have to elevate himself back to Edward. The Clamouring events had always been profitable for their principal organizer. With the travelling show, they stood to make him seriously rich.

Eddie got back to his suite buzzing slightly from the coke. He ordered his second bottle of champagne and drank it unable to concentrate fully on something almost surgically hardcore on the porn channel. He finally dropped off at just past 2 am having snacked half-heartedly on a bowl of pistachio nuts he thought might come back to haunt him in the small hours of the night. Though his final feeling before slipping from consciousness was one of unmitigated pleasure at just how immaculately the evening's Clamouring rite had gone.

It was the smell that awoke him. The stink of decomposition smarted in Eddie Coyle's nostrils and he blinked awake and looked at his wristwatch reluctant to breathe it in. It was 3 am. He'd slept for only an hour. His mouth was dry and the thud of a hangover reverberated dully already inside his skull. He sat up all at once aware of the dreadful conviction that he wasn't alone in the room.

He could hear breathing that wasn't his. A sort of wet-bellows clatter that was raggedly arrhythmic. There was an excited, aroused quality to the sound. In Eddie's ears, it signalled a gleeful struggle.

He raised his head and saw that there was a seated figure in an armchair under a window opposite where he lay. He hadn't closed the curtains fully after switching off the TV and there was enough ambient light in the room to see by, at least in a gloomy, black and white sort of way. At first, it looked to Eddie like his visitor was wearing a mask. His face appeared too pale and sort of granular to be made authentically of skin. Except that it moved and shifted, as though restless and somehow uncertain. Masks didn't do that.

The stench was awful. Eddie's eyes teared up with it. He wanted to heave, but was too afraid for his chest to permit the movement required for that. He was terrified, he realized, in the presence of this pasty, coarse featured, reeking intruder. He didn't dare switch on the bedside light a foot from his trembling right hand. He was afraid of the detail that further illumination would reveal to him. His visitor's hands were disconcerting. The fingers cradled in its lap appeared too long. Then their tips glinted bonily in a shutter flash of moonlight and Eddie realized it was their nails that gave the fingers their implausible length.

'Who are you?'

'You know who I am. At least, you know who I was.'

The voice to Eddie's ears had a slurred, sloppy quality, like an approximation of speech, more an impersonation than the real thing.

'What do you want?'

But recognition was dawning now in Eddie's frightened mind. There was a familiarity about the mannerisms and the posture. The face and the voice were horribly incomplete and therefore wrong, but the figure was tall and thin and the velvet rags clothing his pale limbs was recognizable as the remnants of a suit he'd seen in photographs taken long ago. Decades ago, really. Before his own birth.

Eddie Coyle repeated, 'What do you want?'

The odour was overpowering. It interfered with clear thought, miasmic, polluting, contagious in its corrupt, oozing potency.

The figure spoke again. 'You've summoned me back without a soul, Eddie. So I've come for yours.'

Eddie Coyle swallowed. 'You're James Prentice.'

The figure in the armchair gurgled laughter. 'Not quite. Not yet.'

'You're all wrong.'

That wet chuckle again. 'It's an imprecise science.'

Shienshe.

'This is a dream, right?'

'Of course it is, Eddie,' the apparition said. 'Just a bad dream.'

* * *

Ruthie Gillespie thought that April Mear's reconciliation with her father would likely leave her friendship with Paula Tort intact despite the long decades of persistent deception. April would come to know that only faking his death had kept Martin alive. And that Martin's survival was the consequence not only of Paula's scheming, but of Paula's subsequent, heartbreaking sacrifice.

She thought that Martin might remain in the Scottish Highlands, because he really did love all waste and solitary places. Or he might relocate to somewhere else quiet in the world, his name legally changed to something slightly less attention-grabbing than the one he had. He'd receive regular visitors there. Or he might share his home on a permanent basis. Paula was past retirement age, had nothing further to prove to herself or to anyone else, and was probably intent on making up for a great deal of lost time.

Ruthie didn't honestly think Martin would perform publicly again. He had a voice he hadn't used much in recent decades, so it was likely intact in its power and range. He'd still possess the physical dexterity to play the guitar. The talent wouldn't have diminished. And he still possessed that extraordinary, high-voltage presence that seemed to charge the air in his orbit. He'd sell out stadia if he did decide to perform, either solo or with a replacement version of his original band as their front-man once again.

But Ruthie didn't think he'd do it, for the same reason he'd never cut another record. His gift had been compromised and tainted. He'd heard his Master's voice as his share of a corrupt bit of bargaining and his silence now was the price paid for sincerely repenting that. She thought now that he really had been capable at one time of levitation. That might have been the least of his accomplishments. She sensed he was afraid now of powers in which he'd once revelled because those powers were unnatural. Perhaps he'd fear that performing again might revive them. Permanent retirement was certainly a wiser option than a comeback seemed to be.

She was in Ventnor with Michael Aldridge, four days after reading about the apparent hotel suicide of Eddie Coyle, when she got a call from Frederica Daunt.

'Dad's received an invitation.'

'All fathers love the prodigal,' Ruthie said.

'He's beside himself. New lease of life. Asked me to thank you.'

'I didn't really do anything.'

'We both of us know that's not true,' Frederica said.

'I think most of it was fate, Freddie.'

'Will you come and stay for a couple of weeks in the spring?'

'If I'm invited,' Ruthie said.

'You've got a standing invitation.' Then, 'Anything going bump in your night?'

'Yes. An architect unfamiliar with his new surroundings who can't find the loo in the dark.'

That made Frederica laugh. But she still said, 'Nothing else?'

'It's all stopped,' Ruthie said, thinking, *until the next time.*

She'd taken the call outside the Spyglass Inn. The sunset had painted the water crimson where it descended out over a tranquil sea. Faraway yachts ploughed through the brine indifferent to all but their course. Michael was seated beside her, a serene expression on his face, watching it all, watching nature draw the curtain spectacularly on another autumnal day. A feeling had spread through her she thought might be wine-based, alcohol coursing merrily through her bloodstream, prompted on its path by her beating heart. It wasn't the wine, though, she knew. It was her. And what she really felt, watching the orb on the horizon ripple in its descent, was a sweet and quite straightforward sort of contentment.